Mallory Cook
and the
Road Not Taken

Charlotte Nash

piatkus

PIATKUS

First published in Australia and New Zealand in 2019 by Hachette Australia
An imprint of Hachette Australia Pty Limited
First published in Great Britain in 2019 by Piatkus in ebook format as *Saving You*
This paperback edition published in 2019 by Piatkus

1 3 5 7 9 10 8 6 4 2

Copyright © 2019 by Charlotte Nash

A CIP catalogue record for this book
is available from the British Library.

ISBN 978-0-349-42312-8

Printed and bound in Great Britain by Clays Ltd, Elcograf S.p.A.

Papers used by Piatkus are from well-managed forests
and other responsible sources.

Piatkus
An imprint of
Little, Brown Book Group
Carmelite House
50 Victoria Embankment
London EC4Y 0DZ

An Hachette UK Company
www.hachette.co.uk

www.littlebrown.co.uk

Charlotte Nash is the bestselling author of five novels, including four set in country Australia, and *The Paris Wedding*, which has been sold in eight countries and translated into multiple languages. Her signature style showcases a lush sense of place, rich plot, emotive heart, and a body and soul odyssey for her characters. She is an intrepid traveller with a lifelong love of new experiences and has adventured around Australia and the world for both work and pleasure, including in her pre-writing life as an engineer and medico.

When not writing, she is a connoisseur of beautiful baked goods, gourmet tea, and an eclectic mix of favourite movies. *Mallory Cook and the Road Not Taken* is her sixth novel.

For the latest news from Charlotte, visit:
www.charlottenash.net
Facebook: AuthorCharlotteNash
@CharlotteNash79

Also by Charlotte Nash

Ryders Ridge
Iron Junction
Crystal Creek
The Horseman
The Paris Wedding

For Vic, who keeps my faith in the goodness and kindness of people's hearts

Mallory Cook
and the
Road
Not Taken

Chapter 1

MALLORY COOK HAD LIVED IN THE LITTLE GREEN COTTAGE since the day she'd left school, seven long years ago. She and Duncan had taken it because of the extremely low rent, and because after being rejected from several other prospects, they were rather desperate to find a place to live. It was the cottage or couch surfing, and standing at the end of the long drive, the cottage seemed the better choice.

From a distance, the place had certainly looked like a colonial postcard: all cosy beneath the trees, with a distinguished gable, a wide brick chimney, and an outhouse of firewood promising comfort on cold winter nights. Up close, though, even an enthusiastic real estate agent would have had trouble ignoring the lean in the floors, the hideous mould problem, and the cracks and holes that let in all the spiders. The curtains were so thin that they lit up like ghosts in storms, and the location on an old avocado farm meant they were far from potentially helpful neighbours. But these features had never bothered Mallory.

Only two things really bothered her. The first was the black-cloud storms that thundered in off the sea and collected the cottage in a full-frontal assault every few days in the summer. One of those storms had lashed the windows last night, even though it was autumn already.

The second was the fact that a year ago, Duncan had suddenly moved his fledgling company all the way to New York, leaving his fledgling family – Mallory and their five-year-old son, Harry – to manage on their own. They'd grown apart anyway, he'd said, which was news to Mallory. The shock had been just like one of those storms, only it had taken much longer than a night to blow itself out.

Despite storms and absent husbands, when Mallory woke on this particular Friday morning, she knew today would be the best day of her life.

She danced to the radio as she pulled the limp doona up to make the bed, removing a large bear from under the covers. It belonged to Harry, and she'd taken it with her for comfort last night. But she wouldn't need it again after today. By the time midnight came, her little boy would be back across the hall, tucked in the red racing-car bed they'd painted together. Duncan would be sitting on the lime-green sofa, the one they'd recovered from a skip bin when they were first married. They'd laughed so much that day, delirious with the delight of moving into the cottage, even though Duncan's computer desk had to be made from planks and milk crates. Mallory crossed her fingers, deep in full-fantasy imagining: Duncan would laugh when she reminded him of the sofa's origins. Then she would tell him about her new promotion, showing him he wasn't the only one who could make it. They would talk into the late hours while Harry slept, mending whatever it was that had gone wrong to make Duncan move halfway across the world.

After all, the signs were good. He had finally paid for Harry to visit him in New York, which must mean that the business had stabilised. The round-the-clock stress of being a newly successful CEO, which had made Duncan unavailable so often this past year, appeared to be over. The two of them were flying back today, and Duncan had said that he wanted to 'talk'. Mallory had heard all kinds of apology and hope in his voice. They could work everything out.

Mallory held on to that thought as she shook out her blue work uniform and mixed her first instant coffee of the day. She drank it at the kitchen window, looking out on the chickens scratching about in the grass. Water drops hung like jewels on the shaggy jasmine around the window; it was always in need of a prune. The tiny kitchen, however, was unusually immaculate. The tiled benchtops wiped, all the water spots removed from the single sink, Harry's pictures arranged to cover the rusting cracks on the fridge, and the wonky cabinet door coaxed into a straight alignment. Mallory had enjoyed the temporary calm of her boy being away, but she missed the signs of Harry being home: the half-finished bowl of Weet-Bix on the sink, the drawing pencils and paper on the bench, his favourite blue vinyl chair always pulled out. The house was too empty without him.

She rinsed her cup and checked her diary, supressing the nerves that sprang from reading 'job interview' scrawled across one o'clock. She normally rated job interviews somewhere between the spiders that lurked in the shower and the thunderstorms. And while she was tired of dealing with both of those on her own, the interview was something she could handle. She wasn't even worried about freezing up with nerves, or launching into some awful verbal diarrhoea.

Today, her boys were coming home and everything was right with the world.

The morning seemed full of good omens. Her ancient Corolla started on the first try, and she caught every green light into work.

Her workplace, the Silky Oaks Residential Care Facility, sat on a hilltop looking down on Moreton Bay, its double-storey edifice rising from beautifully kept gardens, with a stand of wild and untamed eucalypts kept at a safe distance beyond the southern boundary. Mallory waved to a gardener who was busy clearing fallen branches, no doubt casualties of the storm, and paused to appreciate the view of two white-sailed yachts out on the sparkling water. Unlike her cottage, everything close up matched the postcard beauty of that view. Silky Oaks boasted white walls, tasteful art, and a gentle smell of lavender and rose petals. And if it was a little too bright and clinical for Mallory at times, the place was certainly organised, clean and efficient. It couldn't have run any other way with Mrs Crawley, Director, at the helm – the same person whom Mallory would face at her job interview.

Mallory wasn't that worried because Mrs Crawley knew her. Mallory had worked at the Silky Oaks Care Facility almost as long as she'd lived in her cottage, seven dedicated years as a staff carer. She was one of the very few veterans, and had seen many other staff come and go. Now, a position had opened for an Engagement Manager, and Mallory wanted it more than anything in the world, beyond having Harry and Duncan back.

She stowed her bag in the staffroom and jogged into the nearest ground-floor resident's room, humming the same boppy pop song. Then she went to work transferring her residents down to the breakfast tables, and chatting with them about the day ahead.

'The kindergarten class is coming at eleven,' she told Evelyn, and Sue, and Mr Burgundy, who'd been a music teacher and still insisted on being called 'Mr'. But his smile was the broadest when he heard the class was coming. Mallory loved these moments with her residents. It was the whole reason she did this job. She was humming again by the time she returned to help strip beds.

'You're in a good mood. What's that you're singing?' asked Bridget in her broad Scottish accent. She was Mallory's closest work friend, serial pusher of baked goods, and occasional font of motherly advice.

'Just the last thing I heard on the radio this morning.'

Bridget laughed. 'I thought you'd still be turning inside out with nerves, after the storm last night. I nearly rang you up to make sure you weren't under the bed.'

'I was fine,' Mallory lied, glossing over the hour of clutching Harry's bear so hard that she'd had fur under her fingernails. She checked her watch; her interview was hours away, but her stomach still flipped.

'I'm sure you'll do well,' Bridget said, when Mallory admitted her nerves.

'What's the worst that can happen, right?'

Bridget shook her head. 'I don't like to think like that, but no one deserves it more. Lord knows you're braver than me. Crawley scares me witless.'

•

Bridget's statement had the unfortunate effect of priming Mallory to notice the intimidating side of Mrs Crawley. By the time the administrative assistant showed Mallory into Mrs Crawley's office, Mallory's stomach had a full crew of tap-dancing butterflies on high alert. The office was neat and tastefully appointed, with plush red chairs, soft tan carpet, and a framed modern art print on the wall. A large window faced out into the garden with a glimpse of the water. For families and relatives, it was probably soothing and orderly. Mallory simply felt out of place.

Mrs Crawley sat reading a letter, her back to the window. She wore a dove-grey suit and black-rimmed glasses. A minimally applied coral lipstick was the only brightness in her face, the skin around her mouth smooth from being a career non-smiler. The air smelled of vanilla, which normally reminded Mallory of Bridget's home baking, but today seemed to reek of foreboding. Mallory tried to sit up straight and not fidget but she could feel her heart crashing around in her ribs, and the cramp developing between her shoulderblades. Finally, Mrs Crawley briskly signed the letter and filed it in her out-tray. She removed her glasses.

'Mallory. Well. Thank you for your interest in this role.'

'Of course,' Mallory said, her tongue so thick she had to force the words out. 'It's just such a dream job. I was really excited to see it come up. You see, ever since I started working here I've wanted to, and I just thought, yes . . .'

She trailed off, aware she was doing the verbal diarrhoea thing. Mrs Crawley was staring at her. Mallory clamped her lips shut and smiled.

After a small pause, Mrs Crawley picked up a sheaf of papers and said, 'Yes, well, your application was certainly thorough. I think it might be useful if I talk a little bit about this position, and what we need from the applicant.'

Mallory sat forward, eager to move on. At eighteen, she'd come needing a job, but Silky Oaks was now her second home. She knew every inch of its white walls and lino floors, and all about the lives of the residents on her roster. She knew the number of seconds it took to get hot water in the tap in each bathroom, and how to pound the third locker in the staffroom when it stuck. She wanted to step up.

'The Engagement Manager is responsible for all the activity programs we run within Silky Oaks for all the residents, including weekly, monthly and special events. That's everything from craft, to film screenings, to group visits like the community choir. It's across both floors and four wings. We need someone who can coordinate a large number of people's needs and resources within a strict budget, and follow through in an orderly way. The residents' lives need routine.'

Mrs Crawley paused. So far, all this had been on the job description. Mallory didn't exactly agree with everything Mrs Crawley had said, but she knew she could do this job.

'Yes, I understand,' she said. 'Because I'm really very passionate about Silky Oaks and the people who live here. I've loved the changes I've helped make and I think I can continue to do that as the Engagement Manager.'

'Good, good, that's all good. You have a lot of enthusiasm.' Mrs Crawley gave Mallory a smile, but it was a careful smile, one that said she didn't quite mean the praise she was offering. Mallory's stomach dipped.

'I have more ideas than what I put in my application,' she rushed on, needing Mrs Crawley to believe she was serious. 'I've managed a tight budget, and I have good relationships with all the elders.'

'We prefer "resident" here,' Mrs Crawley corrected.

'Of course. Sorry. I mean, I'm good with people.'

Though Mallory wasn't quite sure that Mrs Crawley fell into the group of people she was good with. She tried a warm smile, which was usually a safe fallback move. Mrs Crawley merely lifted the bridge of her glasses and rubbed at her nose, as if all this smiling had given her allergies.

'Tell me more about your ideas,' she said as she replaced the glasses.

'Well,' Mallory began, 'I know that many residents are lonely. That was one of the reasons I proposed the kindergarten class.'

Lonely was sometimes an understatement. It happened so often that families began by visiting regularly, but then life took over and those visits dropped away, leaving mothers and fathers and grandparents separated from the people who had defined their life. It broke Mallory's heart. A year ago, in the wake of Duncan's departure, she'd approached Harry's kindergarten teacher and proposed that the class visit Silky Oaks each week. She thought it would be easy, since the kindergarten was just over the hill and behind the trees from Silky Oaks: the very reason Mallory had chosen it. The weeks of negotiations that followed left her sleepless and jittery. But while weekly visits had to become fortnightly, and outdoor activities were abandoned for story time in the lounge, the program was still an unqualified hit. The residents loved it, and so did the children. The residents told fascinating stories, and the children were delightfully spontaneous and unpredictable.

'But I want to take the idea further,' Mallory said. 'The class can't be here every day, and I think many of the eld— residents would love that connection and companionship more of the time.'

'So you're proposing pets.'

Mallory paused, seeing the twitch at the corner of Mrs Crawley's mouth. 'It's been done in some other care facilities, and they have seen these amazing increases in happiness and even less medication. I really think—'

'Yes, I see.' Mrs Crawley clasped her hands together on her desk. 'The thing is, Mallory, this is a management position. And managers have many considerations to make. The kindergarten class has been an interesting pilot program, but it has come at a price, one that I'm not sure you've quite understood.'

Mallory sat absolutely still, feeling small and vulnerable, as though she'd landed in the principal's office. She knew Silky Oaks hadn't been wild about the class visits at first, but she'd thought the success had swept those reservations away.

'The administrative load is very high. All the residents had to have Blue Cards. We had to check insurance and liability, and then there was the guinea pig incident.'

Even under pressure, Mallory had to purse her lips to avoid laughing. A few months ago one of the children had smuggled a guinea pig into Silky Oaks. Bridget had been the one who discovered three children introducing the animal to Mr Burgundy. The children had been teaching Mr Burgundy about the guinea pig, and Mr Burgundy had been suggesting composer-themed names, like Mozart and Brahms, and humming rousing bars from symphony scores.

Mallory had been shown the whole thing on the security tape, and she had been delighted because Mr Burgundy was often so quiet. Just watching him open up over the tiny furry visitor had prompted her thinking about pets to start with. Evidently, Mrs Crawley had neither been fascinated nor delighted.

'I know we had a few problems,' Mallory said carefully. 'But we'll learn from that. And anything that improves the lives of the residents has to be a good thing. Craft is great, but it can't give you that sense that someone else understands you and loves you. I think having animals here could do such amazing things. Even if it was chickens – they could be outside. And a garden – then we could have eggs and vegetables for cooking, really involve everyone in our community. Of course, I'll make a proper plan with all the research supporting it.' She rushed out the last sentence, aware her earnest words were failing to move Mrs Crawley.

'I'm sure you would.' Mrs Crawley gave her another, not unkind smile. 'But that's not the only issue. In a management position, the hours are more regular, but longer. The work schedule can be tough if you don't have much . . . family support to share the load.'

The pause told Mallory that Mrs Crawley really *did* know everything.

Mallory swallowed. 'My husband's just been in New York while his business was setting up,' she said, tweaking the truth. 'He's coming back. Today, in fact.'

'Really? I see.'

A long pause settled, during which the automatic scent dispenser on the wall puffed out a fresh shot of vanilla. Mallory suppressed a sneeze, which nearly turned into tears. It dawned on her that this promotion was not only *not* going to be hers, but that she had probably never been a serious contender.

'Look, Mallory, I will be honest with you. You're a hard worker, and that's something I value. But you're young. Most of the people we interview for this position have university qualifications. I'd like to see you gain some more experience, perhaps we could even help with some courses, and then apply again in another couple of years. When you have a much better grasp of the role. All right?'

Mrs Crawley squared the pages and slotted them into her out-tray.

And that was the end of Mallory's first hope.

•

Bridget found Mallory splashing water on her blotched face in the staff locker room.

'I take it that didn't go well,' Bridget said. Then, when Mallory turned to face her, 'Lord above! What on earth did she say? You look like you've been crying all morning.'

Mallory pressed the damp towel to her cheeks. 'I just blush like this. Mum used to think I'd been sunburned. I was hoping to look less fluorescent before I go back out there.' She sighed. 'And no. She's looking for someone older, and more . . . managerial, I suppose. But she did say she liked my enthusiasm,' Mallory added, trying to find a way to lessen the humiliation. She hung the towel. 'Do you think she might change her mind, if they don't find another candidate?'

Bridget popped an eyebrow. 'I suppose there's chilly nights in hell.'

Mallory winced, deeply wounded. Not just because she really hadn't been in the running for the job, but also that her ideas wouldn't find a ready welcome. How could she keep working here if she couldn't promise better days ahead for her residents? She pulled open her locker, where a series of Harry photos lined the door.

'I'm so sorry, Mal,' Bridget was saying. 'I know how much you wanted this, and you'd have been wonderful. I have no doubts.'

'At least Harry's coming back tonight,' Mallory said, staring at the photo of him holding his bantam chicken in the cottage's backyard, eyes scrunched: his standard response to being asked to smile. She touched the photo, wishing her love to him.

'Wait a minute.'

'Mmm?' Mallory turned to find Bridget with her hands on her ample hips, peering at Mallory's locker.

Bridget pointed a finger. 'What is that?'

Mallory knew exactly what Bridget had seen. The dress was hardly unnoticeable. Blood red, it was covered in delicate embroidered gold flowers. Mallory had worn it to her senior formal, her first date with Duncan. Duncan had said he loved it, loved the way she'd worn the bold colour and short skirt among a crowd of slinky black floor-length numbers. Mallory had kept it in plastic in the back of her cupboard ever since. She'd been seventeen, and it still fit.

She shrugged. 'I'm going straight to the airport after work. I wanted to get changed.'

'Into that?'

'I wanted to look nice,' Mallory said, hoping nonchalance would fool Bridget's Scottish intuition. That it wouldn't be obvious that Mallory was only wearing the dress because of Duncan.

Bridget heaved a sigh and gave Mallory a kind pat on her shoulder. 'Please tell me you're not doing what I think you're doing. You're not thinking of taking him back?'

Mallory closed the locker. 'He wants to talk. I have to give him that,' she said, trying to suppress her hopes of far more than *just talking*.

'Do you really think that's a good idea? I'm not judging, mind. I just care about you. I don't want to see you so hurt again.'

'He's still my husband, and Harry's father,' Mallory said. 'Here, look.'

She pulled a letter out of her pocket. It had arrived two days ago and was already creased from handling. Bridget unfolded the letter, full of Harry's large, childish letters, and a drawing with three stick figures labelled 'Mum', 'Dad' and 'me'. Next was a printed photo: Duncan and Harry together, identical grins on their faces, the same little ruffle at the end of their left eyebrows, holding a homemade sign that read, *Wish You Were Here*. The New York Aquarium was behind them.

Bridget sighed, and slipped Mallory's justifications of love and forgiveness back into the envelope. 'I suppose,' she said doubtfully.

'And he says his company is doing really well. It wouldn't be like before,' Mallory said.

'You mean, like when you were struggling to feed all three of you while he sat at home tinkering with his computer? What would you do, move to New York?'

Mallory hesitated. She hadn't even thought about the details. All she'd wanted was time to talk with Duncan, without the pressures that had been around them a year ago, when his company was taking off. She was certain that if they could just spend some time together, they could work it out. She didn't like Bridget's doubt.

'We haven't settled any details,' Mallory said. 'But I don't want to be that person who couldn't give him another chance. I know you think he bummed off me until he didn't need me anymore, but it wasn't that simple. He was under such pressure. Look at how many people here don't have their families anymore, Bridge. I want mine back.'

Bridget sighed. 'Aye, I understand that. Good luck to you, then. And you'd better wish me luck, too. One of the ladies I'm taking down to the lunch room next took a swing at me last time. I think she didn't like my jokes.'

'Good luck,' Mallory called, sneaking another look at the photos in her locker before she headed back to work.

Once lunch was over and her residents resettled in their rooms for an afternoon rest, Mallory was rostered to cleaning duty in the south wing: a tidiness and cleanliness check of the family lounge, computer room, and small TV room. Mallory moved through the lounge, straightening chairs, re-sticking Blu Tack on the Easter drawings the children had made two weeks ago, and trying not to dwell on the lost promotion. She listened to the news headlines while she changed the bins in the TV room: Trump had tweeted something outrageous again, a volcano somewhere in the Pacific north-west was threatening to erupt, a footballer had won some kind of medal. She shut off the TV.

In the computer room, she tucked the chair into the desk, turned off the monitor and collected a page left in the printer tray. She was on her way to the paper bin when she noticed it was an airline itinerary.

Brisbane to Los Angeles, then Los Angeles to Nashville, it said. That was a big trip. She knew many of the people who lived at Silky Oaks, but she didn't recognise the name at the top: Ernest Flint.

'Is Ernest Flint in this wing?' she asked the nurse who was eating lunch at the desk across the hall. 'I think he might have left something in the computer room.'

The woman made a face. 'Ernie hasn't used a computer in his life. Jock's the only one who's been in there today. Room twenty-six on the second floor.'

Mallory found the door to room twenty-six open, and immediately glimpsed a resident with a difference. The room might have held the same furniture as all the others – the king single bed on one wall made up in a plain blue quilt, a desk under the window. But the opposite long wall had been painted a deep navy, and supported a bookshelf, crammed with books and models and jam jars filled with miniature brushes. More hand-painted military plane and helicopter models hung from the ceiling on fishing line. Jock himself sat at the desk, ringed with neat piles of logic problem books, his pencil poised above a crossword. He was short and wiry, and wearing a worn green fishing hat covered in badges. Under the back, Mallory glimpsed clipped grey hair.

She knocked, and the eyes that swung around were bright blue and wary.

15

'Hello,' she said. 'We haven't met. I'm Mallory and I work over in the north wings. I found a print-out in the computer room and wondered if it was yours?'

She held it out. Jock slowly pushed his chair back.

'Oh, uh, okay,' he said, taking the paper.

The badge at the centre front of his hat was from the Stockman's Hall of Fame. Mallory tried not to stare at the others, or to try to count how many there were.

'Thank you,' he said quickly, folding the paper in half.

Mallory smiled. 'You know Ernest Flint?'

'He's just down the hall, but he doesn't know how to work the computer.' Jock paused. 'I think he's allergic.'

Mallory laughed. 'I'm just glad to see someone's using the computer room. We tried to organise a course last year but there was some funding problem. And I always thought it shouldn't be locked, but they're concerned about theft or something.'

Jock's expression warmed. 'Sounds like standard bureaucracy. Though maybe it's my collection has them worried?'

He gestured at a set of movie cases on the shelf, where *Ocean's Eleven*, *The Italian Job*, *The Thomas Crown Affair*, *The Bank Job* and *3000 Miles to Graceland* poked out their spines.

'Wow,' Mallory said, with a laugh. 'I'm seeing a trend there. Like a good heist?'

'Don't worry. Not planning anything.'

Mallory winked. 'I won't tell anyone. Don't you have a great view up here,' she said, catching a glimpse through the glass. He had one of the north-east windows that faced the ocean, a bright expanse of cobalt blue framed in gum trees. Below, the gardeners were still working on the fallen branches.

'It's not bad, is it?' he said. 'The storms are spectacular. And I can see the sun come up over the water.' He blew out an audible breath. To Mallory, he seemed a little reserved, and was more comfortable now she wasn't facing him.

'You ever paint it?' she asked, nodding towards the paints on the bookcase, and choosing not to think about storms.

'Oh, no, just the models,' he said. 'You know, I've seen you around downstairs, when the kids visit.'

'Have you? I'm sorry if I haven't said hello. I'm always running around making sure no one is missing, and no stray guinea pigs, that sort of thing. I'll try to do better today.' She gave him an encouraging smile.

'Right you are, then.'

Mallory looked around. 'This room is really nice. How did you get the changes past the board?'

Jock gave her a sly smile. 'You know the phrase "better to ask forgiveness than permission"?'

'I see,' Mallory said, nodding and laughing. She admired a touch of subversion. 'You know, these models are very good. Would you ever be interested in teaching a class—' She broke off, and took a breath, remembering that she wasn't going to be the Engagement Manager. 'Well, anyway, my son's very interested in models, though mostly trains. He comes in sometimes when the babysitter drops him off here at the end of my shift. Would it be all right if we came by sometime? Maybe you could give him a few pointers.'

Jock smiled. 'Anytime.'

By the time Mallory left Jock's room, she'd completely forgotten about that piece of paper.

Chapter 2

MALLORY ARRIVED TWENTY MINUTES EARLY TO THE airport, jangling with excitement. She smoothed her hair in the Corolla's rear-view mirror. Was the dress too much? Too late now if it was. She had to force her wobbly knees to carry her all the way to the terminal, changing the welcome poster between hands so that her clammy fingers wouldn't warp the cardboard.

She camped out by the arrivals rail, imagining Harry flying through the door. She would catch him up in an endless hug and press the softness of his hair against her cheek. In her mind, she went over and over what she would say to Duncan, the apologies she'd offer for any part she'd played in him leaving. Two weeks before, Duncan's timetable had been so tight, they'd not even had time for a coffee in the airport café.

'I'm sorry, I can't, Mal,' he'd said then, and he really had looked sorry, and tired too, in his beaten jeans and polo shirt at the end of a seventeen-hour journey. No one would have known he was the CEO of a hot software company he'd built from scratch. 'But we need to talk about everything. Can we do that in two weeks?' He'd given her an uncertain smile, the same one he always used when he wasn't sure of his reception. She'd agreed, nearly breathless with possibilities. She'd known then that he wanted them to try again.

So Mallory was ready to talk, to be calm and mature, and not to repeat the questions of the past year that had so often prompted only silence. Impatiently, she watched a previous flight's passengers dribbling out of customs, searching for their loved ones in the crowd. A few people strode towards the taxi rank alone, and Mallory could only feel sad for them.

Time dragged on, and the crowd thinned. Mallory paced, down to the end of the terminal and back. Oh, why did she have to be early? Waiting was just awful. Finally, the board said the flight had landed. She tried to do the maths in her head. How long would customs take? Half an hour at most, perhaps?

The first passengers appeared after twenty-five minutes. Mallory pushed her way back to the rail, bouncing on her feet with the 'Welcome Back Harry and Duncan' sign ready. She measured each shadow through the frosted glass wall, hope surging with every adult–child pair. After an hour, when she was the only one still waiting, Mallory dropped the sign. Three texts to Duncan had gone unanswered. Had she made some mistake?

She checked the flight number again. The airline. Maybe they were simply stuck in customs. Oh no, had Harry brought in something he shouldn't have? Or worse, had they missed the flight? Mallory groaned at the idea. She couldn't bear having to go home alone again and come back later. But surely Duncan would have let her know? They must just be delayed in customs.

The woman behind the airline's enquiry counter was sympathetic but firm. 'I'm sorry, I can't give out any inform-ation about passengers. Privacy, you understand.'

'But it's my son, and he's only five. I wanted to know if they were still waiting for bags or something.'

The woman's expression momentarily softened. 'He's travelling alone?'

'No . . . with my husband. I'm supposed to pick them both up.'

The woman shook her head. All that she could confirm was that, yes, the plane had landed, and it was the same one as the flight information Mallory had.

Mallory backed away, dejected. How much longer should she wait? The airline counter had told her that passengers couldn't take calls in customs, but she called Duncan's mobile anyway. It went straight to voicemail. Of course. Slightly encouraged, she waited through another half-hour. But when a new flight was disgorging its passengers, desperation set in. She tried his mobile four more times, then scrolled through her phone for the New York number. Duncan had a housekeeper called Maria; maybe she could confirm whether they had made the flight.

The line only rang once before it picked up. 'Hello?' said a male voice. Mallory's relief morphed to confusion. 'Who is this?' the man insisted, his voice thick with sleep. 'Hello?'

She took a quick breath. 'It's Mallory,' she managed. 'Duncan, it's Mal.'

In the long pause that followed, Mallory heard sheets rustling. She imagined him sitting up in bed and rubbing his eyes. 'Mal. It's four in the morning,' he said.

'Did you miss the flight? I'm at the airport.'

'Ah, shit,' he said, as though he'd just forgotten an appointment at the dentist. 'I meant to call you. But then we had this meeting with the VC guys and things were intense for a few days. I forgot.'

'You forgot?' Bright streaks of annoyance and hurt and relief shot through Mallory's heart, forming a muddy indecipherable emotion. 'Duncan, I was so worried! I didn't know where you were.'

'We're right here.' He had a tone now, as though she was being melodramatic. 'But I did mean to call you. Harry's staying here, Mal.'

'What?' Mallory tried to grasp what he was saying. 'Does he want to stay longer?'

The other end of the line muffled, but she could still hear Duncan's footsteps, the sound of a door catch opening and closing. Then the creaking of a leather chair. He must have closed himself in his office.

He let out a sigh. 'Please believe that I didn't want to do this on the phone, but I don't think I can possibly get away for a while. I think it's better for everyone if we keep things as they are right now. Harry's happy. And you'll have an easier time, too.'

'What are you talking about?' she asked. 'Harry's got school on Monday.'

'You're not listening, Mal,' he said, very calm, very reasonable. 'I'm saying he has a school here. We already talked about this possibility.'

Mallory felt her eyebrows crush together. 'When did we talk about it?'

'At the café, at the airport, two weeks ago. When I asked about Harry living in New York. You said you'd be open to it.'

'I never said that . . .' she began, but suddenly she really couldn't remember what she'd said two weeks ago. She'd been so busy thinking about the possibilities with Duncan, of the three of them being a family again, she hadn't even finished her coffee. Had she given him the idea that he could do this? Had she misinterpreted his words as a romantic gesture, thinking he meant the two of them should try again, when really he meant something else?

'I never meant that he would just stay there now,' she said, through a wave of nauseating panic. 'He's supposed to come home.'

'That's not what you said, Mal,' he said, with an exasperated sigh. 'Look, I understand this isn't the best way of doing things. But I really do have it all sorted out. Harry loves it here. He can go to an amazing school just a few blocks from the office. He's already made some friends this last fortnight. He can have a home here that he can only dream about in Australia. Opportunities. We talked about this. He won't have to grow up in such a tiny place, and it will be easier for you too. Of course, I want you to be free to call anytime, visit anytime you like. But him staying here is best for everyone.'

Mallory's back met the glass wall of the terminal with a thud. She pressed a shaking hand to her forehead. What was he talking about? He was the one who'd left her and Harry for his company's big chance in New York. He was the one who'd said their lives had moved apart. She couldn't fathom what he was doing.

'Let me talk to Harry,' she said in a rush. 'Please.'

'He's asleep, Mal.'

She had the awful sense of finality, that Duncan was about to close the shutter on this conversation without any resolution. 'He gets up early. Please. He'll be awake. I just need to hear his voice.'

'He's only just adjusted to the time zone,' Duncan said, firm. 'Now, as I said, you feel free to call anytime you like. He loves seeing you on Skype. We'll need to iron out the small details. We will. But that will have to be later. I've got an early meeting. Take care, Mal.'

With that, the line clicked. Mallory re-dialled, again and again, and heard the engaged signal.

She lowered her phone in cold, stomach-sinking disbelief. A few people milled past with trolleys and bags, oblivious to Mallory's ridiculous dreams now lying like shredded paper at her feet. It had all been a fantasy, just like the faint lingering scent of Harry's shampoo she could almost smell in the air.

Chapter 3

THE NEXT MORNING MALLORY SAT CHEWING HER NAILS IN the offices of Turner & Bodie, a family law firm in the outer suburbs. The air-conditioning was turned off for the weekend, and the atmosphere was thick and still. She was convinced all of this was some mistake . . . but she was also desperate for information. Bridget had made the appointment after Mallory had called her from the airport. Bridget knew someone, who knew someone who was the brother of one of the partners, so another someone had come in specially on a Saturday to see Mallory.

The slim young lawyer across the desk wore a dark suit and a pair of thick-rimmed glasses. While her attire was disturbingly similar to Mrs Crawley's, she managed to exude a calm confidence as she listened to Mallory's story, making notes on her yellow pad. The framed certificates on the wall oozed authority, so by the time Mallory finished speaking, she felt reassured that all the confusion would be over soon.

'Let me recap,' the lawyer said, flicking over her pages. 'After Mr Cook moved out last year, the arrangement has always been that Harry lived with you?'

'Yes. He moved to New York and Harry stayed with me. Duncan said he didn't have the resources for us over there.'

'Has he ever paid maintenance?'

Mallory shook her head. 'He didn't have any income while he was building his business. I was the one working.'

'What about after he moved out? When the business took off?'

'Um, well, he said that they had a lot of start-up costs, and he wasn't drawing a salary yet. And he always looked after Harry while I worked before that, so I think I would have been the one paying him.'

She expected to see judgement, the kind Bridget always served up when Mallory talked about Duncan and his business, which Mallory had bankrolled since she was eighteen. Even after Harry came along, she'd worked nights and weekends to keep Duncan's hopes alive. She had only enjoyed momentary vindication when his start-up attracted a game-changing investment, before he'd moved out. She had walked around like a zombie, devastated and embarrassed, but as the weeks went by, she could see the stress he'd been under with the company, that he needed space for a while. Bridget thought those concessions were madness.

'What sort of man happily lets a new mother go out to work while he sits at home earning nothing?' Bridget had said more than once. Mallory could only shrug.

Now, the lawyer seemed unsurprised as she scratched down notes. She pushed up her glasses. 'From what you've told me, the facts seem straightforward. You've always had full custody by mutual agreement after you separated. Your son went to visit Mr Cook with the understanding he would return yesterday, and now Mr Cook has declared he's taking custody without your agreement. Fortunately, the States is a signatory to the Hague Convention, so we can lodge recovery orders and have them recognised by an American court. We should also apply to have Harry on the Family Law Watchlist, in case they do happen to return to Australia. After that,' she said, 'I'd want to consult one of the senior partners about contacting the Attorney-General's Department to put in place some more long-term measures.'

The complicated terms hung over Mallory like storm clouds, and she hated the word 'separated'. She didn't want to have to do any of this, couldn't imagine how Harry would feel to be dragged through court proceedings. Surely Duncan would realise what a mistake he'd made before it came to that?

'This isn't like him,' she said, hoping desperately she was right. 'Duncan wouldn't take Harry away. I'm sure he's just misunderstood something I said.'

'It's very common to feel that way,' the lawyer said carefully. 'And it is possible, but I don't want you to be surprised if you find that your husband knows exactly what he's doing, and if he's quite refractory to reason. Sometimes people do incredibly cruel and inexplicable things when marriages break up, and it comes as a complete surprise.'

Mallory swallowed, her body rejecting the idea like a bad oyster. 'Okay.'

The lawyer took off her glasses and rubbed the bridge of her nose. 'Mallory, I do want you to be prepared. While the process is clear – we can lodge the documents in a week, and organise a barrister overseas – it's also expensive. Very expensive. And if he decides to challenge, it could become very long and involved.'

Mallory opened her mouth to say Duncan wouldn't have the money, but closed it again. She really didn't know what he had.

'How much?' she asked.

The lawyer named a figure that was most of what Mallory made in a year, then added, 'But if he challenges, more, and the whole process could take months. Are you ready for that?'

Mallory's laugh came out under the pressure of her nerves, before a noose of fear tightened around her throat. 'How could he possibly challenge it?' she whispered. 'I supported him for six years. I worked nights and weekends, even when Harry was a baby. I just can't believe that he'd do this. He always said when the business took off, he'd make it all up to me.'

An involuntary tear spilled down her face. Wordlessly, the lawyer pushed a tissue box across the desk.

'Mallory,' she said gently, 'people do the most hideous things when their families break down. Sadly, this isn't a special case. It's our job to help you.'

'Do you think he's right?' Mallory asked, suddenly full of doubt. 'That Harry would be better off there? That he wouldn't have to see how hard it is to make ends meet? He could afford better schools, all that stuff.'

'That's really not for me to say,' the lawyer said, but Mallory heard a note of disgust. 'Might be better if he'd chosen to send you some of his new riches, or to discuss it with you first. I don't know how he could challenge it, but he might. You are clearly not neglectful, but he could allege something harder to prove, like mental instability, which might mean you have to sit a psychiatric evaluation.

'And that's not all, I'm afraid,' the lawyer continued, her expression grim. 'Even when we recover Harry, you may need a parenting order to ensure he stays here with you. In that case, it could be five times as much.'

It was almost the price of a house. Mallory had no more words. She beat a hasty retreat, saying she would think about it.

•

Mallory spent the journey back to the cottage wondering where she could find that impossible kind of money. All avenues seemed to converge on winning the lotto. When her thoughts took a dark turn towards casinos, she pulled over and walked around on the footpath to get a grip.

She arrived home feeling as though she'd just worked a twelve-hour overnight shift. Autumn was sliding towards winter and a chill blanketed the cottage under the trees, colouring the world bleak. The iron roof was dull, the windows dark, and the shaggy coat of climbing jasmine too heavy for the leaning timbers to hold up. Mallory had the involuntary thought to search for Harry's warmer pyjamas, which led to further tears.

Inside, the rooms were cold and empty, the bare boards creaking. The kitchen bulb blew when she flicked on the switch. She gathered Harry's old bear to her chest, just to have something of him to hold. His toys were all from op shops; every spare cent had gone on babysitters this past year. Now that he'd started school, she had been saving slowly, but she didn't have anything close to the amount the lawyer was talking about, and there wasn't anything to sell. All the furniture was second hand. She and Duncan had been married in a quick civil ceremony, and they'd never got around to a ring. All their friends had been just out of school, so there hadn't been any expensive gifts. Her car was barely worth scrap, and she needed a vehicle for the relief shifts she did at the respite centre. After her mother's habits, she had been too afraid to apply for credit cards. She had only two accounts: one for expenses, the other for savings. Expenses had just enough for groceries before her next pay. In savings, she had the bare germination of a one-day home deposit. It wasn't enough.

Time evaporated in her bewilderment. When she came back to reality, she was out in the yard with an old serving spoon she used as a trowel in her hand, weeds from the vegetable patch in an uprooted pile. The sun was going down, the chickens were happily scratching around for worms, and her fingernails were clogged with dirt. She sighed and returned inside to clean up and face the problem. She had to find a way.

Twenty minutes later, when she was examining online interest rates on personal loans and feeling sick to her toenails, Bridget knocked on the door, bearing a cardboard box of fruit and vegetables.

'Unwanted proceeds of the co-op haul. I thought you could use it,' she said, depositing the box on the kitchen bench and automatically filling the kettle. 'Now, what did the lawyer say?'

Mallory relayed the information numbly, as if she were out of her own body, while Bridget made tea and pushed a mug in front of her. When Mallory finished, Bridget sat back, apparently too shocked to make her customary jab at Duncan.

'Do you think he'll fight it?' she said.

Mallory rubbed her finger over a crack in the countertop. 'I don't know.'

'I was going to say I'd lend you the money,' Bridget said, 'but I never imagined it could be that much.'

Mallory could only shake her head. Regardless of where the money came from, she could be paying it back forever. 'I know you'll think I'm crazy, but I know that if Duncan and I were just able to be in the same place, none of this would be happening. He isn't like this, Bridge. New York's just so far away. It's never the same on the phone or Skype.'

'Well, I'm not sure about that. But I wouldn't blame you if you just got on a plane,' Bridget said. 'What can he do if you just show up?'

Bridget left after an hour, but the idea wouldn't. Mallory paced the house. She'd thought about going to New York before, but not exactly like this. It was supposed to be them all going, together. Mallory had never been overseas. The prospect of going on her own was daunting, and a flight to the States was expensive. Then again, it wasn't as expensive as the legal fees, and if she and Duncan could just talk face to face . . .

She pulled herself up. She couldn't just leave on no notice. What about work? And besides, she should really try to talk to Duncan again. This could still all be a misunderstanding.

She waited for the clock to drag around to nine-thirty, when she opened Skype with a shaking hand and dialled, half expecting no one would pick up.

'Mummy! I heard the beeps.'

Harry!

His voice shot sunshine beams of joy through her heart. The picture took a few seconds to resolve, long enough for Mallory to swipe away her tears. Harry was kneeling on a black leather chair, the one in Duncan's study in front of the computer. 'Hi, baby!' she said. 'How are you?'

For a few minutes, Harry talked about all the things he had been doing – eating hot dogs, going to Central Park and Coney Island and the aquarium, some of the time with Maria because Daddy had been working, but he'd seen Daddy's new office, too, and been allowed to play with the photocopier. He was wearing a shirt with 'I love New York' on the front, the *love* replaced with a red heart. It tore at Mallory: Harry clearly understood nothing about what was going on.

'Daddy says I can stay, so when are you coming, Mummy?' Harry said finally.

'I'm not sure, baby,' she said, choking up. To see his little trusting face through the monitor was too much. 'Can I talk to Daddy?'

'Sure, Mum!' Harry climbed down off the desk chair, and she heard him call for Duncan. The chair slowly swung around, revealing an abstract print on the wall behind. Beneath it was a graceful glass vase atop a wooden cabinet with brass handles. The whole thing looked expensive, and would probably be awarded tens on a renovation reality show.

She eventually heard Duncan, somewhere off-camera, saying, 'What have I said about coming into my office?' Harry's response wasn't audible, but Mallory tensed.

Harry's face popped back into view, looking contrite. 'Dad says I have to get ready now. Bye, Mum, I miss you!'

'I miss you too, baby—'

But he was gone. After a long pause, when Mallory's heart was beating so hard her chest ached, Duncan appeared, a larger, harder version of that same face. He didn't sit down, just leaned on the desk. All she could see was the powder blue of his shirt, a striped pink tie hanging down. A thick watchband she didn't recognise circled his wrist.

He ducked his head into view, straightening his tie as he looked into the screen. 'This'll have to be quick, Mal. We're on our way out.' A little frown of concentration gathered between his brows. His gaze ran off to the left as he clicked the mouse. 'Just closing a few windows. I'm running late.'

A dagger stabbed through Mallory's heart. She took a huge breath, trying not to be rushed. 'This early?' she said, sounding upbeat. 'Must be the big bucks.' Duncan had once joked he wouldn't get out of his pyjamas before nine unless he was being paid the big bucks.

'It's after seven-thirty,' he said, distracted, missing the old joke. 'I've got a meeting at nine downtown, and Harry has a new music class to get to first.' He leaned away from the monitor. 'Harry!' he called. 'Brush your teeth please, sport! Maria's waiting.'

'Duncan, we need to talk. Right now, please.'

Duncan paused, and looked back into the screen.

'I didn't agree to this,' Mallory said. 'I don't know what sort of misunderstanding we had, but Harry can't stay with you. He lives with me, and his school is here. That's been our agreement since you left. You can't just up and change it. He needs to come home.'

'We agreed that—'

'No, we didn't! You didn't ask me about any of this, and I certainly didn't agree to Harry staying there for anything more than the two-week visit. Now, I want to know when he's flying back. As soon as possible.'

A pause. 'Are you finished there?' Duncan's voice was so cold, Mallory shrank. She'd only heard that low, angry voice from him once before, and it brought the memory flooding back. They'd been at a dinner with some potential investors in his company years ago. The night had been a big deal for Duncan, the first serious sign anyone might be prepared to invest in the business. Mallory had known that, but she'd also been so tired that night, shy and wrong-footed at the fancy party, uncomfortable in a borrowed dress. She hadn't known what to say to people and probably wasn't in her right mind, after two bad nights with Harry, a double shift and the stress of leaving him with a sitter. In her nerves, she'd told some stories from her work, and somewhere between Mrs Connelly's enema and Mr King's sailor-swearing, and the polite avoidant eyes of the dinner guests, she realised this probably wasn't appropriate conversation. Duncan's mouth had been very tight as he'd drawn her aside. 'That's enough, Mal,' he'd said. 'For God's sake, I'm asking these people for money. And one of them's the Liberal Party president. Have a bit of thought.'

She'd been so ashamed of embarrassing him then.

Now, trying not to quail, she said, 'He's my son, Duncan.'

'And he's mine, too,' Duncan countered. 'I'm giving him a better life here. You have a good hard think about it, Mal, and you know I'm right. We talked about this. You can't just change your mind either.'

'No, it isn't better! And we haven't!' Mallory said, finally suspecting that there hadn't been any miscommunication at all, that maybe the lawyer was right. 'You can't just take him, can't uproot him from his life here.'

'Settle down,' Duncan said. 'And don't take that combative tone with me, Mal. How do you think Harry will feel to hear you? You're confusing him.'

She frowned. 'How the hell am I confusing him?'

'He needs to settle in here. If he's hanging out for calls all the time, and if you're telling him he should come home, it's mixed messages. You'll just upset him.'

'I'm upsetting my own child by talking to him?'

'Well, yes.'

'I'm his mother, Duncan. He lives with me. He's lived with me his whole life. You took off a year ago. Why are you being such a heartless bastard? Just let him come home!'

Duncan heaved a sigh, as if he was the most put-upon man in the world. 'If you can't acknowledge your part in this, I want you to stop calling.'

'What?'

'At least for a while. You're not helping anyone.'

A bruising fist thumped into Mallory's stomach. 'You can't cut me off and be so unreasonable. I'm speaking to a lawyer.'

Duncan didn't even flinch. 'Mal, I'm *being* reasonable. You're the one being dramatic. Think about it. Really, think. Harry is better off here. And if you try and argue differently, and get lawyers involved, then I'll have to raise my concerns about your fitness.'

Mallory's mouth opened, stunned.

'That's not fair—' she began.

'We have to go. I won't have him singled out because he's the kid late to class. And don't call again.'

The video feed vanished, replaced by the profile photo of Duncan with Harry, incongruously smiling. Desperately,

Mallory hit 'call' again. It rang and rang, and rang out. She tried again, and this time the call dropped immediately. Duncan was now offline.

For a long minute, Mallory couldn't move. Of all the outcomes, this wasn't the one she'd expected. Beyond him cutting her off, she glimpsed that he'd been calculating in doing this. Deliberate.

She sat back in her chair, listening to the kitchen clock *tick, tick, tick*, around five whole minutes. And then, without thinking, she opened her browser and clicked through to an airline booking site. A week ago, when she'd been off in the hopeful dreamland that Duncan might ask her to come to New York, she'd applied for a visa waiver, so there was nothing to stop her. *Click, click* on book and pay.

Bridget had said she would get on a plane. And that was exactly what Mallory was going to do.

Chapter 4

MALLORY MANAGED TO DOZE ON THE FIRST HALF OF THE flight, but the closer she came to Los Angeles, the more sleep eluded her. When the flight attendant was clearing trays from the dinner meal, and other passengers were nodding off under grey blankets, she was thinking through her plan for the fifth time. She had to change planes in Los Angeles, then once she arrived in New York she would take the subway to Duncan's apartment. Or maybe she would have enough cash for a taxi. That might be faster than working out the subway. It wasn't much of a plan, so she spent the rest of her time obsessing over Duncan, and what on earth had happened.

After he'd left a year ago, Mallory had never once gone looking for information about him online; nothing could be worse than reading about his success. Once or twice, she'd idly typed his name into Google and waited just long enough to see the results come back before she closed the window, her heart pulsing with the hurt of his leaving.

But after that last Skype call, she couldn't help herself. She had clearly missed something. When she and Duncan had first met, he'd been an aspiring entrepreneur, a generous, funny man who made her feel like the whole world was made of stars. Something had clearly changed. She had to understand what. She filled the time to her flight finding and saving articles.

His LinkedIn profile hadn't given her much she didn't already know: CEO of Iron Gate Software. His Twitter account was mostly reposts of business-related news articles. Finding anything else was surprisingly hard.

Mallory waded past search results for a few academics and lawyers with the same name. When she eventually found an article mentioning *her* Duncan Cook, it made her eyes cross, full of dry business jargon about market potential and stock options and promising start-ups. Iron Gate was only one of the 'one to watch' companies in the article, but the writer took the time to mention Duncan's energy and all-out commitment to success, yet his down-to-earth casual approach to the workplace. That was still the Duncan she had known: working slavish hours, but opposed to the formal stuffiness of traditional business. Now, reading the article for the fourth time revealed nothing new. She sighed and leaned back in her seat. Outside the window, the world was starless, only the flash of the plane's lights breaking the night.

Far across that darkness, phones were ringing in the Federal Aviation Administration offices all over the USA. As Mallory flew over the International Date Line, an ominous bulge appeared on the side of a volcanic cone near Lassen Peak in the Redding area of California. It was the same mountain that had appeared on the newsfeed Mallory had watched in the Silky Oaks lounge; the US Geological Survey had been concerned about increased seismic activity in the region for weeks. Then, at 5:08 am local time, a lateral blast erupted from the volcano, creating a debris avalanche and a cloud of fine silica and ash fourteen miles high, which began drifting across the USA at the speed of a late-model passenger car.

By the time Mallory next woke to a pink and apricot sunrise on the wing, airspace was being shut down all across the west coast. Emergency services were scrambling to keep daredevil sightseers away from the mountain. The captain made the first announcement: something about a volcano, but they were being allowed to land. Mallory raked her fingers through her hair as the cabin crew served juice as if nothing was happening. Crisis seemingly averted.

But when she spilled out into the LAX terminal, chaos appeared to have set up shop and sold tickets. Customs was backlogged with a great sea of people in subdued silence. After an endless wait in the barely moving line, she finally stumbled through the exit chute, and found more milling crowds. The air smelled of heat and sweat. All thoughts of Harry and Duncan momentarily evaporated.

She rushed down the concourse until she found a set of arrival and departure monitors, the screens awash with red-and-yellow 'Cancelled' messages flashing down the rows. Like so many other stranded travellers, she scanned, hoping against all hope that her connection would be the exception. But, no. Cancelled.

Pushing through the crowds took forever and a stress-flush burned up her neck and cheeks. Great ribbons of people and bags streamed from every airline desk. Complications were accumulating like bricks, building a wall in the way of New York. This couldn't be happening. Seriously? A volcano?

As someone who'd just left the desk walked back along the line, Mallory put out a desperate arm. 'Excuse me, what did they tell you?'

'Everything's on hold,' said the man, with a philosophical shrug. 'The ash cloud is drifting right across the country. There goes my trip to Atlanta!'

When Mallory finally reached the desk, the frazzled clerk could only confirm all the flights to New York had been cancelled and they were organising luggage return. They could offer a flight back to Australia, which she would have to pay for, or she could stay and wait. Mallory asked when the flights would be back, ready to accept a day, maybe two.

The clerk just laughed. 'Ask the volcano!' he said. 'Next!'

Mallory closed her eyes. She was on the wrong side of a foreign country with only a few hundred dollars to her name. For the first time since Harry had left to visit Duncan, she felt truly and utterly alone.

She willed herself to calm down. There must be other options. All the car-hire desks had posted hastily printed signs saying they were completely out of stock, so she connected the free wi-fi on her phone and looked up trains to New York. She bit her lip when she saw the information: it would take nearly three days and cost three hundred dollars. Even so, it had to be better than hanging around in an airport. She would run out of money paying airport food prices in less time.

By the time she'd selected the fare, the site told her that seat had been sold. The next-best deal was a hundred dollars more. She swore under her breath and accepted, plugged in her debit card details, and hit purchase. The screen paused for a long time. Mallory watched, knowing she should not press back or interrupt or even breathe wrong while the electronic brain processed her details.

Then it declined. Mallory said a very bad word.

Muttering, she checked her account balance: enough to cover the ticket. She tried and failed to book three more times. Exasperated, she changed the last cash in her wallet to US dollars and called the train booking service. When the card declined there too, she finally used a handful of dollars to call the bank in Australia from a payphone, nervous about her mobile's credit.

'Ah, well, there's the problem,' said the operator with unnecessary enthusiasm. 'The account has been frozen.'

'Frozen?' said Mallory. 'But how could it be frozen?'

The operator cleared her throat. 'Well . . . sometimes it can be a creditor with a court order—'

'I don't have any creditors.'

'Let me just look in the notes. Oh, I see. Requested by Mr Duncan Cook, the joint account holder.'

Mallory pressed a hand to her head. This wasn't happening. Her skin burned hot against her palm. This wasn't happening. 'Why would he do that?'

'Well, most likely the request was made pending a dispute with the joint account holder.'

'Meaning me?'

'Well, yes. It's just a temporary freeze. It will automatically be removed after thirty days if there's no further action.'

'I'm stranded in LA,' she said, a quiver in her voice. 'I'm sitting in the terminal. My flight's been cancelled and I just want to book a train and I can't because my husband froze my last four hundred dollars?'

'I'm sorry to hear that,' the operator continued professionally after a short pause. 'This must be very frustrating. The volcano seems to be making a mess. I just saw it on the news.'

No matter what Mallory said, or how she pleaded, nothing could be done. She ended the call with her whole body hollowed out to the husk. Duncan taking Harry had stolen her heart, and now this had scraped out the last of her dignity.

Angrily, she dialled Duncan again and again on Skype. No answer. She googled the number for his company in New York, but the receptionist only got through telling her he was out of the office before her money ran out. Mallory closed her eyes against the tears. She was willing to bet that he would never answer her there anyway.

In that moment, standing in a cloud of desperation by the out-of-credit payphone, she remembered a resident they'd had at Silky Oaks a few years ago: Glenda, an American woman with early onset Parkinson's disease. Mallory had taken to chatting to her on the night shifts, and they played cards together, which Glenda insisted was good for her motor skills. Glenda would sometimes tell stories about her life in America, jovial nothings about the wonders of soul food or the coast in her native Washington state, nothing too personal. Then, one night, Mallory had asked how she'd come to Australia. Glenda had gone very quiet, then told her a long black comedy of dominoes: her husband had been diagnosed with cancer; Glenda had lost her job because there was no one else to take care of him. Then, she'd been evicted because she had no job, and nowhere else would give her a lease. The two of them had ended up in a shelter in the middle of a bitter winter, her husband growing sicker and sicker. Eventually, they'd been able to contact a relative and make the journey to Australia, where they'd stayed.

Mallory remembered the faraway look in Glenda's eyes as she said, 'You never know what's going to happen, Mallory. You think everything is fine one day, and then life knocks your knees right out, and you're tumbling down and down, and there ain't a damn thing you can do about it.'

Mallory knew now what she'd meant. Three days ago, her life had been manageable and stable, on track for a promotion and a family reunion. She'd never been aware of how fragile it had all been, and now the card house had collapsed. If she'd just had a credit card . . . but even the thought of credit made her break out in hives. She heard ringing phones and saw the shadows of big men coming to knock on her mother's door. It had never been an option.

With her account frozen, she couldn't even contemplate calling work to ask for an advance. Not to mention that it was the middle of the night in Brisbane. When she swallowed her embarrassment and thought to try Bridget, all the train tickets for the next week were sold out.

Only two choices remained. Fly home, or stay and hope.

•

Mallory sat on the toilet lid, her head slumped to the wall, listening to the repetitive *whoosh* of taps and hand dryers. She couldn't go back to Australia without Harry. She would have to camp here with all the other unfortunates until flights resumed. Just her and the two changes of clothes she had in her duffel bag, currently hanging on the back of the door.

But what if flights were weeks away? What would she eat? Where would she sleep? Mallory squeezed her eyes shut. She was so stupid. She'd been in such a hurry, she hadn't even thought to buy travel insurance.

She tore a square of toilet paper to blot her eyes. Her mission had been struck down by an act of God. Mallory wasn't particularly religious, but she worked with elderly people whose families had often forsaken them. She listened to their stories and wiped their unmentionables. What God would keep a mother – any mother, let alone a carer for the aged – from her child?

Mallory started as someone rattled the cubicle door, probably making sure she wasn't forgetting the waiting line. She swiped her eyes with the rough scrunched paper, sniffed, flushed, swung her bag over her shoulder, and opened the door. A few tired eyes in the queue flicked over her, pretending not to notice her puffy face. She squeezed past to a spare basin between a woman examining her lipstick, and an elderly lady wearing a cardigan in royal purple.

Mallory soaped her hands, thinking over the cash in her pocket. When she turned to the hand dryer, the old woman hadn't moved. She was staring into space, her brilliant white hair finger-waved in the front like a twenties flapper's, giving her face a distinguished frame. She looked fun, Mallory thought, with her bright cardigan and a long red skirt, but tired and lost. One hand clasped some papers to her chest.

Mallory touched her shoulder. 'Excuse me. Are you okay there?'

The woman shifted, her gaze unfocused. She slowly tracked across and finally met Mallory's gaze. After a second, she brightened.

'Mabel!' she said.

Mallory had worked with elders long enough to recognise someone in need of help. She pressed a hand to her chest. 'I'm Mallory. Are you waiting for someone?'

The woman brushed her forehead, as if trying to remember.

'Can you tell me your name?' Mallory asked.

No answer to that, either. Mallory appealed to the waiting line, but everyone shook their heads. The woman clutched Mallory's arm to steady herself, and Mallory patted the hand.

'Don't worry, we'll work it out. May I?' she asked, pointing to the papers. The woman slackened her grip and offered across what turned out to be a small stack of photos. They were old, some faded to sepia, others with folded corners and brown stains. Mallory flipped through pictures of dogs and cats, a goat, and two horses standing by a white fence rail.

'That's Agatha and Christie,' the woman said suddenly, pointing a trembling finger at the horses, her words carrying a trace of a southern accent. 'I have to feed them before dark. They get so riled up, waiting.'

'They're beautiful,' Mallory said. The next was a black-and-white wedding photo, the young couple standing under the spreading branches of a tree. The man wore a suit with a carnation pinned on his lapel, and a shy smile. The woman wore a grin, cat-eye glasses and a smooth white satin dress, her left hand holding a bouquet away, as if she were about to bowl an underarm pitch. On the back, *Zadie and Ernest, Sydney 1968* was written in faded fountain pen letters.

'Is this you?' Mallory asked, searching for a resemblance between the woman before her and the much younger face in the photograph. 'Zadie?'

'The flowers made me sneeze,' the woman said with a tremulous laugh, touching the small bouquet in the photo. 'I had to hold them down like that. I told Ernie that I was fine with it being just us, but he doesn't really understand. He's so set in his ideas.'

Zadie gave Mallory a beaming smile, as if all this made perfect sense. Mallory couldn't help smiling back.

'How about we see if we can find someone to make an announcement? There's plenty of time before dark, and you can tell me more about Agatha and Christie if you like.'

Mallory led Zadie slowly towards the doors, sure that someone would be searching for her already.

The terminal was more congested than ever. Zadie tightened her hand as Mallory paused to look for an airline help desk, and several people jostled past, shifting their shoulders to fit. Mallory reconsidered her plan, worried about them being knocked over, but she couldn't leave Zadie on her own. She was about to collar one of the passers-by when a man in a green fishing hat caught her eye. He was turned away, but clearly searching, back and forth, scanning between groups of people. His hat was covered in badges and with a frayed patch on the back brim, it looked just like the one Jock had been wearing at Silky Oaks . . .

He turned, and they locked eyes with a mutual jolt. It *was* Jock. Wrung out with all the drama, Mallory waved, glad to see any familiar face. And after a pause, with Jock squinting at her across the crowd, he raised a hand.

'Well,' he said, after pushing his way through, 'fancy meeting again like this.'

At the same moment, a booming call came from the left. 'Zadie? Zadie! There you are, thank God!'

The voice's imposing owner limped into view. Mallory's first impression was of a storybook giant: a tall, bad-tempered, grey-haired man with large ears, clearing the crowd with swings of his cane. But he was too neat for a giant – his hair was precisely combed, his checked shirt tucked in to grey dress pants and restrained with a polished brown belt. And despite his stature, he was frail. Mallory could see how one leg dragged, the thinness of the limb through the trouser leg, the heavy lean on the cane.

This man pulled to a stop, looming over Mallory, Zadie and Jock, the four of them creating an island in the slow tide of stranded passengers.

Zadie kept hold of Mallory's arm. 'I found Mabel,' she said.

The giant frowned and, after transferring his cane into the crook of his elbow, reached for Zadie's arm. 'Come on now, Zade. You can't just wander off like that.'

'She was in the ladies' bathroom, looking a bit lost. I'm Mallory,' Mallory added, observing the same heavy brow as the man in Zadie's photo. 'You must be Ernest? I just saw your wedding photo.'

The man with the cane looked at Mallory with a turned-down mouth, as if she'd just told him she'd been snooping around in his bedroom. Finally, he said, 'It's Ernie. Ernie Flint. Much obliged to you, young lady. Now, come along, Zadie.'

46

'Oh!' Mallory exclaimed. '*You're* Ernest Flint. From the itinerary.' She smiled encouragingly at Jock. In the middle of her own despair, this unexpected connection to Silky Oaks was a great comfort. But her declaration only produced a tense stare from Ernie.

'She's the one who found the print-out,' Jock said quickly. 'She works at Silky Oaks. How do you like those odds?'

Ernie's mouth dropped open in alarm. 'She does? What's she doing here?'

'Relax,' Jock said. 'She's not here to take you back. Or are you?'

'Take you back?' Mallory asked, confused, until Jock gave her a just-go-with-it wink. 'I mean . . . no?'

'Excellent, you see, Ern?' Jock said. 'Now, where are you headed?'

Mallory sighed. 'Nowhere, it seems. I was supposed to be in New York. Are you stuck too?'

'That depends,' he said. 'Would you go back into the ladies' and see if someone called Fiona is in there?'

'Fiona?'

'Yes, please. Blue blouse, black trousers, blonde hair in a ponytail.'

So Mallory did. 'Nope,' she reported five minutes later. 'Two Fionas, but none matching that description.'

'Dammit,' Jock muttered. 'I was afraid of that.'

'Who's Fiona?'

But Jock and Ernie were engrossed in another conversation that involved no words, just eyebrow raises, small head shakes and fingers rubbing at temples.

Finally, Jock said, 'What do you think, Ern?'

Ernie gave a one-shouldered shrug. 'It's a foolhardy idea. But if you think she's the only option.'

With that, he led Zadie away. While Mallory was still perplexed by what was going on, she couldn't help but be touched by the way Ernie protected Zadie, even with their slow, limping steps. Zadie looked back over her shoulder and waved. Mallory waved back.

'What was all that about?' she asked Jock.

'Well, you said you're stuck here, right?'

'Yes.' Mallory raised her hands hopelessly. 'I couldn't get a car, or a train, so I guess I'm waiting it out. Maybe it'll only be a day or two. That's possible, right?'

Jock laughed. 'Don't you remember Eyjafjallajökull?'

'Remember what?'

'The Icelandic volcano that blew in twenty-ten. Could be weeks yet, and then there's the backlog of passengers to shift.'

Mallory's mouth opened and closed without a sound. 'Are you serious?' she said faintly. She'd be on starvation rations to last even a week in the airport with her cash reserves.

'What if I told you that we could all leave, right now? We have a car, we just need someone to drive, and to help out. Maybe we can solve each other's problems. How about it?'

'You need a driver?' Mallory frowned at him, waiting for the catch, and suddenly thinking about his heist DVD collection. 'You're not planning on robbing a bank, are you?'

Jock laughed. 'Partner in crime, if you want to think of it that way.'

As Mallory considered his offer, thinking about Harry, she realised that she probably *would* rob a bank at this point, if it meant she could get to New York.

'Let's talk,' she said.

•

'It's just a little road trip, plain and simple,' Jock explained when they were all seated at a café table.

Mallory's hopes dimmed. 'But I need to be in New York as soon as possible. I can't possibly do a leisurely road trip.'

Jock glanced at Ernie. 'We never intended to drive either. Ernie and Zadie are heading to Nashville, and I've my own rendezvous further down the road. So, I figure, you drive us all to Nashville, then you can hire your own car, or fly if they're running again. It'll only take a few days. We'll still get there long before all this flight business sorts itself.'

Mallory gulped her steaming cup of black coffee like it was water, trying to cut through the long-haul fog and work out if this really was an option. Finally, she shook her head. 'I haven't got any money for hiring a car,' she said. 'I'll just end up stranded in Nashville.'

Jock sat back. 'This is your department,' he said to Ernie.

Ernie turned his bushy scrutinising brows on Mallory. He hadn't said much to this point, but he hardly needed to: he had the brand of stare that belonged to school principals and High Court judges. 'I'll offer you a simple contract,' he said. 'You drive us to Nashville. Two thousand dollars is yours when we get there. We'll cover the hotels and meals on the way.'

Jock made to say something, but Ernie cut him off. 'That's the offer,' he said.

Mallory's mind raced with possibilities. 'How long did you say it will take?'

'Four days, I think, down the interstate,' Jock said, showing her a map on his smart phone. She squinted at the screen as he scrolled eastwards across the continental United States. She had no idea exactly how far it was, but she'd already made up her mind. The money was more than enough to fly from Nashville, or drive, or take a bus. She'd still have some cash when she reached New York, which she would no doubt need to fly Harry home. Driving also had advantages: no one could cancel the journey or dictate a timetable.

'All right,' she said. 'But I don't really know any of you from Silky Oaks. What care do you need from me?'

'Nothing really for me,' Jock put in quickly. 'Ernie—'

'Can answer for himself,' Ernie grumbled. 'Had a stroke. Right-side muscle weakness. Help with dressing, toileting, and two-handed activities.'

Mallory noted how he removed the pronouns, so it wouldn't have to feel like he was talking about himself – clearly a sensitive topic – but he was also clear and precise. He seemed to have a grip on everything, which was encouraging.

'Zadie,' he went on, 'has . . . early stages.'

Alzheimer's. Mallory nodded. 'Does she have any problems with balance?'

'Occasionally,' he said. 'Mostly it's memory problems, with good spells of clarity here and there. Tends to be worse in the evening. But her medication is working well at the moment.'

Except for wandering, Mallory thought. But Zadie couldn't wander if they were in a car, and if Jock could take care of himself it sounded very doable.

'And what if her medication—'

'I'm a doctor,' Ernie said, cutting her off. 'If medication needs adjusting, I can look at it.' He wore his scowl like a favourite outfit. 'Will that be all with the questions?'

50

Mallory downed the rest of the coffee. She looked at the three of them. She could say no and stay with the thousands of other stranded travellers. Or, she could take this chance. 'Let's go.'

And that was that. Even with their slow progress through the terminal, Mallory's mood lifted, her chest full of new hope and relief. All around, people were going nowhere, but not her. She was on her way. Crisis averted.

She carried this unsullied optimism right up until Jock fell into step beside her. 'Thank you,' he said. 'Now, tell me, have you driven on the right side of the road before?'

Chapter 5

MALLORY NEVER GUESSED LEAVING LA WOULD BE SUCH
an opera of wrong notes. She had grown up in a distant
suburb of a small city in sparsely populated Australia.
Driving out of the airport at home was only as complicated as
choosing the right exit. She was therefore utterly unprepared
for the scale of Los Angeles, and for the vehicle she'd have
to command.

'That's not a car, that's a tank,' she said nervously to
Jock, staring at the massive vehicle. She'd been tricked by
its description as a mid-sized SUV. Compared to her old
Corolla, it was a gleaming behemoth, with a confusing
array of buttons, a bonnet like a cruise ship, and blind
spots down both sides. It took her ten minutes to establish
the handbrake was actually a foot brake, cunningly hidden
down near her left leg.

'Yeah, but a tank with power steering,' Jock had said,
patting her shoulder.

His reassurance did nothing to help. Mallory was thrown by the smoothness of the ride, the cushy seats that swallowed her, and the overly responsive brakes.

Then there was the right-hand driving.

Everything was backwards, and she experienced flashes of terror every time her subconscious took over and thought she was on the wrong side. This led to swerving, corrective swerving, and jamming on the brakes.

Before they'd even exited the parking lot, she'd flung all three of her passengers forward in their seatbelts. Ernie, folded into the front-passenger seat on account of his long legs, gave her sidelong stink-eye glances and pointedly hung on to the over-window handle. Jock was more patient, a calming voice from the seat behind that said, take it slow, and she would get the hang of it, and joking that at least they knew the anti-lock brakes worked. Zadie's only input was a soft, 'Whee!' after one sudden stop, as if she was on a rollercoaster.

Out on the roads, the traffic was intense, no doubt accepting all kinds of help from the volcano. Mallory drove hunched forward, her knuckles blanched around the wheel, her jaw clamping tighter with each word out of Ernie's mouth.

'You've missed a turn,' he complained for the third time.

'Don't worry, the GPS will work it out,' Mallory said.

'We're just going in circles. At this rate, we'll be in Nashville next month.'

Finally, by some miracle, they reached a freeway, and Mallory negotiated the on-ramp, trying to merge with a tiny gap in the frightening traffic. God, it was like the freeway scene in that *Matrix* movie, except she didn't have superpowers to save her. Still, she could fit . . . just another second. Then, she could relax.

'Merge!' shouted Ernie. 'Merge, merge!'

Startled, Mallory saw too late that the on-ramp had smoothly morphed into an off-ramp. She slipped back and lost her spot, left with no choice but to sail off the freeway again, and into another gridlocked garden of traffic lights. She pulled up with a jerk, her heart thumping, fingers shaking.

'Wonderful. Here we are. Again,' Ernie said.

Tears prickled on Mallory's eyelids. They were doomed to drive in circles forever. Ernie was going on and on about timetables, and how paper maps were the only proper way to navigate, and now he was playing around with the GPS, losing the route, and Jock was telling him to leave it alone. When Mallory saw a service station, she swung in and jerked to a stop.

Ernie looked up. 'Why are you stop—'

'I need to concentrate,' she said, trying to keep her voice under control. 'I'm trying to drive a strange car on these . . . these—' she waved a hand out at the long lines of brake lights '—*bloody* roads.'

'Well, I wouldn't have agreed to this if I'd known you wouldn't be able to *drive*.'

Jock laid a calming hand on Mallory's arm, climbed out and hauled Ernie's door open. 'Time to swap, Ern,' he said. 'GPS needs fixing.'

That's not all that needs fixing, Mallory muttered in her mind, then felt guilty. She prided herself on being able to connect with difficult residents, and there were many of them: people in varying stages of dementia, with hearing loss, with painful chronic conditions that made them grumpy. Or simply those who were lonely and fed up with what life had become, who even wanted to die. She felt a grave responsibility to make their lives better. She resolved to try harder.

Just as soon as they were out of the city.

It took twenty minutes to reach another on-ramp and be properly on their way. Having Jock in the front was an improvement, but it didn't stop Ernie. Should they be in the right lane? What was that the GPS just said? Could they have the radio on to see if there was a traffic update? No, Zadie didn't like the music, turn it off.

Mallory sweated, her shoulders cramped from the tension. The clock showed it was after two before they were climbing up through dry foothills out of the LA valley. She tried to count this as progress and to relax. It looked a lot like Australia, really, when you went away from the coast. Scrub-covered hills, dry earth, and big, big sky . . . and even bigger trucks.

Then they crested the mountain, and Mallory gazed all the way down the pale ribbon road, which vanished into vast plains and distant smoky blue mountains. She wasn't in Australia anymore, and it dawned on her how vast this journey might be. She gulped, feeling all that distance as a yawning space in her chest, swallowing up her courage. Maybe she should have waited in the terminal.

But Harry was out there, on the other side of it all.

'What were you going to do if you hadn't found me?' she asked, her voice trembling. 'Were you going to drive all this way on your own?'

'Nope,' Jock said, 'this is plan C.'

'Plan A was to fly, right?'

'Yes, but certain volcanoes had other ideas. I jumped on the car bookings as soon as I had reception on the tarmac. Knew they'd go fast.'

'So that makes this plan B, doesn't it?'

In the back, Ernie snorted.

'Not exactly,' Jock said. 'Plan B was Fiona. Nice lass from a contract agency.'

'She wasn't,' Ernie argued.

'Yes, she was from an agency, Ernie,' Zadie put in.

'I mean she wasn't nice.'

Jock gave Mallory a grin.

'Was that the Fiona you asked me to check the Ladies' for?' Mallory asked, as she tried to work out the cruise-control buttons.

'That's her. She joined us in Brisbane, but seems she found greener pastures in LA. Left us in the lurch. I think the lure of Hollywood might have been too strong – don't you think, Ern?' Jock said. 'We ran into you at just the right moment.'

'Took our money is what she did,' Ernie growled. 'Hollywood can have her.'

'Wait, she abandoned you in the airport?' Mallory said, aghast. 'Why would someone do that?'

After an uncomfortable pause, Jock said, 'Do you want to explain, Ernie?'

Mallory glanced in the rear-view. Zadie had drifted off, and Ernie was busy wedging a rolled-up jumper against the window as a pillow for her.

'Ern?' Jock repeated. 'Care to shed some light on Fiona's departure?'

'Nothing to do with me,' he said, his voice rough and petulant. Clearly something had happened between Ernie and the mercurial Fiona. Mallory gave Jock an enquiring eyebrow, wondering whether to worry.

'Let's just say there was a . . . personality clash,' Jock said.

Well, that was hardly surprising. Ernie was a tough customer, but this was only for a few days. Mallory finally found the cruise setting, and eased her aching right foot off the pedal. 'Well, she'll end up with a horrible reputation at her agency, that's all I'll say. They'll never give her work again.'

'She probably won't care, if she's in the next Bond flick,' Jock said.

'Bond is British,' Ernie grumbled.

Jock chuckled. 'So, how long have you worked at Silky Oaks?'

'Nearly seven years,' Mallory said. 'I started just after I left school.'

'Pity you didn't have the chance to do something more with yourself,' Ernie said.

'Geez, Ern,' Jock said.

'What? I'm just saying it's not the sort of job a young person chooses to do if they don't have to. Didn't you want to go to university? Didn't have the grades, I suppose.'

Mallory's hands reflexively tightened on the steering wheel, not just because of the question, but also because it thrust her back into that time. Her life had changed so fast in that year after school. One moment, she'd been a happy, carefree teenager, dreaming about all the one-days she'd have. Then came Duncan, being bowled over by love, wanting to support his dreams, and then she had a baby and needed to keep a roof over all their heads.

She took a deep breath. She didn't regret any of it, but neither did she want someone to think she was stupid. She'd had enough judgement from her mother and friends, and Mrs Crawley. 'Actually, I did just fine in school. But I had a baby to support. That didn't leave much room for university. I'll go one day, maybe.'

Ernie grunted. 'Pity that you had to work. Babies need their mothers. Women understood that when I was growing up. Everyone thinks they have to go back to work these days. A little economy is all that's needed.'

Mallory ground her molars. Don't rise, she thought. He's just from an older generation. But another part of her wanted to yell at him that, yes, she hadn't wanted to go to work so soon either, but she hadn't had much choice. 'Economy' didn't go far when you were the only one earning the money.

Instead, she said, 'I love my work.'

'That's really something,' Jock said. 'Not many people can say that, don't you think, Ern?'

'I suppose that's good,' he said grudgingly, but turned to stare out the window. 'You see those trees? The First Lady in sixty-five was responsible for that. Billboards were popping up all over the place, real eyesores they were. So they passed the Highway Beautification Act. Planting trees and shrubs instead. Real vision, that was, in a time where commercialism wasn't so all-consuming. Now, there's a museum—'

As Ernie kept up a patter of highway trivia from the sixties, Mallory tuned out. It was like listening to a schoolteacher. She sighed, trying to ease the muscle aches in her shoulders and arms from gripping the wheel. Only when she realised Ernie had been silent for ten minutes did she sneak a look in the rear-view. She found him asleep, catching flies with his head lolled against the seatbelt.

She blew out a long breath. 'What a day,' she said, rubbing her neck.

'You did well back there.'

She glanced across at Jock. He sat very upright in his seat, his hands resting on his knees, like he was in the front row of a school photo. The brim of his fishing hat was flipped up. 'Thanks,' she said.

'Ernie can be opinionated.'

'Mmm.' Mallory sighed, weary. She didn't want to talk about Ernie, she just wanted to put the miles between her and LA. The road slipped by, cutting a path through the pale, sandy earth of the plain. 'Sure is dry out there.'

'Oh, this is nothing. You wait till Arizona and New Mexico. It's all desert.'

'You've been here before?'

He paused. 'Not for a long time. How are you feeling? Tired?'

'Okay at the moment. That coffee must be kicking in.'

'I'll catch some shut-eye then. But wake me up if you're drooping.'

Soon, the miles were passing to a soundtrack of soft snores.

•

For two hours, she drove across the flat expanse of Apple Valley. Jock didn't sleep long, waking in time to say, 'Last chance for Vegas,' at the turn for the Interstate 40. Mallory finally felt as though they were making progress.

Ernie woke a half-hour after that, launching into serious scrutiny of a highway map he'd bought in the airport, crumpling and twisting the sheet, and muttering. This went on for what seemed like eternity before he suddenly gripped her seat from behind.

'Take this exit,' he said. His hand shot into view, pointing.

'Why?'

'Take it, take it!'

Mallory heard his apparent panic, hooked right and duly took it. The sinking sun cut through her side window, blinding her, and they bounced on the rough shoulder, pulling up down the slip-road with a wheel skid. She twisted round. 'What do you need? Are you in pain? Need the bathroom?'

Ernie sat back, pointing his good hand down the road. No sign of a medical emergency. In fact, he looked rather satisfied. 'Keep going this way now. There's something I want to show Zadie up ahead.'

Mallory pressed her hand over her still thumping heart and glanced at Jock. They'd covered so much ground, why deviate now?

'Maybe we should make a stop,' Jock said diplomatically. 'We can loop back to the interstate and find our overnight port afterwards.'

'That's what I'm saying, we can stop down here. Great place. You'll see it soon,' Ernie said.

Mallory's doubts grew the further they drove. A few tiny towns passed by, handfuls of squat buildings the same colour as the sand. Off the highway, the whole area seemed dreadfully remote. But Ernie had noticeably changed, a small-boy kind of excitement colouring his voice. He kept patting Zadie's arm and saying, 'Do you remember this, Zadie? All this desert? We stopped here, do you remember?'

Zadie looked out the window with her fingers pressed to her chin, a smile echoing the youthful version of her face in their wedding photo. 'Yes,' she said softly, at shortening intervals.

Finally, in the distance, a sign appeared, rising up like a beacon from the flat, grey-yellow desert. It was a block of black, with a big wedge of red, shaped like a sideways mouse cursor. Yellow letters announced *Roy's* with *Motel Café* vertically underneath.

But much like Mallory's cottage, the impressiveness of the sign diminished on approach. The paint was dull and peeling, the neon unlit. She pulled off the road into an empty service station. She could see a cluster of pale blue cottages and a glass-fronted building with a few crowning palm trees, but no sign of activity.

'What on earth is this?' she asked.

'*This* is a cultural icon,' Ernie huffed. 'It's a perfect example of mid-century Googie architecture.'

'Google what now?' Mallory said. She was so beyond tired, her eyes as sore as her heart, and she had no idea what Ernie was talking about.

He didn't answer. He pushed his door open and was soon encouraging Zadie out of her seat. The two of them were halfway across the dusty lot, heading for the café, before Mallory could even work out if the place was open. She peered at some construction fencing in the distance. Down the way, a group of bikers were taking photos. It was kind of creepy.

Jock caught her eye across the cab. 'Did you ever see *Psycho*?'

Mallory shuddered. 'I hate scary movies, but I've seen enough of them to know that the desperate carload of people looking for a place to stay shouldn't stay here.'

To say she hated scary movies was an understatement. Duncan was the one who enjoyed them. He used to trot out gems like *Friday the 13th* and *Scream* and the original *A Nightmare on Elm Street*, scoffing popcorn while Mallory hid under a blanket. She'd been scarred for life just watching the opening sequence of *The Ring*. The music still induced palpitations. Duncan used to dig her face out of the blanket and kiss her on the nose, wrapping his arms around her. 'Come on, watch it, it'll be good for you,' he'd said.

Mallory, feeling fragile as the high notes of a horror soundtrack dug fingers into her nightmares, used to turn her face into his chest until it was over.

She'd been mildly horrified when Harry seemed to have inherited Duncan's inclinations. He loved creepy-crawlies and haunted houses and Halloween, and giggled delightedly when scared. He wielded the bug catcher, marching in to tame lurking shower spiders and release them safely outside, his hair flopping forward as he crouched, watching them scurry off all bandy-legged into the undergrowth. Mallory watched with less fascination, sure each spared arachnid was plotting an immediate return inside, and trying not to think of the shower scene in *Arachnophobia*. The only safe release was directly under the heel of her shoe, John Candy-style . . . if only she wasn't so squeamish about it.

Now, looking about this dusty place, the over-large beat-up road sign made her think of a deep-sea angler fish, luring prey in the dark with a big shiny light. She only knew about angler fish because of Harry. She could see him, poring over a book of undersea creatures, which all resembled the monster from *Alien*.

So lost was she in that image of him that, as she climbed out of the car, she expected Harry to erupt from the back seat and go hurtling across the dust, shouting, 'Mum! Come on! Awesome!'

It wasn't until Jock said, 'Got that right,' that she crashed back into reality. She couldn't even remember what they'd been talking about. Ripping Harry's phantom presence away was enough to knock her breath out. He *wasn't* here. Her little boy was still down that endless road.

I'm coming, baby.

Mallory started as her phone rang. After fumbling the handset in the hope it was Harry, she saw instead a familiar number.

'This volcano is all over the news!' Bridget said, sounding very far away. 'I thought you might be stuck in the airport. Nothing's flying over the US.'

'I was stuck, but I managed to make other plans,' Mallory said, her eyes following two tiny dust devils whirling across the cracked pavement. 'I'm driving.'

'What? All that way?'

'It was that, or go home,' Mallory said, into the crackling line. The connection really was awful.

'Aye,' Bridget said, after a pause. 'I suppose desperate times and all that. I just wanted to know you were okay, and that I'll tell Crawley you had a family emergency.'

'Oh, thank you! I owe you one, Bridge.' Mallory had meant to call work, but with her rapid departure and the whole ash-cloud thing, she'd forgotten. That was all she needed: to come back and find she'd been fired.

'Nothing owed. Just stay safe, okay, duckie? I'll call you later.'

Mallory closed her eyes and let herself slump against the car, her forehead on her arm. Fatigue was setting hard in her bones. Only the jet lag was propping her eyelids open like broken vertical blinds. And yet all she wanted to do was slide into the driver's seat and keep going.

'Hey, Mallory.'

'Mmm?'

Jock was peering at her with concern. 'We'd better call it a day I think. I'll grab a sandwich for you and we'll round up Ernie and Zade, and find somewhere to stay, okay?'

After Ernie's enthusiasm for mid-century architecture, Mallory anticipated the rounding up would take some time. Ernie, however, was already on his way back, red-faced, though Zadie seemed fresher than the long journey should have allowed, as if this place really was a fond memory.

'Been a few changes since we were last here,' Ernie said, grumpy. 'Hotel's closed. Being restored, apparently.'

'When exactly were you last here?' Jock asked.

A pause. 'Nineteen sixty-eight.'

Jock chuckled.

Under a bruised purple sunset, Mallory drove the SUV back into the desert. The sun was well behind the distant low hills, throwing long shadows towards the night. The road out here was lonely, so Mallory minded less that Ernie talked nonstop as they drove.

'Course, the interstates stripped the life out of the old sixty-six, that's why hard-working businesses like that have just died. Such a shame. No one appreciates these things until they're gone.'

'And yet curious how that interstate is also going to allow us to thwart the volcano, and reach Nashville in four days. How about appreciating that,' Jock said.

'That's hardly the point. It's commercialisation at its worst, the scourge of innovative business.' Ernie returned to scrutinising his map, a pair of bifocals pushed down his nose.

'Didn't think you were such a fan of innovation,' Jock said mildly.

'Just stay on this road,' Ernie said, and then continued to report the same at intervals.

Eventually, Jock looked around. 'We do have a GPS, Ern,' he said, pointing to the unit.

'Don't trust it. What if the satellites go down?'

'What if that map you're using was printed in nineteen sixty-eight?' Jock shot back.

Just when Mallory was wishing that both of them would find a mute button, her phone rang again. Hoping it might be Harry, she threw all thoughts of serial killers out the window and pulled onto the shoulder, slipping to put on the foot brake while she groped for the phone, which encouragingly said 'private number'. The car's engine hummed in time with Ernie's grumble as she pressed talk.

'Hello?'

'Ah, Mallory.'

Mallory's heart flopped into the asphalt. She screwed her eyes shut and grimaced. 'Hi . . . Mrs Crawley.'

'I had you on the roster this morning, but Bridget tells me you have a family emergency. How late will you be?'

'Oh, yes . . . you see, the thing is that I had to fly to America. And then this volcano happened. Actually, it's funny, you'll never guess who I ran into. Three residents—hey!'

Mallory's phone flew away from her face, and collected the dash with a thud.

'Jesus, Ernie,' Jock exclaimed. 'Was that really necessary?'

Mallory peered around to find Ernie with his cane raised. What the . . . *had he just knocked the phone out of her hand?*

'What was *that* for?' she demanded. 'You could have hit me in the head!' She retrieved the handset from the floor. Remarkably, the phone seemed intact but Mrs Crawley was gone.

Zadie leaned forward, eyebrows knitted in concern. 'Are you all right, Mabel?'

'I think so,' Mallory said doubtfully. She straightened up only because Jock had confiscated Ernie's cane.

'She was going to tell Crawley,' Ernie said, arms folded.

'What on earth is the problem?' For the first time in this misadventure, Mallory trembled. She was out here, miles from help, with three people she hardly knew, one of whom was a cheap paperback page away from behaving like a lunatic. She stared at the three of them, willing someone to speak.

After a short pause, Jock said, 'Are you going to tell her, or will I? She should probably know, Ern.'

'Tell me what?'

'Keep driving,' Ernie said, sitting back. 'We all need some dinner. Then, we'll talk.'

•

It didn't take long to find the interstate, and Mallory swung the SUV east, the atmosphere so tense she could have played a tune on the air coming from the vents. An hour later, they reached the town of Needles, tucked into the side of the Colorado River. Under a blanket of stars, the main street presented a cheerful array of motels. Jock pointed to one and Mallory pulled in. Fifteen minutes later, the four of them were sitting in the next-door diner, complete with cherry-red booth seats, chrome-stemmed bar stools, and checked napkins. An attentive waitress wore a yellow uniform dress with a white apron, her thick blonde hair caught up in a bouncy ponytail. Mallory felt as if she'd walked onto a movie set, in a scene where the nefarious plan is laid out.

Ernie studied the menu for five long minutes before ordering an omelette to share with Zadie – no onions, no peppers, no chilli, extra cheese, not too hot. Jock ordered a cheeseburger and fries. Mallory ordered the same, because it was the first thing she saw, before pushing her menu away. She kept an eye on Ernie's cane, which he'd stowed on the chair back between the booths.

Finally, the waitress pushed her pen behind her ear. 'All right. Now you just sit back and relax, and I'll take care of everything,' she said with an energy that to Mallory was a dim memory.

'Nice girl,' Jock said.

Mallory shifted her gaze between him and Ernie, and Ernie's cane, and Zadie – who was laying out her animal photographs like cards in Solitaire.

'I guess I'll start.' Jock leaned forward. 'You see, we didn't exactly leave Silky Oaks with permission. That's why Ernie didn't want Crawley to know where we are.'

Mallory, mid-yawn, instantly woke. 'What? You mean, you just—'

'Walked out? Yeah, pretty much.'

'But why? You can take social leave and still have your place funded. There's a clear process.'

'It's more complicated than that,' Jock said. 'Tell her, Ern.'

'You young people don't get it,' Ernie began. 'There's no point when you work for them. You'll never understand what it's like.'

'Try me. Unless you want to lose your driver.'

At that moment, the waitress arrived as smoothly as if she was on rollerskates, passed out three milkshakes, and put a steaming cup of black coffee in front of Mallory. 'Now I know you didn't order it, but you look like you need it, honey.'

Mallory almost cried with gratitude and had to look away so that the others wouldn't see how emotional she was.

'Look, we had a tight timetable,' Jock said, filling in where Ernie wouldn't. 'Silky Oaks takes weeks to process applications. There was no guarantee they'd have let us go. We don't have families to vouch for us.'

'I'm sure that they would—'

'They want to move Zadie,' Ernie said suddenly, glancing at his wife, his words unusually soft and guarded. 'After I had this stroke, we moved in to Silky Oaks together. She still had a lot of good days then, and she still does now, when she's had good rest. But Silky Oaks is insisting she needs a higher level of care in a different wing, and there's no room for me to go with her. My judgement doesn't count with those people, so if they won't listen to me, I wanted this time with her first.'

Mallory couldn't argue with the facts; she knew such things could easily happen. It was one of the heartbreaking aspects of care. But walking out still seemed an extreme move. 'Okay,' she said. 'But flying halfway across the world without telling anyone?'

'Better to ask for forgiveness than permission, right?' Jock said. 'They never would have approved it, Mallory. I think you know that.'

Mallory sighed. Silky Oaks must be frantic, but at the same time, she couldn't help admire the three of them. They'd calculated the odds of doing things by the book, and decided to go their own way. Theirs was a boldness she'd have wanted to champion, if she'd had the chance at that promotion. She would have wanted every resident to know they could be daring and hold firm to the things they wanted to do. She also wanted Silky Oaks to change so that it didn't require such subversion.

'You could have called them,' she said. 'Or posted a note, or something.'

Jock twitched his mouth. 'I suppose. Kind of dents the bravado, though.'

'How exactly did you actually make it out anyway?' she asked as the food arrived. 'I mean, they'd have known you were missing. Zadie must have someone checking on her pretty often.'

'Ah,' Jock said, holding up a chip and squeezing it with pleasure. 'You know, the kitchens at Silky Oaks don't serve chips. But we do have a lot of routine.'

'I don't understand.'

Jock then explained how they'd made a habit for several days of Ernie and Zadie walking down to a bench overlooking the bay, one that was out of view of the main building. How Jock had carefully gone around every window, working out where the cameras were and what they could see. How he'd cultivated a friendship with one of the gardeners, who came around the rear door plant boxes at the same time each day and who, for a quiet fifty slipped into a pocket, was quite happy to pick them all up in one of the golf-carts and ferry them down to the street. From there, they'd taken an Uber to the airport – because Jock suspected Silky Oaks might call taxi companies – where they'd met up with the now-departed Fiona. Ernie chipped in with all the places the plot had nearly come undone, until he was actually smiling, and Mallory was laughing at the audacity of their plan.

Even Zadie was grinning. They could have all been twenty, living up the first day of a road trip. Finally, with the table covered in plates and trays and napkins, Mallory was yawning. Ernie and Jock had both slumped, Ernie with his arm around Zadie, who was slowly sliding the trays into each other, and stacking the plates and napkins.

'You don't have to do that!' exclaimed the waitress, who came back to clear the table and ask if they wanted pie, which they all declined.

Finally, when they were alone again, Jock said, 'Are you going to turn us in?'

Mallory shook her head. 'But I should still call them. Someone should know where you are; someone other than me, I mean.'

'No calls,' Ernie said. 'We have insurance if there's a problem.'

'What does it matter? They can't stop you now.'

'Did you have to tell your landlord where you were going before you left home?' Jock asked.

'No . . .' Mallory conceded. 'But then I didn't pay off the gardener to escape either.'

Jock grinned. 'Fair point. But the rulebook is pretty thick on unauthorised travel. They could probably give away our rooms and stuff. This way, we'll be back before they can put anything in motion.'

'They wouldn't do that,' Mallory started, but then stopped, because she wasn't quite sure. The contracts that residents signed were long and complicated. Who knew what Silky Oaks might be able to do in this situation? Besides, her main concern was reaching New York and finding Harry. Everything else was secondary.

Later, Jock pulled her aside when she came out of the bathroom.

'Look,' he said, 'I'll call Silky Oaks, let them know we're okay and to call off any searches. Just tell Ernie what he wants to hear.'

Mallory nodded. She wanted to end this, needed to sleep; they all did. Either way, she knew she would keep driving tomorrow. So she went back to the table. 'Here, I'll take my SIM card out if it makes you feel better,' she said. She would be temporarily unreachable to Mrs Crawley, but she didn't want to finish that conversation now, and she had the wi-fi at the motel should Harry call.

With Ernie satisfied, they stepped outside into the night, walking the short path between the diner and the motel. Mallory swayed on her feet. Ernie was patting his pockets.

'Can't find the keys,' he said.

'Car keys or room keys?'

'Both.'

Several confused minutes followed of trying to establish where they'd last been seen, until Ernie remembered Zadie had been holding them at the diner.

And that was how Mallory ended up, jet lagged to the teeth, digging through a dumpster near the California–Arizona border. The waitress was sympathetic, bringing a flashlight and helping her pull out the bags.

'You must be exhausted,' she said, after Mallory had told her how far they'd all travelled in the past two days. 'Still, it's real sweet taking your grandparents on a road trip.'

Mallory found the room keys sandwiched between two slices of buttered toast, and the car keys buried in a scrunched napkin.

When she arrived back at the motel, she was shaking with a level of exhaustion she hadn't experienced since Harry was a tiny baby, and she still needed to help Zadie and Ernie change. When she finally went back to her room and fell into bed, it hit her: they'd only driven five hours today, and Jock had told her it was forty hours to Nashville.

Chapter 6

THE NEXT MORNING, MALLORY WOKE TO ERNIE BANGING on the door with his cane, needing help with the bathroom. She stumbled out, disoriented and groggy, and only just managed to do her job. She was so tired, and could have gone back to bed for hours. Jock was the one who saved her, wordlessly pushing a coffee into her hands. He looked far too spry for yesterday's adventures, already showered and dressed, fishing hat in place.

They were on the road again by seven. Mallory spent the first hour rubbing sleep from her eyes and squinting into the bright sun, which rimmed the distant clouds in fluorescent orange.

'Volcanic sunrise,' Jock said, turning on the radio. The news was full of the ash cloud, the airport chaos, and speculation about how long it might all last. Out here, in the sands of the Mojave Desert with its pale earth and vaulted sky, the drama seemed to be taking place in a parallel universe.

Mallory's jet lag, which felt like stuffing in her head, added to the disconnection, but at least they were moving. Zadie especially was having a good day, asking if Mallory had eaten breakfast, and what type of music she liked to listen to.

Mallory stammered halfway through an answer before Ernie interrupted and asked Jock to hook up his phone to the car radio. Soon, *The Eagles' Greatest Hits* was flowing through the speakers.

'I didn't think when I helped you digitise this stuff that I'd have to listen to it,' Jock said, twisting in his seat as 'Take It Easy' began.

Ernie folded his arms. 'What's wrong with The Eagles?'

'What's right with The Eagles?' Jock said, but he was grinning as if this was a friendly argument they'd had before.

'I never liked their music much,' Zadie said, her voice high and clear. 'But Don Henley was a dish.'

'Who's Don Henley?' Mallory asked.

'He played guitar,' Zadie said. 'And he's a conservationist. Do you know the Walden Woods Project?'

'What's that?'

'It's a woodland in Massachusetts,' Ernie cut in. 'Thoreau stayed in a cabin there, and it inspired his book *Walden*. Wonderful story about self-reliance, and simplicity, and that progress isn't everything. Real piece of classic literature. You must have heard of it?'

Mallory didn't even dare ask who Thoreau was. Instead, she caught Zadie's eye in the rear-view. 'You sound very community-minded,' she said, hoping to encourage her.

'Oh, yes,' Ernie said proudly. 'Zadie was an accomplished nurse for many years, and she was a hugely successful fundraiser for charities – hospitals, the RSPCA, homeless shelters. All in her twenties, mind you. She really had the drive to achieve.'

In the pause that followed, Mallory couldn't help feel the implied judgement in Ernie's tone, the contrast of this drive to achieve and her own failures. She did her best to brush it off.

'And is that how you met? At work?' she asked.

'In a way. I went to Nashville in sixty-eight for a conference at Vanderbilt University,' he said. 'Zadie was volunteering at a missionary training college nearby – it had the most lovely grounds. I walked in there one day when it was pouring rain to find shelter, and there she was.'

'Your coat was all dark on the shoulders. From the rain,' Zadie said.

'Yes, that's right. You remember, love?'

'Dr King spoke in the chapel,' Zadie said, the gentle lilt of her southern accent coming through. 'I crept in the back to hear. Daddy was ever so cross.'

'Dr King?' Mallory asked, curious. 'You mean, Martin Luther King?'

'Wonderful Christian man,' Zadie said. 'My father didn't like him much.'

'King did speak there,' Ernie said quickly, 'but that was years before we met, Zade. That was when you were maybe seven years old. I'm talking about after we met, and I'd planned to drive back to Los Angeles. You remember that? I'd bought a car to see the Main Street of America. Zadie had never left Nashville and wanted to go. The rest is history.'

Nineteen sixty-eight. Mallory calculated.

'Fifty years together. That's really something,' she said, trying to comprehend it. That was such a long time, and there must have been ups and downs. Could she and Duncan ever have had that long together? 'Are you going back to visit family now?' Mallory asked.

'We're going to a wedding,' Zadie said with excitement.

'Oh lovely. And—'

'I think that's enough on that,' Ernie said firmly. 'Mallory doesn't need to know our business.'

Mallory sighed as the conversation again derailed. Just when she thought she was getting somewhere. Rounded hills flanked the highway, crowned with green shrubs, and underneath the now overcast sky the desert seemed less forbidding than it did in the open sun. But time went so slowly in silence.

She rubbed her neck, stiff from too little sleep. *Three more days.*

'How old is your little boy?' Zadie asked abruptly.

Mallory dropped her hand and glanced in the rear-view, surprised Zadie remembered. 'He's five.'

'And what's his name?'

'Harry.'

Zadie made an approving sound in her throat. 'Lovely traditional name, don't you think, Ernie?'

'Mallory said yesterday,' Ernie said. 'I was saying how it's a dreadful shame how mothers have to work these days. They don't have any time with their babies when they're young.'

Mallory clamped her teeth, and very slowly sucked a breath. She knew she shouldn't rise, but holding in a rebuttal only intensified her heartache.

'Ernie's an obstetrician,' Jock said quickly. 'He's got opinions on these things.'

'And why shouldn't I? No one thinks about the children. It's all *me, me, me* with young people, handing off their little ones to strangers.'

'I did think about it, actually,' Mallory said tightly. 'I worked a lot of community night shifts so I could be there during the day, and my husband looked after him when I couldn't. I didn't *hand him off* to anyone.'

Ernie paused. 'Your husband? Oh, I see.'

Only then did it dawn on Mallory that Ernie must have assumed she had been an irresponsible teenager who'd got herself pregnant and been forced to abandon her child into care. And worse, he'd judged her for it.

'Yes, my husband,' she said. 'Not that it matters, but Harry never went to childcare for a single day . . . at least, not until this past year. In fact, he's with my husband in New York right now.'

No need to mention the circumstances. He could stuff his opinions.

'I see,' Ernie said stiffly. 'I do apologise if I had a different impression. I suppose you must have worked very hard.'

Mallory wondered if he had a mild superpower for turning compliments into backhanders, or if he just didn't believe her. After all, if her husband was in New York and expecting her, why would she have been stuck in LA without any cash?

'And how about you, Jock?' Mallory asked, hoping to prevent Ernie reaching any conclusions. 'Are you going to this wedding too?'

'Me? No.' He hesitated. 'I'm going straight on from there.'

'Where to?'

Again, hesitation. 'Further north.' Jock tapped his fingers against his knee and reached for the GPS. 'To visit my brother.'

'Where's he live?'

Another pause. 'Virginia. It's a fair drive on after Nashville.'

Hearing his obvious reluctance, Mallory let the subject drop.

'Tell you what though, Zadie,' Jock said a minute later. 'Pretty progressive for the sixties, young woman like you upping and leaving with a man, even if he was a doctor.'

'She was eighteen,' Ernie said.

'Just. Her passport said she was born in nineteen-fifty.'

Mallory glanced in the rear-view. The muscle in Ernie's jaw quilted. 'I'll thank you not to abuse privileged inform-ation,' he said.

'Passport's hardly privileged information. Especially when I helped you get it.'

'Not how I see it. You don't exactly have the authority to—'

'Oh, listen, this one's a classic,' Mallory said, pouncing to turn up the music as 'Hotel California' came on. In fact, she rather hated the song, with its mournful melody and depressing lyrics, but anything to head off a conflict. She'd learned distraction techniques with Harry. After yesterday's incident, she'd insisted on Ernie stowing his cane in the boot, but the last thing she wanted was septuagenarian fisticuffs in a moving vehicle.

After a few seconds, Jock resumed poking at the GPS. 'Sorry,' he said.

Mallory rubbed her forehead, feeling cooped up in the car. 'Let's just make it to the next stop without blows, okay?'

The road ran on across a vast plain where train tracks scribed great arcs, sometimes touching the line of the road before diving off on a different curve into the distance. Triple and quadruple locos pulled double-decker container cars along the lines. Harry had been single-minded about trains since the age of two. Mallory could imagine him pressed up against the window, counting the wagons and calling out the numbers on the engines, and asking to stop to witness the big diesels thundering past.

She hadn't spoken to him in forty-eight hours. Please, she thought, let this drive be flawless. Let me reach him and fast.

•

For a while, they settled into a predictable rhythm for the journey, driving through shifting scenery while listening to a cycle of nostalgic songs and radio news, and then eating roadside food. Rinse and repeat.

Flagstaff, Arizona, flew past within the hour, bringing a landscape of elevated hills and pine forest bright with spring foliage. One mountain even had a snow cap. Then the mountain was in the rear-view, and the plains opened up again, pale green grass stretching from one horizon to the other, the wind rippling the surface like water.

Ernie again grumbled about the interstate, that it cut across the continent, barely touching down anywhere, but Mallory was only too happy to be a skipping stone.

After three hours, they stopped at a lonely petrol station with a Dairy Queen, and Mallory stretched her legs before they sat down to an early lunch. The TV screens were filled with volcano news.

'What exactly is that?' she asked, when Jock dug into a plate of unidentifiable white lumps in a white sauce, with a brown crumble on top.

He scratched his head. 'Biscuits and gravy with sausage, allegedly,' he said. 'It was this, or fifteen different varieties of sugar and peanut butter. Take your pick.' He emptied out a shopping bag loaded with Nutter Butters, Twinkies, Oreos, cheese-filled pretzels, Red Vines, chips, and numerous other glossy foil packets. Ernie frowned his disapproval.

Mallory pushed the packets around and chose one without really looking at it. She wanted to keep driving. After she'd helped Zadie and Ernie to the bathroom, they were nearly back to the car when Jock tapped Mallory on the shoulder.

'Here,' he said, holding out a pair of sunglasses, new tags still dangling off them. 'You were squinting something awful, and we're going to be driving east every morning. Also, I'm sorry about what Ernie said. Don't let him get to you. He's really an okay guy.'

'Thanks,' she said, but she still couldn't help feeling judged and inadequate in Ernie's eyes. It shouldn't have bothered her – after all, she'd encountered dozens of prickly residents over her time at Silky Oaks – but something about Ernie chafed her. Mallory found herself oddly protective of Zadie, and wondered how the two of them could suit each other.

'One more thing.' Jock held out a credit-card sized packet. 'I have a spare phone card. Please take it. Number's on the back. If you were roaming with your Australian one, it'll bankrupt you and you'll need a phone after Nashville. This has data and calls. Assuming you can get reception anywhere out here.'

Mallory was so touched by his kindness, she nearly cried. 'Aren't you worried I'll call Silky Oaks?' she said.

He shrugged. 'Just don't mention it to Ernie, okay?'

Mallory slid the glasses on with a sigh of relief and prepared to drive on, but found Ernie pondering his map, which he'd spread on the car's bonnet and weighted down with his cane. He had a yellowing photograph in his hand.

'I recognise this road,' he said, pointing across to a narrow bitumen strip alongside the interstate.

'All looks the same to me,' she said. 'Shall we go?'

'Look here,' Ernie said, poking the photo under her nose. 'Look at the shape of these hills, that double bump over there.'

Mallory peered at the faded image, and had to admit it did look like the same place. Maybe.

'We stopped here in sixty-eight, I'm sure of it,' said Ernie. 'There's an Indian trading post down there.'

'Doesn't look like anything's down there but tumbleweeds and potholes,' Mallory said, squinting down the tiny road.

'Believe me, it's there,' Ernie insisted as she climbed back into the car. 'Go that way.'

'I don't want to get lost.'

'We can't get lost with that GP-whatsit. The road will join up with the highway again, just a bit further down. Genuine Indian trading post.'

'Selling genuine stuff made in China and Mexico?' Jock said, then as Ernie scowled. 'I'm joking, Ern. Maybe we should just stick to the interstate.'

'I'm telling you this was a proper place with handcrafted goods. Zadie loved it. Be good for her to see it again. Help her memory.'

'I bought a poncho,' Zadie said from the back seat. 'A purple one. With all these squares of black and white.'

Ernie beamed with pure love.

As Mallory took the turn she wasn't happy, but consoled herself that she could still see the interstate. It was right there, across a strip of grassy land, and Jock offered the further comfort that the GPS indeed showed a highway entry only a few miles away.

'After that, it's an hour and a half to Holbrook,' he said. 'Probably stop there tonight, or a little further if you're okay to push on.'

When the sun vanished behind a cloud, she slid the glasses up on her head. On this narrow service road, the vast ocean of shifting grasses grew taller, as if the car was slowly sinking beneath the fronds. The gusting wind tumbled through the grass heads and buffeted the windows. Mallory frowned. That felt like storm winds. Sure enough, when she glanced out Jock's window, she saw a graphite smudge on the southern horizon. Her stomach flipped in a familiar and unpleasant way.

'What's that?' she said in a small voice, pointing.

Jock peered out. 'Looks like weather.'

'A storm?'

'Miles away,' Ernie said from the back. 'Moving slow.'

'Not necessarily a good thing,' Jock said. 'If it moves fast, it's gone fast.'

'Arizona is the lightning death capital of America,' put in Zadie. 'The guide book said so.'

'Great,' muttered Mallory. Why did it have to be a storm? She had visions of the unearthly patterns lightning made on the walls at home, when thunder cracked like splintering bones, and sticks whipped down on the roof. At home she could barely function with that going on, and here they were out in the open.

'What did I say – look!' Ernie said, pulling her back to the present.

A squat white building had appeared ahead. Mallory prepared to eat her words, until they came close enough to see the signs of abandonment. She pulled the car across the broken tarmac of the parking lot, weeds growing tall through the cracks. The building's white walls were yellowed by time and sun, windows smashed into stars.

Ernie was quiet as he climbed out and limped across. Mallory followed. Through one broken window, she could see empty tables and rafters full of cobwebs. A lonely, chipped buffalo figurine lay on its side on the floor, and an unidentifiable heap of fabric – perhaps ponchos made in Mexico – was piled in a corner. Not even Jock said anything.

'I'm sorry, Ernie,' Mallory said.

She did feel sorry for him, standing there before the tumbledown building, his expectations soured into disappointment for a second time. But if he felt such things, he didn't betray them, simply limped back to the car with a shake of his head. Mallory could hear him apologising to Zadie, and she in return patted his arm, the universal signal for *it doesn't matter*, though Ernie obviously thought it did. Mallory almost wished the place had been open, just to see Ernie smile.

Five minutes later, they were back in the car, pulling onto the service road with The Eagles still softly playing. After ten minutes, the road was still narrowing, the pavement cracked and lumpy.

'Shouldn't we have joined back to the highway by now?' she asked, slowing as the car wheels vibrated over the surface.

Jock frowned at the GPS screen. 'We've passed the point it said there was a ramp. Maybe the map's not up to date.'

'What do we do?'

'I guess we either keep going, or we turn back.'

No way was she going back. The interstate was maddeningly close, just across that strip of land and behind its low fence. Trucks burned past at seventy-five miles an hour, making it seem as though the car was hardly moving.

Finally, Mallory spotted an overpass. 'There it is,' she said with relief and accelerated.

'Excellent.' Jock stowed the GPS and leaned back.

Then the steering wheel wobbled. Mallory eased off the accelerator, hearing an ominous *fop-fop-fop*. The wobble amplified and the car sank in the back.

She bit her lip. Please, no. That was *not* a flat tyre; not here, not now. The noise was just because of the bad road. Any second now, when they reached that ramp and its smooth concrete surface, all would be well.

Jock glanced across. 'Feels like a tyre,' he said. 'Better stop.'

Swearing under her breath at the traitorous gods of motor vehicles, Mallory pulled the car to a stop. A few seconds later, she and Jock were staring at the deflated rubber of the rear passenger tyre, slumped like black dough under the wheel rim.

'I've got pins in my back and disc problems,' Jock said apologetically. 'Should I call a roadside assist?'

'That's okay,' Mallory said, feeling the pressure of time. Better to get this over with. 'I know how to change a tyre.'

She did. Once, when she was eighteen and two months pregnant, she'd been stuck after a late shift with a flat. She'd messaged Duncan, who had taken over an hour to pick her up, by which time it was past midnight and she was nearly hysterical. He'd apologised profusely: an unmissable conference call with developers in Chicago. But Mallory had been unpleasantly reminded of her mother, who never knew how to do anything around the house, always waiting for Mallory's father to get around to it, even though he almost never did.

At the time, there'd been a male orderly at Silky Oaks called Chris who drove a vintage muscle car and proudly told anyone who would listen that he'd done it up himself. Mallory had summoned the courage to ask him at lunch.

'You don't know how to change a tyre?' he'd asked around his mouthful of sausage roll, as astonished as if she'd said she didn't know how to brush her teeth. But he'd had kindness. After their shifts, in the staff carpark, he'd taken her through changing every tyre on her car until it was burned into her muscle memory.

She'd been late home, and Duncan had been mad. 'Who's this Chris guy?' he'd asked more than once. Later, Duncan had apologised and said he only felt awful because Mallory should be able to rely on him. But Mallory liked relying on herself, and swiftly learned how to fix leaking taps, adjust door hinges, and pull hair balls and lost toys from drain holes, all critical skills for living in the cottage.

Now, she swiped away chilled sweat with the back of her forearm. She had looked after herself and Harry for the past year, and she would finish this job too. They would all be warm and dry in the next town before long, and she would be in New York before she knew it. *Positive thoughts.*

She popped the trunk, trying not to look to the south, where the storm was spreading, a purple and grey bruise on the sky.

•

Of course, knowing how to change a tyre and doing it were two completely different things. For a start, they had to remove all the luggage to search for the jack and the spare, which were hidden under the floor of the boot. And then the spare turned out to be a dreaded space saver, so they'd have to limp at low speed into the next town and have the puncture fixed before they could drive on.

'Where's the wheel brace?' Mallory said, staring at the empty cavity around the space saver. Gusts of chilly wind buffeted her as she searched, and eventually found the brace cunningly hidden in a side panel. By then, she had a gooseflesh road from neck to wrist.

She lay on the grubby bitumen, trying to push the jack into the correct position. Her face burned with stress; she must have a red-hot flush up to her earlobes.

'It says there should be two notches in the chassis,' Jock called helpfully, the owner's manual open on his lap.

Mallory finally found the spot. 'Aha!' she said, aligning the jack with grim satisfaction.

Raising the jack up was awkward and slow, but soon it was touching the chassis, and she was ready to remove the nuts. After that, she'd jack the car and have the tyre off, then new one on, all done. So much faster than waiting around for help and not a moment too soon. She was starting to feel the irrational storm terror sinking its claws into her, and was eager to reach the next town. The last thing she wanted was to embarrass herself in front of her passengers.

As she was aligning the wheel brace, she heard a distinctive galloping engine roar on the interstate. A motorbike was coming towards them from the ramp ahead, a big black and chrome machine. The rider must have turned off the wrong way, and was now rumbling to a stop.

Mallory kept working, watching from the corner of her eye. A big guy in black leather swung his leg off, spiked his helmet onto the handlebars and came towards them with ground-eating strides. Mallory felt herself shrink. What the hell did he want?

'Howdy,' he said. 'You wanna hand with that?'

Later, she reflected that he might have sounded perfectly friendly. Might have had the very best intentions. But Mallory suddenly wasn't a grown woman on the roadside in Arizona. She was a little girl, back in her mother's house, watching through a split in the curtains while a man like this walked up the overgrown path and pounded his meaty knuckles into the front door. She heard the metallic chink of the door chain, the growling voice that threatened her father about money he owed someone. She felt the *crack* of wood as the man shouldered the door so hard, the chain broke. He'd just been making a point, trying to scare her parents. A minute later, his black boots had carried him out of their yard, but that incident had scarred a deep corner of Mallory's soul.

So now, she moved her body on instinct, blocking the man out. 'No. I'm fine,' she said, her whole body braced.

He took a step back, but Mallory still felt his presence behind her like the gathering storm: big, mean, and to be fled from as fast as possible.

'Got a storm coming in,' he said. 'You see that? And I'm a mechanic.'

She snuck a look at him, his features amplified by her dread. He towered over her, black sunglasses hiding his eyes, but not the yellowing bruise spreading into his left cheek and temple. His chest was absurdly muscular under his jacket. He didn't make any move towards the tyre, but he didn't leave either. Mallory turned back to the wheel, hoping he would evaporate, like the monsters under her childhood bed who couldn't find her if her eyes were closed.

'I'm nearly done,' she lied.

'Well,' he drawled doubtfully, 'if you're sure now.'

'Perfectly, thank you.' Her words were like chips of ice.

Ernie tried to cut in. 'I think we should let this man—'

'Ernie.' Her voice shot out, sharp and clipped. 'I know how to change a damn tyre. Butt out, will you?'

With this, the biker tipped a finger at his forehead as if he were wearing a hat. 'If you folks are fine, I better go run that storm into town. All y'all take care now.'

Mallory held herself rigid until he and his overloud bike disappeared down the road. Then she heaved a breath. Her heart was thundering, her arms jelly, as if she'd just survived a robbery at gunpoint and then decided to finish off the experience with a marathon of push-ups.

She took another breath, but her heart rate refused to normalise. The brace hung heavy from her hand.

'We could have been done by now,' Ernie complained, gesturing with his good hand at the departed bike. 'Why would you turn away a competent man's help?'

Competent man, ha! 'Don't worry,' Mallory said, through her clenched teeth. 'I *do* know how to change a tyre.'

No need to flinch at the lightning flashes, or to feel this was taking too long.

She shoved against the wheel brace, channelling her frustration. Chris had never mentioned that a flat tyre could be so *hot*. She kept catching her knuckles on the scorching rim. And this second-last nut wouldn't budge, no matter how she strained against it. She shifted position, tried again, feeling like her back muscles were about to pop.

'Come on,' she growled. She stood, and leaned all her weight on the brace.

The nut gave, and she fell, her knuckles crashing into the wheel hub. She heard one of them crack, and she tumbled rather ungracefully into the side of the car.

A hand touched her shoulder. 'You hurt?' Jock said. 'Want Ernie to take a look?'

'No, no,' she said, looking up to reassure him. He was holding his hat on against the wind. 'I just slipped. A graze, that's all.'

It wasn't quite the truth. On the surface, it didn't look bad: a sliver of skin had lifted off across the middle knuckle, as fine as tissue paper. But underneath, a deep-purple bruise spread between the first and second knuckle. Nothing seemed broken; she just needed a minute to recover. She tried to make a fist, and it felt like someone was driving a knife through her hand. No way was she going to ask Ernie to look at it.

Zadie wound down her electric window. The dark clouds seemed halfway across the sky now, the front a murky shade of green, much like Mallory's knuckle would look in a few days. An icy water drop flew into Mallory's forehead.

'Mabel,' Zadie said, 'it's going to snow. Just like it did before Christmas.'

'I'm sorry this is taking so long,' Mallory told her, slowly flexing her hand.

'You hurt yourself?'

Mallory extended the hand, hiding her discomfort. 'Just a bruise, see?'

Zadie reached out, and her fingers on Mallory's skin were smooth and warm and reassuring. 'You're a brave girl,' she said.

Mallory had to look away as tears prickled her eyes. Having rebutted an offer of help she didn't want to let Zadie down. 'Thanks,' she said with a sniff, 'But it's not going to snow. We're in the middle of the desert.'

'Mallory.' Jock raised his eyes up to the sky. 'I think we'd better get moving.'

'It won't snow, right?' she asked, far less certain.

'I don't want to scare you, but four years ago there was a snow storm in April. In Flagstaff.'

Mallory tried to pull in a calming breath, but her lungs were stiff. 'Isn't that the place we just drove through?'

'The same.' He shrugged and pointed at his phone. 'Sorry. Can't help that it's all on Google.'

'Great.'

She fitted the wheel brace on the last nut, which was tight, too, refusing to shift. Some lug-nut must have done them up in a shop with a power tool. After her last experience, she applied her weight with her foot. She leaned until her other foot left the ground and she was actually standing on the brace. Uh-oh. That wasn't good. Her weight wasn't enough. Left with no options, she stomped on it.

A metallic *snap* echoed off the road as her foot met the ground again, followed by a *tink* as one part of the wheel brace landed on the asphalt, another in some nearby grass.

Mallory and Jock stared for five shocked heartbeats. The wheel brace had snapped neatly across its weld into two very useless pieces.

She lost it. 'You've got to be kidding me! This is a brand-new car! How could that even happen?'

Jock peered at the broken pieces. 'Well . . . does it say, "Made in China"?'

Chapter 7

MALLORY TRIED EVERYTHING TO FIX THE WHEEL BRACE, or at least make it usable. She lashed the pieces together with bandages from Ernie's first-aid kit, but that couldn't hold up under the torque. A belt was just as useless. Ernie searched the car for the hire agreement and the emergency numbers, before concluding that Fiona must have walked off with them. In the meantime, Jock found booking information in his records and hunched in the front seat out of the wind, mobile pressed to his ear. From the lack of conversation, Mallory concluded that there was either no reception, or he was on extended hold. No assistance was coming soon.

She trekked across the gap to the interstate to try to flag someone down. She got close enough for the trucks zooming past to nearly knock her over, and realised the road had no shoulder. Worse, while there was an entry, there was no official exit. The man on the bike had turned off the wrong way, and any other compassionate motorists were unlikely to make the backwards turn. Icy raindrops spat down. The dark clouds had banished the sun and rebuilt the desert in shades of shadow. As she stumbled back, Mallory imagined them stuck inside the crippled car while the storm thundered through. Her panic rose to horror-movie levels.

She heard an engine above the traffic then, loud, and galloping, and ten seconds later a black motorbike came into view on the other side of the highway, the rider hunched against the wind. Wait . . . was that the same bike?

As it screamed past, Mallory's hopes sank, but a minute later she heard it again, coming back towards them. He took the same illegal turn as before, gunning down the service road, and pulled up.

Desensitised after the first encounter, Mallory had a better look at him, even as the wind whipped her hair across her face. He certainly made an impression, swinging his leg off the machine, a wall of bone and muscle and leather. Raindrops made tiny explosion marks over his jacket shoulders and sunglasses. Rather like that big guy in a movie Duncan had made her watch once. A face with no expression; a machine man, out to kill.

He had parked a little further back this time, as if he wasn't sure of his reception. Then he grinned. 'Thought you said you knew how to change a tyre,' he said, his words running together in a liquid drawl of amusement.

Mallory was still holding the broken back of the wheel brace. She lifted it, as much defence as explanation. 'Well, this broke . . .' she started. Then all the fight went out of her. She was hurt and exhausted. She needed a port. 'Don't suppose you've got one of these in your Harley?' she asked.

He tipped his glasses up on his head. Beyond the ugly bruise on his face, she saw his eyes for the first time – blue, behind thick lashes. 'My Harley?' he said in disbelief, twisting around to point a finger at the bike. 'Lady, that's not a Harley. That's a Rocket Three.'

With the absurdity of that comment, and of being mown down by a storm in the Arizona desert, Mallory laughed. 'That's a "no", then. Perfect.'

She slung the broken brace on the ground, and dropped her head, defeated. Lightning flashed, but the biker abruptly turned on his heel and strode across the land island towards the interstate.

'What are you doing?' she called as he vaulted the low fence and stepped out onto the road, where traffic raced past at alarming speed. Mallory put her hand over her mouth. Zadie's window lowered again and her face popped out, watching with raised brows.

'Oh shit,' Mallory muttered, as she heard the long squeal of brakes and a blaring horn of a red sedan. The biker stepped aside to give the car room to stop. The driver leaned out his window and yelled through a cloud of blue tyre smoke. Mallory heard the 'Are you crazy?' even over the wind.

The biker didn't seem to care. Mallory had no idea what he said to the driver, but the next moment the car had pulled away, performed the same illegal turn and parked near the Rocket. The driver popped the boot.

'Thanks so much,' Mallory called apologetically to the driver, a middle-aged man in worn jeans and a flannel shirt, with curling brown hair sticking out from under his cap, which he kept adjusting as he helplessly looked on.

In less than a minute, the biker had the stuck nut off the wheel with the borrowed brace and the car fully jacked, as though tyre changing just might be his Olympic sport.

Zadie peered down at him from the window. Mallory, with new hope of beating the storm, was determined to be useful and was ready with the spare. Thunder rolled over them like surf crashing on a beach.

The biker accepted the tyre with one broad hand. 'Had to be a space saver,' was all he muttered as he lowered the jack, job done like a pro. He returned the brace to the accosted driver, who took off at speed. Mallory, still attempting to recover her pride, tried to heft the flat into the boot. She couldn't even lift it. A warm hand touched her back.

'Here,' the man said. 'Let me wrangle that.'

His voice was just like the thunder, and he picked up the tyre as easily as a pool toy. The rain-spotted luggage followed.

Embarrassed, Mallory couldn't quite meet his eyes. Jock was the one who stepped up.

'Thanks, mate,' he said, offering the man his hand.

Ernie wound down his window. 'Are we ready now?'

The biker was unhurriedly wiping his hands on a blue cloth he must have pulled from his pocket, and his eyes finally caught Mallory's. 'Your grandparents?' he asked.

'Not exactly,' she said quickly, wanting to transform into something small and furry that could dart off to hide under the swaying grass.

A smile curved his lips. 'Not from around here, are you? Not with an accent like that. Australian?'

All Mallory could do was look at the ground. 'Guess so.'

'Well, Miss Australia, Winslow's still twenty clicks down the road,' he said, shoving the cloth back in his pocket. 'You fixin' to stay? Storm's gunna be a bad one and y'all be lucky to beat it now. Y'all can follow me in.'

So that's what she did. They'd only been moving for a minute when the first front hit. The rain came down in drenching sheets, and Mallory had to slow to a crawl just to see the lines ahead of her, often losing sight of the black bike. The knuckles of her uninjured hand were white against the wheel, and her heart thumped a pulse in the injured one. *Please, don't let it hail. Please don't get lost. Don't roll off the road into a flooded ditch.*

Every time lightning flashed through the glass and the thunder boomed, she had to bite her lip and remind herself that she was a grown adult.

Eventually, the downpour eased and they picked up speed, but it never stopped. After twenty-five minutes, the biker indicated a right exit off the highway. After two quick turns, he pulled under a motel awning, the carpark and street swimming.

Mallory took a long minute to peel herself out of the driver's seat and exit the car. The rain rushed down the gutters in torrents. Several guests were standing under the shelter, just watching. The huge black motorbike leaned on its stand, dripping water into a vast puddle, with no sign of the rider.

Ernie limped inside to sort out rooms, so Mallory helped Zadie out of the car.

'Wait,' she said, as Mallory went to lead her inside.

'What?'

Zadie closed her eyes and turned her face towards the storm, and Mallory realised she was enjoying the cold spray drifting in on the wind. Mallory stood with her, feeling those tiny pieces of the storm, and her anxiety finally emptied out.

She could notice other details, then. Jock staring at a sandy mud puddle forming on the footpath, his mind seemingly far away. The gutters overflowing into silver water ribbons from the roof of a derelict-looking KFC next door.

'It rained like this the day we left Nashville. Water drummin' down on the windshield, and all the fields green and muddy,' Zadie said, then glanced at Mallory, her focus a little off. 'But then, you've never seen it.'

Mallory didn't have the chance to respond before Ernie limped out with two keys, explaining that they only had two rooms and she and Jock would have to share. Mallory couldn't have cared less. By the time she was helping Zadie to the toilet, she was shaking from exhaustion and her stomach was rumbling. None of them had had any lunch.

'I'll go and find where we can get some food,' she said wearily.

'The desk said there's shops across the road,' Ernie said, confiscating the keys and meting out some cash. 'Bring back the receipt. The desk will probably lend you an umbrella.' He paused. 'And maybe you should clean up first.'

Only when she made it back to the room she'd be sharing with Jock did she notice the grease smear across her cheek. Her nails were black crescents, and her knuckle skin was bruising blue and purple under the dirt. She washed up quickly and then trekked through the rain with the borrowed umbrella to fetch sandwiches and instant noodles. Once Ernie, Zadie and Jock were eating together, with Ernie refusing all offers of help, she excused herself and put the 'do not disturb' up on the door.

•

Sitting on the bed ten minutes later, she stared at Skype on her phone. She'd already tried to call Duncan twice. The air in this room smelled rather strongly of smoke and something floral, which added to the claustrophobia of the drumming rain, and her feelings of hopeless inadequacy. She knew she should try to sleep, but she was too wired.

Instead, she went back over the bookmarked articles she'd found about Duncan and his company. The words were soon blurring together. His company was on the rise, blah blah, promising future, blah blah. Contracts in the works. Nothing new. She flicked back to his Twitter feed. Since she last looked, he'd posted a handful of new links. Most were interviews with CEOs or business policy articles that made her yawn so hard her jaw cracked. But the last was a list of nominees for an award run by something called the April Roundtable. Unusually, Duncan had commented on his re-tweet: 'So honoured to be in fine company.'

Mallory read through the piece: Duncan was one of five shortlisted up-and-coming CEOs for a grant and some kind of mentorship from 'some of the country's most successful executives'. The article spent most of its copy talking up the innovative approach of Duncan's software, and had a very clichéd quote from Duncan that winning the award would be a 'dream come true'. Mallory snorted. Duncan's dreams had already come true. How many more did he need?

With angry fingers, she stabbed at the email app on her phone. Bridget had sent a message: *I keep getting your voicemail. Are you ok? How far have you driven?* Mallory replied that she was in Arizona, and that she was fine, she just had a new SIM card. She would try to find out the number. She didn't have the energy to relay the details of tyres and storms.

She had just hit send when, unexpectedly, a Skype call came through, Duncan and Harry's picture lighting the screen.

'Hi, baby!' Mallory's heart leapt with joy as Harry resolved in the chair. He'd had a haircut, the sides and back sculpted into crisp lines, so different from the shaggy head he'd gone away with. She saw someone else leaning in behind him, but it wasn't Duncan: it was a woman with brown hair tucked up behind her head, dark eyes, and a nurse-like bearing.

'Ah,' said the woman. 'It's working, Harry. You talk now, go, go.'

'Mummy!' Harry said, his smile broad and happy.

Tears sprang into Mallory's eyes. She wanted to fling her arms around him. 'Oh, I so wanted to talk to you,' she cried. 'Whatcha doing?'

'We're going to the park soon,' he said. 'And we're having pizza tonight and bagels before school tomorrow. And Brady has a pet spider. It's huge, Mummy.'

'Wow,' she said, but all she heard was, *school tomorrow.* Pizza. Bagels. The new haircut. As if this new life was already cemented, the one Duncan had made for him. All fresh and clean and hopeful, while Mallory sat here with the smell of metallic grease clinging to her skin. She had to concentrate to hold herself together as Harry elaborated on the plans and wondered what a pet spider would be like.

'It all sounds fun,' she said carefully, when he finished. 'Are you feeling okay?' She desperately wanted to know.

'I'm good,' he said, then paused, looking down. 'I miss you, Mummy.'

Mallory could hardly speak. 'I miss you, too, Harry. So much. But you can call me anytime, okay? And I'm coming to see you.'

'You are?' He brightened. 'Daddy said you were too busy to talk.'

Mallory bit down hard on her tongue. 'Where's Daddy now?'

'At work. We're going to the park when he comes home.'

'Is that Maria with you?'

The older woman bent down and waved. 'Hello,' she said.

'Thank you so much,' Mallory said. 'I really wanted to talk to Harry.'

The woman glanced up, as if checking the door. She lowered her voice. 'Of course. All boys need their mother. We keep this call our little secret, okay, Harry?'

He nodded fervently. 'Because Daddy says I'm not allowed in his office without him.'

Both she and Maria knew it wasn't the office that was the problem. Mallory blessed the housekeeper for her daring, as Maria stood sentry while Mallory recited *The Little Yellow Digger* for Harry from memory. Finally, Maria said they should go.

After Harry said goodbye and got down, Maria turned back to the screen. 'You said you are coming?' she asked.

'Yes. I've just been delayed because of this volcano thing. I have a long drive left. A few days.'

'Good. Come soon. He misses you. I will try to find another time to call.'

Mallory held on to this hope, though her voice trembled. 'Tell Harry I love him.'

When the Skype screen closed, Mallory let her phone fall to the bed, tears running down her face. Something about that call had punctured her soul. She had to get away for a bit: Jock would want the room soon, and she didn't want to answer questions about her swollen eyes.

She pulled open the door and turned down the long hallway, heading for the little foyer space inside the motel's back door. The rain was still drumming down, but at least she could see outside. Maybe she could stand under the awning in the fresh air.

But someone was already in the foyer, sitting against the wall with his long legs stretched out, his clothes soaked to the skin.

Chapter 8

Mallory hesitated. The biker had removed his jacket, leaving his sodden black t-shirt to show off muscular arms and a wide chest. That should have been enough for her to turn around, but between his knees sat a king-size bucket of fried chicken. The sight was odd enough for her to pause.

Not that she wanted to speak to him. She didn't want to speak to anyone, not with her red eyes and thoughts of Harry bashing around in her head like moths blinded by a flame.

He looked up and caught her staring. Mallory wanted to die with how much of an idiot she felt. She knew he deserved a thankyou. A short, brief thankyou, and then she would be absolved from his debt. She could walk in the other direction and find her fresh air somewhere else.

She drew herself up and approached, hugging the wall. God, he was a big man, even sitting down. He was tearing into a drumstick with his teeth. Fee-fi-fo-fum, she thought, and almost giggled. Finding the funny helped with the nerves, and anyway, he was a bit too good-looking for a giant.

His hair was standing up in little wet clumps, and she realised from a dark halo on the carpet that his jeans were soaked, too. But the smell of fried chicken was so good she could almost understand why he hadn't changed. Her own stomach rumbled. 'I want to thank you for helping us out,' she said briskly as those blue eyes met hers. 'You didn't have to stop, or to come back for us. It was ... nice, of you,' she finished. There, that would do.

Awkwardly, she awaited a reply, wondering if he was giving her the silent treatment. Then he swallowed, and she realised he'd been avoiding talking with his mouth full.

'And here I figured you weren't real keen to talk to me,' he said. 'But you're welcome.'

'It's not that,' she said hastily, not wanting to appear rude or ungrateful. 'It's just that you . . .'

'Scared you?'

'No,' she said, too quickly. No way would she admit to that.

A smile curved his lips. 'Infringed on your sense of autonomy by offering to help you change a tyre?' The words rolled carefully – almost hypnotically – off his tongue. Mallory frowned. Wait ... was he mocking her? Prepared to be annoyed, she searched his face, but his eyes beneath that awful bruise only held a touch of sympathy.

'Well,' she said. 'Maybe a little.'

'Figured. I've got sisters,' he said. He picked up the bucket with his clean hand. 'Want some?'

Oh, she did. After all the rain, and the stress, she couldn't imagine anything better than a big piece of fried chicken. She edged closer.

'The KFC next door looked closed.'

'It is,' he said. 'Bein' repurposed. But the guy at the counter pointed me to another place that does chicken fried steak. Seems they bought up the old containers. Tastes reasonable.'

'Chicken fried steak?'

'Yeah. You know, steak that's fried like chicken,' he added, when she frowned.

'So that's steak?' Mallory said, still confused, but at least she felt less like crying.

He held up the drumstick, pretending to examine it. 'I'm gonna reasonably assume this is chicken. Damn weird-lookin' steak.'

'I'm so confused right now.' Mallory laughed, but she couldn't quite bring herself to sit down. Something about him was just so intimidating. She stood at the door, pretending to look out into the rain.

'Tell you what,' he said, 'I'm just going to sit here real quiet and listen to the rain. You wanna eat something? You go right ahead.'

He bent one leg so he could rest his arm. Mallory knew she either had to leave or take him up on the offer. Finally, she circled, sat two feet away, and peered into the bucket.

He tipped it towards her, shook it invitingly. She selected a wing.

He snorted. 'That's your choice?'

'What?'

'A wing? The runt of the box. At least take a thigh, or a rib, something with actual meat.'

'I like the runt of the box,' she objected, finding it surprisingly easy to push back against his relaxed manner. 'It's got the highest skin to meat ratio, and the skin is the best part.'

'All right,' he said slowly. 'I'll give you that one.'

They ate in silence for a few minutes, Mallory casting glances at him, slowly making him into a real human, and not a bully boy at her mother's door or a killer in a movie.

'You know you're soaked through,' she said finally, feeling comfortable enough to state the obvious.

'What?' he said, looking down at himself. 'Well, strike me dumb, I do believe you're right.'

She made a face. He was definitely mocking her now.

He gave her a sly smile and said, 'Believe me, I know.'

'Why didn't you change? You know the carpet's all wet under you.'

'What are you, my mother?'

She shrugged, and plucked a piece of tender meat from her wing. It tasted as good as it smelled. 'Eat your chicken,' she said.

He laughed. 'Gotta work on that accent, Miss Australia,' he said, pushing his Texas twang into cliché. 'Eat your *darn* chicken, AJ, or me and you are gonna mix, you hear?'

'Eat your *darn* chicken,' she repeated. The 'r' came out all wrong, but he laughed anyway. 'Does your mother really sound like that?'

'Nah. My mother's English, and a professor of literature in Austin. She wouldn't be caught dead soundin' like that. My dad's the Texan. Now my grammy? She'd sound like that.'

'Really?'

'We're a real big mixed bag of contradictions, our house. As for the carpet, I'm not changed because everything's soaked. Jeans, boots, bag, socks. That was a real lot of water, made it all the way down to my toothbrush.'

'Oh,' Mallory said, feeling bad for him, but she couldn't help a laugh.

'Oh yeah, you laugh now,' he said, feigning hurt. 'After I come back for your broken-braced ass.'

'I'm sorry, it's not funny. And you didn't have to come back.'

He shrugged those big shoulders. 'Wasn't going to leave a lady and her grandpas stuck out in a storm, even one who doesn't want help. When I didn't see you come past, figured there was a problem. Went back to check it out.'

'That was nice of you. Really.' A few seconds ticked by. Mallory kept eating, and glancing at him, surprised by how easily he made her laugh. 'Um . . . what happened to your face?'

'Well, see, I had this disagreement with another guy's fist,' he said, matter-of-fact. He dropped another set of cleaned bones on the lid and dug for a fresh piece.

'I guess that makes sense,' she said, sounding wary.

He shrugged. 'There's always someone who wants to take a swing at the big guy. Usually, I walk away. Just not this time.'

A silence settled, acknowledging the conversation had reached a too-personal territory. Mallory looked for another piece of chicken but, feeling her fatigue, didn't pick one up. She really should go and check on Ernie, Zadie and Jock, and then see if she could take a nap. But she couldn't make herself stand and be alone again.

'They're not my grandparents,' she said over the rain.

'I do remember you sayin' that.'

She took a heavy breath. 'I'm just helping out. I was stuck in LA with this volcano thing. They're going to Nashville and I'm going to New York, so we made a deal to travel together.'

He paused his eating and turned to look at her. 'You just decided to help some total strangers you met in the airport?'

'Not exactly,' she said, and explained about working at Silky Oaks, and their nurse walking out on them, and meeting by chance in the airport.

He nodded. 'So just moderate strangers, then. Why Nashville?'

'Going to a wedding, apparently. Except Jock. He's going to Virginia.'

'Lot of effort, driving across country just for a wedding.'

Mallory chuckled. 'That's nothing. They had to break out of Silky Oaks first,' she said. 'But don't tell anyone. Ernie's a bit worried about being found out.'

He grinned. 'That a fact? Guess it must mean a lot to them. And what about the vet? He the one going to Virginia?'

Confusion pulled at her forehead. 'Vet?'

'Vet. Veteran. Guy with the hat?'

'Yeah, that's Jock. What makes you think he's a veteran?'

'I was in the Marines for eight years, just got out last June. I can spot a military man.'

Mallory frowned. The idea hadn't occurred to her, but now she remembered all those models of aircraft and tanks in Jock's room. For the first time, she realised she didn't understand at all why he was living at Silky Oaks. He seemed far more able than the other residents. It must be the problem with his back – he might not be able to cope in his own home anymore.

'You got a name, Miss Australia?' the man said suddenly.

'Mallory,' she said. 'And you're AJ?'

'In the flesh.' He offered his hand, as if they'd only just met. After a moment's hesitation, Mallory shook. Despite his wet clothes, his palm was warm and dry, and enveloped hers like an oversized glove. She winced at the pressure.

'My grip ain't that strong,' he said, quickly releasing her. 'You hurt that hand?'

'It's nothing,' she said, tucking it under her leg. 'What's AJ short for? Albert James?'

'No.'

'Alexander Joel?'

'It's just what my friends call me. So you can do the same. Now we've exchanged chicken grease and all.'

She laughed. 'So, are you headed home to Texas? I know that's the next state over.'

'Two states over. And no, I'm headed to Chicago.'

'For a holiday?'

'Nope. Just doing a long ride, the old route sixty-six, all the way from Santa Monica Pier.' But there was a hesitation in his voice, the same one that Jock had had when Mallory asked about what he was going to do in Virginia.

'You take a long break from work or something?'

He shook his head, but hesitated again. 'I haven't worked since I discharged. I was supposed to be starting a bike shop up in LA, but it . . . fell through. So I hit the road.'

'Just you and your non-Harley Rocket. What?' she said, when he broke into a huge grin.

'My non-Harley Rocket, that's a new one.'

'You didn't think I'd remember?'

'Oh, I'm correctin' all kinds of assumptions now,' he said. 'Yeah, me and my Rocket. It's a Triumph. That's my mother's English genes rubbin' off on me. What's in New York?'

'My son,' she said before she could think.

'You gonna hit Broadway and Times Square together?'

'He's five.'

'Ah.' He nodded a few times, chewing, as if mentally calculating. 'So, what'd *he* do?'

'Who?'

'Your man. I mean, otherwise, why are you driving across the country with folks you don't know to see your boy? Sounds like a man problem. I told you, I have sisters.'

Mallory's appetite evaporated as he hit way too close to home. She became all too aware of herself: what was she doing, sitting here in a hallway talking to this man? Laughing at what he said? When she had so far yet to travel.

'Thanks for the chicken,' she said, standing up. 'But I'd better go.'

'I say something wrong?' he said. She could hear the surprise in his voice.

'No. I just have things to do,' she said, trying not to look back as she walked down the hall.

She tried and failed to lie down and sleep, her thoughts alternating between Harry, and AJ sitting there in his wet clothes. When Jock came back after twenty minutes, his hat wet from the rain, she gave up.

AJ was no longer in the back foyer, so Mallory went to the desk to ask which room he was in, and knocked on his door. He opened it wearing only a towel, looking like a bodybuilder who'd just stepped out of the shower. Oh. My. Lord.

'I was just, you know, thinking ... I mean, that you didn't have ... I mean, here,' she said, shoving a folded grey t-shirt towards him and trying to find something fascinating about the doorjamb. 'Jock said it's old and he doesn't want it back.' She felt the flush rise up her neck as her words tripped over themselves.

AJ reached out and took the shirt. 'That's a kindness.'

'Least I can do after you helped us out,' she said. Man, her face was on fire now. She tried to be brave and look up at him, but all she found was a pair of beautiful blue eyes staring down from above that incredible body. 'Anyway, I um, enjoy the shirt. Bye.'

Mallory fled back to her room and shut the door, her face incandescent with embarrassment. She slid into the bathroom before Jock, who was watching the cable news, could ask questions. She stared at herself in the mirror, trying to focus on Harry. Thank goodness all the drama was over, and she wouldn't have to see AJ again.

•

The storm beat itself out in the late evening, the sound of falling water replaced with the hiss of all-night trucks cruising down the rain-washed interstate. Jock was already asleep when Mallory returned from helping Ernie and Zadie into bed. The room was dark, but Mallory could have sworn he was still wearing his hat.

She took an age to fall asleep, her thoughts a carousel that rushed around and around, from desperate longing for Harry to the journey ahead, with brief intrusions of AJ in his towel. She almost wished she hadn't taken him that shirt. Maybe he really was some rough-up guy, with that bike and those bruises on his face. Even if he had seemed perfectly normal to talk to. There'd been bruises on his ribs, too. She couldn't believe she'd told him anything about Harry.

She closed her eyes and rolled over with a groan. They hadn't driven as far as they'd meant to, then the whole thing with the storm and the tyre. Her bruised hand had stiffened. It had been more than enough for one day, without mysterious biker men added in.

As she finally drifted to sleep, she prayed for an easier tomorrow, free of mechanical problems and lies from husbands, and dark knights on steel horses. Just let them stay on the road and cover as many miles as they could.

She woke early with thin light streaming in behind the curtains. Jock had already dressed in shorts and a button-down shirt, his hat in place, and was pulling up the bedsheets, smoothing the creases into precise folds, tucking them tight against the mattress. Mallory watched him with one eye open, thinking of what AJ had said about him. He certainly looked like he knew how to make a bed, army-style.

'Mind if I turn on the TV?' he asked, seeing she was awake. 'Just want to catch the headlines. Then I'm out of here. Give you the room to yourself.'

The morning news was still full of the travel chaos. Mallory, dressed in last night's trackpants and t-shirt, threw back the covers just as fervent knocking came at the door. She found Ernie on the stoop, out of breath.

'It's Zadie,' he said.

Mallory ran as though last night's lightning had electrified her whole body. Zadie sat on the edge of her bed, hands braced, her frail shoulders shuddering up and down with each laboured breath.

Mallory's automatic reaction was to hit the emergency button that would bring the nurses, but she wasn't at work now. Sweat gathered between her shoulderblades. Was Zadie having a heart attack? A stroke? Ernie was pacing back and forth, as though he didn't know what to do first.

'Ernie,' Mallory said. '*Ernie.*'

He stopped pacing.

'Have you called an ambulance?'

'Mallory.' Jock stood in the doorway, pointing at a phone held to his ear. 'They're on their way.'

'Okay, good. Ernie,' she said, putting a hand on his arm, 'the ambulance is on its way. What can we do in the meantime?'

'Yes. Yes, all right.' Ernie finally collected himself, easing down on the bed beside Zadie. He tried to feel her pulse but was hampered by his weak leg and arm, which threw off his balance as he held her wrist. 'Stay with me, love,' Mallory heard him say under his breath. 'Please, stay with me.'

The paramedics' arrival brought relief. Mallory was finally able to take stock as they strapped an oxygen mask and ECG dots on Zadie, and asked a flurry of medical history questions. Zadie was already calmer by then. As the medics monitored her ECG, Mallory sank down onto a desk chair for support, wondering what would happen now.

A few minutes later, one of the paramedics came across. 'We can't find any signs of your grandmother having any heart problems. This might just be a panic attack. But we think it's best she be reviewed in hospital.'

He waited, as if asking for permission. Mallory glanced at Ernie, who had Zadie's hand in his as she lay on the stretcher. 'Yes, of course,' Mallory said.

The Little Colorado Medical Centre was only a few minutes away. Once Zadie had been reviewed and settled, Ernie finally left her side and came out of the room. He was pale, his bad leg trembling. Mallory drew him towards a seat in the hallway, afraid he was about to fall.

'How are you doing?' she asked.

'They're not worried. Seems it was a panic attack. It's happened once before, when she's been disoriented. She just seemed so . . . buoyed by this trip and she's usually so settled in the mornings after a rest. I was caught off guard.'

'I mean, how are *you* doing?'

Ernie blew out a long breath and shot Mallory a quick glance. She saw something vulnerable in his eyes. The stiffness seemed to leave him. 'Oh, I'm fine,' he said. 'Nothing to worry about here. Just a little tired.'

'You take such good care of her.'

Ernie looked down at his feet, as if he was considering what to say. Mallory would have put equal money on a profound insight and a scathing rebuke against the hideous carpet pattern. Finally, he shook his head. 'She is the most amazing woman I ever met,' he said. 'Like a shining star. I couldn't believe she wanted to leave home and come all the way back to Australia with me. She left her family here, their farm, with all the animals she loved. That was a big thing for her.'

'I gathered that,' Mallory said, groping for comforting words. 'She seems to have a kind soul.'

'Yes. A big heart. Generous. Selfless. Then she gets this damned disease. And where's the justice in that? After the good she did all her life, and everything else that happened.' He paused. 'I'm sorry if I made some incorrect assumptions about you. I was . . . glad you were there this morning. I couldn't put my thoughts together. Too long retired, I suppose.'

Mallory smiled, a well of gratitude warming her heart, even if Ernie couldn't quite meet her eyes. 'I was glad to be there, too,' she said.

'This trip is for her, you know,' he went on. 'I promised her, and I'll keep that promise if it's the last thing I do. You know—' He paused again, and this time he looked around, as if remembering where he was.

Abruptly, he set his cane and hauled himself up. 'I should go and . . . find her doctor again. It's not like in Australia. They charge you for everything here. Even that ambulance trip will be a bomb.'

'I can do that for you. Why don't you sit and rest and I'll—'

'No,' he said sharply. 'You take a cab back to the motel. Go and be useful. Make sure we're ready to go when they discharge her.'

Mallory closed her mouth. Just when she thought they were getting somewhere the old Ernie had resurfaced. He shuffled a few steps down the hall, then stopped and looked back, as though he might apologise, but he didn't.

Mallory sighed. But she had seen that moment of tenderness in him, and it allowed her to forgive him everything he'd said.

Chapter 9

ON THE WAY BACK TO THE MOTEL, MALLORY FINALLY remembered the tyre, still flat as a pikelet in the boot of the hire car.

'It's sorted,' Jock said, when Mallory flew in panicking, trying to google somewhere in Winslow to take it before Ernie and Zadie were ready to be picked up. Jock was sitting at the narrow desk, still watching the volcano news.

'What? How is it sorted?'

'Took it to a tyre place.'

Mallory frowned. 'What about your back?'

'I mean, AJ took it to a tyre place.'

Mallory felt as if someone had just smacked her in the forehead. 'AJ? The biker guy? But how on earth did he do that?' She laughed. 'That must have been a funny sight, taking a tyre on a bike . . . wait.' She narrowed her eyes at Jock. 'You let him drive the car?'

'Why not?'

'But you went with him, right?'

'Nope.'

Mallory gaped. 'Ernie doesn't even let *me* have the keys alone. What if he'd . . .'

'What?'

'I don't know! Taken off with the car, or run it into a street pole or something.'

'I didn't know when you were coming back. You'd have been worried if I wasn't here. AJ seems a decent bloke. He knows a good mechanic shop. Did you know he's a mechanic? And now the job's done. No harm.'

'Jock, we just met him on the side of the road. He's not even on the car agreement.'

Jock shrugged. 'Neither are you.'

Mallory threw up her hands. She couldn't argue with that and there were no Rocket motorbikes in the motel carpark, so AJ must already be gone.

They were back on the I-40 by eleven, Ernie impatient and insisting on examining how the suitcases had been loaded before they could leave the hospital. Then they were heading east into the tan grasslands shadowing the Little Colorado River. The only evidence of yesterday's storm was the rapidly evaporating puddles in the low spots on the road verge. By the time they had passed through Holbrook and had swung north, heading for the New Mexico border, the land was dry again. Dust devils twisted across the plains.

Ernie and Zadie slept in the back, unsurprising after the morning's events. Mallory was reminded of Harry as a baby, falling asleep in the chugging Corolla as they drove home from grocery shopping on Saturday mornings. She'd often been coming off an overnight respite centre shift, but even on the nights she hadn't slept much, those small trips had been cherished time with Harry, carrying him on her chest around the supermarket. Duncan had stayed at home, madly coding in the rare time alone, and equally exhausted. How they had all survived those early years was a mystery, but she no longer remembered the exhaustion, only how soft Harry's hair had been against her lips.

The thought tied her stomach in a longing knot, and she sighed, a big gush of air, trying to release the tension.

Jock glanced across from the passenger seat. 'That's a wicked bruise you've got on your hand. You do that yesterday?'

'Oh, yeah. It's nothing. Just my memento of the trip.' In actual fact, Mallory was constantly reminded of it every time she knocked the injury into things.

After a long pause, Jock said, 'I know Ernie's a difficult character to like.'

'Careful, he might hear you,' she said, and glanced in the rear-view.

'Nah, he's out. Last month, I took out the piano accordion when he was asleep like that. Never even moved. The staff on the other hand . . . they moved pretty quick.'

'Let me guess – they didn't want you to disturb anyone?'

He tapped his nose. 'I offered to take it down the garden, or switch to the bagpipes, their choice. I don't think anyone found it funny. It's a stern mob in our wing.'

Mallory laughed, but she felt bad for Jock, too. 'That's a shame. You should be able to play.'

'Maybe they have enough to do. More than one of them's refused to deal with Ernie, and mysteriously transferred somewhere else. Fiona didn't even last a day . . . actually, it was negative time, if you account for the date line. Rate you're going, you're setting a record. That's why he keeps the car keys. Afraid you'll bugger off, too.'

'He does have a knack for being . . . difficult. And opinionated.'

'Yeah,' Jock said, nodding. 'That he does. Bit surprised he's gone his whole life without someone breaking that nose of his. Nutter Butter?'

He offered a packet full of dusty-looking biscuits. Mallory took one and bit down on something crunchy and peanut buttery. She wasn't sure if she liked it.

She chewed meditatively. 'So how is it you're friends?'

'I was in my "try something new" phase.'

Mallory laughed. 'Seriously.'

'Because he's always interesting company. Silky Oaks was a logical move for me, but it can be lonely as hell. He's smart as razors. Always have a good yarn with him. Keeps the old black dog away.'

This time, Jock glanced in the rear-view, then reached around and poked Ernie in the kneecap. 'Hey, Ernie,' he said. When he received no response, he lowered his voice. 'See? Out like a light. The thing is, I can't imagine he was always like this. Must absolutely gall him that he can't work anymore after his stroke. And now he feels like he's losing his wife, too. I think that's why he's like he is.'

Mallory grunted, remembering the vulnerability she'd seen that morning. 'I can understand that.' She fixed her gaze back on the highway, watching it slide under the bonnet. Metre after metre, mile after mile. 'It must have been a huge change.'

'I don't know how much someone else can understand the things that really change you,' Jock said quietly. 'The ones that mean you're never the same again. It's always so personal.'

Mallory thought about Harry in that moment. Would this whole situation be something that changed her forever? Would she fail to bring him home? Would it change him forever too? She hated the idea that her little boy, who'd only just started school, would suddenly realise that he couldn't see his mother anymore. No one else would know what that was really like for him.

'Maybe not,' she said finally, trying to steer her mind back to Silky Oaks. 'But we should be able to make better places to live. I had all these ideas.' And she told him about her aspirations to be the Engagement Manager, to bring in animals and new programs that gave everyone a real connection with life. Jock nodded along, making noises of agreement.

'So you organised those kids coming in every fortnight?'

'Yeah, that was me,' she said. 'I read some research that said having animals and children around could literally bring people back to life. You know, because they're unpredictable. Gives you things to talk about and look forward to.'

'Bit like this trip, I suppose.'

Mallory paused. 'Yes, I guess. Except with fewer volcanoes and flat tyres.'

Jock laughed.

'Ernie said this trip was for Zadie, a promise he made. Do you know what that's about?'

'Not exactly. They're very close, those two,' he said. 'He's protective. She's just lovely. On her good days, she'll talk for hours and hours about her animals and her work. Other days, she'll tell me the same story over and over in the present tense, lost in some childhood memory, or not say much at all.' He shook his head. 'Damn terrible disease, isn't it? That's why I do sudoku.' He held up a book of logic problems, folded back on its spine and scratched with pencil marks. 'Keep the old grey matter firing.'

'Seems to be working,' Mallory said, puzzled about Jock. She couldn't quite reconcile his pleasant, capable persona with him living in a care facility. 'Was it your back that made you move to Silky Oaks?'

'Oh, I have some trouble with a few things. Hard to live in a house when you can't lift a ladder. Nice of that AJ bloke to lend a hand, wasn't it? Nice to see a young fella like that with a good heart.'

'Yes. Nice of him,' she replied, but she didn't want to think about AJ. The memory of him was fading nicely with every mile closer to Harry.

'So, what happened to being the Engagement Manager?' Jock asked.

'Oh. They wanted someone else.'

'I'm sorry.'

Mallory shrugged. 'It's okay. Maybe next time.'

'Or maybe you should work somewhere else.'

Mallory didn't answer. She was too busy thinking about all the things she had to do before work even rated on her priority list.

•

The border crossing into New Mexico was marked only with a small green sign. Ernie and Zadie slept on until Mallory pulled into a truck stop near Gallup. After they lunched on Subway sandwiches, Mallory used the last dollars in her pocket to buy a bag of the cheese-stuffed pretzel things that Jock kept offering her, and another of Nutter Butters.

'Stupid addictive American food,' she muttered as she handed across her money. Great time to become a stress eater.

After that, they were back on the road. Ernie requested a new playlist, so the speakers spilled Buddy Holly and Roy Orbison as they ran neck and neck with the freight trains beside the highway. The landscape gradually greened. Fields appeared beside the road with orderly, tractored rows and trees. Low hills replaced the endless plains, and the highway passed through cuttings of dark fractured rock. They flew over the dry bed of the Rio San Jose, and then on, on, through the rising canyon tops of Albuquerque.

When the sun was sinking, Mallory checked the time and was surprised it was nearly six. They'd been driving for five and a half hours, the GPS indicating they were nearing Santa Rosa.

'Should we stop in the next town or keep going?' she asked, hoping to drive on. The light was still bright and they'd lost time this morning. But it had been a very long day for Zadie.

'Probably best to stop,' Ernie said.

She swung off the I-40 onto the old Route 66 towards downtown Santa Rosa, scanning for a motel. She'd just spotted one on the other side of the road when Zadie gave a strangled cry.

Mallory jumped in fright and reflexively braked, pulling onto the narrow shoulder with a skid. 'What is it?'

Zadie flapped her hands, fumbling with the window buttons, frantically looking behind. 'There!' she said. 'Go back!'

Mallory shot a questioning eyebrow at Ernie, but a passing car blared a horn at them for being half out in the lane, so she pulled out again and kept going.

'No!' Zadie insisted. 'No, no! Go *back*!'

'Turn around,' Ernie said. 'She must have seen something.'

Just barely managing to avoid an accident, Mallory found a place to swing through the centre and head back the way they'd come. Meanwhile, Zadie found the electric window button, wound it down, and took her belt off. That set off some alarm in the car, so Mallory had to stop amid the chaos of Ernie trying to prevent Zadie from hanging out the window and a passing truck blasting a horn at them, and incessant beeping. The car rocked to a halt, Mallory's head and heart pounding. Lord, could she catch a break sometime soon?

'How far back?' Mallory asked, when the window had been wound back up and something like order restored.

Zadie could only point through the rear glass. Mallory made another U-turn and stuck on her hazard lights, driving slowly in the right-hand lane so that other cars could pass. It didn't take long.

'That's it?' Mallory asked, pulling over. Decorating a light pole on the shoulder was a large white poster board with a bucking bronco rider and *Clovis Rodeo* in old-west font.

'You want to go to the rodeo?' Ernie asked.

The joy on Zadie's face said everything. Jock tapped at the GPS. 'Clovis is south of here, near the border with Texas.'

'But that's not where we're going,' Mallory said.

'How far?' Ernie asked.

More tapping. 'Less than two hours.'

A hard belt of steel wrapped around Mallory's resolve. The drive was far enough as it was, the time to reach Harry already insufferably long. 'No,' she said. 'We can't add that time. I need to get to New York, and you said you wanted to reach Nashville as soon as possible. We have to stick to the interstate.'

Zadie's eyes dulled, and she stared forlornly at the sign. Ernie was trying to negotiate. They could find another rodeo to go to after they reached Nashville, couldn't they, Zade? But the atmosphere in the car was thick with disappointment, like when Mallory told Harry he couldn't stop to see a passing train. Zadie wanted to go to *that* rodeo.

Tears built behind Mallory's eyes, and she blinked them away, hopelessly conflicted. How could she believe the things she believed about giving elders more of their lives back, see that excitement in Zadie's face and not make the detour? And yet, how could she be Harry's mother if she did?

Jock let the GPS fall in his lap. 'Look, just pull into that servo up the road. I'll run some calculations. We'll need to make a fuel stop anyway.'

•

Ten minutes later, Mallory leaned on the car with a cold bottle of water pressed to her forehead. She hadn't said a word while helping Ernie or Zadie to the toilet. Zadie was now sitting in the car with the door open, mistakenly thinking they were going to that rodeo. Ernie had spent the past minute trying to convince Mallory.

'You do remember what happened the last two times we left the highway?' Mallory asked, ticking them off on her fingers. 'First, we ended up at the creepy abandoned diner, second, we blew a tyre and were nearly scrubbed out by a storm. Things come in threes.'

'Ridiculous superstition. This won't be like that,' Ernie said. 'Jock, tell her.'

'It doesn't add that much time overall,' Jock said, clearly uncomfortable about being put in the middle. 'Yes, we head south-east, but then we turn across the border after Clovis, and come back to the I-forty at Amarillo. Thirty minutes difference to just staying on the interstate all the way.'

'Plus the time at the rodeo itself.'

'Well, yes, a little of that,' Ernie said. 'What if I make it worth your while, a little bonus cash?'

Mallory closed her eyes on a wave of despair. 'It's not about the money.'

At this, Jock slipped back into the car, ending any stake in the negotiations.

Ernie limped a few steps towards the long shadow cast by the service station's road sign, then turned back. 'Can I have a word in private over here?'

Mallory followed with reluctance. In the shade, she folded her arms. 'It's not that I don't want her to go, Ernie,' she said. 'But I need to be somewhere too.'

He sighed and worked his jaw, as if the words had to be wrangled and forced out of his mouth. She hadn't seen him take such a long time to speak about anything.

'You know, I used to think like that, too,' he said finally. 'All my working life. I always had to be somewhere else.'

Mallory opened her mouth to argue this wasn't about *work*, but he held up a hand, appealing for her patience. His voice became low and full of regret.

'I wasn't a very good husband to her, Mallory. She trusted me, left home for me all those years ago. Moved to a new country where she didn't know anyone. Then I spent our life together working. Always working.'

He paused, then gave a laugh that was more like a startled bray. 'Oh of course it wasn't what I intended to do. I thought when the next stage of my career was done, I'd have more time. When residency was over, when college exams were over. When I moved into private practice. But it never changed. I used to tell her that babies don't respect schedules, and that was why I was always at the hospital. There was always a crisis to sort out. She said she understood.'

He paused again, took a breath, and briefly caught Mallory's eye. Something about him seemed so diminutive under the distant hills. 'Then one day, she's having trouble remembering who I was. And I realised that I wasted all that time with her. I always made her promises – we'll go on this trip, or that trip, but it never happened. I think I broke every promise I ever made her, including the very first one.'

Mallory rubbed her face, moved against her will. This was clearly her cue to ask. 'What was the first one?'

'To get married in the Wightman Chapel in Nashville.'

Mallory looked up. 'So this wedding . . .'

'It's ours,' he said. 'I always believed once was enough, but it's my last chance to make it all up to her, just a little bit, for all the things I promised and never did. She wanted to get married in that chapel, and that's what I'm going to give her.'

Mallory put a hand to her forehead, laughing and shaking her head. 'Here I am, wondering what the next awful thing is that you're going to say to me, and it turns out you're a romantic after all.'

She meant it as a compliment, but Ernie made a sour face and huffed. 'You young people don't know what love is anymore,' he said, but even his grumpiness couldn't dent Mallory's new view of him.

She shook her head. 'I think you're just saying that to make sure I know it's still you in there.'

This time, Ernie smiled and raised a hand, a small gesture, asking for forgiveness, for compassion, to be given all the things that he himself was struggling to give. 'I don't know what's going to happen to us when we return to Australia. I don't know how long she's going to remember me. I would never have done this for me. But since we began, she's said more, remembered more than ever. If she wants to go to a rodeo, I want to take her. I'd like you to help me. Please.'

He set his mouth, as if uttering that last word had been tantamount to spilling his blood all over the Santa Rosa soil.

Mallory tipped her head back and breathed in dust and diesel fumes rolling in off the road. Really, she was helpless in the face of his declaration. And Jock said it wouldn't add much time.

She sighed. 'Better tell Jock to load up the GPS,' she said. 'We don't want to get lost.'

●

They took Highway 84 south. For the first half-hour, the setting sun cut long grey bands across their path, the purple and magenta sky competing with the red earth fields that stained the road a dusky orange. To Mallory, it seemed the twilight would never end, each stretching shadow pushing her further from Harry.

After nearly an hour, the sun was finally gone. They drove through Fort Sumner and the GPS's cheery voice directed them onto Route 60, the road painted in the last pink blush of day.

Mallory stifled a yawn.

'Stop if you see a motel,' Jock said.

'It's only another hour to Clovis.'

'It is. But you're tired. Pull up when you see one.'

'I'm fine, it's not that far.'

'Mal.'

She glanced across. He had a kindness in his eyes. 'Pull over, okay? It's been a long day.'

They spent the night at a Super 8 with rendered block walls and deep green carpet. Jock magicked meals out of the motel reception. Mallory meant to work out the time zones to try Skyping Harry, but the next thing it was eight in the morning and she was lying on the bed with her shoes still on. She hadn't realised how exhausted she was. She flew out of the room in a panic, thinking that Zadie and Ernie must have needed something by now. As it turned out, they were just waking too, so she took care of their showers and toilets.

By the time they'd all eaten breakfast, it was nearly ten, and Mallory's mood was as black as her coffee. The sun was depressingly high as she turned the car east on Route 60. The only thing that buoyed her was Zadie, who had insisted on being dressed in a pair of white jeans, a purple button-down blouse, and a pair of flat-heeled cowboy boots, which were so supple and well-worn they must have been favourites for years.

'She hasn't wanted to wear any of that for ages,' Ernie said with approval. 'I was only hoping when I packed it.'

Such enthusiasm couldn't help but be contagious. Along the hour's drive, the highway cut through tiny, neat towns and joining roads that ran off through golden pastures and were swallowed in the curve of the earth. Fields gradually replaced the pastures, until Mallory drove into the wide streets of Clovis, bustling with horse floats and pick-ups, and good-looking people in jeans and cowboy boots.

When they took a wrong turn, Jock asked directions to the showground from a pair of young cowboys sitting on the tray of their truck, one of them strumming a guitar. Something about the smile the guitar player gave them, and his wishing them a good day and tipping his hat, shot a ray of sunshine into Mallory's mood, and unexpectedly she thought of AJ. It must be the accent.

'Look at that roan,' Zadie said from the back seat, pointing out yet another horse to Ernie. 'Just like Silver Dollar. Lovely mare.'

When they drove into a dusty, grass-studded field that served as the rodeo parking lot, a marshal took one look at the three passengers and directed them to a park near the entrance. As she stepped out of the car, Mallory was swept up into the excitement. Everyone who passed seemed to have a patriotic light burning: American flags adorned bumper stickers and belt buckles, flew on flagpoles and on t-shirts, and were drawn on faces. One horse had red, white and blue ribbons woven in its mane. The air smelled of fresh leather and smoke and turned earth. Competitors passed by with numbers on their backs and tasselled chaps shimmering down their legs.

Then Mallory pulled up short. Standing in the shade of a food stand, being admired by more than a few passers-by, was a shiny and rather unmistakable Rocket motorcycle.

Chapter 10

'Did you see that?' Mallory asked Jock as they slowly ascended the grandstand stairs.

'What?'

'AJ's Rocket, parked down there.'

'I did,' he said cheerfully. 'Nice ride, that.'

'Do you think he's following us?'

'AJ? Nah, he called to see how we'd gone with the repaired tyre. Mentioned we were going this way. He said it sounded interesting.'

Mallory frowned. 'When did he call?'

'Oh, while you and Ernie were talking at the servo back in Santa Rosa. Gave him my number in Winslow in case we had problems with the tyre.'

'Can we please focus on the task at hand?' Ernie said. 'We don't need to go any higher, Zade.'

Soon, they were seated with a good view of the ring, with several kind people making room on the end of a row. Jock sat on Mallory's left, with Zadie and Ernie to her right.

'I didn't think to bring my hat,' Zadie said, looking wistfully around at the sea of western headgear.

'It would certainly go with that shirt,' Mallory said. 'Though that's the extent of my knowledge. I've got no idea about anything they're doing down there.' She watched as two riders in the ring worked to cut a calf from a pack, and rope it front and back. One rider then jumped down to tie the calf's legs together. Mallory pitied the small helpless animal.

'It's roping,' Zadie said, more lively than Mallory had ever seen her. 'Cowboys started all these games to be faster at their jobs, but I never liked it. Didn't like to see the little calves branded or tied down on the ground like that.'

'No, I imagine not,' Mallory murmured. Down in the ring, the animal was freed quickly, and trotted off seemingly unharmed while the crowd applauded a good time. She found her eye roaming around from time to time, wondering if she would spot AJ. 'What do you like, then?'

Zadie's cheeks plumped. 'Barrell racing.'

They didn't have to wait long to see some. Mallory had to admit it was exciting, the horse and rider flying down the ring, skidding around the three barrels in a clover-leaf pattern before the crowd cheered them home. Zadie sat up straighter, following every round with intense fascination.

'I wish I could still do this,' she said. 'I used to beat my brothers. And oh, how they hated to lose!' She laughed.

Mallory laughed too, and then stopped abruptly as she spotted a tall man in black jeans climbing the stairs. As he rounded the corner, though, she saw it wasn't AJ.

'Fancy some lunch?' Jock said. 'I saw a barbeque downstairs. Want to come, Ern? Got an idea for you. The girls will be all right here for a while.'

'Yes, sit with me,' Zadie said, patting Mallory's knee.

To Mallory's surprise, Ernie went with Jock, the two men taking their time to descend, Ernie feeling for each step with his cane. Mallory's stomach gave a little lurch watching them, like it had every time Harry had wanted to climb somewhere high. Please, she thought, don't let them get lost, or slip on a cow pat and break a hip, or be fleeced by some country scam. She had only vague ideas about what went on at rodeos.

'Does your little boy ride?' Zadie asked, in the next lull between competitors. 'I think you said you had a little boy?' A frown creased her brows.

'Yes,' Mallory said. 'We talked about him in the car. He's five. And no, we don't ride. No horses at the cottage except in storybooks.'

'Oh.' She sounded disappointed. 'What about a dog?'

'No dogs yet,' Mallory said. Harry had started asking for one a year ago, right after Duncan had left. Mallory had resisted because she could only just manage to do everything they needed now. She didn't know how to add another family member into the mix. The chickens didn't count because they mostly looked after themselves. 'He does like our chickens rather a lot, though. He worked out how to pick one up when he was two. I don't know who was more surprised, me or the chicken.'

Zadie chuckled and nodded in approval. 'Sounds like a boy. I was terrified of the rooster in our coop. He was a mean old bird. I steered clear. My brothers would chase him, and he'd chase them right back. One time, he nailed one of them right in the caboose!'

Mallory laughed. 'Bet he was sore after that. Did he learn?'

'Not much. Our house was like a zoo. My brothers were always in scrapes.'

The arena event had now moved on to steer wrestling. Below, a rider burst from the gates at one end of the ring, chasing a steer, then hurled himself onto the animal's neck. Zadie followed the action without a word for three rounds.

'What's your husband do?' she suddenly asked.

Mallory was taken aback and, in her surprise, evaded reality. 'Oh, he's a computer guy. He makes security software. He started the company when he left school and now he, uh, runs it, I guess.'

'And what's he like?'

'He's a good father,' she began, then had to stop because tears threatened to close her throat over. 'He, um, he's dedicated and clever. And he works hard. Long hours.'

She didn't want to talk about this, not while her feelings about Duncan were so muddled, swinging from anger to nostalgia like the needle of a lost compass. In all the reading she'd done, she hadn't come up with an explanation for what he was doing, and that drove her the craziest of all.

'Ernie works long hours,' Zadie said with a gossamer touch of sadness. 'His patients keep him busy.'

Mallory glanced towards the stairs. No sign of Jock or Ernie. 'Does he like his work?' she asked, curious.

'Ernie needs a purpose. He doesn't know what to do at home. Can't sit still a minute before he's lookin' for somethin' to fix, some garden bed to dig up or things of mine to meddle with.'

She chuckled. Mallory cast a sidelong look towards Ernie's empty seat, thinking how difficult a man like that would find life, now that basic balance was a daily problem. 'That sounds practical, but exhausting.'

'Mmm,' agreed Zadie. 'He always says he'll be able to cut back soon. He needs his work, but sometimes you need to just sit. Not run away from your own thoughts. One day it will happen. That will be better for us both, don't you think, Mabel?'

She had a faraway look in her eyes. Mallory squeezed her hand. She wanted to reassure Zadie that Ernie wasn't working anymore, to remind her about the wedding that Ernie said she'd always wanted. But Mallory had a sense that Zadie wasn't in the present moment, so she took a softer approach. 'Will you be seeing your family in Nashville?'

Zadie shook her head slowly. Mallory didn't know if that meant that there wasn't any family to visit, or that they didn't get along.

'What about back home in Australia? Will anyone be worried about you being on this big trip?'

Zadie's focus seemed to return. 'What's there to worry about?'

'I mean, anyone who knows you live at Silky Oaks. Any children?'

'Ernie was always working,' Zadie said again, and Mallory instantly regretted the question. She'd felt safe asking it because Zadie had asked her. Maybe that was why Ernie felt his position so keenly; if they'd wanted children but his career had always come first, it must be a point of sadness.

Zadie turned back to watching the ring, and though the sadness seemed to linger like smoke over the outdoor barbeques, after a few more rounds of horses kicking up dirt and cowboy bravery, Zadie seemed to recover her spirits.

Mallory was grateful. She looked at this woman with her kind eyes and purple shirt, her pictures of her beloved animals, and could only think how cruel it was that age could slowly take her mind. Mallory started thinking about her ideas for animals at Silky Oaks again, and how it could work even if she wasn't the Engagement Manager. Maybe she could start with encouraging the management to accept pets that new residents wanted to bring with them. If she still had a job when all this was over.

Jock and Ernie returned ten minutes later, Jock bearing foil trays of carnival food and a plastic bag of sweating water bottles.

'This looks . . . interesting,' Mallory said, surveying the food.

'You see, what you've got here is all five food groups,' Jock said. 'Meat, grease, starch, gravy and seasoning.'

Mallory shot him a worried look, thinking about Zadie choking, or salt load on old kidneys, or food poisoning putting a vomit-stained delay on the drive.

'There's roast potato, pumpkin and creamy beans in this one,' Jock said, as if he could hear Mallory's thoughts. 'I'm pretty sure those are all vegetables. Is that right, Ernie?'

'Botanically speaking, pumpkin is a fruit,' he said distractedly, as most of his attention was focused on sitting again without falling. He blew out a breath once he was down, and gave Jock a conspiratorial nod. Mallory had never seen him so chipper.

Jock then reached for a bag Mallory hadn't seen, and handed Ernie a crisp white western hat, its brim artfully rolled.

'And this is for you, Zade,' he said.

Zadie's delight could not have been more complete. Mallory swapped seats to allow her and Ernie time together admiring the new hat, and reminiscing about rodeos past, while Mallory and Jock ate. Despite the universally mushed appearance that all takeaway food seemed to absorb from its packaging, it was delicious: soft, smoky barbequed pork, creamy potatoes and beans, sweet pumpkin.

'This is really good,' she said between mouthfuls.

'I know. Find a good food cart, set up forever,' Jock said. 'Zadie's having a good day, too.'

'We had a long chat,' Mallory said, and Zadie was still going. She and Ernie were discussing a high school rodeo association event where she and her brothers had all competed. Something about breakaway roping, and her brothers' team roping and steer wrestling, and two horses named Gravy and Biscuits.

Mallory was surprised when she checked the time and saw two hours had already passed. 'How much longer do you think they'll want to stay?' she asked Jock. 'I was thinking we might start driving again in an hour.'

Jock hesitated, looking guilty. 'About that . . .'

'What now?'

'Ernie's organised with some official downstairs to give Zadie a tour of the yards, and there's a street concert and dance tonight he wants to stay for.'

Mallory put her face in her hands, her fingertips digging into her temples. Why couldn't Ernie just stop to discuss it first? 'We were just supposed to be here a few hours,' she said through her fingers. 'You said it wouldn't set us back much.'

'I know,' Jock said, shifting uncomfortably. 'It does add a day. But to be honest, maybe a rest isn't a bad thing. I was really worried about you driving last night. And the three of us aren't spring chickens. Besides, I don't have the heart to say no when the two of them look like that. Do you?'

Mallory sighed. While she momentarily sympathised with the long-departed Fiona, and fantasised about taking the car and leaving them all here, she knew that they wouldn't be driving on until the morning.

•

The street party was a raucous affair that had spilled out from the showground and into the roads outside. The pavements and footpaths were crowded with jeans, boots and cowboy hats in every shade. Walking back from a drinks stand with bottles of water, Mallory had to take swift evasive action as a teenage girl flew past, her headwear in shocking pink. The hat was the same colour as the fading streaks of the volcanic sunset, which was lending a romantic backdrop to the party. From a temporary stage straddling the tarmac, lilting country music set a smooth celebratory mood.

Still, Mallory found it difficult to relax. While her companions had slept during the afternoon at the motel, she had sat on her bed and googled flights and buses from Nashville to New York, and then the route from LaGuardia to Manhattan. Bridget had emailed again: *I'm thinking of you every hour. Let me know you're safe when you can.* Mallory had written back: *I'm at a rodeo in New Mexico, can you believe it? But tomorrow we'll be across Texas. I'll be in NY in three days.*

After she'd sent the message, she'd stared at the Street View of the front of Duncan's building, burning the image into her mind. Three days, and she would be there. She had to be.

She had meant to sleep, then, but instead she'd returned to puzzling on Duncan himself. Driven by the conversation with Zadie, Mallory had re-read the piece about Duncan being nominated for the April Roundtable award, scouring for clues. Was Harry somehow an advantage to him? The award had been running for over a decade, but aside from announcing winners, there wasn't any history to read about. Mallory typed 'April Roundtable' into Wikipedia. It was a lobby group, working to ensure the government passed pro-business legislation. Mallory snorted. Just Duncan's crowd; he loved to bang on about what the government should or shouldn't be doing for businesses. Mallory had often tuned out, bored to a stupor. With a peal of regret, she wondered if that explained part of why Duncan had walked out: was she just not the right sort of wife for him? She wasn't sophisticated. That had been a secret fear in her heart ever since that disastrous dinner party. But while it still hurt to think he'd rejected her for being herself, it hardly explained his actions with Harry.

She'd fallen asleep worrying at the question, but woken after two hours, surprisingly refreshed; Jock had been right about her needing the rest.

Now, she sat on one of many hay-bale stacks along the footpath, tapping her toes to the music and waiting for Jock to come back from 'checking out the place'. At a nearby table, Ernie and Zadie watched the dancers. The two of them seemed amazingly spry after their own afternoon naps, as though they could keep going until midnight. Zadie had changed her shirt, but the new western hat was still proudly in place. Ernie held Zadie's palm with his strong hand, his head bent towards her, two glasses of sweet tea untouched before them.

Mallory checked the time. Jock had been gone a while. She pretended to watch the dancers. Several girls in short dresses and western boots laughed and twirled on their partners' arms. Mallory gripped her elbows. Ernie and Zadie would be fine for a minute if she went looking for Jock. Better to be doing something than sitting here alone.

She sensed someone staring. She twisted around but no one was behind her except passers-by. On the dancefloor, everyone was intent on their partners. Then she glanced far left across the road, and there was AJ.

He was leaning against an awning post, wearing a cowboy hat. He'd shed his leather jacket, and instead was making art of a pair of blue jeans and a stretched grey shirt. In fact, she may not have recognised him, except that he had such an unmistakable bearing. You couldn't be that tall and not stick out, especially when you were the only man standing still in an ever-moving crowd. His blue eyes held her, a small smile on his lips.

The flush rose up Mallory's neck before she could form a single thought.

He raised a beer bottle in her direction. She gave a half-wave in greeting, then glanced away, rubbing the back of her burning neck. An upbeat song wound to a close, and she clapped with the crowd for something to do. She didn't look back across the street until the opening bars of the next song were flooding from the speakers. He was still there, glancing back from the dancers as if he'd been following her gaze.

He pointed towards the dancers, then gestured across at her, and back at himself. Finally, he raised a palm. The question was clear.

Mallory shook her head. 'No way,' she said, though he couldn't possibly hear her. She was not going to dance. Certainly not with someone she barely knew. Especially with him.

He shrugged philosophically, and Mallory relaxed. She hated dancing. She remembered a boy in her class in high school pestering her to do some lively number at a bush dance. Her face had been incandescent by the end of her long string of refusals, and then he'd called her a bad word under his breath. AJ's straight acceptance of her refusal gave him points in her book. She glanced at him again. He was taking a long draw on the bottle now. Man, he looked good in that hat.

Jock still wasn't back. Maybe she should walk across the street and say hello. But the more she thought about it, the more she wondered what to say – beyond thanks for fixing up the tyre in Winslow – the less her legs would be commanded to move. She sighed, and checked on Ernie and Zadie. Another older couple had sat down at the table, and Ernie was busy gesturing – making introductions, it seemed. They certainly looked like they were having a good time.

Yes, Mallory thought, she would go and say hello. But when she looked back across the road, he was gone. She scanned the footpath. No AJ. And she was suddenly disappointed, as if it was sad to think that glimpse across the street would be the last she ever saw of him.

She stood up and brushed down her shirt more times than it needed, trying to decide whether to turn right, or left and walk all the way around the dancers.

And then someone stepped in beside her, and she smelled soap and spice.

'You reconsidering that dance?' he said.

Mallory looked up at him, at that amused smile on his face, and had to sit down again. 'No. I was just . . . stretching my legs.'

'I see,' he said, and sat down beside her, his weight nearly upsetting the bale. He stretched his legs out. He was still wearing his motorcycle boots, and they reached all the way to the gutter. 'Fancy meeting you here,' he said.

'Still the side of the road, I guess,' she said, looking around the footpath. 'But at least in better circumstances.'

He laughed. 'Yeah. That they are. Beer and everything. You want one?'

Mallory shook her head. 'I'm not much of a drinker. Where on earth did you get that hat?'

AJ put his beer down on the footpath, removed his hat and balanced it on the bottle. 'The Rocket's saddlebags are deep.' He nodded at Ernie's table. 'Whole party still together?'

'I sure hope so,' Mallory said. 'Jock's been gone a while. I'm starting to wonder if I should check on him.'

'You worried?' AJ stretched up to look across the crowd, sounding as though he'd mount a search party if she said she was.

'Not really,' she said. 'At least, not yet.'

'All right, then.' His body relaxed, and he leaned back. 'I never thanked you for the shirt.'

Mallory finally noticed he was wearing Jock's old grey shirt, the one she'd given him in Winslow. Now it was tucked neatly into his jeans, with a belt so thick it looked like it had been cut from a cart harness.

'I didn't recognise it. Looks different on you,' she said.

'I would think.'

'Well,' she said, trying not to marvel at how he made a worn piece of cloth look so reinvigorated – possibly it was the stretching across his biceps. 'Certainly didn't think you'd fit in any of mine.'

He laughed, a low rumble. 'Now there'd be a sight. How's that hand of yours?'

Mallory glanced down at the still-purple bruise. 'Doesn't hurt anymore. Jock told me you had our tyre fixed. Thank you. You didn't have to do that.'

'I had the time. Had to wait for my kit to dry. Your not-grandma was okay then? Jock said she was at the hospital.'

'Zadie. Yeah, she was. She's drinking sweet tea now like it never happened.'

'Southern classic,' AJ said. 'Look, here's trouble.'

Mallory glanced at the table to see Ernie pushing himself up on his cane and drawing Zadie out of her seat. The other couple were already heading towards the dancers. Mallory tensed, ready to leap across and help, but Ernie had managed and was now steering Zadie, very slowly, to the floor.

'Seems she had a panic attack,' Mallory said, watching and praying they wouldn't trip on the kerb or slip on the straw strewn around the tarmac. 'Ernie was keen to leave once they discharged her. I didn't see you at the hotel when we came back.'

'I found a laundromat. You ever seen a duffel bag going round a dryer?'

Mallory laughed, then cleared her throat.

His eyebrows drew together. 'I'm sensing that laugh is about more than my duffel bag.'

'Hard to imagine you in a laundromat,' she said, to avoid

telling him she was battling a flashback of him standing in the motel room door in his towel.

'Why's that?'

'Well, you know,' she gestured up and down his huge frame. 'You're this . . . big, tough guy.'

'And so I can't do laundry? Oh, lady, do you need to see a Marine Corp. First thing you learn after cleaning floors with a toothbrush. You're not a tough guy if you can't harden up and wash your own clothes.'

'Gosh, Bridget would love you,' she said.

AJ's eyebrows tweaked. 'Who's this Bridget?'

'Someone I work with, back home. Never mind.' Mallory smiled, and finally felt her muscles unwinding. While her subconscious might keep reminding her that he looked like a bully, all evidence seemed to suggest otherwise. His physical presence faded after a few minutes talking to him. He seemed so normal. Even charming in his own way. She didn't know what she'd been worried about with him standing across the street. It had been like this last time, too: afraid to talk to him, then finding it easier than she'd imagined. 'I guess I just don't think of a guy like you like that,' she said.

He nodded. 'I know. Like I said last time, you look like me, people tend to make assumptions.'

'When you found us on the highway that first time, do you know what I thought?' she said, feeling the need to confess why she'd behaved so irrationally.

'Now, there's a handsome, mechanically minded man. I should reject his help immediately?'

She laughed. 'Seriously. You reminded me of that movie. About the killer robot? You know, the one with the big guy on the bike? Plus, I hate storms and I wasn't really thinking straight. Maybe you did scare me, a little. Sorry.'

'Hold up.' His eyebrows rose. 'Are you talking about *The Terminator*?'

'That's it!'

One side of his mouth tugged up. 'Great movie,' he said. 'But *The Terminator*'s a cyborg, not a robot.'

'Same, same. Whatever, I don't like horror movies.'

'It's not a horror movie,' he said, in that slow drawl, utterly serious. 'Have you ever actually seen it?'

'Yes, of course. Well, sort of . . .' Her dim memories of that particular movie night were somewhat interrupted by Harry's crying and Duncan's commentary, and at least some time hiding under the blanket. 'Big dude chases some woman across a city, lots of guns and explosions, and she barely gets away at the end?'

She was a little bit proud of how coherent that sounded. AJ shook his head, then tipped his chin towards Ernie and Zadie, who were now doing a shuffling dance in a close hold at the edge of the floor.

'I bet *they* know the plot better than you do. You've got it all backwards.'

'How's that?'

'It's a romance, not a horror story.'

Mallory's incredulous laugh exploded like a firework. 'Yeah, right.'

'For real. Kyle Reese and Sarah Connor.'

'That's the most ridiculous thing I've ever heard.'

'Well, now, seeing as you don't know how to change a tyre, I don't expect you to follow,' AJ said.

'Hey! I know how to change a tyre.'

'That a fact?' he said, grinning.

'I do! At least, when the equipment doesn't decide to *break*,' she muttered.

'I maintain my point. Kyle Reese is a soldier who travels through time for Sarah. But since you haven't really seen it, you wouldn't know.'

'Only you would think that movie is a love story.' Mallory glanced down at his abandoned beer, peeking out from under the hat, and wondered how many he'd had tonight, and how she'd come to be at a New Mexico rodeo, arguing about romance and robots with a leather-wearing biker.

AJ shrugged. 'Soldier volunteers to protect a woman he's never met, but whose picture he's been carrying for years. He has a one-way ticket. He's prepared to die for her. Sounds like true love to me.'

He pressed a hand over his heart in illustration, but Mallory wasn't thinking about the movie, or the rodeo, or anything anymore except the photo of Harry in her own pocket. The slow honky-tonk faded as her stomach curled up. Harry was the one she would die for. What was he doing right now? Was he in bed, asleep already? Eating dinner? Missing her? Was he asking for her, and being told that she was busy? Or did he believe, somewhere in his heart, that she was on her way to find him?

She had to believe that. Especially here in the midst of this rowdy street party, surrounded by people having a good time when she only wanted to be somewhere else. And that made her want to cry, again.

'How about that dance?' she said, standing suddenly. Anything to avoid thinking about the things she could do nothing about right now. The embarrassment of dancing was a lesser evil than crying in front of this man she hardly knew. AJ didn't hesitate except to retrieve his hat, following her to the edge of the floor, where all the women were elaborately twirling to the lively beat.

Mallory stopped short. 'I don't know how to do that,' she said. 'I might not have thought this through. Maybe we should—'

AJ took her hand, and the next second he had moved her into a dance hold. And even though he was so much taller than she was, and she was thrown by the warm feel of his hand on her back, a minute later she was managing to shuffle almost on the beat. 'Nothing to it,' he said. 'You never learned to dance?'

'It wasn't on the Bayside High curriculum,' she said, trying not to stand on his feet. 'I think Ernie and Zadie are more coordinated than me. How is it you know how?'

'A mother obsessed with English Country Dancing . . . and the unfortunate fate of being tall enough to partner my older sisters. Don't ask me about the cotillion. I don't like to talk about it.'

Mallory giggled despite herself, and trod squarely on his foot. 'Sorry! I didn't have any brothers.'

'Don't you worry. These boots can take it. You want to try a turn?'

'I think I might break an ankle,' Mallory hedged, watching a nearby woman neatly spin under her partner's arm, tasselled skirt flying. 'Is that why all the women are wearing boots?'

AJ laughed, and as a long note wound the song to a close, Mallory found herself in a momentary peace. All her problems still existed, but at least she'd wriggled out from under their weight for a few minutes. The next number began with the slow rhythm of a ballad, and AJ drew her closer. Mallory fought the urge to rest her head against his shoulder.

After a few beats just listening to the music, he said, 'You don't really want to be here, do you?'

'What makes you say that?'

'Your face.' He shrugged. 'And circumstances. If you'd had an easier way to New York, I reckon you'd have taken it.'

'Close,' she said softly, and looked away, trying to push the anguish down, counting pale strands of straw to distract herself. It didn't work. She was tired of keeping everything inside.

'He froze my accounts,' she said. 'My husband, I mean. When you guessed it was a man problem, you were right. I landed in LA with the volcano thing happening and I had no money. It was the middle of the night back home and I didn't have anyone I could borrow from. I need to reach New York. This was just what happened.'

'You couldn't charge it?'

'Oh no, I don't have credit cards,' she said quickly. 'People ask me all the time how I cope, but really, it's much easier without.'

He pulled away just a little so he could look at her, in a new and considering way. 'Fancy my sisters could learn a few things . . .' he began, then, 'But this ain't about them.'

'It's my mum, you see,' Mallory rushed out. 'She has this problem. With gambling. She probably has ten credit cards and they're all maxed out. She's always been like that and . . . God, I can't believe I'm telling you this.'

A breeze caught her hair and cooled the back of her burning neck. She was locked in by the understanding in his blue eyes. Now she'd started confessing these things, she'd fallen over a cliff and couldn't stop.

'Growing up in that house,' she went on, 'it was just broken promises, and being afraid to answer the phone or the door because of the debt collectors. Sometimes, they were big guys in leather jackets. I swore I would never let Harry grow up feeling scared like I was. So I don't have credit cards, don't borrow money unless I absolutely have to. I knuckle down and make it all work.'

She shook her head. 'I shouldn't have told you that,' she whispered, feeling exposed, and knowing her face must be bright red. 'God, I'm so embarrassed.'

AJ said nothing for a long minute, but his arm tightened around her. 'That why you don't like horror?'

'I don't know, maybe.' She shrugged. 'I suppose you do?'

'Not my first choice, but in the right mood it feels good to be fake-scared. I've seen worse things in real life than in movies. Except the Japanese ones. Those are messed up.'

'Like *The Grudge* and *Ringu*?'

'Thought you said you didn't like them.'

'Yeah but Duncan does,' she said. 'We had lots of movie nights. Not really my choice, but yeah.'

'Your husband made you watch them anyway?' His accent came out strong.

'Not exactly.' She paused. 'He thought it would be good for me, a kind of therapy. Can't stand storms or horror movies, so I needed hardening up, apparently.'

'How'd that plan work out?'

She dropped her forehead momentarily to his chest, finally laughing in irony. 'Terrible! Still can't stand either one. I'm a hopeless case. He always said I was too much like a mouse.'

AJ's hand moved up, hugging her to him, as if they were more to each other than strangers who'd met on the side of a stormy road. When Mallory raised her head, he looked down on her with a smile. 'Well. I guess the man never saw the mice that hang round a military camp. You don't mess with those critters.'

She laughed again. Somehow, in just that one line, he'd managed to take the sting out of Duncan's long-ago assessment of her. And it felt so good to laugh.

'Even so,' AJ said, 'I kinda miss being on a base.'

'Oh?'

'Yeah. It's like a family there, home away from home. It was my whole adult life until last year. Kinda hard to move on.'

Mallory absorbed the tinge of loss in his eyes, and thought of the new and sometimes bewildered residents at Silky Oaks, who'd left their lives behind, and often not by choice. 'That must be a tough adjustment. But your family will be glad to see you, won't they?'

He paused. 'Actually, I haven't been in touch with them in a while now.'

'No?'

He shook his head.

'You don't get along?'

'Oh, we get along fine.' He was the one looking away now, unable to meet her eyes, and his fingers were moving in a repetitive circle on her lower back. 'It's just been . . . a tough time.'

Mallory guessed, with intuition born of her many years in caring, that something had happened, something more than simply having left his military life behind. Normally, she would not have asked, but here they were dancing together. He was warm against her, his voice a touchstone in the night and the music and everything else in a world spinning around her.

'Has this got anything to do with your bike shop falling through?' she asked. 'That must have been disappointing.'

'Sorta, yeah,' he said, but the slow song was winding up, and he stepped away from her, shutting her down. Across the floor, Ernie led Zadie back to the table. Mallory had a sense of closing time, and she didn't want that, not yet. She wanted to know what had happened. They stood there, facing each other, stuck between dancing and departing, between the intimacy of trusting a new friend and the glossy dismissal you gave to a casual acquaintance.

'You hittin' the road again in the morning?' he asked.

'Yeah,' she said, feeling absurdly miserable. 'You?'

He nodded, and just when it seemed they were about to part as strangers, he smiled at her from under the brim of his hat, and reached out for her hand. Mallory's heart lifted so fast that she reflexively bit her lip, avoiding . . . well, what? To avoid feeling like she was flirting with him?

'You be sure and avoid those service roads,' he said, his smile turning cheeky. All she could think about was how his hand felt around hers.

'We couldn't get two flats on one trip, could we? Fate's not that cruel?'

'Fate's crueller, darlin',' he said, leading her back to the hay bale. He let go of her hand so that he could retrieve the beer bottle and peel the label from the glass. 'You got a pen?'

'Um, I think so.' A habit from her job. She dug in her pocket, and came back with a biro, a freezer marker and a small ball of blue lint. She shook the lint away, embarrassed, and offered the pens. He took the marker, which looked much like a toothpick in his fingers, flipped the label over and wrote on it.

'This is my cell,' he said. 'In case you run into any more problems. You take care now, Mallory.'

His fingers briefly brushed her hand, and then he sauntered away, leaving her staring after him, a twin glow on her skin and in her heart. After a long minute, she went searching for Jock. She found him sitting in a chair not too far away, his back to a shop wall, hat pulled down on his forehead. To Mallory, he seemed wan and downcast.

'Nope, completely fine,' he said, when she asked him about it. 'Probably just walked a bit far. We heading back?'

Chapter 11

THEY DROVE OUT AT SIX-THIRTY THE NEXT MORNING. THE sunrise sky was an oil painting: brilliant red and streaked with long horizon clouds, fading into the last Prussian blue of night.

After the excitement of the rodeo, Zadie seemed a different person. She hummed in the back seat, smoothing the sleeves of a brilliant fuchsia shirt that Mallory had helped her into and, prompted by the passing fields, described the family home she'd grown up in outside Nashville. Rolling green hills, streams that ran through the valleys like showers of crystal, woods where she had wandered with dogs or with Eric the donkey, so tame he didn't need a lead rope.

'Sounds beautiful,' Mallory said. 'Like a fantasy land.'

'Beautiful and magical,' Zadie agreed. 'But hard work, too. We only had a washboard and a wringer to start with. I can remember Mamma stoking up the coal furnace in the basement. And her bringing the big tub outside in summer for me to play in. I always wanted to be outside. Making fairy houses and dreamcatchers in the woods. Even the Bell Witch didn't worry me, though my brothers were scared halfway to Texas.'

Mallory's arms crawled with goosebumps at just the name. She'd seen enough horror movies to fill in the gaps. Jock was the one who asked, 'What's the Bell Witch?'

'Poltergeist,' Zadie said. 'Lives in the woods. But I never saw it.'

'Perhaps we could talk about something else?' Ernie said.

'Yes,' Mallory said quickly, keen to steer well away from poltergeists. 'Let's talk about the rodeo.'

'Real community event, wasn't it?' Ernie said, settling back. 'That's the way that people used to connect with each other. Real, face-to-face conversation. None of this facetweetering rubbish.'

Jock laughed. 'You mean Facebook. And Twitter.'

'Whatever they're called,' Ernie said, waving his good hand dismissively, though he still seemed in fine humour. 'Young people spend far too much time stuck in computers. I never even brought a computer into my practice. You look people in the eye. We got along just fine without computers for as long as I can remember.'

'What about the space program?' Jock said.

'What about it?'

'Well, they had to use computers, and thanks to them we've got this little beauty.' Jock patted the GPS unit. 'Never be lost again.'

Ernie harrumphed. 'Except when it doesn't work.'

'You weren't complaining when I used a computer to book this trip.'

'Maybe not that *you* heard.'

Mallory laughed. Jock shook his head, but he was still smiling.

'I like the net,' he went on. 'You can find out all kinds of interesting things about people. Take Silky Oaks. I know practically who all the visitors are, and most of the staff in our wing. Just look them up online and boom! There's their photo, and a picture of their dog, and their kids, and their resumé. Some of them have their whole profiles visible.'

'How dreadful,' Ernie said.

Mallory snuck a look at Jock. 'Sounds like we need to do some training on privacy settings.'

'Maybe. But it's fun. Mal, back me up on this.'

'Me?' Mallory said.

'Yes. You keep in touch with your friends on Facebook, right?'

Mallory blew out a breath. *Which friends would those be?* 'Actually, not so much. I, um, don't really find it good for keeping in touch with people. My friends from school and I moved pretty far apart, and I see my work friends almost every day. I also don't want to put Harry's pictures up online.'

'Very sensible,' Ernie said.

What Mallory didn't say was that she had no interest in her school friends' pictures of holidays and university graduations, and they would no doubt have no interest in seeing any of Harry. When you were the only person in your class who'd married and had a baby right out of school, everyone else thought you were strange. She was probably the one they had all laughed about when they caught up at cafés on weekends – Mallory, the one who had a baby now and was working to support her nerdy husband who had a pipedream of running a company one day.

Besides, no one who hadn't had children was interested in hearing about the minutiae of daily difficulties – 'sleep deprivation', 'parenting' and 'work/life balance' were highly theoretical concepts for most people under twenty-five. They all seemed to have strong opinions, but no practical experience. Although the online mothers she'd found were worse, having both the strong opinions and the certainty of their own narrow experience to back them up. Mallory had decided to stay away from online communities. She'd learned to ask the older mothers she knew through work any questions, and otherwise she and Duncan had muddled through. The only time she'd felt the urge to drop a boastful post on Facebook was when Duncan's company had finally taken off. She'd been so grateful she hadn't when he'd walked out only weeks later.

'Well, I don't know what I'd do without it,' Jock said, a little more quietly. 'I can talk to other people who paint models. Or find out how to make mashed potatoes taste like they came from a restaurant. You've only been at Silky Oaks six months, Ern, and you've got Zadie. You'll work out how lonely it can get. This time next year you might want to be online, and then you'll find out you have to ask to use the computer room, because the damn thing's locked. Mallory understands, don't you, Mal? She's got plans for Silky Oaks.'

'Oh?' Ernie said, voice swimming with imminent disapproval.

'More aspirations now,' Mallory said hastily. 'I was hoping to be promoted, but it didn't happen.'

'She's the one who organised the kindergarten visits,' Jock said. 'Says the spontaneity is good for people.'

'*You* organised them?' Ernie said.

Mallory sighed. 'Yes. But that will probably be the end of my changes. I had plans to try and have animals – pets – for everyone who wanted one. And gardening, maybe green power programs, an artist in residence, things like that. But I doubt any of it will happen now. Mrs Crawley wasn't impressed.'

'I should think not,' Ernie said severely. 'The costs and the administration must be extraordinary, not to mention the health aspect.'

Mallory pressed her elbows into her sides, feeling as though she was back in the interview room with Mrs Crawley. 'What health aspect?'

'The animal dander and droppings! Not to mention parasites.'

Jock snorted. 'Oh, come on, Ernie. People live with pets every day. What makes us so special we can't have them?'

'It's just not appropriate. It's not appropriate for the class to visit either.'

In the rear-view, Mallory could see Zadie reach a hand to Ernie's knee. Mallory knew she should probably leave this alone when he was so worked up. But she was still smarting after Mrs Crawley's dismissal and her shattered dream.

'Isn't it appropriate to make everyone's life better? This isn't just me making things up. There's research from places overseas that do things differently. Those facilities have lower needs for medication, lower rates of injury and mortality, not to mention the elders are happier. Isn't that appropriate?'

'Elders,' Jock said. 'Oh, I quite like that. Sounds so distinguished.'

'I like it too,' Mallory said quietly. 'But Silky Oaks' policy is that we call everyone "residents", so that's what I do.'

Ernie had said nothing. Finally, he grumbled, 'And where are all these magical overseas places?'

'Here, in the States,' she said. 'And Canada and some other places. I first heard about it on a podcast—'

'That's like the radio, Ern,' Jock said.

'—then I found a lot of information on a website. It's even run by a doctor. They have data and programs and . . . lots of ideas,' she finished, feeling despondent. She really had wanted to see if Silky Oaks could embrace some of those ideas.

She asked Jock to put the radio on, and kept driving. Ernie stared out the window. After two hours, they had left the suburban crush of Amarillo behind and were almost out of the northern wedge of Texas. As they passed the state line into Oklahoma, Mallory stopped briefly to let them all stretch their legs. She sipped on a bottle of water, listening to the rush of the highway. When two motorbikes zoomed past, she wondered if AJ had left Clovis, and whether he had already turned north towards Chicago.

They ate lunch at a truck stop near Clinton. Mallory was cramped from the hours behind the wheel, but their progress on the GPS map was satisfying enough to buoy her spirits, and Jock raided the truck stop's shelves for what he called 'driver sustenance'.

'Don't worry, I got Nutter Butters in there,' he said, and Mallory didn't know whether to thank him for feeding her growing habit. Nothing that addictive could be good for you.

Ernie and Zadie were both dozing within a half-hour. Mallory drummed her fingers on the wheel as they slowed for roadworks. She glanced over at Jock. 'I wouldn't have picked you for google-stalking the visitors at Silky Oaks.'

He gave a small smile. 'They keep the visitor book right there in the open. Easy to find out the names. I'm always glad when people come. Lots of folk there don't have anyone.'

'How about you?'

He shook his head. 'I got an ex-wife, and two kids somewhere. They don't really want to know me.'

'I'm so sorry,' she said, surprised.

He shrugged. 'My ex remarried when the kids were little. They call him Dad. It was all a long time ago now.'

There was an uncomfortable pause.

'I've been meaning to ask you about your hat for ages,' Mallory said, trying to redirect. 'Do you fish?'

'Nope, can't say I do.'

'Have you, um, had it a long time?'

'Ages,' he said, tugging on the brim. 'Got it for Christmas one year, and started collecting the badges. Have to keep the bald spot warm, eh?'

He smiled, but too quickly. He clearly didn't want to talk about his hat.

'Did you say your back was the reason you, ah, moved in to Silky Oaks?'

Another pause. 'Partly. I volunteered myself. Wasn't really a good idea to be on my own anymore.'

'But now you're going to see your brother. You excited?'

The length of pause this question prompted was just as uncomfortable as the mention of Jock's estranged family. 'Yes,' he said finally.

'Did he move to the States, or did you move to Australia?'

'We're both originally from upstate New York. Little dairy farm there, near the Finger Lakes.'

'Really? You sound pretty Australian to me.'

'Left when I was young.'

Mallory knew he didn't really want to talk, but she was interested, and keen to help the time pass. 'Did the whole family move, or just you?'

'Just me, I guess. I thought I wanted an adventure.' Jock tipped his head back on the seat rest and gave an audible swallow. The skin over his face was drawn, his mouth turned down, as though he was ill.

'You feeling okay?' she asked.

'A bit queasy.'

'It wasn't something you ate? I wasn't sure about that breakfast.'

Their breakfast had been ambiguous burritos that Jock had organised with the motel, most of which Mallory hadn't eaten.

'Just a little heartburn,' Jock said, pressing a hand over his chest. 'Maybe I should have gone easy on the Red Vines.'

'Do you want me to stop?'

'No, keep driving.' But his shoulders gave a little shiver.

'Too cold?' Mallory reached for the air-conditioning controls which, in line with Ernie's instructions, were blasting frigid streams into the cabin.

Jock waved her away. 'No, it's fine.' He sounded really tired. They cleared the roadworks, and Mallory accelerated.

'How much further do you think we can go today?' she asked after a few minutes.

Silence.

'Jock?'

'Mmm?'

'How much further do you think we can drive today?'

'Oh, right.' He sat up and consulted the GPS, taking a very long time. 'Less than two hours to Oklahoma City,' he said finally.

'That'll only be early afternoon. Where's another three hours after that?'

He tapped away, but it took an age with him pausing to stare out the window. Mallory wondered if the connection was slow. 'Fort Smith, just over the Arkansas border,' he said.

'And how far from there to Nashville?'

Tap, tap, tap. 'Shade over seven hours.'

Seven hours. A day's drive. Mallory let out a breath, her spirits revived. Ahead was smooth road, and the green fields of Oklahoma spread around them to the horizon. The dry landscape of the west had transformed into lush grass and trees. Another day, and she would be done with driving. She could be on a plane or a bus to New York tomorrow night.

'Good,' she said. 'That's good.'

Anticipation fizzed in her blood like bubbles from a shaken soft drink. Tonight, she would ask Ernie for half the money he'd promised and use it to book transport. Between now and then, as the road slipped by, she would think about how good Harry would feel in her arms, and what she would say to Duncan ... What would she say to Duncan?

'There's not much to tell,' Jock said abruptly.

Mallory, deep in simulated conversations, had to wrest her attention back. 'Sorry?'

'About where I'm from. Upstate New York.'

'Oh?'

'It's just like all the clichés.'

'I'm afraid I don't know any,' she said.

Jock shifted in his seat. 'Rolling hills. The Finger Lakes and the Susquehanna River rolling through the valley. White snow in winter, green in spring; red and orange and yellow in autumn. Postcard stuff. And the sunsets . . . even this volcano doesn't have anything on them.'

'Sounds lovely.'

'Yeah, it was. Extreme, too. Winter could be brutal. I can still remember not being able to feel my fingers as I walked down to the milking shed. We used to crack ice off the water troughs.'

'Who's we?'

'Then the summers, they could be so hot the tar on the roads would melt. But it was slow, slower than the cities anyway.'

'Like around Silky Oaks? Growing up on the Bayside felt a long way from the city.'

'Yes. It doesn't have the same scenery, but the pace, yeah.'

Mallory heard movement in the back and glanced at the rear-view. Ernie was rubbing his eyes. 'Where are we?' he asked as Zadie slept on.

'About an hour from Oklahoma City,' Jock answered, and turned towards the window again.

'What are you talking about?' Ernie asked.

'Upstate New York,' Mallory said.

Ernie grunted, like this didn't interest him in the slightest.

'So, how often have you been back?' Mallory asked Jock. From the longing in his voice, it sounded like a place that was in his blood, that he wouldn't allow to go without him for too long.

'Never. Never wanted to before.'

Mallory swallowed her surprise. 'Still have family there?' Something about his description left her with desperate questions.

'Not anymore,' he said.

'Let's stop in Oklahoma City,' Ernie cut in.

'Sure, but just for a rest if everything else is fine,' Mallory said, finding it difficult to leave the conversation with Jock. 'We're going through to Fort Smith for tonight.'

•

Jock never did finish his story. Zadie slept on and on through the rest of the drive, only waking for the afternoon stop. She didn't seem quite herself when they unloaded at the motel, near the heart of Fort Smith, Arkansas. Mallory had to support her elbow all the way from the car to the room, a distance of only five metres that seemed to take an hour. Zadie refused a shower and claimed she wasn't hungry, and so Mallory settled her in an armchair while she brought in the rest of the bags and helped Ernie with the bathroom.

'She might change her mind,' Mallory said, as they finished. 'Must feel better to clean up after the drive.'

'Well, if we'd stopped in O-City like I wanted to,' Ernie began, then cut himself off as if realising that ship had sailed. 'But I suppose we stopped in Clovis. She really enjoyed that, really did.'

'I know,' Mallory said, washing her hands and then pushing the bathroom door open. 'Sounds like she was quite a competitor when she was young.'

'Goes with growing up on a ranch in Tennessee,' Ernie said.

'Did she keep up with that in Australia? I used to see signs for rodeos coming to the riding school when I was a kid.'

'For a little while,' Ernie said, glancing over at Zadie, who was staring into space, her eyes drooping. 'But we lived in Sydney for a long time. Hard to keep horses in the city.'

Mallory took a breath. 'By the way, Ernie, could we have a chat about my pay?'

'Oh?'

Mallory's heart thumped a bass line in her throat. She so hated discussing money. 'You see there's a problem with my Australian account, so I wanted to ask if you might convert some of the money into a booking for me. A flight or a bus.'

'That wasn't our arrangement.'

'I know. But it would really help if I know when I can leave for New York tomorrow.'

Ernie was busily unzipping the case, bracing his hip on the bed for balance. 'I'll think about it. We'd better organise some dinner, now.'

'Okay,' Mallory said, then took another look at Zadie. She crouched and put a hand on the woman's arm. 'Are you hungry, Zadie?'

No answer.

'How about we have something to eat, then do showers later?' Mallory said. She gently pressed her fingers against the delicate skin of Zadie's forehead. No fever. Mallory rose, feeling both frustration and guilt. She wanted the day to be over so she could look at flights, but maybe they'd driven too far and Zadie was exhausted. 'I'll round up Jock, then we can decide what we might like to eat.'

She walked the seven steps to the next room door. It was ajar, so she pushed it open.

'Jock?' The room was vacant, the bathroom door closed. She knocked. 'Jock?'

No answer. She tried the handle and it opened to the empty bathroom. She stepped back and looked around. Jock's bag was exactly where she'd left it, just inside the door. Normally when they stopped, he took the bag to the cupboard straight away and then began moving the furniture, so that his bed was tight in a corner. It was slightly odd, but Jock liked things a certain way. This time, nothing had been touched. No toiletries laid out in the bathroom. Very un-Jock like.

Mallory stuck her head back into Ernie and Zadie's room. Ernie looked up from his seat on the bed.

'Did Jock say he was going somewhere?' she asked.

'Probably having a poke around. He likes to do that in a new place.'

Mallory frowned. The motel's street entry faced a vaguely industrial area with warehouses. There was no sign of Jock. He had never gone anywhere without mentioning it before. He always seemed like a responsible, no-surprises kind of person. Mallory keenly felt how little she knew about him.

The thought was a blunt finger, prodding her in the back. She quickened her steps, walking around the motel complex without luck, a cold, prickly sensation spreading in her stomach. She went back to Ernie.

'You need to tell me if he ever had any problems at Silky Oaks. Wandering off? Becoming disoriented, anything like that?'

'Well . . . not that I've seen,' Ernie said, but in a way that told her he might suspect there was an issue. He dug in his pocket and produced a small notepad. 'Here, try that number. That's his mobile.'

It rang out three times before Mallory found the phone, on silent, still in the car.

'Great.' Mallory put her hands on her hips, thinking. Hopefully, she would find Jock coming back from a nearby servo with a packet of gum. But otherwise, she was going to have to go searching, and leave a woman with dementia in the care of her stroke-weakened husband. Perfect.

'Shit,' she muttered under her breath. 'Look, stay here. I'm going to look for him.'

Ernie didn't argue, so Mallory trotted out to reception and asked them if they'd seen Jock leaving the complex.

'Oh, yeah,' said the woman behind the counter. 'Walked out not long after you arrived. I think that way.' She pointed down the street, towards a red-bricked post office.

Mallory went that way, and was nearly run over when she forgot to look right instead of left crossing the road. The post office was closed, its large carpark deserted. She circled around to the monument behind the motel, dedicated to a General Darby and featuring a sculpted man on a motorbike. Mallory had a fleeting thought of AJ, before she began asking random strangers. No one had seen Jock. Finally, she retreated to the motel and asked Ernie for the car keys.

'Look, keep my phone if it makes you feel better,' she argued when he first refused. 'It'll take three times as long if we all go.'

'Your phone isn't worth that much,' Ernie said.

'It's my lifeline to my son,' Mallory said sharply. 'Give me the damn keys.'

She took the car out a minute later, intending to drive widening loops around the motel. Trouble was, she wasn't good enough with the whole right-hand-driving thing, or keeping track of where she was without the GPS telling her where to go. After only ten minutes, she was lost.

CHARLOTTE NASH

Thinking she could find her way back by turning around, she instead found herself on a long street that ended in a carpark. With another car right up her tailpipe, she drove all the way through and out the other side, and onto a road by a huge cemetery, its trees overhanging the fence and a carpet of headstones disappearing into the distance. Mallory shivered. A graveyard.

She tried to search among the trees as she went, and ended up in the wrong lane to turn off. She slowed down to allow another car to overtake her, corrected her mistake, then in a lapse of concentration drove down the wrong side of the next street.

She was just thanking God that no one was coming the other way when a siren blared from behind. Mallory jumped, and saw the red and blue strobe of police lights through the cabin.

Oh, dear God.

Her heart went instantly into thundering panic, however much she told herself to stay calm. This wasn't home, where she held her breath at every RBT, expecting the clapped-out Corolla would be slapped with unroadworthiness. At least this car was a good one. Then she remembered she was in a strange country, and that she'd just been driving on the wrong side of the road. In someone else's car.

No, panic was perfectly acceptable.

The cop took a while exiting his patrol car, and by the time he arrived at her open window, and asked the standard licence, registration and insurance question she'd seen in the movies, her calm adult veneer was cracking like a dropped egg.

'Um,' she said, fumbling with her wallet. She extracted her licence and handed it over. 'That's my licence. The, um, the car's rented.'

The cop turned her fancy orange, smart-chip Australian licence card over in his hand. 'What is this, ma'am?'

'My licence. It's Australian. I'm from Australia,' she added uselessly.

He inspected the card for a long time. 'Where did you rent the vehicle, ma'am?'

'Los Angeles airport,' she said, but her lip wobbled. The cop's face was hard, his expression immovable, like AJ's had been when they'd first met. She had an image of being thrown in the lock-up, not being able to find Jock or get back to Ernie and Zadie – and, worse, her progress to New York delayed again. 'I, um, I think the rental documents are back at the motel,' she whispered, knowing the documents had disappeared with Fiona and regardless wouldn't help without her name on them.

'Do you know why I stopped you?'

Mallory took a breath. 'Yes. I know I was driving on the wrong side. I think I forgot. I'm out looking for my grandfather and I've got two other elderly people back at the motel and I didn't think it would take this long but I got lost and, and . . .'

Her throat constricted so much that she couldn't get any more words out. She pressed a hand over her face, helpless. When she looked back again, the cop's expression hadn't changed; he probably saw ten criers a night. The shame of potentially losing her composure was just enough for her to pull herself back together. She sniffed back the tears. 'I'm worried about him being missing. He left his phone at the motel. I just want to find him.'

'How long has he been missing, ma'am?'

'Well,' she said, with a hiccup, 'I've been driving around for an hour or so. We arrived in Fort Smith maybe a half-hour before that.'

She gripped the wheel, knowing that *man missing for an hour and a half* wasn't breaking news. The officer's unimpressed expression confirmed it.

'Step out of the vehicle, please, ma'am.'

Dying of mortification, Mallory pushed the door open, her heart now officially breaking speed limits, her limbs shaking. She stumbled over her own feet before she managed to close the door, which must have been an excellent argument in favour of her sobriety. As the officer took her through tests, she was gawped at by every passing pedestrian and vehicle occupant. With still enough light for everyone to get a really good look at her, she wanted to creep back into the car and disappear into the tiny space beneath the front seat.

'That will do, thank you,' the cop said eventually. 'Wait here, please.'

He retreated to the patrol car, the chunky utility belt rocking with his steps, and then Mallory could hear the intermittent crackle of a radio. Was he calling for back-up? Would he come back and slap her in cuffs? Impound the car?

And Jock was still out there, somewhere alone in Fort Smith.

Chapter 12

THE COP STRODE BACK DOWN THE PAVEMENT. MALLORY held her breath.

'Ms Cook, can you describe your grandfather?'

She blinked. 'Uh, yes, he's about my height. Um, blue eyes—'

'What was he wearing?'

'Green shirt,' she said, stretching her mind back. 'Grey shorts with a brown belt, I think. Oh, and his hat! He wears this green fishing hat, with badges all over it.'

'His name?'

'Jock.' She didn't know his last name. But the cop didn't press the point.

'All right, Ms Cook. Here's what's going to happen. You're going to follow me to the Sheriff's Office. We'll take it from there.'

Mallory's heart lodged squarely in her throat and refused to budge. She didn't know what to make of this. The cop obviously didn't think she was drunk, or he wouldn't be letting her drive. Maybe this was just how they impounded cars. She imagined so many doom-and-gloom scenarios that after she'd parked and followed the officer into the building, she was floored to see Jock sitting in a plastic chair in reception. His shoes and socks were muddy and bits of grass clung all the way to his knees.

'Jock!' She rushed across, dropping down before him so she could look him in the eye. 'I was so worried.'

'I'm sorry,' he croaked.

The officer was talking to someone behind the counter. Mallory looked up as a woman in uniform came out into the foyer.

'Where did you find him?' Mallory asked.

'He found us,' the woman said, a note of exasperation in her voice. 'He walked in here about twenty minutes ago, asking for Mallory. We told him there wasn't anyone here called Mallory. All we've been able to get out of him since is that he's sorry. We were about to take him up to the hospital.'

'Thank you,' Mallory said, her relief transforming back into concern. What the hell was going on? Jock wasn't running a temperature. Maybe he'd had some kind of episode, like a seizure, and then he'd been confused. But she'd never heard of anyone wandering around for an hour like that after a seizure. 'I'd better have him checked out.'

The officer let her off with a warning, actually managing a sympathetic voice when she told him that they were driving all the way to Nashville. 'You take care, now,' he said as she loaded Jock back into the car. 'That's a hell of a long drive.'

Mallory waited until the officer had pulled his car out of the lot before she wrestled with the GPS and set the destination back to the motel.

'I don't need checking out,' Jock said before she could pull away.

'It's not optional at this point.' She dropped her hands from the wheel. 'I still don't understand what happened.'

'I got lost.'

'After walking off without telling us?'

He shrugged. 'I needed to get away.'

'Why? What happened?'

He didn't answer. Mallory drove, took a corner the GPS ordered, then another.

Finally, he said, 'It was that conversation in the car. I don't normally talk about any of those things. They . . . get on top of me sometimes. Run loops in my head.'

Mallory leaned back in the driver's chair. Up until now, she'd been under the impression he lived at Silky Oaks because of physical limitations. Now, here was a whole other side of reasons. She thought about his sense of humour. She'd known other residents who deflected attention away from their problems by being funny, and wondered if Jock did the same thing. 'I'm sorry, Jock. But I still need to get you checked out.'

'Why?'

'Because they thought you were confused, and maybe you were. Because I can't keep driving tomorrow unless I know you're fine.'

He folded his arms over his chest. Great, this was going to turn into an argument, and more delay. The wanting for Harry swept at her, a fierce undertow, while the rest of her was stuck in the deep immovable sand of this driving arrangement.

A minute later, she pulled into the motel. 'Look,' she said, turning the engine off, 'don't say *no* just now. Let me go check on Ernie and Zadie, make sure they don't need anything, and we'll go do the dinner run together.'

He didn't answer, but his crossed arms drooped. Mallory pushed her door open – she'd take acquiescence if she couldn't get agreement – and knocked on Ernie and Zadie's door. When no one answered, she had to dig through her pockets for her key.

The room was empty.

The door creaked as she pushed it wider, checking all the corners. She noted one bedspread was wrinkled, and a bag lay askew in the corner. Lord, what *now*?

That was when the woman from the reception desk stuck her head into the room.

'Good, you're back,' she said. 'I'm supposed to tell you they've gone to the hospital. The lady wasn't well.'

'Zadie?' Mallory repeated dumbly.

'Yes. Was an ambulance here and everything.'

●

They waited in the busy ED for hours. When Mallory thought to check her phone, she found three missed calls from Ernie, all from when she'd probably been on the footpath with the police and had left her phone in the car. Ten pm rolled around before a doctor came to review Zadie. He took a five-minute history and ordered some tests. Twice in that time she became agitated, and it had taken all Mallory's and Ernie's compassionate soothing to calm her. They finally had to take her to a corner of the waiting area to play Allman Brothers Band songs before she settled.

Jock waited patiently, subdued, but otherwise as if nothing had happened. He was the one who provided the phone and the playlist. When Zadie was finally called in and disappeared with Ernie, Mallory was still holding the phone, as Dickey Betts sang about crossroads in the dark of night. When in the next breath, he was singing about somebody waiting, Mallory shut it off, rubbed her face and sat beside Jock.

'What happened tonight, really?' she asked him.

He shrugged, as if he didn't know what she was talking about.

Mallory blew out a breath. She was tired, so tired. Her need to reach Harry was a slavedriver holding a whip to her heart, but Jock's disappearance had thrown her. Suddenly, a whole bunch of new potential problems stood in her way of reaching New York.

'If I called Silky Oaks and asked to read your file, what would it say?'

'Hopeless case. Do not resuscitate,' he said.

'This isn't funny! I was so worried. Don't make jokes about that.'

'I know. Sorry.' He rubbed a hand over his face. 'It would say that I have "turns". That's a nicely imprecise medical term, innit?'

'What kind of turns?'

'Things get overwhelming, and I need to get away. I walk and I walk. Eventually, I come round.'

'Overwhelming . . . like with flashbacks?' she guessed, wondering if this was a trauma-related reaction. She'd seen a few residents over the years with parts of their lives they wouldn't discuss for just that reason.

Jock's expression closed down. He looked at the floor.

Mallory handed his phone back. 'Forget that. Is this why you live at Silky Oaks?'

Another shrug. 'Plus my back. I was being real about that. Look, I had a mate who used to look out for me. When he passed on, I was lonely more than anything. I went to Silky Oaks because at least there's people to talk to, and if I have a turn, I'm not on my own.'

Mallory's chest ached for him. 'All right, I believe that. How do we make sure you're safe tonight, and for the rest of the trip?'

After a pause, Jock said, 'I've got some pills, for when it gets on top of me. I'll take one when we get back. Sleep like the dead.'

'What sort of pills?'

'Valium.'

'Fine. But don't make jokes about the dead. We're sitting in a hospital.'

'Yeah, okay.'

There didn't seem anything else to say. She walked away and sat down to wait. Jock put in a set of earbuds and leaned back in a chair with his eyes closed. Another half-hour passed before Ernie shuffled out to find them, shaking his head.

'What?' Mallory asked in alarm, thinking the news must be bad.

Ernie pulled himself up with great dignity, and Mallory glimpsed the doctor he must once have been. It was then that she noticed the purple bruise on the crest of his cheek.

'She's going to be fine,' he said. 'She has a urinary tract infection, and the fever's probably responsible for her disorientation.'

Mallory sagged with relief. 'It took so long, I was sure it was really bad news.'

Ernie grunted, and lowered himself into a plastic waiting chair. 'Never complain about the health system in Australia, that's all I can tell you.'

'What happened to your face?'

'My what?'

'Your face. It's all bruised. Did you fall?' She reached up to gently touch the edges of the mark. What had happened while she'd been out looking for Jock? As a carer for the aged, she lived in fear of falls and the bone breakages they caused. 'I'm sorry I left in such a hurry.'

His silence stretched so long that, at first, she thought he was angry, that he blamed her. Perhaps she deserved it. How would she have felt if he'd broken his hip, or if Zadie had?

Then Ernie gave a heavy sigh. 'It wasn't your fault,' he said roughly. 'This isn't the first time it's happened. She's had UTIs off and on over the past year, and the disorientation always comes with it. She doesn't know where she is, or who anyone is. Understandable that she's scared, and lashes out.'

Mallory's voice dropped. 'That's how this happened?'

'She didn't mean it,' he said firmly. But his mouth wobbled. Awkwardly, he pulled a handkerchief from his pocket and rubbed at his nose. He took two deep breaths, holding himself together.

'I'm sorry I wasn't there,' Mallory whispered. 'I should have been there.'

'He all right?' Ernie asked, nodding across to Jock, who was still reclined in the chair, eyes closed. 'He told me he has episodes sometimes. I didn't want to say before, in case it wasn't that.'

'Yeah,' Mallory said. 'He says he's okay now though.'

She wasn't sure she believed it, but what more could she do? She couldn't frogmarch a grown man to the doctor. They sat a while in silence.

'I've been thinking a bit about what you said in the car, about the animals,' Ernie said. 'I might like to look at that research. Zadie lost her last dog, Melville, just before we moved to Silky Oaks. That was very hard on her. He was a wise old thing, that dog. She'd just lost him, and then I had the stroke.'

'A lot of upheaval,' Mallory said.

'Yes.'

'I really am sorry I wasn't there tonight,' she said again.

Ernie nodded, and somehow she knew he forgave her. 'They want to keep Zade in overnight with a drip and antibiotics, but she can go tomorrow. Maybe we could be moving again by lunchtime.'

'You want to keep going?'

'We can't stop here.'

Mallory rubbed her eyes. After today, she realised how alone she was out there on the road with the three of them. They'd been lucky so far. What happened if the next time Zadie had a problem they were somewhere remote, and there was no knight in shining bike leathers to step out on the road and get her the metaphorical wheel brace she needed?

'We'll stop more often for the bathroom,' she said. 'And make sure Zadie keeps up her fluids. We don't want this to happen again.'

Ernie nodded. 'You should go and get some rest. They're letting me stay here.'

'They are?'

'The amount they charge, they bloody well are. I have to deal with the insurance now. Come back in the morning. There's enough nurses around that I'll be fine.'

He shuffled away.

Back at the motel, Mallory showered and brushed her teeth, but her mind was still whirling and awake. She checked on Jock and found him asleep facing the wall, his hat still in place, bed again moved into the corner. A thick folder sat on the bedside table. Holding the folder down was a nearly spent block of paper, turned upside down, with a heavy pen resting on top. Mallory thought about flipping that block of paper over to see what was on it. Just for a second. Just to feel like she wasn't all alone and knowing nothing.

She padded across the carpet and stepped out the door. The night was still and quiet, but for the electric buzz of lights. In New York, it was after one in the morning – she couldn't call there, even in the small hope Harry might pick up. But she needed to talk to someone. In Australia, it was the late afternoon, but she was mildly terrified about how much a call might cost. Instead, she dug in her pocket and came up with the crumpled beer label from the rodeo.

Her hand trembled as she dialled, and when he picked up, she nearly dropped the phone.

'Hello?' His voice was gruff, as if she'd woken him. 'Hello?' He cursed, and she heard footfalls; he must be moving to find better reception.

'AJ,' she said, finding her tiny voice.

All the noise down the line stopped. 'Mallory?'

'Yes. I'm sorry to call so late but I just wanted to talk to someone and I thought maybe you would be up, so—'

'What's wrong?'

'Oh, nothing,' she said, but her voice rose so high on 'nothing' that her lie was obvious.

'Didn't throw another tyre, did you?' he asked in his deadpan drawl.

She managed a wry laugh. 'No, no, the car is still in one piece. Survived the police and everything.'

'Police? You tellin' me you're in the lock-up now?'

'Close,' she said. 'Some dodgy motel in Fort Smith.'

He chuckled. 'Give me the name. I'll be there in half an hour.'

'Why, where are you?'

'About half an hour from Fort Smith,' he said.

'You don't have to do that.'

'You got me interested now,' he replied.

'It's nearly midnight.'

'And yet look at me, puttin' on my boots.'

•

He rolled up twenty-five minutes later. Mallory heard him coming from two blocks away, the characteristic gallop of the Rocket's engine like a beacon through the night. She was sure that the whole complex would be awake by the time he'd pulled in and killed the motor. When he handed her a helmet, she handed it straight back.

'I don't need that.'

'Now, you might be over twenty-one,' he said. 'And this state might let you ride without one, but not wearing it is as stupid as it is dangerous. Take it.'

'I mean, I'm not getting on that bike.'

'You'd rather hang around here, communin' with the warehouses?'

'No, I just don't think I should go anywhere.'

'Why not? We ain't goin' far.'

'Because . . .' *Because I don't trust you? Because I don't do things like this? Because I have responsibilities?* Weary of excuses, she stuck her head back into the room and found Jock still in his deep sleep. She wrote him a note in case he woke up.

'I'm surprised you didn't wake him,' she said, returning outside. 'I can pick you coming a mile away.'

'It's the triple engine,' he said.

'What does that mean?'

'The Rocket has three cylinders, not two or four. It produces a good balance of low-end torque, and high-end power, plus a characteristic note. That's what you can hear.'

'That's all fine and good,' she said, as she tried to climb gracefully up onto the pillion seat, 'but if they find my body tomorrow, Jock's going to hunt you down.'

'Just how dangerous do you think I look?' AJ asked.

'No comment,' she muttered, not needing to point out the black jeans and leather jacket, his towering height and square jaw.

'That's all right, just imagine you're in a horror movie,' he said as he started the bike up. The engine was so loud she wasn't sure if he was laughing or not.

She forgot everything but hanging on, in what seemed to be perfectly rational terror. They passed two blocks before Mallory realised he was riding at a sedate pace. She slowly relaxed her arms and let the night air, balmy with spring, slip over her face. So, this was what riding a motorcycle was like. Wind in your hair, body out in the open. Easy and free. Well, free to fall right on the asphalt . . . but still, free. She could see why AJ liked it. Once, a long time ago, she thought she'd like it too.

She'd had that particular conversation with Duncan when she'd been a few months pregnant with Harry. They'd been in the middle of painting over the cottage kitchen's hideous aqua-blue walls.

'I think I want a motorbike one day,' she'd said.

Duncan had laughed and dipped his brush. 'Yeah, right.'

'I'm serious.' She painted over the same spot, feeling the flush rise up her neck. She didn't want to change anything, but that didn't mean she wasn't apprehensive of the restrictions that a baby would bring so early in their lives. She wanted Duncan's assurance that life could still be exciting and spontaneous.

'Babe,' he'd said, 'they're dangerous. Why would you want to put yourself in that position when you've got a young kid who needs you?'

'I said "one day".' But her chest had felt all shrunken and empty.

Duncan had seen the look on her face. He'd come and put his arms around her, still holding the paintbrush. 'Hey, don't be like that. Once this business takes off we can do so many amazing things. Let's just focus on that, huh?'

And he'd dotted her nose with his brush. Mallory had laughed and tried to get him back, and soon they were racing around the house and motorbikes were forgotten. She hadn't remembered that conversation until now. She frowned, thinking of other times like it, when Duncan had persuaded her to abandon an idea in favour of his plans. At the time, she'd always seen his point: they did have restrictions to deal with. Now, she realised that while he'd said he loved her big ideas, they'd never actually acted on any of them. Duncan's plans had been everything.

Now, here she was, after he'd left and taken Harry, riding a dangerous motorbike with a dangerous-looking man. Maybe it was the cathartic act of rebellion, or just needing to fling the past week off her shoulders, because she wanted to throw her hands out like Kate Winslet on the bow of the *Titanic*.

'Glad you didn't,' AJ said when he'd pulled over at the end of a quiet street and she'd told him. 'Wouldn't want you to have collected a street sign. But I do understand the feeling. You honestly never ridden before?'

'Never,' she said, accepting his hand so she could climb down. They were at the edge of the city, alongside a vast park with a stone building etched in light from the full moon. 'Where are we?'

'Historic site. I had lunch here earlier when I came through town. Real pretty. Come on.'

He led her across the road and grass, then downhill, until they passed over a set of train tracks, and then up again through a cutting where moonbeams split the deep black shadows. Mallory followed with growing apprehension. It wasn't that she believed in werewolves, or ghosts – but if she had, then she imagined they would lurk in a place like this. Maybe it was pretty in the daytime but right now it just seemed spooky.

AJ climbed up a knoll, where the ground became more open under the trees and the night was calm. Mallory was just appreciating the peace when they crested the rise and she unexpectedly saw water. A little way down the bank, they found a bench facing out on a river. Mallory sat. The leaves shifting in the treetops sounded like soft rain. The water shushed by, and had the lustre of silk. Insects hummed, and a distant channel light marked time with little flashes of green. Mallory could see a road bridge some way up the river, but here you would hardly know a city was just a few blocks away.

'That's the Arkansas River,' AJ said. 'Much nicer than warehouses. Now, then. Spill.'

'Spill what?'

'Your bad day. Didn't ride all the way here to listen to some bullfrogs.'

So while distant headlights scribed the highway over the water, Mallory told him about Jock, and her encounter with the police, and then Zadie and the hospital.

AJ chewed on a plucked piece of grass. 'Jock say what happened?'

'Nope. I'm not even sure he knows. That's why I didn't really want to leave the motel, but he took a sleeping pill, so he'll probably be out till morning.'

AJ grunted. 'He's been through something, that guy. I've seen friends like that.'

'Yeah, I guess so.'

'Point of life, ain't it? Everyone gets dealt a hand, some good, some plain awful. I think that was the first thing I learned in the Marines – after how to do laundry, that is. Never know which one you're gonna get.'

'Laundry or a bad hand?' she asked.

He laughed. 'Either one.'

'Tell me about it,' she said, meaning to be ironic, but AJ leaned back.

'Well, take me, now,' he said. 'One day you're leaving the Marines, planning to start a bike shop. The next year, all that's folded and you're riding across the country looking for what you're supposed to do now. Best laid plans are ripe to be undone.' He threw his hands up behind his head, and snuck a look at her, as if assessing how she would take this.

She could only sympathise. 'Yeah, I guess they are. So what happened?'

He shook his head, and she heard the catch in his voice. 'I ain't a talker, not about that. I want to hear about you. That's what I'm supposed to say, right?'

Mallory laughed, but it gave way to a sigh. 'Well, I just thought we were getting somewhere. That I'd be in Nashville tomorrow night and on a flight to New York. Or at least a bus. And instead . . . I'm wondering if I'll never make it at all.'

She stood up, wishing she was back on the bike with the roar of the engine drowning out these thoughts. Harry's absence was a void in her chest, made so much worse because she hadn't heard from him.

She paced across to a series of information plaques over-looking the river. In the dappled moonlight, she couldn't read the smaller words, but it was something about the Trail of Tears. An illustration showed a Native American woman carrying a child to her chest, head down against a harsh winter wind. The next showed a funeral, a tiny basket lowered into the ground.

Emotion slugged Mallory like a punch in the dark. She could hardly breathe. She pressed a hand to her chest, desperate for Harry. She couldn't suck the tears back in this time. She put her head in her hands and cried, silently at first, then great racking sobs that tumbled through the air and down to the river.

She tried very hard to pull herself together. God, how embarrassing. She did *not* want to cry in front of him. When she heard the creak of him standing up, she almost thought he was leaving, that he couldn't bear witnessing her make such a fool of herself. But all he did was take her arm and sit her down again.

'I'm so sorry,' she said, over and over as she tried to wrestle the tears under control.

He dug in his jeans pocket and offered a rough-cut piece of cloth. 'Here. Might be some oil on it. Can't guarantee it wasn't used last to wipe a dipstick.'

Mallory laughed. A hiccupy, half-hysterical laugh. 'Some gentleman you are,' she said, but she managed to take the cloth. It was checked cotton, probably torn from an old shirt. And while it smelled faintly like the last greasy mechanic's shop she'd been in with the Corolla, somewhere underneath was a familiar floral scent. Like furniture polish. Something clean and bright to focus on.

Her sobs dried up, and AJ rested a hand on her back, familiar and comforting, as he had been when they'd danced at the rodeo. Warmth flowed into her skin, and she almost put her head down on his chest, wanting him to fold his arms around her, to be safe in his embrace.

Because she *did* feel safe. Not the kind she'd felt with Duncan, where she could always count on him to be upbeat and tell her what she needed to hear to make it through; this was deeper and calmer. A knowledge that this man was honest, said what he meant, and was brave enough not to shy away from danger or from tears.

Finally, she dried her eyes, dabbed her nose and folded the cloth into squares. 'I guess you don't want this back.'

'You can keep that one.'

'I am really sorry,' she said again. Man, all she'd done today was apologise.

'Holding it in gives you an ulcer, or somethin'. Don't be sorry.'

'I'm just not sure if I can take any more of the last few days.'

'You know, everyone in boot camp thinks about giving up. But people are stronger than they think. You are too. You're just bein' tested. That never feels good, but doesn't mean you won't make it.'

'Maybe.' She listened to the insects humming on the water, looked up and found the moon peeping through the branches of a tree. So beautiful; but beauty wasn't comforting. 'It's more than that, though. I know I told you that I had no money because my husband froze my accounts. But that was after he decided to keep Harry in New York without asking me. One minute, my five-year-old son is living in my house and I'm just putting things back together after my husband leaves, and the next, Duncan's got him. And there's nothing I can do about it, except show up.'

AJ's face was all hard lines as he frowned in the moonlight. 'So that's what's really going on?'

'I know, I know. You're going to ask why I let him go in the first place.'

'Nope.'

She paused. 'You weren't?'

'He must want to see his father. There more to it than that?'

'Yes and no. See, I married Duncan when I was eighteen, almost right out of school. He was twenty, just finished uni, and working on a start-up business. It was going to be a big thing, going to make him heaps of money.'

'Did it?'

'Not right away. We knew that it was going to take a while. So I did a short course in aged care and went to work. Once the business was up and running, I was supposed to be able to go back to study, or whatever I wanted to do. Then I found out I was having Harry, and we got married. And that was the next four years – I worked, he worked on the business.'

'Then what?'

She shrugged, trying not to feel that what had come next had been predictable. 'The business took off about a year ago. Duncan was working more than ever, lots of conference calls to New York and Chicago, lots of odd hours. We hardly saw each other for months, tag-teaming around Harry and work. One day, a few weeks after the big important deal went through, Duncan just sat me down and told me he couldn't keep living like this. That we'd grown apart. That he had to move to New York anyway and it would be best for both of us to split, at least for a while. And he left.'

'Did he come back?'

'Once, about four months after that. It was really awkward. Harry was desperate to see him. He cried every night for a week after Duncan went back to New York again. I think it was worse than if Duncan had stayed away. I pretended everything was fine.' In fact, Mallory had cried for a month, but only ever where Harry couldn't see her.

AJ leaned forward. 'So, how'd you end up here?'

'Duncan suddenly asked if Harry could visit over the Easter holidays, that he'd pay for the fare.' She sighed. 'I said yes because I thought that was a good sign. And because he told me that he'd been thinking about us. That when the visit was over, he wanted us to talk. I thought he meant about getting back together. Maybe even about us moving to New York with him, finally.

'God, I actually thought that.' She laughed, but it had no humour. 'Anyway, after they missed the flight home, Duncan told me that he thought it was better if Harry stayed in New York, that he didn't think I was the best parent now I was on my own. The only thing I could do was get on a plane.'

She felt the same despair she'd felt that night in the airport – only this time, it made her angry. She pulled off the end of a grass stalk. 'I'm so stupid to have let him go,' she said, and flung the grass towards the water. It fell short. 'Typical,' she muttered.

AJ chuckled. 'You're not. And as far as your husband goes, sounds like a lucky escape to me.'

Mallory's head jerked around. 'What do you mean?'

'You're a brave, generous woman, going out and supporting him for all those years, even if he did deserve it, and I'm not sure he did. He took off and left you just when his luck came good. That's not a man who loves you. That's not responsible, or treatin' someone right. Heck, that's not even a man. You still wanted to be with someone like that?'

'He's not a bad guy,' she said, feeling indefensibly defensive, despite everything that Duncan had done. 'It's not that simple. He was under a lot of stress. And he is a wonderful father. He looked after Harry every night so I could work.'

'A man can be a good father and be an awful husband. Man, if I had you to come home to, it'd be everything I wanted. Just for example,' he added, as if he didn't want her to take the wrong impression.

CHARLOTTE NASH

Mallory glanced at him, surprised and moved. She'd
always thought of her home as chaotic and in need of repair,
striving to be better than it was. But through his words, she
could think of her little cottage as a warm and loving place,
perfect as it was, without need for excuses or improvement.

'Anyway, I'm just saying I think you're better out of that
situation than in it,' he said. 'Maybe the only thing you're
guilty of is not realisin' it a year ago.'

Mallory said nothing, thinking. When had Duncan
stopped being a good husband? She'd always thought he
was the voice of reason in their relationship, the slightly
older man with a clear vision for how to get ahead. The
qualifiers she'd just given AJ had been in her head for a
long time: excuses for Duncan leaving, thinking he'd had so
much to deal with, or even that it had been her fault. But
. . . had he used her? The idea hurt so much, she shoved it
away. What did it matter now, anyway? If she and Duncan
had never split, at least she would have had Harry in her
arms tonight. She ached to hold his small body against her,
to cradle his soft head before he was too old to want hugs
from her anymore.

'Or maybe you want to tell me to mind my own business,'
AJ said, dusting his hands. 'And take you back.'

'No,' she said quickly, not wanting to be alone with her
desperation just yet.

'You got a picture of your boy?'

Mallory showed him several on her phone, then fumbled
in her pocket for the letter she'd been carrying since Brisbane.
She unfolded the envelope, withdrew the photo of Harry and
Duncan and handed it across. 'This is the most recent one.'

AJ had to get his phone out and angle the camera flash over the photo to see it.

Finally, he handed it back and gave a low chuckle.

'What?' she said.

'You and your being scared of horror films, and saying you're not strong enough for this. Look at what you're doing. You worked to support your man all through his big dreams, all with a kid to raise, and kept going when Mr I've-got-a-degree-in-SOB split town. Then when he tries to take your boy away, you're not sitting at home cryin' all night. You got on a plane.'

'Well, to be fair, I actually called a lawyer first,' she said.

'How'd that work out?'

'More expensive than a plane ticket,' she said, finding a small laugh. 'And even with volcanoes, ten times slower.'

'Typical. My point is, you remember what I said about *The Terminator*?'

Mallory rolled her eyes. 'Yeah, it's a "romance",' she said sourly, making air quotes.

'Forget about the first movie,' AJ said. 'You need the sequel – Sarah Connor protecting her son. The warrior mother. That's you.'

'Yeah, right,' she said. But however ridiculous it sounded, she couldn't help the warmth that his words put in her chest, or the tears of new resolve that prickled in her eyes. Perhaps she could get through this. Maybe she was strong enough. If wanting something enough could make it happen, nothing would keep her from New York.

She squeezed her eyes shut. 'All I wanted to do tonight was to see his face and hear his voice, to know he's still there waiting. I haven't heard from him in days. Duncan cut off

189

communication.' She didn't mention that she'd tried to call Harry every day, and failed to reach him, and was silently praying for Maria to find another chance to call.

AJ grunted, as if this wasn't a surprise. 'Where do they live in New York?'

'Here,' Mallory said, flipping to the address on the letter. 'Two Bridges. You know it?'

AJ swung the light from his phone to read the address. 'I think it's right downtown, near the Brooklyn Bridge. I've been to New York a few times, but it's a big place.'

Mallory tucked the letter away. 'You on the road again in the morning?'

'Yeah. Turning north for Chicago. Guess we won't be crossing paths again after that.'

'Guess not,' she said. For just a moment, their eyes lingered on each other, and Mallory felt again that unmistakable burst of sadness. He had given her something in listening to her, and the connection that had grown between them resisted so easy a parting.

His smile was gentle. 'I guess we'll always have Fort Smith. Come on. It's gettin' real late.'

They retraced their steps to the bike, AJ's leather creaking in the night air, each of them walking more slowly than they needed to. As AJ handed her the helmet, Mallory said, 'I thought the sixty-six route to Chicago peeled off earlier, in Oklahoma. Jock was talking about it in the car.'

'It does.'

'So why are you here?'

He shrugged. 'I wanted to avoid roadworks on that section. Ty wouldn't have liked the change, but that's just tough.'

'Who's Ty?' she asked.

AJ was reaching for his helmet, stuck on the handlebars. He slowed, as if the name had seized his whole body. 'My brother,' he said slowly, as if he'd spoken without thinking. 'I was supposed to do this ride with him, but it didn't work out. Come on, I'll take you back.'

He had Mallory to the motel less than ten minutes later. She made him park on the street to avoid waking up the whole building, and handed over the helmet.

'Thanks,' she said, feeling the awkward push-pull of wanting to hug someone, and not knowing if this was the time. AJ seemed to have retreated into himself. She swung her arms, wrong-footed. 'Well . . . take care on the road.'

'You too,' he said. Then, just before he pulled away, he looked back at her. 'I hope I see you again, sometime.'

She watched until the Rocket's tail-light disappeared around the corner.

The room clock read one in the morning. Jock was still asleep, having barely moved at all. Mallory set an alarm for seven and lay down on the covers, curled around the empty Harry space in her chest.

Five minutes later, her phone chimed with a text.

AJ: *Asleep yet?*

She wished. Though his message was almost as pleasant as a dream. Mallory sent: *Obviously not.* Then with some alarm: *Not riding and txting are you??*

AJ: *Pulled over. Had to make a call.*

Mallory glanced at the clock again before replying: *Who do you call this late? Roadside assistance?*

AJ: *Funny, Miss Australia.*

Then: *A friend. Lives in NY actually. Works nights.*

Mallory rolled onto her back. The screen was the only glow in the darkened room.

Mallory: *Is this normal for you? Riding around after midnight calling your interstate friends?*

AJ: *Distinctly abnormal actually.*

Mallory: *?*

AJ: *Actually I don't know what normal is now, after the Marines.*

Mallory read over the message three times, then wrote: *Well, what would you like normal to be?*

A pause stretched. He had to be thinking. Then he sent: *I like things quiet. Work a good day in the shop, rebuilding engines, stuff like that. Then home to a nice fire, sweet tea and company.*

Sounds nice, she sent, smiling at the image, then thought about him out there on the road somewhere, alone in the night, so far from the cosy fire he wanted. She remembered what he'd said earlier.

Mallory: *I'm sorry your brother couldn't do the trip with you.*

A very long pause.

AJ: *Me too . . . But then, maybe I wouldn't have met you.*

Mallory bit her lip, a little pleasant glow in her chest.

AJ: *Remember, whatever happens, you'll do right.*

In the dark room with her worst fears for company, she said: *I don't know about that. I mean, look at my track record.*

AJ: *If I was as determined as you, I'd be in Chicago by now.*

Sigh. Mallory wanted to believe him.

AJ: *And if that fails, just remember Sarah Connor ;)*

Mallory could visualise him grinning. She relented: *I'll try. Ride safe, okay?*

He sent back an emoji of a bike helmet.

Mallory waited for sleep to drag her under, and tried to imagine herself as a warrior. She'd been avoiding thinking about how to deal with Duncan once she reached New York. She didn't want to think about the possibility she would go home alone. Now, for the first time, she thought maybe she was strong enough to meet him. She had to be. Perhaps she had been all along – it had just taken someone else to see it.

Chapter 13

MALLORY WOKE JUST AFTER SIX-THIRTY, WHEN LIGHT
spilled around the block-out curtain and a shaft landed
directly across her face. Jock was still asleep.

She rose and rubbed her eyes, feeling unusually awake
despite the short night. She pulled on her jumper and took
her phone into the empty next-door room. It was still early in
New York, but she hadn't heard from Harry since Tuesday,
and it was Saturday now. She dialled Duncan through
Skype and got no response. She paused only a second before
she picked up the room phone and dialled the apartment
number. It rolled to messaging, so she hung up, feeling jumpy.

Jock was groggy after the Valium. By the time both
of them were ready and back over to the hospital, it was
pushing nine.

'Still waiting for the morning round,' Ernie said. He
looked absolutely awful: the bump on his cheek had spread
purple under his left eye, and his right was almost as bruised
with fatigue. His good hand shook on his cane.

'How much sleep did you get?' Mallory asked.

'I don't sleep much anymore. But Zadie's doing much better. Can't imagine they'll want to keep her any longer.'

Mallory's spirits surged. Maybe they could travel a few hours today. If Ernie didn't pass out first and need to be admitted himself.

'You and Jock better have some breakfast,' she said. 'I'll sit with Zadie.'

After he went, Mallory pulled up the plastic chair alongside the bed. Zadie looked so much brighter than she had yesterday: her cheeks pink and full, her blue eyes clear. She was wearing a bland hospital gown, but someone – Mallory guessed Ernie – had tucked the imperial purple cardigan around her shoulders. A drip ran into her left wrist. Mallory twinged with guilt, wondering how she hadn't noticed the deterioration yesterday.

'How are you feeling?' she asked.

Zadie gave a quivery smile. 'I'm swell. There's squirrels outside the window.'

'Are there?' Mallory craned to see out the frosted glass. Nothing moved in the streetscape outside, but who knew what squirrels got up to. 'How many did you see?'

'I'm not sure. But Mabel would have loved them.'

Mallory paused. She'd assumed that Zadie had simply misheard her name, but now she wondered if Mabel was actually someone else. Perhaps one of her beloved animal charges – a dog, or a horse, or a cat, perhaps the predecessor of Melville.

'Zadie, would you like to tell me about Mabel?'

Zadie paused and looked up at the ceiling. 'I went to visit her once, when Ernie was late coming home from the hospital. I had to climb over this big black fence, because the gates were closed. I can't imagine what anyone would have thought if they saw me. Later, Ernie saw a rip in my coat. I told him I'd been climbing a fence—'

The *swisssshhh!* of the bed curtain cut her off. A bank of people stared in, led by a tall, balding man with a stethoscope around his neck.

'Morning, Mrs Flint,' said the doctor, reaching for the chart at the end of the bed. 'How are we?'

Zadie smiled, but Mallory saw the apprehensive tug in the corner of her mouth, the way her fingers groped for the edge of the mattress. Mallory gently took her hand. 'It's all right, Zadie, this is the doctor.'

'No fevers since last night, good hydration,' he said, flipping chart pages, brisk with busyness. Another member of the hovering medical team was scribbling notes. 'Is she taking oral fluids? Good. We can have that drip out now, thank you. Continue with P-O A-Bs on a script and we can discharge by noon. All right, now, let's take a quick look.'

He came around the bed and unslung the stethoscope, listened cursorily to a few places on Zadie's chest, then patted her arm and raised his voice a little. 'We're going to send you home this morning, Mrs Flint.'

Ten seconds later, the whole crew had moved on to the next curtain. Mallory blew out a breath, relieved they were gone. Zadie loosened her grip and caught Mallory's eye. In that look, Mallory glimpsed the whole woman Zadie was: the one who had left home young, who had loved her husband but been lonely in her marriage, who didn't want to now be fading into old memories. Who didn't like being in hospital any more than anyone else.

196

'What was I saying?' Zadie said now, with a small frown. 'About climbing over a fence,' Mallory said. 'To visit Mabel.' 'But you're right here,' she croaked.

'Well, we must have been talking about me, then,' Mallory said, playing along. But she wasn't sure where Zadie was right now, or if she knew what she was saying. Mallory rubbed her eyes; she could hardly believe it was only five days since they'd left LA. It felt like five months. Please, she thought, please let us make it to Nashville.

•

They left nearing lunchtime, pulling back onto the I-40 in the subdued mood of people who'd survived a storm, and knew how lucky they were not to be living under a tarp. Ernie slid on a pair of dark glasses that made him look more like a mob don than a retired doctor, but which covered his bruise, so Mallory kept the thought firmly to herself. She stopped every hour to make sure Zadie had enough fluids, used the bathroom, and took her medicine at the right times. In between, Mallory thought about Harry, and about Duncan, ever puzzling on why he was doing this. She never arrived at any answers.

The highway was forested now, like driving through a tunnel of trees. The road only opened through small suburban centres, and the sprawl of North Little Rock. Progress slowed. The stops made a four-hour drive into six, and the sun was low in the sky as they flew out over the flat plains at the edge of Arkansas. Then the road lofted into a long bridge, and the Mississippi spread beneath them, the towers of Memphis glinting like fire-touched brands in the volcanic sunset. And there, to the left of the road, a perfect glass pyramid reflected a wedge of orange sky.

'What on earth is that?' she asked, awed.

'I have utterly no idea,' Jock said, pulling out his earbuds. He'd spent the entire drive plugged into his phone, saying little.

'Ha, they built it,' Ernie said, slapping his leg. 'I'll be damned. Architect had an idea for that in the fifties. I read an article about it. But everyone thought it was crazy.'

'Guess not,' Mallory said thinking Harry would love it. She imagined him, straining forward in the back seat, trying to see, pleading to be taken closer. For Mallory, the raw need to see him was more than she could stand. 'We're stopping here,' she said, taking the downtown exit off the interstate. 'I need to make a call.'

Ernie actually rubbed his hands together. 'Just what I was about to say. Zadie and I stopped in Memphis when we came through in sixty-eight. We're only a few hours from Nashville now, and we should celebrate the last night. Shouldn't miss the southern food.'

Mallory glanced in the rear-view. She'd never seen Ernie enthusiastic about food before. He'd always treated it like fuel, eating sandwiches or roast or salad with the exact same expression on his face. His main concern had been Zadie – that she was getting adequate nutrition, that her food was easily swallowed. Mallory could only guess that it was either nostalgia, or excitement at nearing the end of the trip.

'Ernie,' she said.

'Mmm?'

'Before any culinary adventures, can we talk about my pay? I'd like to try for a flight tomorrow when we arrive, or another car. That okay with you?'

'Sure, sure. I can give you cash, if your account still has an issue. Or we can split it between that and a booking. Whatever you want.'

Perfect. Mallory's shoulders dropped in relief. Sorting out the money had seemed like a dreaded fence between now and tomorrow. But in just a few words, she'd scaled up the side and could now look over into what came next.

They found a hotel and checked in within half an hour. Ernie booked Mallory her own room, but her heart was heavy as she sat on the bed. It was after eight in New York and she knew the call she was about to make wouldn't be answered.

As if the universe had heard her wish, an incoming Skype lit up. Mallory pounced on her phone, gasping for joy when she saw Harry in the desk chair. He was wearing his Batman pyjamas, hair damp. His face was bright and furtive, as if he was up to no good.

'Mummy,' he said softly.

'Hi, baby,' she said. 'Why are you whispering?'

'When are you coming, Mummy?' A plea, a begging tone she hadn't heard before.

'Soon, baby,' she said. 'Really soon.'

His little face crumpled. 'I miss you, Mummy. I want you here!'

Mallory's soul broke like a raw egg. 'I miss you too, baby. I love you so much.'

But Harry couldn't be placated. He was crying now, with fat tears on his cheeks, hands outstretched, as he'd done as a toddler. Mallory would have moved time and continents to leap through the screen. Instead, she had to watch. She wanted to tell him how close she was, that he could see her tomorrow. But too much had happened already; she couldn't risk letting him down.

She could only say that she loved him so much, that she would see him soon. It destroyed her to see it wasn't enough to comfort him.

Then a shadow fell across the desk. 'What's going on in here? What did I say about my office?'

Duncan.

Mallory's heart sank like an ingot of iron. Duncan came into shot, glanced once at the screen, then lifted Harry out of the chair. Mallory could hear him shushing Harry and reminding him it was bedtime. Harry had dissolved into hiccups and slurred *Mummy please*s.

Mallory hated Duncan in that moment, with an unbridled passion. She would never have kept Harry from him, never in a million years. She had to clench her fist to stop from breaking down. She heard a female voice: Maria, trying to soothe Harry. But that voice should have been Mallory's. She felt the tears rolling down her cheeks, that last image of his distraught face etched on her retinas. She was so upset, so furious that she wasn't there, that she had ever let Harry out of her sight to end up here.

Duncan leaned back into the screen, swiping a hand through his hair.

'That wasn't necessary,' she fired at him. 'I'm his mother! He only wants to see me. Why are you being so awful?'

'I told you not to call,' he said, and shut the screen. Skype hung up.

Mallory began to shake, an all-over involuntary tremor. Her throat was parched. She snatched up a glass and thrust it under the tap, but misjudged. The glass smashed against the faucet and fell into a pile of shards in the sink.

All she could think about was that conversation she'd had with AJ, where he'd said that everyone had something terrible they'd been through. Would this be the thing, a year from now, ten years from now, that had broken her? Would her life be defined by a son she lost, who she tried to reach through thousands of miles and goddamn volcanoes, and yet never saw again?

Duncan was behaving like a stranger, pretending that they'd never painted a nursery together. Acting as if she'd never massaged his aching shoulders after he'd worked in every scrap of Harry's nap time. As though nothing mattered to him now except having his way, and to hell with anything she thought about it.

She stared at the broken glass. Her heart may as well have been in as many pieces.

A knock came on her door, and she straightened, sniffing.

'Mallory?' Jock's voice, etched with concern.

After a pause, she called, 'Yeah?'

'You all right in there?'

'Just a sec.'

She ran the tap and splashed the water over her face, fumbling so much in avoiding the glass that she soaked her collar. She snatched up a rough towel and dried herself, but her eyes were still red and swollen. She only opened the door a few inches.

'Sorry, I was washing up and broke a cup,' she said. 'Do you need anything?'

Jock's expression was hard to read. Probably she wasn't fooling anyone, but he was kind enough not to say anything.

'Ernie's okayed a dinner venue – best ribs in the country. Figured it was the last night and I'd treat everyone. He's even allowed us the keys to get take-out.' Jock jangled the set. 'Anyway, he's still on the phone arranging something in Nashville. Wondered if you needed more time with your call?'

'It's done,' she said quickly, and though she had no desire to eat, 'where are we going?'

Chapter 14

To Mallory, the evening inched by at the pace of a slow Elvis number. Jock actually played Elvis in the car on the way to The Bar-B-Q Shop, because he said it was entirely appropriate in Memphis. The restaurant turned out to be a restful cave, with red walls, dark wood and high ceilings, and a host at the door who greeted them in a soft southern voice and called her ma'am. The whole place made her think of AJ and those moments with him in the cool air by the river. Jock bought them giant glasses of iced sweet tea to drink while they waited at the bar.

'Oh, that's really good,' Mallory said, taking huge gulps. Sugar really was the balm that soothed everything.

'Have you never had sweet tea before?' the waitress said, when Mallory asked her if it was a house specialty. 'Well, you're in the south now. Every southern woman's got a pitcher of sweet tea in her fridge, though we like to think ours is special.'

Those few minutes of sitting with Jock inside the restaurant were tranquil, but the mood didn't last the drive back, even with the intoxicating smell of barbequed pork. Perhaps the sugar was wearing off. Mallory could feel the weight of her conversation with Harry settling on her, the need to get moving again straining against her impotence to do so. She needed to settle things with Ernie.

They ate around the motel's pool, still closed from the winter but with a pleasant view of the apricot sunset. The smoke and spice smell of the tender meat promised delicious eating, but Mallory picked at her food. Jock and Ernie ate with unusual gusto, licking sticky fingers like children, and Ernie reminisced about songs from the seventies that Mallory had little knowledge of, often waving a rib as he did. Zadie slowly ate her way through a side of beans, appearing to enjoy the novelty and singing odd lines from songs she recognised. Three slices of homemade pie waited.

Mallory tapped her foot. She hoped that at any moment, Ernie would remember they hadn't discussed the money before the dinner run and would make some opening statement about it himself. If she brought it up again, would he think she was being pushy and his good mood evaporate? She silently chastised herself for treading so carefully, but it didn't help her to form the words. So much for AJ's notion of her as a warrior woman. She couldn't handle Duncan on a Skype call. And now she was waiting and waiting to ask Ernie about her pay.

She'd nearly worked up the courage to break into the conversation when a phone rang in Ernie's pocket. He then made a lot of drama about finding napkins to clean fingers before he could retrieve it, by which time the caller had hung up. Ernie examined the screen.

'I can't make sense of this, Jock,' he complained. Another five minutes went by as Jock tried to explain how to bring up the missed call. Finally, Ernie grunted in satisfaction.

'I better phone them back. It's the agency in Nashville.' And he limped slowly away to the other side of the pool.

While he was gone, Mallory rallied her courage.

'Where are you staying in Nashville?' she asked as a lead-in when Ernie finally came back.

He wiped his mouth and examined the remains of his dinner, as if wondering whether to eat more. 'Oh, a hotel close to town, right near the university and Scarritt Bennett.'

'What's that?'

'The training college. Where Zadie used to volunteer. Where the chapel is.'

'Beautiful chapel,' Zadie said, her voice a little croaky. 'The stone makes voices into angels.'

'And you have someone to take over from me?'

'All taken care of,' Ernie said. 'She's meeting us at the hotel.'

'What time is she going to be there?'

'Oh, we'll confirm all that in the morning. When we have a better idea of arrival time. No rush.'

Mallory's legs involuntarily tensed, as if she needed to run. Yes, they said, there is a rush!

'Can I call them to do a handover now? Make it smooth for everyone tomorrow?'

'That won't be necessary, thank you,' Ernie said, refusing to look at her. 'We can cover any of those things when we arrive.'

Mallory chewed her lip. 'About that,' she said, realising she'd have to be more direct, 'can we talk about my pay? You remember I said there was a problem with my account.'

'Yes, I remember. I said in the car it was fine.'

'And the ticket booking?'

Ernie's phone rang again. Mallory kept chewing her lip as he once again limped away to talk to the caller. Another fifteen minutes ticked by.

'Zadie, that was the lovely director at Scarritt. She has some ideas for the wedding,' he said, coming back.

Mallory let it go. She and Jock cleaned up while Ernie laid out the plans with Zadie, and then Mallory helped Zadie back inside, and to the bathroom, checked she'd taken all the right medication, and helped her change into her nightdress. Ernie was on the phone again, upbeat and discussing a cake.

Mallory brushed Zadie's hair, hoping that Ernie was about to wind up the call. Her dinner, meagre as it had been, sat heavy in her stomach.

'Well, I'm beat,' Ernie declared as he ended his call. 'Time to hit the hay.'

Mallory cleared her throat. 'Ernie, can we finish talking about my pay?'

'How about in the morning? Don't worry, you'll get your money.'

She felt a barb of resentment. He was behaving as if she was hassling him about something that didn't matter. 'It's just that I wanted to make a booking. And I might need the rest in cash. I didn't know if that would take time to organise.'

Ernie's jaw worked. 'Shouldn't be a problem. Might have to call the bank to work out how to make a large withdrawal here.' He sounded uncertain.

'Jock could help with that,' Mallory said quickly. 'It's important I head to New York tomorrow and I didn't want any surprises. I can go and find the booking, and we could take care of that now?'

'In the morning will be fine,' he said. 'We're all tired now.'

'But what about the time zone? Morning here is the middle of the night in Australia. The bank might not have anyone to answer a call tomorrow. It's midmorning right now. Best time to call.'

There was a pause, in which Ernie heaved a sigh. 'I understand you're worried about this, but I'm not making any more calls tonight. We'll have plenty of time to work it out in the morning.'

A moment later, Mallory found herself on the outside of the closed door, not knowing what to do. What could she do? Bang on the door and insist that he make sure he could pay her tomorrow?

But what if he couldn't, and she was left waiting . . . or worse: stranded again while yet another man held her hostage with money.

Her gut clenched in a double fist, and again she thought of that awful Skype call. Harry's tears, and Duncan's unyielding attitude. What exactly was she planning to do when she reached New York? The vision in her head – that she'd knock on the door of the apartment, that Harry would rush into her arms and that they would both then leave for the airport – was missing a lot of pieces. What would Duncan really do when she appeared?

Warrior woman.

Ha.

What a joke.

'Ernie holding out on you?' Jock asked, when he saw Mallory's face.

'Says we have to talk about money in the morning.'

Jock grunted. 'Ernie's cagey about things like that, but he won't stiff you. He follows through.'

Mallory sighed. Jock would think the best of his friend, but by Ernie's own admission, the whole reason he was here was that he'd made a long career out of not following through on promises, even to the wife he so clearly loved.

'And if he doesn't, I'll see you right,' Jock added.

Mallory smiled her thanks as she felt a buzz in her pocket. Hope went off like a firework inside her: maybe Harry had sent her a message.

Instead, there was a text.

How's the mission, Sarah? Did you make it to Memphis? AJ.

A warm comfort folded over her, as if she'd pulled on an old cherished jumper after an hour's freezing in a winter wind.

Just, she typed back. *How's the road to Chicago?*

Funny thing about that, he said. *Not on the road to Chicago.*

Mallory's heart took this as a signal to begin thumping. *Where r u?*

Want to go to Silky O'Sullivan's and do a Diver? AJ typed.

Mallory had no earthly clue what that meant, but she typed. *Where is that?*

Memphis.

•

Mallory declined all AJ's suggestions of hitting the famous eateries of Memphis, citing that she'd already had ribs for dinner, and even those weren't sitting well. Instead, she asked him to take her to the pyramid by the Mississippi. She knew she wouldn't be able to sleep, and needed to do something to dissipate the jumpy impatience in her bones. She wasn't sure if she saw it, or simply imagined Ernie watching their departure from behind tweaked curtains like a disapproving father. Jock had heard the Rocket, stuck his head out of his room to wave, and promptly gone back inside.

A ride on the Rocket wasn't what she needed, but maybe it was the next-best thing. All the way to the pyramid Mallory threw her head back, letting the wind and the big growling engine strip away her frustration over Duncan and Ernie. When they arrived, underneath the bridge pylons that soared over the Mississippi, she peeled off her helmet and said, 'Jock didn't call you, did he?'

'Call me?' AJ stuck his own helmet on the handlebars and peeled himself off the seat, boots creaking. He'd had a haircut somewhere between Fort Smith and now, and the clean edges emphasised the hard lines of his face, the weight in his shoulders. God, if he wanted, he could probably snap her like a twig.

'About me.'

'Maybe he did. If he had, what would he have said?'

After trying to work out if that was an admission, or a clever turnaround where she would have to show her hand first, Mallory said, 'Why aren't you on your way to Chicago?'

'I'm going the long way round.'

'Too many roadworks?' She shot him a questioning eyebrow, and he gave her a lopsided grin, which only stirred that spark of longing she'd felt in Fort Smith. Somewhere in her subconscious, she knew that he was here because of her, even if she wasn't prepared to acknowledge it. Instead, she set off for the pyramid, which rose beyond the elevated freeway. The side was marked with a huge sign that said, *Bass Pro Shop*.

'Well. This is different,' she said, five minutes later, standing inside.

The pyramid's interior began with a long hall, lined with dark wood that opened into a vast cavern. The roof was high enough to dwarf actual trees, which were hung with twinkling lights and moss, and sheltered an undergrowth of sporting goods. There was a lake – an honest-to-God lake, with boats and everything – and rock walls, and a ring of cabin-style hotel rooms elevated off the main floor. The colour palette was muted brown and green and warm wood, the colours of the forest and camouflage. And rising up in the centre was a truss-framed elevator, lit in sparkling green.

'Now you're going to tell me why you wanted to come here,' AJ said. 'I don't pick you for a hunter.'

'I thought it would be a museum or something.'

'I guess a sporting goods megastore is "something",' AJ drawled.

'Well, it's a different something,' she said, disappointed. She'd been counting on a place she could tell Harry about.

'I think the word you're searching for is "incongruous",' said AJ. 'Want to go up the top?'

He jerked a thumb towards the ceiling, so high over their heads it was lost in a haze.

They rode the lift to the lookout. In the gathering night, Memphis was a sea of twinkling lights meeting the east bank of the Mississippi, the roads like jewelled bands. Mallory ran her eye all the way west, down all the miles she'd already travelled. On that side, the river owned everything, and it was dark. Now, she had to go east, towards the light, and fast.

AJ only let her brood on the view for five minutes before he leaned on the rail beside her. 'Something's happened.'

'Why do you say that?'

'It's a gift. You going to stew that pot all night, or spit it out?'

Nothing like a bit of subtlety.

'Harry called me tonight.' She then told him about the rest of it, managing to get through the story in a short time without crumbling to tears. 'I suppose I should have seen this coming,' Mallory rushed on, when AJ said nothing and kept his eyes on the view. 'I can't bear the thought he might be punished for calling me.'

'Where are you going?'

Mallory stopped, realising she was on her way inside without even thinking. She turned back and blew the air out of her lungs.

'I don't even know! I'm shackled, and I hate it. I can't go anywhere until we reach Nashville, and I need Ernie to pay me so I can leave from there.' She broke off, not wanting to revisit the conversations about money.

She told herself they'd arrive in Nashville by midmorning tomorrow, and then she'd be free. Ernie would pay her, and she could find a way to New York the same day. It had to play out that way.

'That's a real serious frown you've got going there,' AJ said.

Mallory's thoughts turned. 'Tell me something. Say Sarah Connor was in my situation. What would she do?'

'It would probably involve high-powered weapons.'

'Typical,' Mallory muttered. Fantasy was all very well, but Hollywood couldn't help her now.

'You're wrong, by the way,' AJ said.

'About what?'

'Thinking all this is your fault.'

'I didn't say that.'

'Yeah, you did. About ten different ways now.' He ticked them off on his huge fingers. 'You said you should have seen this coming. That if you hadn't let Harry go, this wouldn't have happened. But your ex is an asshole. Probably of long standing. Nothing you did changes that.'

Mallory took a breath to argue, but instead she found herself staring at him, his blue eyes gleaming back at her in the fading light. Something in his words held truth, and held her, reaching to the marrow of her bones. She nodded, slowly.

'Something changed, though,' she said. 'He left us a year ago. Why do this now? I just don't get it. I was reading that he's up for some award, but so what? His business has been growing all this time.'

AJ shrugged. 'Who wants to know the mind of an a-hole?'

'Please don't say that. You don't know him.' But she didn't want to talk about Duncan anymore. She ached for AJ to put his strong arms around her and tell her everything would be fine. To hold her up, just while the fear that she was about to fail wore itself out.

AJ gave her a look that managed to say how vanishingly little he cared about Duncan. 'Don't have to know him. I know you.'

For a second, she thought he was going to kiss her, then he looked away, the thick muscles in his neck stretched like ropes. Who was she kidding? They'd just met a few days ago and were going in different directions. And what the hell was she even thinking, while Harry was still in New York? As Mallory silently remonstrated herself, AJ was quiet, his thumb working against the railing. Finally, he cleared his throat.

'What's your plan after Nashville?' he said, as if it was a military operation.

'If there's no flights, I guess maybe a train—'

'That'll take more than a day,' AJ said. 'But then, it's also a long drive.'

Mallory told herself she could drive all night if she needed to, if only she could bank a good sleep tonight.

'The others are staying in Nashville?'

'Ernie and Zadie are. Jock's heading on to Virginia.'

'How's he doing that?'

She shrugged again. 'Didn't ask. Maybe he'll hang around until the flights are back on.'

This seemed to bring their conversation to an end. As darkness gathered around them, the river was a silvery shimmer under the moon. A beautiful setting for an awkward pause. Mallory dusted off her hands, and abruptly the gravity of what she was doing, and the excruciating effort of all the positive thinking fell on her like a boulder. She braced her hands on the railing.

'Oh, God,' she whispered. She put her forehead down on the cool metal. 'Oh, God, what if this doesn't work?'

'You'll make it work,' AJ said, and that warm hand was on her back again.

She shook her head. What if the car packed up between here and Nashville? What if Zadie needed admitting again? What if Ernie never paid her? What if, what if? She heard her breath coming in gasps, the panic of losing Harry crushing her lungs.

'You want to know my real name?'

Mallory straightened. 'What?'

'You heard me.'

'You're AJ,' she said. But the panic had neatly derailed. 'Which is short for . . .?'

'Angus Jordan?' she guessed.

'Nope. Ajax.'

Mallory blinked. 'Ajax? As in the cleaning product?'

'Ajax as in the *Greek god*,' AJ said, giving her a dirty look. 'Cleaning product,' he muttered.

'Actually, Ajax wasn't a god,' Mallory said. 'A hero, yes. Not a god.'

'You a schoolteacher now? I should call you "Miss Australia" again.'

'I've seen *Troy*, and Harry was just getting into Greek mythology. We read this book . . .' She trailed off, trying not to go back to the dark place.

'Then you'll love that my sisters are Hera, Athena and Livia.'

Mallory laughed despite herself. She poked him in the centre of the chest. 'So what's your last name?'

Her voice came out huskier than she'd meant, and he glanced down at where she touched him before he answered. 'Archer,' he said softly, covering her hand with his.

'Ajax Archer?'

'Mmm-hmm.'

'That's like an alter-ego name,' she said, a little breathless. 'You haven't got a cape in the Rocket, have you?'

His grin was slow. 'Nope. What you see is what you get.'

Ajax. It suited him. And now he was looking at her with soft eyes, and she wanted to fold herself into his body. But she couldn't do that. She wasn't here for that. She removed her hand, but he squeezed her palm briefly before she could turn away.

'I'd like to see you again sometime,' he said.

'You would?'

'When all your stuff is sorted out. Yeah, I would.' His face was serious. 'I can't stop thinking about you.'

'But I'll be back in Australia.'

'They have these things called airplanes,' he drawled. 'It's not a foolproof system, as you know, but they work most of the time.'

Mallory was too surprised to blush. 'It's thirteen hours flying. And why on earth would anyone want to visit Brisbane?'

'Aside from you being there?'

Mallory did blush now, her ears burning like torches. Lord, he was serious.

'Every place's got somethin' worth seeing. Something unique and beautiful, or that has a story, like this wacky pyramid. Come on now, ain't there anything you think is worth seeing in Brisbane?'

Mallory wrinkled her nose. Brisbane had the reputation of being the big country town of Australia, the unsophisticated northern city that could never compete with Sydney. And worse, she lived in the 'bogan east', hardly a tourist mecca. Duncan had been itching to leave as soon as he could. Great things happened someplace else, that was what he'd said. Then again, Mallory hardly honoured what Duncan thought anymore.

'I suppose the bay is beautiful in the morning, when the sun is shining on the water and yachts go sailing by. Or in the early evening, when the sea breeze is fresh. There's islands out there with sandhills and lakes. At least, I think there is.'

'You've never been?'

Mallory shook her head. Her mother had never been the going-places-and-doing-things sort. She'd been the let's-pretend-we'll-do-it-but-never-will kind. The times Mallory had been places had been with other people . . .

'Oh,' she said. 'Riverfire!'

'Come again?'

Mallory straightened, excited. 'Riverfire. It's this huge fireworks night. I went once when I was sixteen, but it's on every year in the middle of town. It was amazing. To start, they had this fighter plane come in low, right over the river, and this big flame roaring out the back.'

'Afterburner,' AJ said. 'Was that an F-111?'

'That's it! And then the fireworks, which just go on and on. They light up three bridges across the river, as well as the barges, and they go from the tops of the buildings, too. It was just . . . wow. They don't have that fighter plane anymore, but there's big army helicopters, I think. I saw it on the TV.'

Mallory could almost feel the grass under her fingertips again, and smell barbeques and tomato sauce. She and her schoolfriend had crammed themselves into the crowd that night, in the perfect position halfway between bridges, buoyed in their near-adulthood independence and, for Mallory, a rare night out. They'd worn glow bands on their wrists and danced to the soundtrack, while the sky exploded into coloured stars.

'So,' AJ said, 'you're telling me that there's a fireworks show with military aircraft and you didn't think it was worth mentioning? When is this thing?'

'September. Just when the weather's turning warm again.'

'Well, book me a seat.'

Mallory gazed into his blue eyes that were so fixed on her, almost believing this could happen. She knew then that if they had met in any other circumstances, if the timing hadn't been so tight, her worry not so desperate, then he would have kissed her now with an intensity that would have knocked her knees out. It was almost enough for Mallory to forget what was at stake. She hated herself for that.

She pushed away from him, even though it hurt to avoid his proposal. She just wasn't capable of thinking that far ahead right now. 'I should get back.'

AJ didn't argue, but when he pulled up in front of her motel room, he stopped her before she went in. 'One more thing,' he said.

'Yeah?'

He paused. 'Before I go, I want to tell you about Ty.'

•

Mallory didn't know what possessed her to invite him in. Maybe it was curiosity, maybe that she understood this was something sensitive, and she didn't want him to talk about it in the carpark of a motel. Or maybe it was simply to delay him leaving – to entertain, even for just a few minutes, the idea of him in her room. Even so, when he looked around and said, 'Don't worry, I'm not planning on any ill intentions', she couldn't help feeling a little disappointed.

She busied herself making very bad instant coffee for both of them, then perched on the small desk chair. He took the end of the bed across from her, his coffee untouched.

'So Ty's your brother?' she prompted when it seemed he couldn't begin.

'Yeah. *Was* my brother.'

The hairs on Mallory's arm rose. She put her cup down. 'Was?'

'Ty always wanted to do Route Sixty-six,' he said. 'He loved all that old-school America stuff. Old cars and bikes. And food trucks. Southern barbeque, burgers, lobster. Boy loved to eat. He was my little brother, but we were real close,' he added, as though this wasn't the most important detail.

'What happened?' she asked.

'We planned the trip, all the way through our last year in the Marines. See, we'd joined up the same month, planned on getting out together, too. We were going to do the old Sixty-six from LA to Chicago, then ride all the way back to California through Montana and set up our shop. We had the lease all set, all the money saved up.'

He paused, as if regretting starting this story. Finally, he started again, but his words were tight and deliberate, as if he were keeping a great emotion at bay. 'A few days before we got out, Ty picked up this bug that laid him out. We thought it was bad food at the base, but it just got worse. Eventually, he ended up in hospital with pancreatitis.'

He pronounced the condition with a slower drawl, injecting it with foreboding. Mallory waited as AJ swung the cup around in its saucer.

'He was supposed to be there just a couple of days. The doctors said he'd need fluids and rest, but then they found the cancer.'

Mallory froze. 'Oh, AJ, I'm so sorry.'

His head tipped back and he stared at the ceiling. 'The cancer was already advanced when they found it. Doctors said that was typical. Ty was convinced he was going to beat it anyway. At least, at first. Took a few weeks for him to realise that wasn't going to happen.'

Mallory held her breath, scared to disturb this painful story he was choosing to tell her.

'It's a terrible way to go,' AJ went on. 'If it was me, I'd be asking for the clean end. But we don't let people out like that, do we? Real terrible way to go.'

'And you had to watch,' Mallory said. 'That must have been awful.'

AJ blew out his breath. 'Yeah. Sure. And I wasn't always the best at it. I tried to be there for him, but I was angry too. I was pretty painful for everyone else to be around.'

Mallory abandoned her chair and sat down beside him. 'No one's good at difficult situations. You should see how many families don't come around anymore for their parents and grandparents once the going's hard. If you stick at it, you're doing fine.'

'I dunno, maybe,' he said, hunched over on himself now. 'I also kinda shut down on everyone since he passed. Couldn't face the rest of the family, so I flew out straight after the funeral. Eventually made it to LA, picked up the Rocket and hit the road. Haven't returned anyone's calls. I know they're worried. I know that isn't the best way to go about it, but that's where I'm at.'

Mallory put a hand on his arm, sensing how badly he needed comfort, how this experience had burned him with grief. 'Give yourself time,' she said gently. 'Maybe this is just how you need to deal with what happened. Some people gather their friends around them. Some people ride Rockets across the country.'

She was encouraged by the small smile that touched his lips.

'You'll know when you can reach out to your family again,' she said. 'And it's nice to be honouring your brother by doing the trip you both planned.'

AJ unfurled, his blue eyes not looking quite so sad. 'That's how I tried to see it. Other times, I'd be guilty that I'm here and he's not. It's weird without him around. Hurts. I didn't think I'd enjoy the ride, but I started anyway, 'cause I needed something to do.'

'Did it feel good just to be going somewhere?' she asked. 'That's how I felt when we finally got out of the airport in LA.'

'Yeah, sorta,' he said. 'And I ended up with more to do than I expected. Changing tyres, dance instructing, Memphis tour guiding.'

Mallory laughed. 'You think you might open the shop after all, even without him?'

He shrugged. 'Don't feel right anymore. Been wondering if I should do something more like some of my ex-military friends. They go into all kinds of different things. Surveillance. Security. Private protection. Maybe I could do that.'

Mallory thought for a minute. 'Doesn't sound like the quiet life you wanted.'

'Maybe not. But it's something.'

'I'd give anything to have my quiet life back.'

AJ leaned forward. 'The thing is, Mal, I didn't bring up all this stuff to talk about what I'm planning to do next. I figure that's my problem. But I wanted you to realise something about where you're at.'

'What's that?' she asked warily.

'What happened to Ty was awful, but it was also goddamn random and uncontrollable. And so's this thing that's happened to you.'

Mallory stopped nodding. 'Wait, that's not the same thing.'

'It is.'

'It's not. You're talking about *cancer*. Of course that's random. This is stuff with my husband. Of course I could have changed how it all went.'

'You're missing the point.'

'Am I?' she said. 'What's the point?'

'It's not about what you coulda done, it's the idea you did something wrong. You didn't know this was where it would all lead. How could you? We don't go around assuming people are going to screw us over. At least, most people don't,' he said. 'Ty wasn't a hundred per cent for a couple of months before he first went to hospital. Subtle stuff. Maybe stuff only his closest friends would have noticed. But I didn't say anything. If I had, maybe they'd have found that cancer earlier. Maybe he'd still be here. But I try not to think like that. It'll make you crazy. Real crazy, I mean, not can't-change-a-tyre crazy.'

Mallory rolled her eyes. 'This again!'

AJ grabbed her hand, as if in apology. Mallory stilled. 'None of us did anything wrong,' he said, his blue eyes earnest. 'We couldn't have known, because we didn't have a crystal ball. It makes me mad as hell, don't get me wrong.

I want to punch everyone who looks at me funny because Ty didn't deserve what he got. But it wasn't my fault. You're still beating yourself up about stuff that happened last week. None of that is going to help you. You screwed up in trusting this guy? Okay, fine, just don't do it again.'

Mallory frowned. She couldn't just let herself off like that. Harry was still in New York, the whole horrible situation still in flux because she hadn't been more careful. It wasn't like that for AJ. As awful as it was, his brother had died and he couldn't change that now. AJ had to believe that he hadn't done anything wrong, or how could he live with himself? Not that she would ever say that to him.

Her situation was different. She still had the chance to fix her mistakes. That possibility was what pushed her out of bed in the morning, what kept her eyes open when she was flagging behind the wheel. It kept her hopeful, knowing that it was not too late, yet.

Or was it?

The thought was on her so quickly, Mallory had no chance to push it away. What would 'too late' look like? When Duncan left New York with Harry, and she didn't hear from them again? Would her last memory of her son be seeing him crying for her on a pixelated Skype window?

Misery came down like a dark sack over her head. She dropped her eyes as tears welled, imagining standing in the doorway of an empty apartment in New York with no idea where they were. Of it all being her fault.

The mattress dipped alarmingly as AJ shifted. After last time, Mallory didn't bother with the '*I'm sorry*'s. She didn't even try to pretend she wasn't upset. She leaned into him, letting his solid weight hold her up. He twisted so that his arm came around her back. With his other hand, he gently turned her face up. He smelled of leather, and a wood and spice aftershave.

'You didn't do anything wrong,' he said softly.

His face was just inches from hers, his crisp blue eyes certain. His skin was brown from the sun, slightly paler around his eyes from his sunglasses. Underneath his crooked nose, his lips were full and smooth.

As her heart hammered under her breastbone, Mallory said quickly, 'There's one thing I don't understand. How come Ty was Ty, while the rest of you are Romans and Greeks?'

His smile curved, but his voice was a murmur. 'It was short for Titan. Neither of us really owned the names we were given. Stop changing the subject.'

'What was the subject?' she said, because looking in his eyes like this, she was barely keeping a coherent thought in her head.

'You didn't do anything wrong,' he repeated. 'Say it for me.'

Mallory hated that 'say it with me' mantra. She'd once been convinced to go to a gym class with a friend from work, and the instructor had been a big one for what he called 'positive affirmations'. Out loud. With gusto. Mallory had never gone back. She believed in positive thoughts, but she liked them in her head, thanks very much. She sounded ridiculous yelling them out loud. She wasn't going to say it. She compressed her lips and her nose wrinkled.

AJ laughed. 'You look like a rabbit when you do that.'

Mallory smiled, enjoying the rumble of his laugh. He really had a killer smile up close. She bit her lip.

His smile tweaked on one side. 'I like it when you do that. But don't think I'm letting you get out of it,' he said.

'Do I have to?'

'Yes. Say it. "I didn't do anything wrong".'

She rolled her eyes. He really was an asshole. 'I didn't do anything wrong.'

'Now, like you mean it.'

'I didn't do anything wrong,' she shot back at him, her eyes flaring with annoyance. But something about the force of the words made a difference, unburdening her.

He stared at her with a satisfied smile, as if he'd really enjoyed making her say it.

'Damn you,' she muttered, thumping him on the chest.

The blow made no impact. Instead, he pointed to his eye, the bruise now nearly gone. 'You want to know how I got this? When I went to California to pick up the bike, I figured I'd put the shop up for sale. Then I went drinking. When the first guy came up all full of himself, I didn't walk away. Pity I didn't see his friends. It was a stupid thing to do, and I think I got off light.

'When I woke up and looked in the mirror, I knew I wasn't in my right head. But I still couldn't call home. As soon as I sobered up, I got on the bike and started riding. Figured it was that or wind up worse. Then I met you.'

He caught her hand, and held it. 'You reminded me how important family is. I called my sister last night for the first time in two months. If I hadn't met you . . .'

Mallory blushed, suddenly feeling how close he was, how his admission so clearly signalled feelings he had for her. His aftershave was probably the kind in those ads where women were powerless against its allure. She hadn't forgotten Harry or what she was doing, but she wanted AJ in a way she'd never felt before, not even for Duncan.

'Mal.' His voice was low and rumbly now. She knew that if she didn't get up right at this moment, he was going to kiss her, and she didn't know what she was more afraid of: that she wouldn't want to get up again, or that she might never see him again.

'Mmm?' She didn't dare move.

His eyes had a tenderness she'd never seen before, a window into a heart that just a few days ago she wouldn't have believed was there.

'Mal,' he said again, his eyes dipping. 'Mal.'

His lips grazed hers, softly, exploring. Mallory experienced the shock of his touch through her whole body. Tentatively, she returned his kiss, and the second time, he made the kiss hard and hungry. Mallory's heart thundered and heat rushed into her thighs. Her lips parted because her breaths needed the space, just as she needed his kiss for her soul. She could think of nothing else in that moment but the caress of his tongue, the sounds of pleasure from his throat, the feel of muscle in his chest and shoulders.

He was sure of himself and, for the first time, she felt utterly desired. She had no doubt about his response, or hers. The phrase *real man* flitted through her mind like a swallow. His hands dropped to her waist, his fingers stroking her back, then his palms travelled down over her hips. In one motion, he lifted her, and split her knees around him, so that their bodies pressed together. He reached for the buttons on her shirt, his breath hot against her neck.

Mallory pulled back, pressing one hand to her burning face, hardly believing what she was doing. He gave her a languid, lopsided grin, this huge man in black jeans and biker boots, as he deliberately undid her top button, then another. She couldn't help smiling back at the unguarded pleasure on his face.

'What happened to no ill intentions?' she said.

'And you believed me? I've never wanted a woman more in my life.'

But as he reached halfway down her buttons, she thought about tomorrow. About him leaving, and never seeing him again. And she couldn't face it, couldn't be raw over him too. Mallory put her hand up to stop him undoing more buttons. It was impossible to be these two people at once – the woman who wanted this man, and the mother who was trying to reach her son.

'I can't do this,' she said. 'It's not that I don't . . .' She fished around, trying out *like you*, *want you*, but nothing fit. '. . . *you know*,' she tried. 'But . . .'

Something flickered in his expression. She pulled the halves of her shirt together.

'I know, I get it. This wasn't a good idea,' he said.

She hugged herself, made cold by those words. She climbed awkwardly off his lap, trying not to notice when he adjusted the front of his jeans. He was on his feet an instant later, collecting his keys, and Mallory was suddenly bereft at the idea of him leaving. 'AJ, wait.'

He looked across with raised eyebrows.

'I'm no good at this stuff,' she said. 'I've only been with one man my whole life, and—'

'Mal, I do get it,' he said. 'I'm not the guy who acts all entitled because he can't understand where you're coming from. I guess I was just wrong about taking your mind off it.'

'I don't want my mind off it.'

'Yeah.' He nodded, but she was still uneasy. If this had been Duncan, there would have been complaining, or hurt remonstration, something that would give her a twinge of guilt. Without it, this exchange didn't seem complete.

'I'm going to ride along with you tomorrow,' he said. 'Make sure you get to Nashville. Because you better believe I'm taking a raincheck.'

Then he was gone, out into the Memphis night, the Rocket roaring away. Mallory regretted letting him go. On a loop her mind played Marc Cohn singing about walking the Memphis streets, just as it replayed the kiss with AJ over and over. She didn't know if he meant what he'd said, or if he'd just said it so he could leave. But whichever it was, Mallory knew that after that kiss, she would never be quite the same again.

Chapter 15

THAT NIGHT, MALLORY DREAMED ABOUT HARRY STANDING at the end of a long road under black storm clouds, his little legs extensions of the twin yellow centre lines. *Mum*, he called. She heard it echo. He was turning, searching for her, his legs tangling in the road lines. *I'm here!* she called back. But he couldn't hear her. She ran towards him, but the distance between them never closed. The harder she ran, the more the road stretched, until he was nothing but a speck on the horizon. She stopped, knowing that she could never reach him. If she wanted to keep even that distant vision of him, she would have to stay right where she was.

She woke shaking, tears in her eyes and great sobs in her throat. The clock read 5:17 am. It was barely light outside, but she knew she wouldn't be going back to sleep.

She took a hot shower until she stopped shaking, dressed, packed up, and it was still early. Intending to take a walk until a more decent hour, she was surprised to find Jock already up. He sat in the doorway of his room smoking a cigarette, tendrils of smoke curling up and over the brim of his hat.

'Caught me,' he said, stubbing the end out on the edge of the concrete and pocketing the filter.

'I didn't know you smoked.'

'I don't, really. Haven't had one in years, but you never forget how. Acquired it from a generous man in room twenty-two. Devious, I know.'

'You did?' Mallory tried to imagine Jock, a short, elderly man of seventy-odd, bumming a ciggie from a guy in a parking lot. 'That does sound devious. Ernie's probably going to notice.'

'Probably,' Jock said. 'I'll brush my teeth three times and he'll still complain about the smell. I'd offer you one, but you look wired enough.'

'Only for three more hours,' Mallory said, counting down their arrival in Nashville. 'I'm going to check if Ernie's awake.'

Ernie, as it turned out, was already up and, in striped pyjamas, was slowly packing his case with one hand. The bruise on his cheek had turned a sallow yellow, but at least it was fading. Mallory held her tongue about the money until she'd guided Zadie to the shower and toilet. When Zadie was dressed and settled in one of the chairs by the window, Mallory repeated the process with Ernie, but she couldn't very well have the conversation when he was half-undressed.

When she finally decided it was no longer inappropriate, she said, 'Ernie, about our conversation yesterday?'

'Yes?' he said. 'Did you find a flight?'

'They're not flying yet,' Mallory said. 'I found a hire car company with plenty of reservations instead. I could take the rest in cash.'

'Sure, sure,' he said, returning to packing. 'I'll need to organise some things, of course, take a little time. But we've only a few hours to go. I was thinking we could take Zadie out for breakfast before we drive.'

Mallory swallowed a wad of frustration. 'What things do you need to organise?'

'The cash you asked for. Banks won't be open for a while, yet.'

'You don't need a bank. You can just take it out of an ATM,' she said.

'I prefer dealing with a real person.'

Mallory hesitated. How did she tackle this? Maybe she had to compromise.

'Look, can I make this car booking on my phone, and have you pay for it? Then that part will be sorted and we could visit a bank once we're in Nashville. We don't have to delay driving then. We can head off while it's still early, and cool.'

'No need to rush now,' Ernie said, irritation roughening his voice. His case-packing became jerky and a pink flush crept across his temples. 'You agreed to take payment once we reached Nashville. After the last woman ran out on us, you can't blame me for being careful.'

'I just want to know I have a car waiting,' she said, unable to avert this becoming an argument.

'You said they have lots of reservations. Why don't you take cash to the counter? Then that's only one transaction. Easier for everyone. You'll have your money by tonight.'

Mallory felt as though an explosion had gone off in her head. *Tonight?* Harry's tear-stained face was in her mind. No, she couldn't accept this. But Ernie was all drawn up, the way he got when he was asserting his pride of independence, refusing to be persuaded. Near the end of his own journey, he seemed not to care about anything else.

'Excuse me please,' Mallory said, and ducked out to Jock's room. A moment later, she brought Jock back with her. 'Ernie, Jock will sit with Zadie. I'd like to have a word in private.'

Ernie's eyebrows arched, and he looked at Zadie before acquiescing. He moved through the door with a long-suffering air, and it seemed to take an age until they were inside the next room. Ernie declined a chair and leaned on his cane, so Mallory stood awkwardly between the beds.

'I'm sorry, Ernie, I just can't wait until tonight,' she said, knowing she would have to make her case, and fast. 'I need to leave as soon as we get there.'

Ernie wrinkled his nose, as if allergic to being hassled. 'We don't have to be so hasty. We need an orderly handover, and Zadie mustn't be harried in the new place.'

'I understand, and I'll do a proper handover of course, but I can't wait any longer after that,' Mallory said, finally deciding she'd have to offer full disclosure. 'Look, three weeks ago, my son went to New York to visit his father, who left us over a year ago. Harry was supposed to come back for school – instead, my husband decided he would keep Harry with him.'

She went on, laying out the details as quickly as she could. The things Duncan had said, the conversation she'd had with the lawyers. Her accounts being frozen. And finally, Duncan shutting her out and telling her not to call again. She fiddled with her phone the whole time, intensely uncomfortable, but needing to say her piece.

'So I hope you understand I can't wait. Please. You can help me get there. I've done everything you asked, including stopping at the rodeo. I'm not asking for you to pay the cash early, just the car booking, so I can leave without delay.'

Ernie shifted his weight. 'I thought it must be something like this,' he said. 'Didn't make sense otherwise. Why would you be stuck in LA if your husband was in the country?'

Mallory held her tongue, waiting for his agreement.

Ernie went on. 'And what is it you imagine you'll do when you reach New York?'

Mallory blinked. 'Take my son home with me.'

'Just like that?'

'Yes.' Her voice was screwed down tight. Why was he asking this? 'He's my son.'

'He's your husband's son, too,' Ernie said, now looking around for a seat. He limped a step and settled himself in the desk chair. 'Now, I know you'll think I'm old-fashioned, but children need stability. You should take this opportunity to have a real adult discussion with your husband, work out your differences. Not enough people do that these days. You're all willing to just throw in the towel.'

Mallory opened her mouth, aghast. Another second went by before she managed, 'He's free to have an adult discussion after we're back at home.'

'Won't it be confusing to be yanked here, there, and then back again? A good mother thinks about it from the child's perspective.'

A good mother.

'Besides,' Ernie went on, 'you'll forgive me for saying this, but I hope you'll take it in as advice. You can't possibly be able to focus on your family while you're entertaining . . . other company. You have to ask yourself if you're really putting your priorities in the best order.'

232

'What on earth are you talking about?' she said.

'That biker,' Ernie said, gesturing towards the window. 'I saw you go out on his motorcycle last night. It's hardly becoming to your situation. What would your husband say?'

Mallory's neck burned with mortification and anger.

'That has nothing to do with this,' she said, breathless at his presumptions.

Ernie held up a don't-blame-the-messenger hand. 'Maybe not. But you're still a married woman. In my day, that meant something. We didn't play around when times were rocky. We stuck it out. We behaved appropriately.'

'Didn't seem to object to AJ when he was changing our tyre on the side of the road,' Mallory hit back. 'And I needed a friend to talk to last night.' Why the hell was she justifying herself to Ernie?

'Talk? Oh, *I* see.'

Mallory's chest boiled, until the pressure hit eleven. '*My husband* left *us*. After I supported him for years. Then *he* decided to do this without discussing anything with me. Don't talk to *me* about appropriate behaviour.'

These words shot like bullets from Mallory's tongue, but Ernie absorbed them as if she'd thrown feathers. 'All the more reason for you to be the one to bridge the gap. A man needs—'

'What?' she said, sharp. 'A man needs bloody what? A meek woman who agrees with everything he thinks?'

Ernie sighed heavily, punctuating his words with his good hand. 'If you'd let me finish, I was saying a man needs to feel *useful* to his family. Able to provide for them. Now, isn't it possible your husband felt sidelined all those years that you were the breadwinner? Now he's in a position to fulfil his natural role, you have an opportunity to mend any misunderstandings. Young people need to learn how to stick together through the bad times. Take it from someone who's been married for fifty years.'

Mallory laughed, incredulous. 'Stick through the bad times? What on earth would you know about that?'

'I know very well what it's like to—'

'No, you don't,' she said flatly, leaning forward on her toes as if she could pummel him with syllables. 'You don't know anything about what it's like to do what I did. To work through sleep deprivation and exhaustion, and never be able to take a break because other people were depending on you. To put aside things you wanted, for them.'

Ernie's face turned beet-red. 'Of course, I do,' he said, thumping his hand into his chest, his voice finally rising. 'I was a doctor. I worked double shifts, triple shifts. I answered calls at all hours of the night. I saved lives. You think *you* know about people depending on you!'

This conversation was clearly not going in the direction he'd anticipated, Mallory saw that. And now all pretence at tolerance was gone, she was only too glad to skewer him.

'But you didn't do it with a baby at home,' she said, pointing her finger at him. 'You didn't do it while you were trying to breastfeed. You didn't come home after a shift and go straight into another because you don't get any time off as a parent. And you didn't do it on a minimum wage. You had a nice stuffed wallet every week, and you could buy your groceries and fix your car, and never worry about whether you could pay the electricity this month. You didn't spend a month eating biscuits out of the work kitchen freebies because you had to fix your clapped-out car, just so you could work another underpaid overnight shift. You hid out in your ivory work tower, probably having a grand time bossing around nurses, and never going home because it suited you.'

'Now just a minute—'

Mallory sensed she had already crossed a line, but she was so angry with him, so angry at the circumstances of her life and his belittling, that she couldn't stop herself. She ploughed on like one of the giant diesel trains she'd seen on their first days of driving, rage granting her power and unstoppable momentum.

'You know what? No wonder you feel like an awful husband, because sure as anything you're a damn horrible person. Thank God you never did have any children. Because what the hell would you know about any of it?'

She hiccupped on the 'hell', which somewhat lessened the punch of her verbal blow.

And then she stopped. Something in the atmosphere had broken. All the blood had left Ernie's face, his open mouth the shape of an inverse crescent moon. He looked as though he was operating on himself without anaesthetic.

Mallory was suddenly aware of herself, trembling all over, having a pointless argument with an old curmudgeon who would never change. She knew she had a bare second before she broke down into tears.

'Good luck getting to Nashville without me,' she said, and walked out the door.

•

She strode off down the street, not caring where she went, pushing her anger out through the pavement and muttered curses, increasingly more profane and increasingly less muttered.

Poor Zadie! Imagine being married to a man who was so sure of himself, so invested in his sure-of-himself career that he'd never come home during your life with him. And now you were fading out and needed help to the bathroom and soft food, he hauled you off on a trip across America.

Selfish, unfeeling man.

She strode across BB King Street, and down the hill before reality pulled her up. Where exactly was she going?

She stopped dead between two grey concrete parking lots. She still had no money. No way of getting from here to New York. She could keep stewing all the way to the river if she wanted, and then she'd be left with standing on the edge of the road with her thumb out. And she'd just torn strips off the man who was supposed to pay her.

'Shit,' she muttered.

For a minute, she entertained wild notions. Asking Jock to make a break for it with her. Holding up a bank. Asking Jock to help her hold up a bank. Taking the car keys and leaving Ernie to find someone else to drive him the few more hours across Tennessee. Then maybe holding up a bank.

All of them seemed to end up with red and blue flashing lights.

Could she beg AJ to take her on his bike all the way to New York? But he was supposed to go to Chicago. And what about Jock?

She rubbed her face. 'Shit.'

She needed a friend, someone to talk her down off the cliff. Or out of the felonious plans, at least. And there was really only one person she could think to call.

Bridget picked up so fast, she must have had the phone in her hand. 'Mallory! Oh, thank goodness. I was starting to panic about you.'

Mallory was completely undone by the joy in Bridget's voice and didn't get out more than a 'Hi' before she was bawling.

'What's wrong now?' Bridget said. 'Oh, you poor wee thing, what's happened?'

'Oh, nothing,' Mallory said, her voice trembling. 'I'm in Tennessee.'

'Well, that sounds grand. I think you made the right choice. The flights are still grounded. So, what's upset you?'

'Oh, just an entitled man being a bastard,' she said, not wanting to spend the time explaining about Ernie, Zadie and Jock, and the whole arrangement. 'And a money problem.'

'I'll send you some,' Bridget said. 'How much do you need?'

Mallory swelled with gratitude, even as she said, 'There's a problem with my accounts, Bridge, so you can't. Besides, it's only a couple of hours to Nashville and I'm picking up some money there.'

'You let me know if you change your mind.'

'It's so good to hear your voice,' Mallory said. 'I'm sorry, I know it must be nearly midnight.'

'You call anytime you need.'

When the call ended, Mallory sniffed and turned around, feeling mutinous but resigned. Going back might be the most distasteful choice, but it was also the most logical. It took twice as long to walk back. When she arrived, AJ and Jock were standing round the Rocket in the carpark. The boot of the car was open, Jock's luggage already loaded.

'We were taking bets,' Jock called. 'I said you'd gone for a walk, AJ thought you'd split.'

Mallory snuck a look at AJ, whose expression rested in an easy, open smile. In her bad mood, seeing the obvious affection in his face only made her more wary and jumpy.

'I was hoping you'd at least come back with coffee,' Jock said, sounding casual, but Mallory saw the question in his eyes, and he came close enough so that no one else could hear. 'Ernie's all in a flap, saying you'd walked out.'

'Just stretching my legs,' Mallory lied, forcing a composure that was as uncomfortable as a corset. She had to do this for Harry.

When Ernie appeared in his room doorway, Mallory couldn't look at him and had to focus on a spot behind his shoulder.

'Bags ready?' she asked brightly.

His frown deepened, but he made no comment as she marched into the room. His cane clicked across the floor as she swung the case lids closed. Zadie was still sitting in the same chair by the window, her teacup empty on the side table. Mallory skirted around the hovering Ernie, and sank down beside Zadie.

'Do you need the bathroom before we go, Zadie?'

Mallory continued to ignore Ernie as she went about making Zadie comfortable for the journey. She chatted on autopilot: how they were on the last leg of the trip today, and before lunch she'd see her home town again. By the time she walked Zadie slowly out to the car, Jock and AJ had all the cases loaded, and Ernie was waiting stony faced in the back seat with the door standing open. The atmosphere around him prickled like dry static.

Three more hours. That's all it was. They could pick up breakfast somewhere, and she'd be unhitched from this wagon by noon.

'You want me to show you the best way to the interstate?' AJ asked, pulling his helmet down. Mallory tried not to look at the thick arms inside his leather jacket, the lips that had kissed her last night. Or notice the frosty stares Ernie was giving him from the back seat.

'If you can swing past a drive-through, go ahead,' she said. AJ pulled out of the carpark in a lazy arc, the Rocket thundering, even at the slow pace that allowed Mallory to catch up. Ernie heaved a disapproving sigh.

Mallory clamped her molars.

They were back on the interstate within half an hour, with the smell of cooked eggs in the cabin. Not far outside the Memphis limits, the country rushed in to meet the highway, all green fields and shaggy trees. Thin ribbons of rural road shot arrow-straight on both sides, dotted with small white houses.

'Pretty. Hard to imagine it's a tornado hotspot,' Jock said into the tense silence.

'What?' Mallory asked, ducking her head to scan the sky, which was pale blue from horizon to horizon and streaked with white clouds.

'Dixie Alley,' Zadie said in the back. 'We always had a shelter at the house. My father dug it in the side of the cellar.'

'You ever use it?' Jock asked, twisting around.

'Once or twice,' Zadie said. 'We pretended more.'

Jock twisted back to the front. 'Don't worry, Mal, tornadoes occur most often in spring. Needs to be the right weather conditions, or something.'

After the storm in Arizona, Mallory didn't even want to think about the possibility of a freaking *tornado*. The way her luck was going, there would be two waiting around the next corner.

'Can we talk about something else, please?'

'I guess, if you want.' Jock sounded disappointed.

She stared ahead, where AJ was easily sitting on the speed limit, the seat of his jeans making a pleasing shape across the Rocket's saddle. She remembered the last time she'd driven behind him, when he was being soaked to the skin in the storm, and imagined what could happen to him in a tornado. With flying trees and cows and trucks. She'd seen *Twister*.

A lump lodged right in the base of her windpipe, like a stopper in a bottle. She couldn't think about him like that. Couldn't care so much about him. 'Fine,' she said, needing distraction. 'How do we know if there's a tornado?'

'I dunno. I've never seen one, except on the telly.'

'Why'd you bring it up, then?'

Jock laughed. 'Just making conversation. Don't worry about it. Odds are low we'd ever have a problem. Doesn't even look like rain today.'

That was all well and good, she thought, but things could change fast. One minute, you think you want to get back with your husband and he might be open to it, and the next he's taking your kid overseas and telling you to never call again. Better prepared than surprised.

'What would we do if we saw one?'

'I don't know exactly—'

'Here.' Mallory threw her phone over to him. She wasn't up for more silence. 'I've been using the wi-fi at the hotels so there's heaps of data left. See if you can connect and find out.'

They drove on through the green fields towards Nashville, Jock trickling in tornado information, occasionally clicking his tongue when the data dropped out. Zadie was leaning towards the window, her eyes jumping as she followed every tree on the side of the road.

After two hours, despite Mallory's enthusiasm to push on, she pulled them into a truck stop and made sure Zadie had water to drink, had a bathroom break, and took her medicine. It wouldn't do to drop her off with any lingering problems. Who knew if the new carer would be patient enough to make sure she was properly clean, that her underwear was untwisted, and that none of the elastic in her clothes was caught or the fabric bunched so it could rub and create a sore. When Mallory helped Zadie back into the car, the old woman looked up with such an appreciative smile that Mallory felt guilty. She tried not to think that it would be the last time she did any of this.

Then again, she wouldn't miss bloody Ernie, still stonily silent. Even when Mallory made gestures of goodwill – albeit motivated by concern that he might not pay her after all – he didn't give. He refused all offers of coffee, and pointedly sat with Zadie so that neither Jock – who'd clearly been tainted by association with Mallory – nor Mallory could share the table.

Only AJ managed to make her smile about it.

'What's crawled up his rear end?' AJ asked. 'Man's givin' me looks like I'm making his ass itch.'

'Thinks you're unsavoury,' Jock said.

AJ scratched his head philosophically. 'Well, man's probably got reasonable judgement.'

When Mallory went to the bathroom, AJ was waiting for her after she emerged.

'Hey,' he said softly. Or at least, what AJ probably thought was softly.

'Hey,' she said, aware she'd barely said two words to him all day.

'What's really going on with Ernie?'

Mallory compressed her lips, then gave in to the chance to complain. 'He behaved like a dick and I let him have it. Now he's stewing.'

AJ laughed. 'Nothing like being a man and sucking it up.'

'I might have insulted his integrity,' Mallory said, though she wasn't sorry. Far from it.

AJ leaned in, sliding his hand to rest on her hip. 'Wanna duck around the back and make out until you feel better?'

His eyes had that wicked gleam in them. Mallory's stomach dipped at the idea of his big body against hers, that feel of his lips again. If she'd been a teenager, she'd have been there in a heartbeat. But she was an adult with things to do. She forced herself to look away.

'We call it "pashing" in Australia,' she said to take the sting out of her refusal. 'But right now, I have to get back in that car.'

His smile broadened in approval, as if only a woman who could refuse him could be worthy of him. As if he'd taken the night to think about it, and decided he really did want her after all. 'See?' he said in a murmur. 'Warrior woman on a mission.'

'Stop it,' she said firmly under her breath, but felt his absence as soon as his hand slipped away.

They were moving again ten minutes later, into the last hour of the journey. Minute by slow minute, the interstate gradually widened like a river at its delta, until they flew over the Nashville suburbs and immediately into a traffic jam.

The GPS guided them, crawling, down an exit into the heart of the city. Mallory wriggled the car down tight back roads, and onto a wide avenue. The streets had an easy restfulness among these trees. She imagined summers sitting on porches, and autumns with leaves crunching underfoot. It had probably looked exactly the same back in the sixties when Ernie had come here as a young man and seen Zadie for the first time.

Finally, they pulled up at the swanky-looking Kimpton Aertson Hotel. Zadie turned her gaze across to where the Vanderbilt University grounds met the road.

Ernie watched her expression, and even Mallory heard his excitement. 'Do you know where you are?' he asked.

'Home,' she said, her smile like sunbeams.

Chapter 16

Zadie's delight at her return to Nashville was overshadowed by the speed at which events turned once they pulled up at the hotel.

Ernie was out of the car almost as soon as the wheels came to rest, stumbling on the pavement in his haste. Mallory flung her door open on reflex, but he'd recovered against the car and gave her such a dirty look that she let him go. He drew Zadie out of her seat, tucked her arm through his, and made for the doors into the hotel foyer.

Mallory unloaded the bags while Jock, who hadn't been afforded any goodbyes either, leaned against the car. He raised his eyebrows at her. Mallory shrugged and handed the cases to a hovering porter. She was angry, and hot, and ready to leave. AJ had parked ahead of them, and pulled off his helmet, waiting in the Rocket's saddle. Even wearing a film of dust like a second skin, he was more appealing than facing Ernie.

Better get this over with.

She stepped through the doors into the hotel foyer, self-conscious in her t-shirt and jeans amongst the thick carpet, columns and uniformed staff.

Ernie and Zadie had reached a set of plush couches, where a woman in wide white trousers and a pressed pale blue shirt was shaking Ernie's hand. She had blonde hair clipped back behind her head, and a warm smile – she must be Mallory's replacement. Mallory liked her instantly, and couldn't help feel sorry for her in taking over at this moment.

'Dr Flint, I'm Belle, from the agency. They asked me to meet you here. I've just come down from the medical centre,' Mallory overheard.

Ernie's chest swelled; he was clearly impressed. Mallory didn't hear his question, but Belle's response was audible. 'No, I'm a medical student now, with four years of nursing before,' she said. 'And I've been with the agency for five years. Now, how shall we get acquainted? Oh, are those your travelling companions?'

Ernie twisted stiffly and gave Mallory a quick up-and-down. She folded her arms across her travel-crushed shirt as Belle strode over.

'Hi,' she said, with her broad southern warmth. 'I'm Belle. You must be exhausted after that drive, but I was hoping we could do a handover before you move on.'

'That won't be necessary,' Ernie cut in, trying to catch up. 'We'll manage quite well, thank you.'

'Mabel came with us,' Zadie said.

'So I see,' Belle said, giving Mallory another smile.

'I'm actually Mallory,' she said, holding her hand out limply. 'I can fill you in on whatever you need.'

'Belle,' Ernie said. 'I'd like you to drive Jock and Mallory into town, please, and then bring the car back. We'll wait here while you do.'

The air tightened. Belle gave him an uncertain glance, 'Right now?'

'They're quite in need of getting on quickly. We don't want to hold them up. So please do as I ask.'

Belle accepted his instruction. 'Okay, then. Will you wait in the foyer, or shall I see you up to the room first?'

'We'll wait.'

Ernie began to turn away, but was hampered by Zadie, who seemed confused, eyes darting from Ernie to Mallory and Jock, and back again.

Mallory took a breath. 'Ernie,' she said. 'About my—'

'Here,' he said, digging in his pocket. He dropped an envelope onto the couch arm, and pushed it in her direction, his weak hand shaking on his stick. 'That's what we agreed. Come along now, Zadie.'

Mallory's shoes squeaked on the foyer tiles as she closed the gap to that envelope. The packet was thick in her fingers, but she couldn't help the regret in her heart at the look on Zadie's face.

She simply had to walk out the doors with Jock and Belle, who was telling him about the airport chaos in the wake of the volcano. She tried to feel only relief that she was finally on her way again, to tell herself that New York was just a short journey away. And then she opened the envelope.

'You all right, honey?' Belle said with a concerned look, as they slipped through the Nashville streets five minutes later.

Mallory closed the envelope. Ernie had been good to his word: he'd given her the money, all right. In crisp, colourful

Australian notes. They smelled vaguely of mothballs; he'd probably pulled the cash from a sock. When she'd first seen the thick pile, she'd been overjoyed at the freedom the money represented. Then she realised she couldn't spend it, and she couldn't even bank it without a working account. She tipped her head back, fighting tears, as if Ernie had managed to punch her right in the nose.

'Just tired,' she managed.

'Since we have some time, is there anything I should know?' Belle asked.

Like, Ernie's a pedantic, miserable jackass, perhaps?

'Zadie is lovely, but there's a few things to be aware of,' Mallory said instead, and briefly filled Belle in on the incidents on the road, care notes, and Zadie's love of animals. 'That's about all I can tell you,' she finished. The roar of the Rocket underlaid the whole conversation. AJ had wordlessly followed them, clearly expecting a proper goodbye before she departed, but all Mallory could think about was how she could deal with the money situation. Her thoughts seemed to be moving so slowly.

'You end up making that car booking?' Jock asked her.

'No,' she said quickly. 'We didn't get that far. I'll just have to walk in.'

Belle recommended a hire place and they emptied out in the street, between a storage centre and a winery outlet. Jock gave Belle his thanks and told her she could go. Then he extended his hand to Mallory.

'Well, here we are. Thanks for everything,' he said. 'Come and say hello again when you get back home?'

Mallory shook his hand with her stomach sinking. Everything was happening too fast now. She was about to be alone on this sidewalk with a packet full of useless cash. She sensed she was missing something, but her desire to leave for New York was short-circuiting her thoughts. Jock hovered, clearly waiting for a reply.

Eventually, as AJ was striding up from parking the Rocket, Jock checked his watch. 'Aren't you going in? I'd like to see you on your way before I head anywhere. I'm sure the big fella would, too.'

Mallory finally admitted her problem. 'I, uh, can't yet. Ernie gave me Australian cash, and I don't have credit cards. I don't suppose you'd want to swap for local money?'

She offered Jock the envelope, her cheeks burning. He peered in. 'I'm not carrying that much cash,' he said. 'But we'll just take it to an exchange. Easy.'

Mallory smacked her forehead. 'Why didn't I think of that?'

'Because you're exhausted,' Jock said gently. 'Come inside and make your booking. I'll pay, then you give me a lift to an exchange, and you can pay me back.'

AJ put a hand on her shoulder. 'Mal,' he said, 'give me the cash. I'll go exchange it for you. The Rocket's faster around town anyway. By the time these guys put you in a truck, I'll be back.'

Mallory looked at him, tall and muscular in his jeans and leather jacket and full-attitude sunglasses. How different he'd turned out to be from what she'd first thought of him. She handed him the money, and he roared off down the road. Watching him go, she felt a sudden qualm and looked at Jock for reassurance.

'The way my luck's going, I'm wondering if I'll see that money again,' she said.

'You will,' Jock said. 'Your luck's about to turn. I can feel it.'

•

The rental company didn't agree. In fact, they were none too happy about taking cash. When Jock pushed on Mallory's behalf, eventually they said they might be able to do it, with extra paperwork and time to do a credit check. But with that hurdle over, and Mallory handing over her driver's licence, the clerk realised she was only twenty-four.

The man held up his hands. 'Sorry, we can only do a cash hire for over twenty-fives.'

'My birthday is next month,' Mallory pleaded, and nearly told him that she'd been driving a rental car for the past week across the country and – with the exception of a flat tyre, which was all Ernie's fault anyway – that car was still fine and dandy. Thankfully, she realised it would hardly help to admit she'd been driving unauthorised or, at best, pretending to be the long-departed Fiona.

She also managed to stop Jock before he offered to pay for her. The clerk had already closed that down; any hint that the credit-card holder was not actually going to be with the car would turn this fool's errand into something more serious.

Jock finally admitted defeat, and a quick few phone calls to other rental agencies proved that this rule was universal: no one was going to rent a car for cash to Mallory.

Jock was very quiet as they left the office and trekked back to the footpath. Mallory leaned against a lamppost to wait for AJ. She would have to try the train station, or the bus after all. She'd ask if AJ could drop her off.

'Train takes a while,' Jock said. 'Even if you got on today, it wouldn't arrive until the day after next.'

'Stupid huge continent,' she muttered, furiously googling. 'Are you sticking around town before you go? I never looked up where Virginia is.'

'It's about four hours south-west of New York,' he said after a pause.

'That's quite a trip from here too, then. Were you going to take a bus?'

'Not sure yet,' he said, but in a way that told Mallory he knew but didn't want to say.

She stared down the road. 'AJ's been gone a while.'

'Forty minutes.'

'Stuck in traffic, do you think?' Mallory said, knowing AJ always split the lane between cars if he could.

'I'll wait with you until he comes back.'

They passed another twenty minutes sitting on the grey sidewalk, Mallory flicking between bus and train timetables on her phone. Just when she was sure that AJ was on his way to Mexico with her money, she heard the Rocket.

She knew the moment he pulled in that something was wrong. He moved stiffly kicking out the stand. She'd watched him do it a few times and it was always a smooth, automatic movement, a lift and push of his heel. He swung himself off with reluctance, and took a moment to shift his jacket before he came over.

'What happened?' she asked.

'Nothing. Here's the cash. The exchange was a bit steep, but at least you're all in green now.'

As he handed an envelope across, she noticed the scuff mark across the shoulder of his leather jacket, and an angry red scrape under the stubble of his chin, bright with blood.

Her stomach rolled tight. 'You had an accident?'

He dusted at the short-cropped hair over his head. 'More of an incident.'

'Your chin's bleeding.'

'Some truck on the forty-one forced me out, by the park there. Had to swerve to avoid a parked car, so ended up off the road and she tipped over in the grass. Suppose I rolled a bit.'

'What!' Mallory exclaimed. 'You must be hurt! You're walking like you were run over by a bus.'

'I'm fine,' he said, stepping away as she tried to examine his face more closely.

'But we have to take you to a doctor. Maybe you hit your head.'

AJ's eyebrows shot up like skeet pigeons. 'I didn't. You know how many times a day someone cuts you off, or pulls out in front of you, when you're on a bike? I'll give you a hint: it's a lot. I rolled on the grass. And thanks to that, the Rocket doesn't have a scratch. I'll have to check her over properly—'

'I don't believe you. You fall off and come back bleeding and you want to check the bike but not yourself?'

Mallory could hear the hysterical edge in her voice, but she couldn't control the way her heart went into spasms at the thought of him being blindsided by a truck.

'I'm sayin' it ain't necessary.'

He did seem fine. He really did, and yet she couldn't shut down the thoughts of how he might not have been fine. She imagined him falling just a bit to either side of where he had, and collecting a lamppost, or not making his swerve and hitting the parked car, or being crushed by the truck. The idea was like a javelin thrust through her body. She pressed a hand to her face, shaking, realising how much she cared about him.

And she couldn't care about him. She didn't need one more bloody complication in her life right now, couldn't have another unresolved situation where her heart was all tangled in knots. She couldn't be looking over her shoulder for him when she needed her eyes on the road ahead. After all, how much did she know him? It was stupid to have formed such an attachment to a man she'd only just met.

'I can't do this,' she said.

'Mal,' Jock said, 'he seems okay.'

'No,' she said. 'I can't do this. I can't do any more than make it to New York right now. I appreciate your help, but I can do this just fine on my own. Get checked out, don't get checked out, but I have to go, and I don't want you to follow.'

'Mal,' he said, 'it ain't like that—'

She held up a hand, but she couldn't quite meet his eyes. She sensed she was being unfair, but the urge to get away, to be on her own again, where she relied on herself, was too strong.

'Look, I don't really know you, and this was never where you were going in the first place,' she got out, though her voice cracked and a tear broke loose from her right eye. 'So feel free to go do what you meant to. Head to Chicago. I need to be on my own.'

She held her ground, though her heart was screaming to take it all back. The hurt in his eyes killed her. But she couldn't take it back. Harry meant more to her.

After a painful pause, AJ offered Jock his hand. 'It's been a pleasure, Jock,' he said, as they shook. 'You take care, now. You too, Mallory.'

The last three words were soft, and he managed to inject them with such regret that anyone would have thought she'd broken his heart. Her own hardly felt better. She snuck a look at him when he was almost back to the Rocket, his swagger dented by his limp. A hard ball of anguish stuck in her throat but Mallory bundled every feeling she had for him tight, and told herself she didn't care about his leaving. It was the right thing. He kicked over the engine and roared away.

The silence was an echo of the options she had left. She would have to take a taxi to the station, where she'd probably find the train wouldn't take cash either.

None of this would be relevant if she had a working account. Why on earth had Duncan even frozen it? Unless . . .

She pulled out her phone and thumbed to the banking app. The flight booking was one of the last transactions on the savings account. *Duncan had seen it.* Mallory was sure of that. He wouldn't have known where she'd booked, but he could guess. So he'd done it deliberately, to throw difficulty in her way. That was low.

But it also meant he'd had days of forewarning, to plan how to counter her, even if she made it to New York. Mallory closed her eyes and begged whatever deities were not currently distracted by volcanic events and rigid car rental policies to please give her a sign that everything was not lost.

Beside her, Jock blew out a breath and squinted down the road. 'Well. What now?'

'I don't know.' Her chest ached with the pressure of so many emotions. Desperate longing for Harry. Regret over

AJ. A lingering slug of Ernie's judgement. 'So much for luck changing.'

Jock grunted. He was oddly quiet, especially after he'd tried so hard with the rental staff to get her a car. He looked down the street again, then at her, something undecided in his eyes. A gust of wind blew across them, and Mallory shivered as it dried the sweat on her neck.

Jock blew out another breath.

'Come on,' he said finally, and about-faced into the rental office driveway.

'Jock, don't, you heard what they said,' Mallory called, jogging after him. 'I'll get a train. Maybe we can split a taxi for wherever you're going. You don't have to wait for me.'

She really didn't want another pointless conversation with the rental people, but Jock didn't stop. He pushed inside and went straight up to the counter. Mallory braced, anticipating the conflict. The desk clerk's automatic smile was already dimming.

'I'd like to rent a sedan, thank you,' Jock said, pushing his licence and credit card across the counter.

Mallory struggled to realign the expectations in her head. 'What are you doing?' she whispered.

'Hiring a car.'

'But you can't drive, can you?'

'Sure I can.'

'Then why didn't you before?'

Jock drew her away from the counter. 'Ernie didn't want me driving. It was part of the agreement we had. Didn't want to be a passenger with someone who was at any higher risk of a heart attack or stroke than necessary, or something like that. You know how he is. I apologise for never taking any of the load off you.'

Since Jock had both age and credit cards on his side, the paperwork was all done with very little fuss, and soon he was being shown towards an immaculately clean, late-model sedan. Mallory realised that there could only be one reason why Jock hadn't told her he was hiring a car: he wanted to drive alone. But if Virginia was only hours south of New York, it must be on the way?

She hung back with her bag as Jock checked the car over, wondering what he was intending to do. He was certainly capable, more than he looked. Maybe he really was planning on robbing a bank.

'Can you drop me at the train station?' Mallory finally asked.

'Don't be silly. I'm not leaving you alone after all of *that*,' he said, waving his hand to indicate AJ, and quite possibly the entire last week of her life. 'You can drive with me as far as Virginia. After that, you can take the car on to New York.'

'Really?'

'But you have to understand something. I'm not taking it easy to get there. I'm picking up a few things here, and then I'm going straight through until I'm there. Got it?'

Mallory's heart lifted like a rocket off a launch pad. She gulped, wondering if this could be true. She could be in New York by lunchtime tomorrow. It must be too good to be true.

'You aren't robbing a bank or something, are you?'

'Thought about it.' He actually smiled, then his expression turned serious. 'I just want to be there tomorrow. That's the shape of it. If you're in, let's go.'

Mallory was not about to argue. She put her bag in the back seat and slid into the passenger side while Jock adjusted his mirrors. The atmosphere in the car wasn't like it had been all the way to Nashville. Urgency was like pepper in the air, a permeating irritant with only one remedy: moving on down the road. It was then she realised that Jock had just as big a reason to be here as anyone, and she really knew nothing about it.

Chapter 17

THEY WERE ON THE HIGHWAY SOON AFTER, FOLLOWING A flying stop at a supermarket. Mallory had to share her footwell with a plastic bag full of bulk lolly bags and cakes – liquorice allsorts, peppermint bullseyes, Twinkies, Tootsie Rolls. Unused to having her own money to spend, Mallory had a much smaller bag containing two apples, two packs of Nutter Butter bites, and a Gatorade. It seemed enough to sustain her overnight.

For the first three hours, they passed through broken trees and golden grass beside the highway. The sun went down in a blaze of red behind charcoal clouds. Mallory scanned through the radio stations, and heard everything from Keith Urban and Taylor Swift to a tornado warning for west Tennessee. She leaned in, consulting the GPS, trying to work out if they were anywhere near it.

'That's behind us,' Jock said eventually. 'Don't worry about it.'

He was driving like a man who'd never done anything else. After so many hours behind the wheel, Mallory would have appreciated the break, except that the transformation was unsettling. It was as if Jock had ceased to be the affable, kind and funny man she'd known this past week and revealed a secret identity, one that might link to the man who had disappeared in Fort Smith. They were on track to reach Virginia by the early hours of the morning, but it seemed a very long journey ahead, all the air of the cabin sucked up by an invisible elephant that neither of them were talking about.

'What address can I program in?' Mallory asked, but Jock only shook his head.

'Tell you when we're there.' He focused singularly on the road. When the dark hills in the distance were slowly snuffing out the last daylight, Mallory had to fill the silence.

'Do you want to know why I'm really going to New York?' she said.

'Figured that was your business,' Jock replied, but she saw the circulation return in his knuckles as he eased his grip on the wheel. Maybe he wanted to talk.

'My son is five,' Mallory said, her voice flat, like she was talking to a priest in confessional. 'His name's Harry. His father – my husband – left us a year ago, and moved to New York because of his business. A few weeks ago, Harry went to visit. We'd agreed he'd go over the Easter holidays. But he never came back.'

Carefully, factually, she laid out the rest as she had with AJ and Ernie. Duncan telling her Harry wouldn't be coming back. Her consultations with the lawyers. The flight. The volcano. 'The rest you know,' she said. 'Well, most of the rest.'

'I'm sorry,' Jock said. 'You must be frantic.'

Mallory stared at the road. Her skin felt hard in the cold air blowing from the vents. 'No,' she said. 'It's so much more than that. I'd been thinking all this time that I just needed to get there. But I just realised Duncan probably saw that I booked a flight, so the account freezing was deliberate. Even when I get there, I don't know if I'll be able to take Harry home.'

She looked down at her lap, where she had made fists of the worn fabric of her jeans, and her index finger had pushed a hole through the time-softened denim. 'Duncan has money now. He can pay for lawyers from here to whenever. What chance do I have?'

'But you're Harry's mother. Doesn't matter what happens between parents, nothing changes that.' There was a long pause, marked by the yellow flashes of road marks vanishing into the hood. 'I was a pretty absent father, so I know enough to know what a mother means to a child. She's the one that hangs on when everyone else fails them.'

Mallory stared through the bare ghost reflection of Jock in the windscreen. The mountains had no outline anymore, the night an undefined black. She took a breath.

'Sometimes I wonder if Duncan's right,' she said.

'About what?'

'Maybe Harry would be better off with him.'

'When do you think things like that?' Jock asked.

'When I wake up in the night,' she said. 'When I forget where I am, I guess.'

Jock grunted. 'Can't trust anything you think between midnight and sunrise, believe me. He's not going to be better off without his mother, even for all the money in the world.'

Mallory absorbed this scintilla of reassurance. 'But I used to joke about it, when we were together and Harry was really little. Sometimes, after a really long shift, when I was exhausted, I used to ask Duncan if we could send Harry back. I never ever meant it,' she said quickly. 'It was a joke. We both used to laugh because we knew we didn't mean it, but life would feel easier for a minute. Then, this past year, I got in the habit of telling Duncan how hard it was in the few conversations we had. How I couldn't pay the power bill because I had to pay the babysitters first, or because the Corolla was in the shop again, things like that. I said it because I hoped he'd feel guilty for leaving. But a clever lawyer will probably say Duncan misunderstood. Or Duncan could just make something up. My mother has a gambling problem and Duncan knows all about that.'

She sighed. 'I thought I knew him,' she whispered. 'Now I have no idea what's going to happen. I don't really know if I'll even see Harry again.'

She pulled up her knees, feeling the depths of her fear. Her sock feet gripping the seat had holes in the toes, and the new rip in her jeans showed a shadow of skin. She was wearing out on this journey. Would there be anything left of her by the time she reached New York? And it could all mean nothing.

Jock cleared his throat. 'In that bag, in the back, there's a folder. Pull it out.'

Mallory twisted around. Jock's black backpack was on the floor behind the driver's seat. 'This one?'

'Yes.'

The folder was a cream Manila wallet, thick with pages. Mallory had seen it once before, on Jock's nightstand. 'What's this?'

'Open it.'

When she flipped open the wallet, she saw handwritten lines, dated at the top right and addressed to East Homer, NY. She slid out the top sheaf and saw *Dear Mom* in scratchy letters. Over and over, each one, *Dear Mom*. 'Letters?' she said. 'Are these yours?'

He nodded. She could see the way his shoulders were tensed, his gaze ahead, focused only on the road. He detached one hand and rubbed it over his face, knocking his hat up an inch, the movement jerky with repressed emotion.

'I left the farm in sixty-five for the army. My little brother came with me. We both wanted to go and make a difference in Vietnam. My mother,' he said, pausing to take a breath, 'she was fairly horrified by the whole thing. Didn't want us to go, particularly Ben. He was only sixteen.'

'That's so young,' Mallory said, apprehensive about where this was going.

'It wasn't so rare,' Jock said. 'Lot of boys went. There were some younger than that, who forged their records. My mother couldn't stop us, but she made me promise to look after Ben. I can still see her standing there as we went, still hoping we'd see sense, or at least if I would. Her voice is in my head all the time. "Look after him, Johnny. You keep him safe." She was afraid for us. She knew better than we did.'

Mallory's back crawled with goosebumps. Jock's voice was as thin and flat as her own had been only five minutes ago.

'We ran into trouble in this village in the middle of the night. Small arms fight, and the two of us ended up in this bombed-out hut. Wasn't much of it left, just a corner of wall. I ran in there, Ben came after me. We couldn't see nothing. It was all confusion and fire and panic. I was standing against the wall, right in the corner, when he was hit. He was right by my shoulder. I heard the breath go out of him.'

He paused to breathe out a great huffing sigh, trying to get control of himself.

'I was taller than him, see? My head was above his, and I took a ricochet.'

He put up a hand to his fishing hat, then hesitated. 'You'll need to turn the cabin light on,' he said. 'But I don't blame you if you don't want to look.'

Mallory reached for the light, her heart thumping, as Jock slowly pulled the hat away.

'Oh, Jock,' she said.

The scar was old, white and knotted, running in a crescent from above his ear, up and back over his head, and arching forward to meet where his hairline had once been. The skin in the curve was sunken, enough to draw shadows in the oblique light, skin that must cover only bone.

'Wasn't so bad when I used to have hair,' Jock said. 'People didn't notice it, kids didn't stare at it. But for the past twenty years, it's either been hats or toupees, and to be honest the toupee is worse.'

He tried to laugh, but the corners of his mouth tugged down. 'That hit I took wasn't even that bad to start with. Had a concussion, they reckoned. Next day, I was throwing up and they had to drain a bleed. It got infected. But that was nothing to finding out what had happened to Ben.

'Because I know, that if we'd been switched places, it would've been me who took all of that hit. I'd have ended my time right there, and Ben would've gone home to Mom.'

Jock swiped a hand down his face.

Mallory inhaled against the tears running down her own. 'How old were you?' she croaked.

'Eighteen.'

She gasped. She couldn't even fathom the idea of people shooting at her now, let alone willingly, and at the same age that she'd been bowled over by Duncan's charms. She hadn't known anything about anything. Hell, she'd only learned how ignorant she'd been in the past week, and learned it the hard way.

'You were just babies,' she said, angry. 'The bloody government should have been protecting you, not shipping you off to some . . . bloody war.'

She knew her words changed nothing. There was no justice. She knew that from all the folk she cared for whose families never saw them, who had served their country but had found living at peace so much harder to do.

'What happened when you went home?' she asked, bracing for the answer.

A long pause. A truck bowled past them, its engine thrumming like a great heart. Its tail lamps dragged away into the distance until they vanished around a long curve.

'I didn't,' he said.

She looked through the reflection of him in the window. 'You didn't?'

'I landed in San Francisco on a rainy day in January. A few hippie protesters were there with signs, and no one seemed to want us back. I kept getting bumped off flights to

New York. I took it as a sign. So when I ran into someone I knew in the airport who was marrying an Australian girl in Sydney, I turned around and flew the other way, and I stayed. We set up in a business together, but I wasn't any good at it. After a year, we fell out, and I went north. Tried a bunch of things, but never felt settled anywhere, really.'

Jock glanced across, as if gauging whether to keep going. She met his eye. In the long shifting shadows inside the cabin, she could imagine his face younger. Could imagine him feeling lost so far from home, the same way she'd felt on this entire journey but so much worse.

'Must have been so hard to move on after what happened.'

'Yeah. I had nightmares for a long time. I was always jumpy. Angry, too, at everyone and everything. Eventually, I learned the things that set me off, avoided them, wrote a lot of stuff down. Finally went to therapy. But there was always something a bit . . . wrong, in here, too, something the shrinks can't fix.'

He tapped the side of his head.

'A bit slower with speaking, and sometimes I'd muck up the words. People didn't know me from before, so they didn't notice, but I could tell. That's why I started doing the logic problems, then sudoku, and into computers. Keep what I have together.'

'I would never have guessed.'

'Not now, I guess not. When you reach the age where half the people around you are having memory problems, or balance problems, or continence problems, my mediocrity finally has the chance to shine.'

He smiled across at her, and she saw plainly how he used humour as a shield.

'You're not mediocre,' she said, her voice catching. 'You're kind and organised and brave. You pulled off a breakout under Mrs Crawley, for goodness sake.'

He chuckled. 'Yes, I did.'

'I'd never have made it this far without you,' she said softly. 'You gave me a chance in LA, and you've made jokes and kept me sane, and then you let me drive with you when I know you wanted to do this by yourself. You're not mediocre. Not to me.'

He sucked in a breath and looked away, clearly too moved to say anything. Mallory desperately wanted him to believe her.

'Even if that were true, I couldn't face going home, not without Ben,' he said. 'After Vietnam, I wasn't the kid who'd left that clean little dairy farm with a white-walled church. The more years that went on, the worse it seemed. Thought it was best to move on, but everything I touched went bad eventually. Got married, but it all went sour when the kids were barely out of nappies. She left me for a better-functioning model, and I don't blame her. I wasn't anything to write home about. So the kids grew up without me, and they were probably better off for it. I wondered if either of them would find me when they were adults, but they never did. By the time I was sorting myself out in therapy, it felt like too much time had passed. I didn't want to push myself into the lives of my kids, who never really knew me. And I didn't see any point in going home.'

Mallory hugged herself, imagining the depth of sorrow she would feel if Harry never returned. 'You're going now,' she said.

'I don't want you to think I didn't miss her,' Jock said, his voice thick. 'I missed her every day. Thought about her every day. I wrote all those letters. Sometimes she'd find out an address for me and she'd write back. She'd tell me about the farm, and that she hoped I was all right, and that she loved—' Jock broke off, and cleared his throat. 'But I was always moving on somewhere else. Every year, I'd think about the leaves turning gold in the fall, and the sun kissing the hills at sunset in summer, and I'd think, maybe next year.'

Mallory looked down at the folder, scanning the lines underneath *Dear Mom*. They were all the same, too. *I'm sorry I'm not there*, they began, and then went on with descriptions of how the season was changing again, or what book he'd been reading, or what ages his children were. The things she imagined a son wanted to write to his mother about. She imagined a woman growing old as these letters came in.

'But I left it too late,' Jock said. 'She was ninety when she passed away, two years ago. They, ah . . .' He paused, and Mallory could see how his eyes gleamed with tears. 'They told me they found her with those letters,' he said, choking up. 'That's why I have them. She'd kept them all together, and she passed away holding a bunch of paper. I should have been there. I wish I could make it up to her, wish I could have been a better son.'

Mallory put her hands over her face, tears flowing down her cheeks. 'Oh, Jock,' she said, her heart breaking for him. 'But she knew, you understand that, don't you? She would never have stopped loving you, and she would have understood why you couldn't come back. I know that's true. And I'm sure she's watching over you now.'

Jock sniffed. 'Don't let Ernie hear you saying things like that. He doesn't believe in that sort of thing.'

Mallory folded her arms. 'Well, I do. A mother knows these things. She'll understand the time was never right.'

'Maybe,' he said, but she saw his shoulders relax a little. 'I'll see her again soon enough.'

'So why go now?' she asked.

He raised an upturned, philosophical hand. 'I just woke up one morning thinking that I didn't want to wait anymore. My health's not what it was. Then Ernie came and asked me about booking flights to Nashville. Seemed a sign.'

'Sounds like it,' Mallory murmured. 'What about your other brother, the one in Virginia?'

'I don't have another brother.'

'Oh. So why are you really going to Virginia?'

'I'm going to rob a bank.'

He gave her a sidelong glance, and a smile. A smile that said he was trying, despite all the cracks in his soul, to tell her that there was still hope because he could still find things funny. Mallory laughed, even in her confusion.

'I hope you brought me a ski mask,' she said.

He did laugh, then, and when it died away, he said, 'Have you heard of Arlington?'

A chill ran down Mallory's arms. In her mind, she saw scenes from movies, of caskets draped in flags, and tombstones in long straight rows.

'My brother's buried there,' Jock said. 'It's in Virginia. That's the reason I'm here. I'm going to see him. Then, I'm going home.'

●

Mallory let him drive until nine, when they pulled in at an all-night truck stop for coffee, which they drank standing under a neon light buzzing with bugs. After that, she took the wheel, and he fell asleep. She drove on for three hours, scanning the radio for company that she didn't find. A dozen times, she hallucinated that she could see the ghostly rear tyre of a cruiser ahead, always just out of the headlights. When the witching hour clicked over on the car clock, the GPS was reporting less than two hours to go. Sleep was threatening to fall on her with the weight of a twelve-pound hammer, so she took an exit to Love's Travel Stop.

Jock woke as soon as the car stopped.

'We're only a couple of hours away,' she said. 'But I need to sleep and so do you. Come on.'

The truck stop gave them directions to a cheap motel down a nearby B-road. The manager wasn't too happy at being roused for a late check-in, but Mallory didn't care. She shoved a fist of cash at him and fell onto the hard mattress, her alarm set for five in the morning. Sleep eluded her. Several times, she almost got up and went to Jock's room, wanting to find new words to reassure him that his mother would never have stopped loving him. She knew it must be true, because she was a mother. But what could she say to convince a man who'd been carrying such guilt for fifty years?

When the alarm went off, she felt as if she'd only slept for two minutes. Dawn was lighting the horizon with streaks of honey gold and blue, revealing the green hills they'd been driving through during the night. Today, somehow, she had to be in New York.

They drove back to the truck stop for a greasy breakfast that she didn't taste. Jock at least seemed in better spirits.

He had dressed in long black pants, impeccably ironed, and a crisp white button-down shirt. Next to him, in her crushed blue work trousers and a shirt she'd worn three times already, Mallory felt like some type of barnyard animal.

She took the wheel. The sun rose right in their eyes, and the trees that flanked the interstate resembled an oil painting of smeared green and flecked gold. They passed roadworks with silent machines sitting idle, and long stretches of empty highway, before noise barriers signalled they'd reached the suburbs.

'When we get there,' Jock said, 'you can just drop me at the entrance. Don't waste time. Just keep going all the way to New York.'

'And how will you get home?'

'I can hire another car,' Jock said.

Mallory shook her head, though she wanted nothing else. 'No,' she said. 'I'm not dropping you off. And I'm not letting you drive on alone. I'm coming with you, then when you're ready, we'll drive to New York together. You can drop *me* off. You have to go that way, right?'

He stared across at her. 'All right,' he said. 'If that's what you want.'

Mallory wasn't sure whether she had done the right thing. She didn't know if her presence would be an intrusion. But he had shown her the letters, told her his story. A tornado would have to go through the road in front of her to keep her from making sure he wasn't alone today.

For the last part of the drive, clouds thickened in from the east, throwing a blanket over the sun and bringing herald raindrops that spatted down on the windshield. By the time she pulled onto Memorial Drive, the sky was in full threat mode. It seemed rather fitting.

From the road, the Arlington National Cemetery wasn't visible until the last moment of approach. The drive took them out along the edge of the Potomac, the city of Washington, DC, rising across the water. The long avenue was lined with boxed hedges and ended with a white marble building. It reminded Mallory of Canberra, where she'd been once on a school trip. The beautiful, wide streets, the marble and stone architecture. Green expressions of life were everywhere. Only the sombre atmosphere and the steely sky signalled a resting place for the dead.

Finally, they pulled into a vast and nearly empty parking lot. Mallory turned the engine off, and the silence flooded in.

'I can't go in there,' Jock said, his voice flat.

'Not yet,' she said, glancing at the dash clock. 'But when they open in about ten minutes, you can.'

He shook his head. 'I think I was wrong about this.'

She couldn't help seeing in his face the terror of a small boy. All the years he'd blamed himself for something he could have no blame in. It should have been his mother sitting here beside him. It should never have had to happen at all. And so, she told him what she would have told Harry.

'I know you will, because you've come this far,' she said. 'You've gone on this long journey and now you're right at the end. This feels big, but the hard part is really over. All you have to do now is walk through the door. And I'm going to do that part with you.'

Please let that be enough. Let him face this thing that's plagued him and find some peace in it. Let this journey have meant the things he wanted it to mean.

'Okay,' he said, a few minutes later. 'But promise me something.'

'What's that?'

'I want to do something for you. When we reach New York, and you find your little boy, let me help you out.'

'How?'

He shrugged. 'Moral support, or whatever you need. You said yourself you don't know how it's going to go. You'll be in a strange city, on your own, and your husband is holding all the cards. I did a lot of therapy, learning how not to get into arguments, how to stick to facts. Even how to give the other person what they want, if it gets the outcome you need.'

Mallory grunted.

'I know – it kills you to do it, but sometimes you have to. My point is, we can go through some plans of how you play it, what you say, how you react. How to keep your head level when you'd rather lose your mind.'

'You would do that?'

'You've done a lot for me. Let me help you.'

Mallory pressed her hand to her chest, unable to speak. The weight of not knowing how she could deal with Duncan eased. Jock nodded, and as if this sealed the deal, he pushed open his door and climbed out. The Virginia air was crisp, whipping the threatening rain into their faces. Mallory stopped him only long enough to hand him his jumper against the chill, then they were walking together up to the stone stairs. Columns rose above them and beyond, past three doors each crowned with a half-moon arch. There, they waited the few minutes to opening, as a group of schoolchildren trekked up the same stairs.

The security process helped to break the tension; it was hard to disappear inside your thoughts when someone was asking you for ID. Since they hadn't brought bags, they were ushered to an express line, and so they left the noise of the children far behind. When they stepped outside into the grounds, Mallory ran her eyes over the trees and lawns, and the gardens. In the distance, a large crowd of people were dressed in white. It took her a long minute to realise those weren't people through the trees, but the first of the rows and rows of headstones. The great tide of respect and remembrance washed over her then, and with it, sadness and loss and grief, all the way to the bedrock. Her heart squeezed.

'Which way?' she asked, slipping her hand through Jock's arm.

She walked with him as far as the right section, where he asked to go on alone. She watched him pace down the long rows of headstones, his short legs lifting over the grass, his head bowed and tipped slightly to one side, and thought how many people had moments of bravery that went unwitnessed.

She turned away and walked the solemn steps to the Tomb of the Unknowns, where a soldier kept vigil. She huddled in her thin jacket, watching him pace the platform like a restless ghost, undeterred by wind and rain. Somewhere on the squally breeze, she could hear a sombre bugle, something like the final notes of the 'Last Post' ringing out.

By the time she'd returned to where she and Jock had parted, she'd witnessed at least one funeral, and several cars circling the network of streets. The scale of it all overwhelmed her. She saw each stone and counted a mother, a father, siblings and friends. She quickened her footsteps, not wanting to be alone anymore. She needed to see another person with warmth in their body like she needed to take her next breath.

She saw him, coming back up the long row, the wind whipping his suit pants against his thin legs. He stood straighter than he had before, but his steps showed effort. She lifted a hand, and he returned the wave, and they met beneath the trees.

'Did you find him?' she asked.

Jock nodded. He blew out a long breath, winded from the walk. Then another, twisting around to look at the path he'd walked up. 'Yeah.'

He kept her gaze but raised his hands helplessly, as if he couldn't say any more, as if there were no words for what this all meant. Mallory wasn't sure if she saw absolution in his expression, but the rain came then.

'I told him . . .' he said finally against the downpour. 'I told him . . .'

Mallory understood. She stepped forward and held on to his arm as the water chilled her to her bones. She knew that he meant *I told him I was sorry. I told him about all of it. I told him I was going home.*

They waited for a slow procession of funeral cars that hissed past, before they made for the cover of the buildings. Jock was still trembling with the release of emotion he'd held in so long, his eyelashes wet with raindrops. He shook his head. 'I should have done this years ago,' he said, water trickling down his temples.

'You weren't ready before.'

He looked at his feet, then up at the falling sky. Pressed a hand to the centre of his chest and gave a long slow blink. Then his legs buckled and he fell to the stones.

Chapter 18

AFTER A WEEK OF LONG DAYS AND SLEEPLESS NIGHTS, Mallory watched what happened next almost from outside of herself. Jock didn't respond to her voice, to her shaking his shoulder, and when she felt for his pulse, she wasn't sure it was there. She screamed for help so loudly that she had to cough before she could give the first breaths of CPR, her hands slipping in the wet.

A gardener heard her, she learned later. Before five minutes had gone by, she had two doctors take over her efforts, and staff assuring her that an ambulance was coming. There must have been some hope, because they loaded him and sped away. Then Mallory was running, her throat raw, back to the carpark.

When she arrived at the hospital, she was told he was still in the ER and to take a seat. Mallory was soaked through. There was grass on her shins and stuck to her cheek, and her hip was bruised where she'd run into the car door in her haste. She had come too far to be told to stay away. The nurse didn't stop her when she found the bay where the doctors were talking in urgent voices about blood pressures and fibrillations and bypasses as the monitors beeped. Mallory simply walked in, told them he was her grandfather, and pulled up a chair. His eyes were closed, a plastic tube and bag taped to the corner of his mouth. A nurse squeezed the bag at regular intervals, keeping her head turned to the discussion.

Mallory felt a black despair blooming inside her. She inched her hand around wires and tubes and found his shoulder.

'Jock,' she whispered. 'Don't give up. I'm here.' She thought she saw a flicker in his eyelids, but she couldn't be sure. So she told him again, then again and again, until the first alarm went off and the doctors moved back in.

He died at eleven minutes to eleven. The specialist took her to a room with a window to explain that the heart attack had simply damaged too much of his heart. That the muscle couldn't function enough to sustain him. That they had done all they could, but it hadn't been enough.

Mallory let the blackness overtake her, otherwise she would have come apart in a million ungatherable pieces. She couldn't cry; her grief was too deep, her anger at the injustice too wild and frightening.

Then came the paperwork. Arrangements had to be made for the treatment bills and the funeral. Roused by unforgiving administration, Mallory told them she'd find the travel insurance documents; she knew Jock had carried them, after all Zadie's medical issues.

She walked around and around the carpark in a daze, unable to find the car. She had a vague memory of parking it hastily, throwing open the door, but nothing else after. Did she have the wrong level?

Eventually, she realised it was simply missing. Not only that, but she also didn't have the keys. Was it possible she'd left it open, maybe with the keys in the ignition? Either way, the car was gone. And with it had gone her bag, and Jock's, the documents, and all the money that she had left.

She faced the churning sky, her mind throwing up positive thoughts that the rest of her brain shot down like clay pigeons. She couldn't find a silver lining in this. This life was all hard, unforgiving edges. Every hardship dug in, bruising until it hurt to think at all. She was car-less and still four hours short of New York, with only a few dollars in her pocket, and alone again. She couldn't muster the energy to swear. She turned back for the hospital, not even feeling the storm on her back.

This was where her warrior self would fall, because not all of them made it home.

•

Mallory endured the next hour in defeat. The hospital allowed her to use their phone so that she could call the Australian consulate, who gave her further directions. As soon as that call ended, she pressed the hang-up catch. A nurse was still speaking to some police officers who had come about the car. Mallory sighed, checked the time, and dialled the Silky Oaks number, knowing that Bridget would probably be on the night shift.

'Mal?' Bridget said, breathless, after Mallory had asked for her friend. 'Are you there?'

'Not exactly,' Mallory croaked. She pressed a hand to her forehead. 'Look, Bridge, don't ask me about why I need this, but go find Jock's file, will you?'

'Jock from upstairs in the south wing?' A pause. 'One of the residents who flew the coop?'

'Yeah. I need his next of kin.'

Bridget put the phone down, and Mallory heard rustling and the thud of the filing-room ladder before Bridget came back on.

'Next of kin, next of kin . . . here we go.' A long pause. 'Ex-wife, but someone's made a note saying only to call in a dire emergency. Mustn't want to be contacted.'

'He mentioned he had kids,' Mallory said. 'Anyone else there?'

'Nope.' Another pause. She dropped her voice. 'So you've seen him? Mal, you weren't *in* on this escape plan of theirs, were you? Mrs Crawley's been reading the riot act around here, even after we heard they were fine.'

'No, I wasn't in on it.'

'Then how—'

'He's dead, Bridge.' Mallory pinched her nose hard to stop herself from crying. 'Look, I ran into them in the LA airport when the volcano thing was happening, and we drove together. I'm in Washington, DC, now. Jock had a massive heart attack. I'm trying to deal with funeral directors and I need to know if there's anyone else to call.'

Bridget blew out a breath. 'Oh my Lord. Wait, let me dig in the back and see the original application. It asks for extended family.' Rustling. 'Yes, here we are. Lists a mother in East Homer, NY. Address only.'

'Give it to me anyway.'

'Oh my, bless my soul,' Bridget said.

'What?'

'This admission record is an inch thick with assessments. PTSD, it says. From Vietnam. Terrible business, that. The poor wee man.'

'I know,' Mallory said, her heart twisting for Jock.

'Well, now,' Bridget went on. 'God-willing, he's in a better place. Now, you give me the details of the hospital there, and anyone else you've been talking to. You don't need to liaise with everyone. Silky Oaks was his primary residence.'

Mallory gave her the names and numbers. Handing over the responsibility didn't feel right, but she was so tired she knew it was better this way.

'Okay,' Bridget said briskly. 'We can take over the arrangements. You've got important things to do.'

Mallory slumped. 'Thanks, Bridge. But I'm not sure I'm going anywhere now.' She wasn't sure she'd be getting out of this chair. She filled Bridget in on what had happened with the car. 'I think I've given up.'

'Rubbish,' Bridget said. 'I've never met anyone in my life less likely to give up. What can I do? Do you need that money?'

'How about an IV of caffeine?'

'Seriously.'

Mallory shook her head. 'Pray for me that the police find the car. I have to go, Bridge.'

Someone must have been listening because when Mallory stepped out of the room, the police were waiting. They'd found the car, abandoned a few miles away, a little banged up and with the contents of the bags strewn all through the boot. The police had kindly collected her belongings in a huge plastic bag. Mallory repacked them; she didn't need an inventory to know that the cash was gone. And because the car was rented to Jock, she couldn't get it back either. That particular mess was going to descend into a tussle between Jock's travel insurance and the hire company. She handed Jock's insurance documents over to an administrator who was talking to Bridget, and then Mallory had nothing left to do. She wanted to slump down right there on the white linoleum; she was so tired it would have felt like a feather mattress.

Yet, Bridget's words and Harry's face wouldn't leave her. She counted the cash in her pocket: thirty dollars, just enough for an overnight bus. It left near midnight and arrived in New York unspeakably early. In the end, she asked the police for a lift to the station. Jock was gone. Harry was still here. She had one last chance to put herself in the same city, to throw herself over the threshold.

Her phone was at half-charge, all she had since the car thieves had taken her charger. She would have to turn it off and conserve so she could navigate at the other end. Only when she reached Union Station, with its grand, vaulting honeycomb stone walls, did she see the text messages. She went up the coach steps as she read them, the bus engine rumbling under her feet.

AJ: *Don't leave yet.*

AJ: *Please. I'm on my way back.*

These first two were from yesterday, when she'd been in Nashville, a time that seemed a year ago now. She didn't need to be reminded of him, but she regretted how they'd parted. She hadn't wanted to hurt him like that, and now, with her heart so bruised over Jock, she felt worse about it than ever. Another three messages had come through later.

She read them as she wedged herself in an empty row near the back of the bus.

AJ: *I think I know where you're going.*

AJ: *Arlington, right?*

AJ: *I don't want this to be how it ends.*

If she hadn't been so ragged, she'd have agreed with him. He had given her confidence when she'd needed it, and comfort, and muscle. She owed him a reply.

Me too. But I'm nearly there. Sorry AJ. Wish me luck.

Then she deleted the last three words and replaced them with *Switching off now.* Wishing was not enough and luck was fickle. Because if a man who had held unreasonable guilt for fifty years could be taken at the last post of his greatest journey, then a mother could also lose her son for reasons beyond her control. What she needed was pure brute effort, for this big diesel engine to carry her through the night.

•

Mallory managed a few hours of broken sleep on the bus before she jerked awake, afraid she might miss the stop. Suburbs and petrol stations and warehouses flashed past through Baltimore, dark with night. Then came the bright lights of Philadelphia and a dozen other, unknown urban hamlets. The world seemed full of lights, now, glittering through trees and on every passing truck. The only place without them was overhead. Mallory didn't know if it was clouds, or if the glow of the east coast neon was simply too bright for stars, but the sky was a dull grey void.

She ached for her tiny cottage in Australia, with its nights blanketed in stars and the scent of jasmine.

She knew when they reached New York, because the speed fell. They crawled past blocks and blocks of buildings, moving ever deeper into the urban jungle, until finally the driver wound down the gears and pulled into the kerb.

Mallory stepped out under a towering building, feeling so tiny on the imposing grey street. She turned a slow circle, shivering in the cool air. The sky was lightening, but among the wall of buildings she had no idea if the sun was up. Two men in threadbare clothes stirred in a camp under the awning. Her stomach growled with hunger, her eyelids scratching with every blink. Now what?

She turned on her phone, and brought up a map to calculate how far it was to Duncan's apartment. Over an hour's walk, it said, way downtown. Mallory frowned: it couldn't possibly be that far, could it? But after only a few minutes, she realised how large the blocks were. She closed her eyes, feeling so stripped of energy she could not take another step. But she must. At least it would still be early when she arrived, so Harry and Duncan would both be at home.

Eventually, she found Broadway and followed it south. She began to stumble in her exhaustion, her eyes crossing when she tried to read the screen. She had nothing left to lose except Harry. That one, singular purpose drove her on. At about halfway there, light spread through the pale grey sky, and urban sparrows came out on the hunt. Early morning commuters began passing on the footpath. After forty minutes, she found the edge of Little Italy and Chinatown. There, she sensed the Hudson River ahead, where the high-rises thinned into open sky over the water. She'd reached Two Bridges.

She quickened her steps, and her heart lurched when she spotted the right street sign. The building looked nothing special from the outside, just a tower of red brick across the road from discount stores, pharmacies and dry cleaners. The entry was secured, but with a steady stream of people leaving for the day, it wasn't difficult to catch the door and slip into the foyer.

Her legs had all the strength of cooked noodles as she rode up the elevator. When the doors opened on the right floor, she edged into a cream hallway with dark wooden doors. She stopped in front of 422, took a breath, and knocked.

Chapter 19

MALLORY HEARD THE HOLLOW *THUNK THUNK* OF HARD leather heels on wood, and shook out her hands, bracing for Duncan to open the door even as she strained to hear Harry running up behind him.

But when the door opened, an unfamiliar man wearing suit pants, a crisp button-down shirt and thick hipster glasses looked out.

'You're late,' he said, making a pointed glance at his wrist. 'I hope you know that another minute and I was calling the manager. You'd better get started, and go get your gear.'

Mallory hardly heard him. 'Is Harry here?'

'Who's Harry?'

'And Duncan?' Mallory looked past him into the apartment. The hall was empty. So was the just-visible living room. She must have the wrong place. She dug in her pocket with shaking hands, bringing out Harry's letter with the address. 'Isn't this four twenty-two?'

'It is.'

'My son's supposed to be here. My husband lives here.' She offered him the letter as evidence.

The man gave it only a cursory glance. 'Must have given you the wrong address. This place is empty. I thought you were my cleaning contractor. We have a showing this morning.'

Mallory blinked, stepping backwards. Was she too late?

'The people who lived here before, where did they go?' she asked.

'Guy moved out a month ago and now the landlord's selling,' said the agent, taking out a slim mobile. 'Now, sorry, I have to chase this cleaner.'

The door closed firmly in Mallory's face. She checked the number three more times, then went back down to the front door and checked the street number, and the street name too. She had the right place. None of the numbers were ambiguous. No ones that could be sevens, or sixes masquerading as zeroes. Duncan's handwriting was scratchy, but the numerals were careful.

Mallory closed her eyes, despair filling her. She'd taken Duncan's word on the address. All this time, she'd been striving to reach this place, and Harry had never been here. She looked out into the vast jungle of New York, where the trees themselves were merely undergrowth to the buildings, and knew he could be anywhere. The next logical move was to find Duncan's office, but Mallory hadn't wanted to go to the seat of his power, where he could easily refuse to see her. She sank down on the kerb, her energy spent.

She sat there long enough for the street to become busy, and for traffic to grow to a dull roar, with sirens, and the trains rattling on the Brooklyn Bridge. A familiar note rumbled in above the horns: a distant, galloping rumble. Sounded just like the Rocket.

The note came closer and closer, until . . . yes, there was someone pulling up a Rocket right outside the building, another tall rider in black leather. Maybe it was a requirement in the Rocket shop if you wanted to buy one. She rubbed her eyes. Damn if that didn't look like AJ. Maybe that was a requirement, too.

Then the rider pulled off his helmet and it was him. Mallory found herself running down the sidewalk, scattering pedestrians, overcome with the relief and joy and hope of seeing him here.

'Slow down,' he said, after her garbled greeting. He sat her on the Rocket's saddle with both her legs on one side, as if the bike were a giant park bench.

'There's no one there,' she said, pointing up at the building in despair. 'Just some agent who said it's been vacant for a month. I'll have to find Duncan's office, but I want to find Harry and I have no idea where he is.' She couldn't voice her worst fear: that she might not find him at all.

AJ held up a finger and put his phone to his ear. His brows were drawn down, his menace assisted by the thick scab on his chin.

'When's the last time you saw the mark at that address I gave you?' he said into his phone. 'Uh-huh. Uh-huh. You sure? Okay.'

At this point, AJ twisted around and lifted his hand in a small wave showing little of the stiffness from his accident. Mallory was astonished to see a burly man, sitting on a bench across the street and smoking, wave back.

There was another flurry of questions from AJ and long silences as he listened. Mallory gave him a questioning look. *What on earth is going on?*

'Where's the office? Text me that address,' he said finally, before ringing off.

He slid the phone back in his pocket. 'Okay, you see that guy across the street? He's been watching this address.'

'What?' Mallory asked.

'You remember I told you I have a lot of ex-military friends who went into surveillance and security? When you told me what was happening, I called my friend Zak and gave him the address. He put someone here to watch.'

'You did? Why?' Dimly, she remembered a text from him about calling a friend in New York.

AJ shrugged. 'After what your ex pulled with your boy, who knows what else he might do? Seemed a good idea to keep an eye on things. Duncan's picture is easy to find on the net especially after we could confirm from your photo, so they knew who to look for. It wasn't hard.'

'So is Duncan actually here after all?' Mallory asked, confused. 'Was it the wrong apartment or something?'

'No, Zak said they've only seen him here once, and then only collecting mail. But they tailed him from his office to an apartment uptown, right on Central Park. That's where he lives.'

Mallory grabbed AJ's arm to stop herself keeling over in hope. 'And Harry?'

'Zak says Duncan is at the office early and takes Harry along. They've seen them leave this morning. An older Hispanic woman arrives at the office to take him to school around eight-thirty.'

Mallory's voice trembled. 'What time is it?'

'It's ten past eight.'

•

Mallory would never have made it through the honking New York traffic without AJ manoeuvring the Rocket around a maze of gutters and gaps. She had no idea how he was navigating. Maybe the enigmatic Zak was feeding him directions through a speaker in his helmet; nothing seemed out of the realms of possibility anymore.

As they wove through the streets, she had no idea what she would do at the other end. Nor when AJ set her down on the pavement, and she climbed three steps up to a set of glass doors. He'd offered to come with her, but Mallory refused: she wanted to see Harry alone, and suspected AJ's presence might create difficult questions, especially with Duncan. All she knew with certainty was that the next few minutes would be something she'd never forget. And that if she wasn't out with Harry in fifteen minutes, AJ would be coming in as back-up.

The lobby was an expanse of clean white tiles, the company logo on the reception desk shiny with newness. A mezzanine walkway stretched across the back wall of the foyer, railed with glass, and a spiral staircase dropped down like a giant tree root between two elevators. To Mallory, it was stark and lifeless.

But Harry was here, and that was everything.

She tucked her hair behind her ears, knowing her clothes were crumpled. The desk attendant was sipping a coffee and gave Mallory a wary eye.

'Welcome to Iron Gate Software,' she chirped, script-like. 'Can I help you?'

'Duncan Cook, please.' Mallory's heart flip-flopped at saying his name, and she tried not to let it show on her face.

The woman popped two surprised eyebrows, as if Mallory had just asked for a meeting with the Queen. 'Mr Cook isn't in the office right now.'

'I know he's here,' Mallory said with unnatural calm. 'Please tell him his wife is here. I need to see him right away.'

'O . . . kay, I'll check,' said the woman as she picked up the internal phone, her tone no doubt meant to prepare Mallory for disappointment. 'Um, Cathy? There's a lady in reception who says she's Mr Cook's wife.'

She spoke in a hushed voice, as if Mallory wasn't standing right there listening to every word.

Mallory waited, the seconds seeming endless. What would she do if Duncan simply wouldn't see her? Barge through to the lifts and search the building? She snuck a look at the elevators, but she couldn't see a call button. She noticed, too, the security guard who was standing inside the front doors. She hadn't seen him before. Her odds of making a run for it seemed poor.

She felt the flush begin rising up her neck. Her whole body felt like it was inside out, her nerves exposed to every raw sensation. The tiles, so hard through the thin soles of her sneakers; the air blowing in cold currents across her forehead, the clickety echo of the receptionist's nails on her keyboard as she waited for a response.

The woman replaced the phone and gave Mallory a surprised smile. 'He'll be right down,' she said.

Then feet came striding across that mezzanine, and there was Duncan, turning to spring down the spiral stairs.

•

As soon as Duncan's feet met the lobby floor, he smiled. A broad, unexpectedly sunny smile, as if Mallory was welcome and expected. She was so tired and confused in that moment, that doubt stole the words she had ready to hurl at him. Had she read this all wrong? How could this be the same man who had cut off her Skype call just days ago?

Despite everything, she felt herself smile at him, just the way she'd imagined responding when she'd been waiting at the airport almost two weeks ago. He looked so normal.

'Mal!' he said, in what one of those article journalists had described as a charming, warm and professional manner. 'You're the last person I expected to see.'

'Duncan,' she said, trying to hold her calm, but her heart was crashing around in her chest. This was wrong, his words out of step with everything that had happened between them. Or maybe it was just pity, because she must look like she'd been wearing these clothes for a month.

He glanced towards the receptionist. 'Becca, can you make an appointment for Mal later today? It isn't a good time now.'

Then Mallory noticed the tips of his ears were bright red. He was uncomfortable too, and trying not to show it so he didn't lose face. She'd watched him do this many times, on difficult conference calls and when talking to potential financiers. Mallory's doubts vanished. He might look calm and easy to everyone else, but she knew he wanted nothing more than to get rid of her. He was trying to deflect her, and to avoid a scene. He'd always been good at dodging arguments.

'Where's Harry, Duncan?' Mallory asked.

The receptionist was watching, her big kohl-rimmed eyes peering out from the side of the monitor. Duncan made the corners of his mouth bend again, a good approximation of a smile.

'Really, Mal, you've caught me at a bad time, on my way to a meeting. But you can come back later and we can talk then. Becca, will you order the lift, please? Third floor. See you, Mal.'

He stepped away. Mallory could hardly believe how he was trying to blow her off, as pleasantly as he could, and that he couldn't see how obvious it was to her.

'Don't walk away from me,' she said after him, angry. 'I'm your wife and I just flew halfway around the world and drove across a continent to be here. I want to see my son. I'm not leaving until I do.'

The next part seemed to happen in slow motion. Duncan turned with his hands in his pockets, looking down, as if considering what response to give. The lift doors slid open. Mallory saw the security guard ambling towards her. Duncan must have given him some kind of signal.

She saw with clarity how events would play out. Duncan would disappear into the lift while the guard, probably assuming she was some delusional vagrant, escorted her out. Duncan would stand behind his big company. She wouldn't be let in the building again. If you give up now, she thought, you'll never see Harry again.

She had witnesses here.

Duncan had come from the mezzanine.

She took a chance.

'Harry,' she called.

Well, *that* got a reaction. Duncan spun, strode back towards her and took her under the elbow, trying to guide her back towards the desk. 'He's at school,' Duncan hissed. 'Let's go, now, Mal. You need a shower. You're embarrassing yourself.'

Mallory tried to shake him off, but he was too firm. Instead, she refused to move, so that Duncan nearly tripped over. She sensed a large presence behind her.

'Everything all right, Mr Cook?' The security guard.

Mallory snapped. She was *not* going to be held back from Harry by these two men.

'*Harry!*' she screamed. Her voice shot across the foyer like an arrow.

They were trying to hustle her towards the door. Mallory dropped her weight, though it was a last-ditch effort. In a second, she'd be out.

Then came the small running feet above, on the mezzanine. Mallory would have known it was Harry from the barest glimpse, even with his hair cut short, and the cap, and the fancy jeans. He was her little boy, coming to her call. He threw himself on the rail of the mezzanine, peering down with wide eyes. 'Mum!'

'Harry!' It came out as a primal cry, a sound that carried all the hope and love she had for him, and all the grief of her long journey. Then he was flying down the stairs, his legs a blur.

Harry was too swift to be caught. He pelted across the tiles, dodged Duncan and threw himself into her. Mallory folded around him, pressing his warm body against hers.

His hair smelled of strange shampoo, his clothes of foreign washing powder, but underneath all that, he was still Harry. Her body felt like armour around him, holding him as he cried and laughed and tried to ask her where she'd been and where she'd come from.

A long time passed before Mallory was aware of anyone else. Of Duncan, trying to reason with Harry to come away, of the receptionist staring, of the security man backing off. When Duncan began to speak sharply, telling Harry to do as he was told, Mallory finally climbed to her feet and rounded on Duncan.

'No,' she said. 'Don't you dare scold him. Not for this.'

Duncan would never keep Harry from her again.

She didn't really have the faintest clue what to do next, except take Harry away from here. The security man clearly didn't seem to want to get between a little boy and his mother, so it seemed possible to just walk out.

Then Maria, Duncan's housekeeper, came through the doors. Obviously mistaking the situation for a happy family reunion, she launched into overjoyed exclamations at meeting Mallory and seemed so oblivious to the tension that the receptionist went back to work and Duncan stood with his hands on his hips, as if taking stock.

AJ chose that moment to enter the lobby, complete with leather jacket and sunglasses. Mallory, who'd been so worried about the impression AJ would create, found she couldn't care less. Nothing mattered beyond Harry. When AJ asked Mallory if everything was fine, Duncan sounded practically level-headed when he said, 'Who the fuck are you?'

'Uncle Bob,' AJ replied, deadpan.

With AJ's appearance, Duncan gave Mallory an I've-had-enough-of-games look. 'Harry has to go to school,' he said. 'Maria, he's going to be late.'

Mallory wanted to scream at him that Harry's school was back home in Australia, with all the friends who'd missed him for the past two weeks. Instead she held her voice level. 'Harry is coming with me, back home to Australia. If you want to change how things are working between us, you talk to me about it first. This whole episode is over. We're going now.'

She was trembling, but she felt strong with Harry's small hand in hers. Triumphant. When he gave her a questioning look, she was able to smile back and encourage him towards the doors. They were leaving.

'You'll be hearing from my lawyers,' Duncan said, his voice a parting volley. 'And good luck taking him anywhere without his passport.'

Chapter 20

DUNCAN'S WORDS CHASED MALLORY DOWN THE STREET. Shit, shit, she hadn't even thought about Harry's passport. After half a block of Harry trotting to keep up, she stopped on the corner and finally registered that Maria and AJ were following. Maria's phone was ringing. After answering it, she gingerly held out the handset. 'Mrs Mallory? Is for you.'

Expecting Duncan, Mallory steeled herself. 'Hello?' she said, curt.

'Mrs Cook? I'm Duncan's attorney.' The voice was deep and commanding, but held a certain note of apology. 'I'm calling to—'

'You can bugger off,' Mallory said, still hot in her anger. 'If my supposed husband thinks he can take my son away from me without a word, and freeze my accounts and give me a wrong address, and then hide behind his lawyer, he's got another thing coming. I just drove across the country because of a bloody volcano. You haven't got anything to scare me.'

There was a pause.

'I do understand your frustration,' he said smoothly. 'And there are obviously conflicts to resolve. I just want to confirm that you have Harry with you now?'

'Yes,' she said tightly.

'Mr Cook wanted to convey again that Harry is expected at school today. The school will check Harry's whereabouts if he doesn't attend. Do you intend on taking him?'

'I don't know,' Mallory said, wrong-footed.

'Well, if you do, Mr Cook has agreed that for the time being, Harry will remain with you, so you must collect him at three this afternoon. Furthermore, I am advising a mediation meeting to discuss the ongoing custody arrangements, tomorrow, at a time that suits you. Will you agree?'

Mallory fumbled, not knowing what to say. She wanted this resolved quickly, but why did they need a mediation? Duncan was in the wrong. He had to give back the passport. 'I guess,' she said finally, hedging because the silence had stretched too long.

'Good. Give me your direct number and I'll be in contact with the details,' the lawyer said.

Mallory handed the phone back to Maria with a tight pressure between her ribs. AJ raised his eyebrows.

Harry tugged at her hand. 'Mum?' he asked. 'Are we going to school?'

Mallory bent down to look him in the face. She smiled, though she wanted to crumble. Holding herself strong for him was the hardest thing she had done in all the miles she'd travelled. 'Do you want to go to school, bubby?'

Harry's big blue eyes flicked uncertainly. 'Well, I am *supposed* to . . . and it's Emily's birthday today. She's bringing cake.'

Mallory found herself walking the three blocks to the school, Harry skipping and pointing out landmarks and asking questions about what would happen now. Mallory imagined that anyone watching would have seen nothing out of the ordinary: just a mother taking her little boy to class. Except that they were trailed by a housekeeper and a big man in leather, whom Maria had taken a fast shine to. Then again, this was New York. Maybe AJ would be mistaken for a bodyguard.

At the school gate, Harry asked if Mallory would be there when the day was over, and she promised she would. He ran in, happy, but Mallory stayed in the crisp air, hung with the sounds of playing children and small flitting birds, long after he'd disappeared.

'You want me to have some people come and watch the place?' AJ asked.

Mallory, a little unnerved, shook her head. 'The lawyer said it was fine.'

'Then you need a shower, and a regroup.'

In the end, Maria took Mallory to a hotel where she knew the owner and handed over a credit card.

'I'll pay you back,' Mallory said.

'This card is Mr Cook's, for my expenses,' she said with a shrug. Then she embraced Mallory. 'I'm so relieved you came. Harry missed you so much. I worried for him.'

So Mallory accepted her paying; she figured Duncan owed her that much.

The hotel was boutique and quirky, with rooms named after golden Hollywood movie stars, none of which she knew. Her room was large, with tall, wooden-shuttered windows, two beds of clean white linen, a thick carpet, and a newly renovated bathroom. After the budget motels on the road, it seemed an absurd luxury.

Maria had work to do, but AJ stayed, flipping through his phone and making calls while Mallory took a shower and changed, though neither act did anything to relieve her anxiety. The few hours since she'd first arrived in New York had been so packed, it felt as though a whole week had passed. And still, she couldn't go home.

'So what are you going to do?' AJ asked when Mallory emerged from the bathroom, her hair limp from the steam, feeling every inch of her exhaustion. She sank down on the bed and stared at the wall.

'I thought when I made it here, this would be over,' she said slowly. 'After everything I went through . . . the volcano, and the drive, and Ernie, and then Jock, and the car being stolen, and Duncan giving me the wrong address. After all that I thought, when I see Harry again, this will all be over. Now that's happened, and Duncan's *still* holding something over me!'

'Wait, wait, back up,' AJ said. 'Your car was stolen? And what's this about Jock?'

'Oh, right.' Mallory rubbed a hand over her face. She could still smell, faintly, the Washington hospital waiting room. Could still see Jock's face against the white hospital sheets. 'I have to tell you some things.'

She filled him in on Jock's sudden death, her voice shaking. The news stilled AJ, so Mallory ended up telling him the whole story, all the things Jock had told her on the overnight drive. AJ listened with his head bowed, only speaking to ask, 'Then what?'

'Oh, man,' he said when she finished. 'I don't know what to say to that.'

'I still have all the letters. But I don't know what to do with them. He didn't have any family left.'

'Leave it alone, now,' AJ said. 'He's gone to a better place, and he'll understand you've got more pressing concerns. Now, who was that on the phone before?'

'Duncan's lawyer,' Mallory said. 'He wants to set up a mediation for tomorrow. I want this all sorted out, but I can't help feeling like I don't know what I'm doing.'

She started pacing.

AJ pulled out his phone again. 'I'm going to make a suggestion.'

'Does it involve more of your surveillance friends? Because I'm not sure how I feel about you having all these people at your beck and call, watching.'

AJ grinned, as if this was a compliment. 'Don't be uneasy. They're all upstanding people. But no. My sister, Livia, is a lawyer. I want to call her, have her come up here and help you out.'

Mallory hesitated. 'She would do that?'

'For me? Probably not. But if her AWOL brother calls, asking her to help a woman I met, you bet your life she'll want to come up here to meet you. Whatever the cost.' He was already scrolling through his phone.

Mallory shook her head. 'Why are you doing this?'

'Because I'm the better man.'

She took him in, all six-feet-four leather-jacket-wearing him. She'd found him on the side of the road. Or, more exactly, he'd found her on the side of the road. He'd offered her food, and solace, and transport, even after she'd twice told him to take a hike. She didn't know how she felt about the fact that he'd called people he knew and organised to have Duncan watched – such abilities implied a large group of friends, possibly with particular skills, and she'd seen that movie – but without him, she wouldn't have seen Harry today. That was everything to her. And now, he was offering more. She tried to find the words to thank him for all the things he'd done, but she had none. All she could do was press her hands to her heart, lift her eyes to whatever deity had sent him, and watch him grin at her in return.

'Liv, it's me,' he said, wandering across the room as he spoke to his sister. At the volume of Livia's response, AJ held the phone away from his ear, giving Mallory a slow smile that could have set the room on fire.

The rest of the school day sped past. She caught two hours' sleep while AJ went out. Then, at his suggestion, she opened a brand-new bank account online, her first act of financial independence since she and Duncan had married. She hadn't even thought to do it before. He took another call from Livia, then Bridget called Mallory, sounding tired.

'What time is it there?' Mallory asked.

'Very early,' she said, yawning. 'But I can never sleep on the night shift, and I wanted to let you know the funeral details. We just had confirmation – it's this Saturday.'

'I doubt I'll be back in time,' Mallory said sadly.

'It's going to be at Arlington.'

Mallory paused. 'Really?'

'Jock's file states he wished to be buried with his brother, so that's what we went for. That was an interesting process, let me tell you. Crawley and I have run up quite the international call charges today, but at least the travel insurer was happy – less for them to do, I suppose.'

'What about his family?'

Bridget sighed. 'I *did* track down his ex-wife, but she didn't seem very receptive. Bit sad, isn't it?'

'Yes,' Mallory said, staring at the tenement building across the street.

'Will you be able to go? I take it you aren't in New York yet.'

'Actually, I arrived this morning.'

Bridget gasped. '*And?*'

Mallory filled her in on the whole situation, including that she was meeting with a lawyer later and had mediation tomorrow. Bridget only seemed overjoyed that Mallory had seen Harry. She still existed in Mallory's old reality: that everything would be fine now.

'There's nothing better, is there?' she said. 'Holding your boy again. Oh, I've got all goosebumps thinking about it.'

'If only it was that simple.'

'Yes. Well, speaking of not being simple, Mrs Crawley would like a word. Can I put her on?'

Mallory sat up very straight. Mrs Crawley was the last person she expected to be around on the night shift.

'Short-staffed,' Mrs Crawley said, by way of explanation. 'Besides, this situation with Jock has been taking priority. Bridget says you met by chance in America. Any sign of the other two? We had a call early on saying they were fine but haven't heard anything more.'

'I last saw them in Nashville. They have a wedding to go to,' she said carefully, wondering how that news would go down.

Mrs Crawley grunted. 'That Ernie always was a difficult one. I'll be needing a phone number, if you have one. And when are you coming back? The news says flights are starting up again soon, and continuity is important for the residents.'

Mallory took a breath. 'The thing is, I'm in New York now. And this family situation isn't resolved yet. There's a problem with my son's passport.'

'Are you going to ask me about an advance?'

'No, no,' Mallory stammered. 'But there is a problem with my account too. You see . . . my husband froze it.'

'I see,' said Mrs Crawley slowly, no doubt fast reassessing all the happy-family assurances Mallory had given her in the promotional interview.

'He's also the problem with my son's passport,' Mallory said.

Mrs Crawley clucked her tongue. 'Men. Have you got a new one?'

Mallory glanced at AJ, who was furiously texting over by the window, his body leaning against the frame, legs reaching halfway up the shutters.

'Account number first, please,' Mrs Crawley said briskly.

That was when Mallory realised Mrs Crawley meant a new bank account and not a new man.

'I expect you not to mention this to any other staff, but I'll re-transfer your last pay immediately,' Mrs Crawley said. 'We can work out any overpayment later. You've always been reliable, and you can't be in a foreign country with no bank balance.'

Mallory sat a moment in stunned silence after she put down the phone. It was reassuring to know she would have some funds coming to her new account. Who knew that Mrs Crawley had such compassion?

AJ slid his phone into his pocket and picked up his jacket, shrugging it on. 'Liv's taking a train in an hour. She'll call Duncan's lawyers and ensure any communication goes through her. I'll meet her at the station and bring her here so you can meet.'

'Okay,' Mallory said.

'After that, I'm heading upstate. Check out Jock's home town, see if there's anyone who knew him. Be back day after tomorrow, I guess.'

'You're going to ride all that way?' *You're leaving now?*

'I thought I'd give you some space,' he said. 'Let you focus.'

Mallory realised in that moment that they had reached a fork in the road, where each of them went in a different direction. She couldn't argue; in a way, it was what she wanted. She didn't know how long the situation with Duncan and Harry would drag on, and neither she nor AJ was able to make promises. Yet however true that was, she couldn't help the sadness of knowing she was losing his companionship.

'Thank you for everything. I can't tell you how much it's meant.' *How much you've meant.*

'Well, I'm glad I didn't leave you on the side of the road either,' he said with a smile.

She tried to laugh, but her voice choked. 'I'll always remember you.'

He put his arms around her, dropping his lips to her hair. 'Easy there. I'm not gone yet.'

She shook her head. 'But this can't really go anywhere. You're working out your life too. I don't even know if I can go back home. Even if I do, we'll be an ocean apart. I can't make promises.'

'I wouldn't ask you to,' he said softly. 'But I'll never forget you either.'

Their embrace lasted a long minute, a final acknowledgement of the unwanted but necessary ending.

Mallory was the one who pulled away. 'I have to pick up Harry soon.'

AJ nodded. 'I'll still see you tonight, when I come with Liv.'

If only the simple joy of having her son back in her life didn't come with the black cloud of uncertainty. Mallory's optimistic nature counted on tomorrow's meeting resolving all the problems, but for the first time, she wasn't sure. Life had a habit of being more complicated.

She sighed. Speaking of complications, she steeled herself to call Ernie.

Chapter 21

LIVIA WAS THE SORT OF PERSON THAT MALLORY ADMIRED in an utterly unenvious way, because she was so positive and helpful. Mallory was energised in her presence, as if Livia echoed the way Mallory saw the world, only she had a law degree from Stanford and not a certificate II from Bayside TAFE.

At five-foot-two with long, glossy black hair, and in a sophisticated slim-fitting blouse with pinstripe pants, Livia was a physical antithesis of AJ. In fact, if Livia hadn't had the same intense blue eyes as her brother, Mallory would have been convinced they were no relation at all.

She also seemed uncommonly sensitive to circumstances. By the time she arrived, Mallory was wrung out. After negotiating the subway system with Harry back from school and hearing all his questions – why wasn't she staying at the apartment with Daddy? Who was AJ? Who would be taking him to school tomorrow? – all Mallory wanted was an evening watching television with her little boy, and losing herself in the joy of having him with her again. Trying to forget about the problems until tomorrow. The last thing she wanted was a lawyer to remind her. Instead, when Mallory answered the door with Harry clinging to her leg, Livia simply introduced herself.

'You must be exhausted and you've absolutely enough to deal with tonight,' she said firmly. 'I'll come back tomorrow after school starts and we'll go through everything then. The meeting isn't until one. In the meantime, if you need anything, this is me.'

She handed over her card. AJ was standing in the hall, looking down at the floor with a small smile on his lips.

'I can't thank you enough,' Mallory said, grateful to tears. 'I thought AJ was joking when he said his sister was a lawyer.'

Livia had looked around at AJ then, a very sisterly assessing look that Mallory couldn't quite interpret. Then Livia gave Mallory a smile. 'We'll talk about *that* another time. Get some sleep, now, won't you?'

'I'll give you a ride,' AJ said to Livia, as she turned to go. 'I'm heading out of town.'

'On that noisy machine of yours again? No thank you. I'll take a cab, like a civilised person.'

AJ shot Mallory a smile. Then, as Livia disappeared around the corner, he paused and blew Mallory a kiss. On impulse, she put out a hand to catch it, and pressed it to her heart. He closed his eyes with a hand to his chest, before he turned and went. She stood in the doorway for five long seconds, wondering if she would ever see him again.

The next morning, the first thing Mallory saw was Harry, sleeping in the room's second bed. She lay very still, watching him, the same way she had checked he was still breathing as a baby. She began to think about how it could all go wrong from here, and had to clamp down on the thoughts before they could ruin the peace.

Dropping Harry at school was worse than it had been the day before, and then she had to negotiate the subway back to the hotel alone. Livia showed up ten minutes later, bearing two coffees and a slim laptop. They sat on the bed Harry had slept in nearest the window, and Mallory apologised about the lack of chairs.

'It doesn't worry me. A bit more comfortable than an office. Besides, this isn't stuff you want to be talking about in Starbucks.'

'Where do I even start?' Mallory asked, lost.

'At the very beginning.'

The morning flew by as Mallory went right through her relationship with Duncan, and everything that had happened in the past few weeks. Livia took notes on her laptop, nodding frequently, interrupting only to ask clarifications, her ankles crossed and her eyes never looking at the keys.

When they finally finished, Livia put her laptop aside. 'Okay. So let me ask you this: what do you want to happen here? What's the best-case scenario for you?'

'To have Harry's passport, and to go home.'

Livia waited. 'That's it? What about financial support?'

Mallory closed her eyes. 'I don't want to reach for things I didn't have before. Yes, it would be great if he came through after all the promises, but I just want to be on that plane home and to know this can't happen again. I can't even think about more than that right now.'

Livia nodded. 'Duncan's not in a legally strong position here, but what your lawyer said in Australia is true. If we have to go to court, it's going to get expensive very quickly. Let's hope he really is open to negotiating.'

Mallory bit her lip, and asked how much Livia's time would cost.

'Don't you worry about that.' She smiled. 'I shouldn't say this, but AJ must be fair in love with you. We've all been worried about him since Ty. He took it really hard, been unreachable out on that motorbike. Mom was convinced he was lying in a gutter somewhere. Let's just say we're all happy to hear from him. Seeing him with that smile on his face, well, that's a bonus better than any money. I think he's started on his healing road. So let's leave it at that.'

Mallory blushed and was struggling to convey that she and AJ weren't really anything to each other when Livia held up her hand. 'But let's not sway off topic. What we really must talk about is some techniques you might need. To prepare you for how this might play out. I don't think for a minute this is going to be easy.'

Mallory hunched around herself. The idea of negotiating with that new Duncan, the one she didn't really know, scared her. Despite her moment of clarity in his lobby, she really hadn't worked him out. She wanted to hide, but she'd lost the option to run away the moment Harry had entered the world.

'Okay,' she said with a deep breath. 'Where do we start?'

•

With Livia by her side, Mallory arrived at the downtown mediation centre feeling positive in a way she hadn't since the morning of her failed job interview. All she had to do was follow Livia's advice, and everything would turn out well. *Picture yourself being calm and unemotional about everything, no matter what he says. Stick to the facts. They're on your side here. If you're feeling overwhelmed, tell me and we can take a break.* Mallory repeated it under her breath. Please, let her collect Harry this afternoon with the news they were going home.

But when they entered the small meeting room just before one, it was empty except for the independent mediator, an older man with greying hair and a creased face. Mallory had met him briefly a half-hour before in a different room, when he'd introduced himself and run through what would happen. She had nodded along, trying to take it in, and wondering if Duncan was about to hear this same speech, or if he was already briefed and waiting. Now, after all the preparation, the one scenario she hadn't banked on was Duncan not turning up.

'We had confirmation,' Livia said. 'Let's just wait a while.'

Minutes ticked by until Mallory's calm transformed into jangling anticipation. She couldn't remember a word the mediator had said. Finally, after twenty-five minutes, Duncan appeared, wearing a charcoal suit but no tie, and in the process of ending a phone call.

'Sorry, urgent work call,' he said, sliding the mobile into his pocket.

Mallory looked around; she'd been expecting that he would bring his lawyer, too, the man with the commanding phone voice. The fact he'd come by himself should have been reassuring, but she felt as though she'd missed something important. Or that she was being unfair, somehow, in having Livia here.

The mediator began by reminding them both that they were here to reach an agreement if possible, and that he was impartial and would simply facilitate the discussion. Mallory was surprised to find herself angry at this short and very reasonable speech, as though they'd come to this discussion on an even footing, instead of her only being here at the end of a very long and ridiculous journey that Duncan had caused.

When Duncan leaned forward, almost eager, she couldn't help the resentment it stirred in her. They were on his home turf, even though he was the one who'd broken their agreement.

'I just want to take Harry home to Australia,' Mallory said, collecting herself when invited to speak. 'To do that, I need his passport. That's all I'm looking for.'

Duncan said nothing, and Mallory found herself elaborating.

'I mean, I've flown here and driven across the country all because Harry didn't come back when he was supposed to. If Duncan wants to change the arrangement, we can talk about that when we're all at home.'

She fell silent. She hadn't meant to say that much.

'I'm going to ask that you address each other rather than me,' the mediator said. He said it gently, but Mallory felt the burn of remonstration creep up the back of her neck.

Duncan cleared his throat. 'You really didn't have to do any of those things, Mal. Getting on a plane? Driving across the country? I didn't even know you'd left home.'

He sounded so reasonable, as if she had been completely crazy to do any of it. Rebuttals flew to Mallory's tongue. That he hadn't left her much of a choice, that he in fact *had* known, he must have. She only hesitated because she couldn't decide which one to start with.

In the silence, Duncan spread his hands. 'If I'd known how strongly you felt, we'd have had a conversation about it. You gave me the impression Harry staying here would make things better for you. Your showing up here yesterday was really unexpected, and disruptive to my business. That performance in my lobby created a lot of questions and embarrassment. And it's confusing for Harry.'

'How strongly I felt?' Her voice came out like an explosion. 'I'm his mother! How did you think I'd feel when you just decided to keep him here? When you told me not to call again? I tried to talk to you on Skype and you cut me off. Twice!'

Mallory knew that she shouldn't have become emotional, but the anger was shooting out of her like air from the neck of a loosed balloon.

'I didn't say anything of the sort,' Duncan lied calmly. 'I said you were free to call anytime, and to visit. I just didn't think you'd do it without telling me.'

'You said that in our first conversation. Later you said not to call again, even when Harry called *me*, obviously upset.' The flush was burning along her jaw and up her cheeks now, her eyes full of tears.

'This is exactly what I'm talking about,' Duncan said, still level. 'We had conversations and you never once told me that you were coming.'

Mallory paused, knowing he'd turned it all around on her. 'You told me not to call, so how could I? And what if you decided to, I don't know, take off?' Oh, she hadn't meant to say that.

Duncan's eyebrows shot up, his expression incredulous. 'Mal, my company is based here. Where else would I be?'

'But you weren't. You weren't at the address you gave me.' She was almost crying now.

'A change of postal address, an easy mistake. Look, Mal, I have to say I have had very real concerns about the pressure you've been under.'

'So you freeze my bank accounts? Is that how you help?'

'I did no such thing.'

'The bank told me you did. And I think you did it because you saw the flight booking.'

'That's fantastical speculation,' he said. 'But since you're raising the topic of money, I know how hard it's been for you, having to shuffle babysitters to make work shifts—'

'That's not a problem now Harry's in school. It wouldn't be a problem at all if you'd—'

'—and not being able to afford uniforms and school camps. It's in Harry's best interests to live here, where he can have access to an excellent school, and opportunities. I thought you agreed. And if necessary, I'm happy for a court to decide whether I'm right.'

'Do you need a minute?' Livia's hand on Mallory's arm was the only thing that prevented her outburst. She was afraid now, really afraid, because if Duncan was only interested in going to court, she didn't have the resources to pursue him.

Livia drew her across to the other side of the room and spoke in a low, calming voice. 'He's pushing your buttons,' she said. 'Stick to the facts. You can beat a pillow to death later with all the rage you're feeling. Think of him as a robot, if it helps, someone who isn't going to be swayed by how you feel because, odds are, that's true.'

Mallory closed her eyes. The mention of robots made her think of the conversation she'd had with AJ about Sarah

Connor, and him calling her a warrior mother. She could almost hear the gentle hum of the insects by the Arkansas River. Then she thought of Jock, reassuring her as the night slipped past them on that long drive to Arlington. She was here because of how they'd helped her. They'd believed in her. She had to be smarter about this, honour the things they'd done.

'I'm just going to go to the bathroom,' she said, and slipped out of the room. She spent five long minutes, sitting on the toilet lid, thinking about Duncan, about Harry and about Jock. She could see him, as he'd been with her outside the gates of Arlington, offering to help.

Saying that sometimes you have to give the other person what they want, even if it kills you.

All Mallory had ever wanted was for her family to be together. But she and Duncan weren't the same. So, what did he want? Maybe this was all about ego, paying homage to his new status as a success.

When she came back, she took her seat, and a deep breath. 'Okay, where were we?'

'I don't know if we even need to do this,' Duncan said, leaning back to button his jacket. 'If we can't talk like adults I think it's best if we let a judge decide. Otherwise, we're just wasting our time.'

Mallory looked him over. With his charcoal suit, his fingers resting on the chrome arms of the chair, he convinced her he was a shrewd businessman. He could have walked onto a movie set and played the part. Such a long, long way from the scruffy, flannel-wearing computer guy with big aspirations she'd first fallen in love with. Something in her would always love the man she'd thought he was, would admire the idea of him as a persistent and determined person pursuing his dream. But that wasn't the man before her. He'd forced her into the most desperate fight of her life. That should have counted for something, but Livia was right: he didn't care about those feelings. So Mallory tried something new.

'Duncan,' she said, keeping her voice level, 'you're a wonderful father to Harry. He adores you. I know that you wouldn't want to see him put through the stress of court any more than I would. So I think we should try to work things out here.'

After a pause, Duncan said, 'I guess we can try.'

'I know that you miss Harry,' she said. 'And you have his best interests at heart when you want him to live here with you. I know how much you regretted your own school experience, not having opportunities you wanted, and you don't want him to have to go through the same things.'

Duncan was quiet now, watching her, though Mallory couldn't tell what he was thinking. Jock had been right: it was killing her to say these things. Killing her to ignore the unfairness of what he'd done.

'My job is in Australia,' she went on. 'I love my work, and I want to go back to it. If Harry and I go home, I'd be happy to talk about him coming here regularly.' She paused and took a breath, feeling like she was stepping off a crumbling cliff. 'Or, I'm not against moving here.'

That earned a reaction. Duncan's lips parted as if he needed to make an urgent point, but no words came out. Instead, he laughed. 'Move here? Mal, be serious.'

'I am,' she said. 'You want to see Harry, and he'd be right here with me. I know it's not the Bayside with all the wild areas and the beaches and creeks, but I hear Central Park is pretty amazing.'

'But you wouldn't be able to work here,' Duncan said, leaning forward, spreading his hands as if this was an impossible proposition. 'You wouldn't be able to afford it.'

'Well, I guess we'd have to discuss those arrangements. I'm sure that with your company doing so well, Harry and I could afford to live here.'

Duncan sat back again. Mallory's heart was thumping in her chest. Moving here was absolutely not what she wanted to do. She didn't want to leave the little cottage, didn't want to leave the work she'd been doing in Australia and move to a strange city. New York dwarfed her, full of power and money she couldn't even fathom. But she would do it for Harry.

'I thought this wasn't about money,' Duncan said tightly. 'You started off saying this was just about going home. Now, of course, you're looking for how much you can get from me.'

Mallory shook her head. 'No, but eventually we'll have to sort that out. I was happy to support you when you were developing—' She cut herself off and started again. 'Look, this is about Harry.'

Duncan's jaw was working now, chewing while his mind processed what she'd said. He hadn't anticipated this, Mallory realised. He had never thought she would make this offer.

'What do you think, Mr Cook?' the mediator asked.

For a bare second, Mallory thought he would agree.

Then Duncan sighed, and pushed back his chair. 'I'm sorry, Mal, but that just won't work for me. I'm happy for you to visit with sufficient notice. Harry can stay with you while you're here, but when you fly home, he stays. He's settled in his school now, and that's best for everyone.'

'He has friends at his school in Brisbane,' she said, scrambling. 'He told me he misses them. He's only been here three weeks.'

The edge of Duncan's eyebrow flickered. 'Why don't we ask him?' he said lightly, leaning his hands on the table but not sitting down again. 'If he wants to go back to Australia with you, fine. If not, I'll pay for your ticket and for visits twice a year. That's fair.'

Mallory took a breath. She'd nearly fallen for it. 'Duncan, he's *five*. He can't decide what pair of pants he wants to wear in the morning. It's not fair to ask him to make a decision like that. I know that we can work this out between us. We worked out how to raise him when I was working nights and you were trying to start up your business. We can do this. Together.'

Saying those words after everything he'd done was like swallowing glass, but she made herself do it. If this really was an ego trip, then she'd make him feel however he needed to for him to cede some ground.

And for another second, Duncan looked as though he was considering it. Then his lips compressed.

'Mal,' he said, 'I didn't want to do this today, but I don't think that it will come as a surprise. I want a divorce.'

Mallory had a sudden sensation of falling. She hardly heard as Duncan apologised, saying he had another meeting to go to, and that he wanted any further discussion to be through his lawyer.

'We'll just have to look at other avenues,' Livia said, when they were outside again, sun shining on the dour mood.

'Which means court.'

'Yes. He doesn't have a leg to stand on, but he's going to make you work for it.'

Mallory felt sick. She'd failed: not only failed Harry, but failed Jock and AJ's faith in her too. Meanwhile, Duncan was off working towards business awards and new contracts.

'There's no justice,' Livia said. 'I'll have to call some people, put together some numbers for you.'

Mallory nodded, but she wasn't thinking about court, or going home, or any of that. She was thinking about how, for just a moment, she thought she'd understood Duncan, and how wrong she'd been.

•

The afternoon raced away, filled with finding a park for Harry to play in, and then searching for a laundromat for the subsequently grass- and dirt-stained trousers. When she and Harry returned, the hotel reception called out that she had two messages waiting. She glanced at the paper slips: both from Ernie. They must be about the funeral. Yesterday, Belle had been the one who picked up the call, and Mallory had been relieved to avoid speaking with Ernie himself. After the day's events, he'd been the last person she wanted to talk to.

When she swiped her door key, the room phone began ringing. 'Hello?'

'Mallory.'

Her stomach dived at the gruff voice. Ernie, too persistent on his own agenda to give her time to call him back. She sank down onto the edge of the bed. 'Yes?'

'I needed to speak with you,' he said stiffly. 'It's Zadie. She isn't doing so well.'

Mallory felt a pang. 'She's sick?'

'No, but she's . . . not the same after you left.' Ernie fell silent, as if he expected her to respond. Or perhaps he was just choking on his words after what he'd said in Memphis.

'I didn't realise how it would affect her,' he went on finally. 'Belle is very competent, but she hasn't the same bond with Zade.'

'I'm sorry to hear that.' Mallory rubbed her palm over her forehead. After the events of the past days, she had no energy left for this. 'Do you want me to talk to her on the phone?'

'No, no.' A pause. 'She's resting now, and I didn't want to raise her hopes if she knew I was calling you.'

'What were you hoping for, then?' Mallory's voice was flat. 'Because after I offered my husband everything he said he wanted, he just asked me for a divorce, so I'm fairly preoccupied with other things at the moment.'

'I'm sorry for your troubles,' Ernie said.

'I'm sure.' Mallory thought about hanging up on him.

'You might not think I'm sincere, but it was not my intention to make it harder for you to continue your journey. Jock sent a message about you having to change the payment, and the difficulty in hiring the car. Fair tore a strip off me over it. I didn't realise how much you'd be inconvenienced.'

'The money was stolen in Washington, so it wasn't like I had it for long,' Mallory said, feeling tired and over it. The particulars of their argument seemed months ago, even as the resentment lingered. She picked at a thread on the bed cover. 'But I'm in New York anyway now, so I don't want to go over this again.'

'All right,' he said. 'I wanted you to know that I've called Silky Oaks. I've reassured them about when we're coming back. I've made sure they know you did an excellent job in helping us out of a bind, and your discretion at my request. I've taken complete responsibility.'

'I appreciate that,' Mallory said, thinking it would have been a scene to witness: Ernie and Mrs Crawley going head to head.

'The thing is, it would mean a great deal to Zadie if you came to the wedding. We've moved it to next Wednesday, when the chapel was free. And, you know, for my eye to finish healing. There isn't really anyone coming.'

Mallory sighed. 'We have Jock's funeral on Saturday. And I have Harry to think about. My situation here is difficult enough.'

'Well, bring him along,' Ernie said quickly. 'He could be a page boy. We won't be able to come up to Jock's funeral, however much I want to. I don't think I should put Zadie through another trip at the moment. I'll pay for you both to come.'

'That's a nice offer—'

'I should, anyway. When we made the agreement with Fiona, it was for more than I gave you. I want to be honest about that.'

Mallory frowned, marvelling at what had brought on such a burst of disclosure. He really did sound like a different person, but she remembered the difficulties he'd caused. If she was ever going to protect herself, it was now.

'I'm sorry, Ernie, I can't. There's just too much happening here. I wish you and Zadie well.'

'Think about it?' he pleaded, as she put down the phone. 'For Zadie?'

Chapter 22

MALLORY TRIED VERY HARD NOT TO THINK ABOUT ERNIE'S call through the next day. She didn't like imagining Zadie unhappy; it reminded her too much of working at Silky Oaks, when a resident desperately wanted something that she couldn't give them. She had to remind herself that Harry was her priority. She could only spread herself so thin.

Returning from the Thursday school run – already an alarming kind of new normal – she was just putting her bag down when her mobile pinged. Her heart gave an unpleasant jump: would it be lawyers again, or the school? Or Ernie?

Instead, she found a text from AJ.

Back in town.

She stood there, staring at the message, wondering if she should even answer it. Was he just letting her know out of courtesy? Hadn't they, just two nights ago, acknowledged that whatever was between them wasn't to be?

How are you? she sent back, her chest teeming with butterflies.

Tired. Filthy, came the response. *Need shower and bed. Didn't sleep much last night.*

Mallory smiled, despite the tiny flips of disappointment as all the butterflies in her chest crashed to earth. He must be going back to whichever mate's place he'd crashed at. *Sleep well then*, she wrote.

Can I come up instead?

The chest flip became a full skydive. Her fingers hovered over the screen, trembling. *No*, she should write. *No, that wasn't what we agreed.*

Before she could write anything, he wrote again. *I know what we said before I left but I want to see you again, even if it's the last time. Or say the word and I'm gone.*

Mallory's finger hovered over the screen, knowing this might not be wise. But she wanted to hear about where he'd been, to have him put his arm around her, to lose herself in the way she felt about him, even if it never happened again.

When she threw open the door, he was still in his black jeans and leather jacket, his hair crushed from his helmet. Dark flecks of grease, bugs, mud and goodness knows what else were caught in the stubble on his cheeks. He smelled like a boys' locker room. Somehow, he was still the most attractive thing she'd ever found on her doorstep.

'How did it go?' she asked, trying to temper herself.

AJ didn't seem in the mood for talking. He reached a hand for her waist, pulled her to him, and rested a kiss on the top of her head, as if he'd been riding for hours just for this moment. Mallory leaned her head against him, closing her eyes to fully absorb the warmth of his touch.

'I'll tell you all about it,' he said, pulling back so he could step inside the door. 'After you tell me about your meeting.'

'Still no passport. And he asked me for a divorce,' she said with a helpless shrug.

AJ scanned her face. 'How you dealin' with that?'

'I feel as if I should have seen it coming. It's the master-stroke, really, isn't it? When he sees that none of the usual tactics are working, he goes for the one thing that might be enough to take my knees out.'

'And was it?'

Mallory closed her eyes. 'Let's not talk about it, all right?'

'Sure.' AJ paused. 'Did he say why he did it?'

'I'm not sure I'll ever really know. But when he gets an idea in his head, he's tenacious about it. He's always been that way – wanting to be a high-flyer. He probably does believe that Harry will be better off here. When I see that fancy school, I can *almost* see what he's thinking. It's driving me a bit nuts.'

'Then maybe you could use these.' AJ dug in his jacket. 'I figured it would be either celebration, or commiseration.'

He pulled out two DVDs.

Mallory laughed. '*The Terminator*, and *Terminator 2*? I told you, I don't like scary movies.'

'After the last week, you won't find these scary. Can I take a shower? I smell like last-week's garbage and I've got half the road on my face. Unless,' he added, 'you want me to leave.'

'No,' she said quickly, and thought she saw him grin as he headed for the bathroom.

She tried not to think about him behind that thin wooden door, peeling off his clothes and starting up a spray of hot water. When he'd kissed her, he'd planted some visceral memory of the feel of his muscle under her hands. She tried to make the idea of him in her bathroom less sexy. He was probably having to duck because of the ridiculously low shower head. But then the idea of him cursing in that low, dangerous voice just made her thighs all liquid. She looked around helplessly for distraction, and her eyes landed on the bath towels, still arranged artfully with a face washer and wrapped soap at the end of the bed.

She tapped on the bathroom door, her heart thumping against her breastbone. 'AJ. Do you, um, need a towel?' *What a lame excuse.*

No answer. He probably couldn't hear over the water.

She raised her voice. 'AJ?'

'What?'

'Do you need a towel?'

A beat of silence. 'Not sure.'

'You're not sure?'

She heard him laugh. 'Come in. You'll see.'

Mallory tried the handle and cracked the door open, the thumping in her chest now rivalling the Rocket for volume. Inside, the air was thick with steam. It hung in a dense white cloud all the way to the bottom of the mirror. No wonder he wasn't sure. She could barely see the outline of him behind the glass. A warm brown suggestion of flesh. But she could tell from the width of the blurred torso, and the angle of his head, that he was looking at her.

'Well, don't be shy now,' he said.

Mallory stood gripping the edge of the door, a last lifeline. The thick air settled wetly against her skin. 'Don't you use the cold tap?'

'I like it hot. Are you bringing me the towel?'

'I don't have it. It's still on the bed.'

He chuckled. 'Are you bringing me *you*, then?'

Mallory let go of the door.

Later, she lay in the crook of his arm on the couch as the last credits of *The Terminator* rolled across the screen, swiping at the tears on her cheeks.

'Told you,' AJ said, softly by her ear. 'Love story.'

'That's so horrible. He can't die at the end. Why on earth did you think this would make me feel better?' She sniffed, turning over to face him.

His expression was compassionate. 'Yeah, I know. But that's the story. You don't always end up with the father of your child.'

'That's the lesson, huh?'

'Too soon?'

Mallory sighed.

AJ extracted his arm from around her and sat up. 'I didn't find anyone.'

'Sorry?'

'In Jock's home town. I asked around everywhere. Lots of people knew his mother, but she passed a couple of years back. Found some distant relations, but they didn't know him.'

'None of them would come to the funeral?'

'One couple would have, who remembered Jock and his brother growing up, but they are both in their nineties. Wasn't going to happen. But I did find the house.'

Mallory sat up to look as AJ opened the pictures on his phone. Even on the small screen, the beauty of the place came through: under clear blue skies was a shining grass field around a painted white cottage, neat as a dollhouse, a grove of apple trees running into the distance. Other pictures showed sheds, an overgrown back pasture, and old chicken coop.

'It's beautiful,' Mallory said, flipping back over the pictures, bittersweet. 'I wonder what will happen to it now. I can't believe he didn't make it after waiting all those years.'

The pain of Jock's unfulfilled quest, without Harry here to comfort her, stopped her breath. AJ pulled her to him.

'I know. I called my mom twice from the side of the highway. I think she thought I'd hit my head. She kept asking what had happened. Maybe that's her now,' he said, pulling his vibrating phone from his pocket. 'Nope, it's Zak.'

He got up to answer the call, and Mallory stretched, and straightened the cushions. AJ wasn't saying much in the conversation. Lots of 'uh-huh', and 'yeah'.

'What?' Mallory asked when he hung up. 'You don't look happy.'

'This is just my thinkin' face,' AJ said. Then, 'Do you want the tape from Duncan's foyer?'

'What tape?'

'Security footage, from the day you went to his office. There's two cameras in there, and they show everything that happened. You, him trying to move you on, and Harry. Zak says it's quite touching. And quite clear about what Duncan was trying to pull.'

Mallory frowned. 'Why does Zak know anything about it?'

'Like I said, lots of the old crew went into security. They know each other. Wouldn't have been hard to find the man who works there. Zak can get you the tape.'

'Why would I want it?' AJ hesitated, long enough for Mallory to put together what he was thinking. She wrinkled her nose. 'You're suggesting I blackmail him.'

'I'm not suggesting anything. And I don't particularly believe it's a good idea. But maybe you want that tape anyway. Ask Liv, at least. See if she thinks she can use it.'

Mallory made a non-committal noise. She was weary with not knowing how the legal situation would play out. She didn't know whether to be comforted or unnerved by AJ's network of friends. If only they could help with extracting a passport. But while men in leather jackets had worked in scaring her parents, Mallory knew Duncan would be immune to such threats, and she would never want to play those games anyway.

'Am I going to meet this mysterious Zak?' she said finally. 'It feels weird him going to all this effort on my behalf.'

'He owed me a favour.'

'I'll have to send him something nice. What does he like?' she asked.

'Irish whiskey or old Hollywood movies, take your pick.'

She laughed, slightly cheered.

'Speaking of which, Sarah's all alone now,' AJ said, shaking the second DVD box. 'Don't you want to see what happens next?'

'I kind of do,' Mallory admitted. 'Does it involve explosions?'

'Does it ever.'

'Happy ending?'

AJ hesitated. 'Happy for her, I guess.'

'I'll take that,' Mallory said, leaning into him again and trying to take this momentary pleasure for what it was. It wasn't like every day an attractive man turned up to use her shower. She didn't want to think about what happened next, how many more nights the limbo might drag on for, and when life would return to normal again. She would take normal over anything in the past two weeks . . . except maybe for AJ. Her heart twinged whenever she thought about how impossible it was that anything could happen with him, how they both knew it.

These hours with him were a bubble, a thin perfection that wasn't meant to last. So she held herself in the moment: the smell of him, clean soap and warm skin, the solid comfort of his body next to hers. The way that smile of his went all the way through her body and turned her inside out. Someday soon, when they were oceans apart and she was back in the tumbledown cottage, she was going to need these memories of him.

When the movie reached the part where Sarah was escaping the asylum, Mallory pondered the security footage on-screen. Thinking. When the film ended, she turned off the credits and sat up.

'She's quite relentless, isn't she?' Mallory said.

'Sarah Connor? Yeah, she sure is committed. Has to be, against the machines.'

Mallory sat there, thinking through all the things that she'd read about Duncan since Harry had failed to come home. The award he was nominated for, all the little references he'd made over the years to his aspirations, his ambitions, his politics. She saw him now with an uncommon clarity: he *was* the same man that she'd always known. A driven, self-assured man who had to win. Success hadn't changed him, it had just put him in a different league. Nothing that she said to inflate his ego would sway him if it meant he had to give in, to return Harry's passport.

So what the hell could she do about it?

'Would you give me Zak's number?' she said. 'I'd like to speak to him in person about that tape.'

'Sure.' AJ flipped through his phone.

'And I'll need the address for Duncan's apartment, the real one.'

AJ paused. 'Are you sure that's a good idea?'

Mallory laughed. 'No, probably not. But I can't sit here hoping. I have to do something.'

'You want me to come with you?'

'Did you see Sarah Connor needing a man?' she said, nervous at the very idea of what she planned to do.

AJ raised an eyebrow. 'Well,' he said slowly, 'lookee what monster I've made here.'

•

She waited until evening, when she could be reasonably sure Duncan would be home. He'd always been the type to work late. Maria agreed to come and sit with Harry, and Mallory told them both she just had to pop out for an hour.

She left them watching a classic re-run of *The Sound of Music* and walked to the nearest subway station, nerves beating a tattoo in the pit of her stomach. She'd been in New York for less than a week, and already it felt like a year. It couldn't become an actual year, so she had to do this.

The address was right uptown, on the edge of Central Park, in a building that loomed over her, thrusting out its stairway and double doors in sleek grey stone. She stepped up to the security point and pressed the apartment button.

After a very long pause, the speaker crackled. 'Mal?' Duncan said, sounding surprised.

Mallory looked up. There must be a camera somewhere. 'Yes. Hi,' she said. 'Can I talk to you?'

Another long pause. 'Come up,' he said finally. 'I'll authorise the lift.' The door buzzed.

The elevator was a fancy affair without any buttons, just a panel in the lobby for a key card. The doors opened for her anyway. Mallory began to feel sick as the lift took her up and up to the fifteenth floor. She was only too aware of what she was up against. And if she failed, she might be calling this city home for a very long time.

The doors opened into a hallway of plush cream carpet. Duncan was waiting in the open door of the apartment, still in his work suit, though he'd loosened his tie and shed his jacket. Mallory swallowed.

'Mal.' He appraised her warily. 'Harry's not with you?'

She shook her head. 'I'm here to talk, without the lawyers. Can I come in?'

He stood aside and she stepped past him, and into apartment Nirvana.

'Wow.' She couldn't help the exclamation. Down a short hall, the broad expanse of living space opened luxuriously onto floor-to-ceiling windows, framing the night-time city, glittering with lights. A pale leather couch at one end of the room complemented a floor rug, like a sophisticated Zen garden.

'You like it, huh?' He'd followed her in, skirting round to her right, where a sleek modern kitchen opened off the living space. Perfectly at home.

'Impressive,' she said slowly, hating herself for saying it. She felt so tiny amid all this display, but at least she understood what all this was about now. It was the apartment of a winner. Of someone who liked to display his power.

'Drink?' he offered.

She shook her head. 'No thanks. I'll keep this short.'

'Okay. So, you changed your mind?'

Mallory, for a moment, couldn't work out what he meant. 'About what?'

'About Harry staying here. I meant what I said today about going to court. It's not personal, Mal. I want what's best for Harry.'

Mallory sucked in a breath, keeping her temper in check. 'I'd think of it more as a change of tack.' She turned away from the view. 'You know, this apartment really is impressive. I only think I've appreciated these last few days how much this kind of life is what you really wanted.'

'Who wouldn't want it?' he said, pride creeping into his voice. 'Long way from a broken-down cottage in Australia.' He cut himself off, as if realising how tactless he was being.

'Where we lived, you mean,' she said, realising now the extent of his ambition to leave the life they'd had behind.

'I didn't mean it that way,' he said quickly.

'Maybe not. But you did mean what you did with Harry. I believe that you think he'll have a better life here. That he wouldn't have to deal with all the problems you had to deal with growing up. The thing is, I don't think you've thought it through in the long-term.'

'You know me better than that. I have every option thought of for him.'

'I didn't mean for Harry,' she said. 'I meant for you.'

Here it was, she thought. This was the moment she had to gamble on how much she really did know him. That success hadn't changed him, not really. When they'd been together, his power over her had been love, and she'd willingly allowed him to use it, so that they always did what he wanted, to move him closer to where he was now. Now that she no longer loved him, he was using his money and his position instead. Her gamble rested on how high he really wanted to reach.

'You see, I'm not going anywhere, Duncan,' she said. 'I'm going to stay here until I have Harry's passport. I meant what I said, too.'

Duncan sighed heavily. 'Why make this messy? Court is going to bankrupt you.'

'I'm not talking about court.'

He frowned for the first time, as if he'd missed something. Mallory took a breath. 'If you want to hold Harry's passport, and play hard, then I'll be outside your office every day, telling anyone who'll listen about what you did.' Duncan straightened, defensive with his arms crossed over his chest, but Mallory went on. 'I'll tell any journalist, any blogger. I'll start Facebook campaigns. I'll find whoever you're doing business with, and they'll know about how your wife supported your dreams for years, working while you built the business, enabling you to move to New York. How you then left. How you took her son without her agreement, froze her accounts, and after the lengths she went to come here, you're still holding on to his passport and threatening to take this through the courts.'

'You wouldn't do that, Mal, it's not your style,' Duncan said unsteadily. 'Besides, sounds like an unbelievable tale to me.'

'The tape is pretty believable.'

'What tape?'

'From your office lobby. Plus, there's a number of concerned bystanders who remember what happened.'

Mallory had found Zak amazingly helpful and extraordinarily well connected. Within a couple of hours, he'd located a number of people who worked at Duncan's office building and who remembered Duncan trying to hustle out his own wife, and the reunion with Harry.

'I didn't want to have to do this,' Mallory went on. 'You're right – it's not my style. But you changed me the moment you took Harry.'

Duncan scowled. 'You can't stay forever. You'll just end up deported. This is a no-win move.'

'Maybe,' Mallory said. 'But I've been doing some reading about the April Roundtable, that award you're up for. They're a pretty conservative group. And I know how much you enjoy politics. I think you want to run for office. Maybe not soon, but one day. How do you think it will go down that you did this to me and Harry? I make enough noise, it's always going to be on your record. Easily discoverable. It'll never go away for you. Your company can be the best in the world, but you'll still be the man who left your wife and then abducted her son. All because you have to win this fight with me.'

Mallory rubbed a hand over her forehead, wrung out. 'Now, Harry and I are taking the train down to a funeral at Arlington on Saturday. I won't do anything until that's over. But come Monday, I'll be making calls.'

Duncan's jaw was working, not finding any words to come back at her with.

'I'm going now. I'll show myself out.'

She was nearly to the front door, feeling him shadowing her steps, when he said, 'What's the deal with that biker guy?'

'None of your business.' Mallory kept walking.

'It absolutely is my business. If you're still insisting that Harry—'

Mallory faced him. In that moment, she remembered again Jock sitting in the car beside her, telling her that he would back her up, help her to stay calm. She sent a prayer of thanks for the strength the memory gave her. She kept her voice level. 'Duncan, I supported us all for years, until you walked out. You took Harry away, and made it as hard as possible for me to find you. You're not entitled to opinions about someone who helped me out.'

She felt strong now, strong enough to acknowledge how absurd all this had been.

'Guess you got lucky with the whole ash cloud thing,' she said. 'Unless you were making sacrifices to some volcano god.'

His face was the colour of ash. She'd loved that face, once. She knew all its tics, the way he pushed his tongue around over the top of his teeth when he was thinking hard at his computer. She knew now that he was angry, and cornered.

'I don't think this is funny,' he said.

'Maybe you should try driving across the country. That was pretty funny. But don't think for a moment that I'm bluffing. I'd die for Harry. Giving you some bad press will be a walk in the park, and no one's going to think you're the good guy here. You want to win this one? You give him his passport back.'

She walked away, making it down the space-age elevator and into the street before her legs gave out. She had to sit down for five whole minutes, more nerves than woman, sick right past her stomach and to her ankles. She had no idea if it would work.

Chapter 23

Jock's funeral, two days later, took place under open blue skies, the crisp spring wind mellowing towards summer, and the grass of Arlington a brilliant green. They met in the administration building, a tiny party of three: AJ, Mallory and Harry, who was bug-eyed and full of questions.

The casket team were six smartly dressed soldiers in blue, who slid Jock's flag-draped casket from the hearse and onto the caisson. Two black horses pulled it away, and Mallory took Harry's hand and fell into step behind, AJ beside her.

She glanced back and saw a large group of men pouring from the administration building, no doubt heading to some other, larger funeral. Tears stung her eyes, and she sniffed, holding Jock in her heart. She'd only known him a week, but she wished there were more people to remember him. Then AJ caught her hand and squeezed, and she looked back again to see the men following in a long column, four-abreast, that didn't seem to end. Some wore suits and others had leather vests over their shirts, long wiry beards and bald heads. But they marched in proud silence, many with medals on their chests.

'Who are they, Mummy?' Harry whispered.

'I don't know, baby.'

'I made some calls,' AJ said, keeping his attention on the caisson in front.

The echo of all their footsteps carried Mallory to the graveside, where she stood with her hand in Harry's, while AJ and the other men held salutes as the casket was lowered. She didn't take in anything the priest said; she focused on the corner of the flag lifting in the breeze, and remembered the kindnesses Jock had shown her.

A rifle volley cracked the air. Tears slipped down her cheeks as the bugler played 'Taps', and Harry squeezed her hand and leaned his head against her leg.

Mallory accepted the folded flag and the condolences on behalf of Jock's absent family, and then the service was suddenly over. She found herself surrounded by the men who had followed, who turned out to be from veterans' groups and motorcycle clubs, many of whom had been to Vietnam or Iraq or Afghanistan, and would remember a fellow soldier when there was no one else to do it.

Harry was fascinated, asking about the medals they wore, and the casket team, and the caisson, and the horses, and why the flag was folded like that, and a dozen other questions. Mallory answered where she could, watching him with relief and pride. She'd been concerned that he would be troubled by the funeral, but he seemed to accept the process better than she had. She resolved not to make taboos, and tried to be matter-of-fact. Yes, Jock was someone she'd known who had died. He'd died because he had a heart attack. That was something that could happen to people when they got older. Harry frowned at this, and she caught him looking between her and the older men who'd attended the funeral. 'Will any of them have heart attacks?' he asked. All she could say was that she didn't know, but that everyone died, eventually, but usually not for many years.

And just when Mallory thought they were about to go down the rabbit hole of death and whys, Harry asked AJ if he could ride the Rocket when they returned to New York.

'Kid's got good taste,' AJ said as they walked back to the administration building.

'Please don't encourage him onto dangerous machines this early,' she said, but now she was thinking about AJ and Jock. Jock's grief had been a burden, a binding chain of survivor's guilt. AJ was still dealing with his loss, but it seemed his grief might take a more easily carried form. Perhaps it was because he had his family; perhaps it was just the person he was.

'Disapproval makes danger more alluring,' AJ said. 'Now, how about pancakes before we head anywhere?'

'Yeah!' Harry cheered, then remembered he was supposed to be quiet and respectful. He tempered his enthusiasm to a more modest *yes* under his breath, accentuated with a fist pump, like a victorious tennis player.

Mallory was about to give AJ a good-natured scolding when a staff member approached and asked if she was Mallory Cook, and told her that someone was waiting for her in the visitor centre. Mallory, thinking that there must be some point of administration she'd missed, pulled up short when she saw Duncan standing by an alcove of plush seats, his hands in his trouser pockets, his suit jacket wrinkled up behind his wrists.

'Dad!' Harry said, running over with an exuberant welcome. 'Are you coming for pancakes too?'

'Pancakes, huh?' Duncan caught him up in a bear hug.

Mallory approached, a tight band of trepidation across her chest. This had to be about what she'd said the other night. She sensed AJ dropping back to give her space.

'How was the funeral?' Duncan said, in a surprisingly conciliatory voice. Or maybe that was just how voices disappeared in this room, with its ornate columns and vaulted glass ceiling.

'There were horses, Dad,' Harry put in. 'And a kay-sun.' He pronounced the syllables broadly and carefully.

'Sad,' Mallory said, bending to kiss Harry's head, to cover her nerves. 'But not as sad as I expected.'

Duncan nodded slowly, searching her face. Mallory wondered if he could see how hard her heart was beating.

'You didn't come down specially?' she asked, trying to keep her voice neutral.

'I had a meeting in Washington moved up at short notice. Possible government contract. Big deal. Wasn't hard to come across the river.'

He looked down at his feet, as if he were trying to decide something. 'I thought about what you said.' He sounded as though they'd discussed the colour scheme for a new kitchen, or which restaurant would host his Christmas party. But then he squinted off to the side, in a look Mallory knew: he didn't really want to say this. 'Were you serious about Harry visiting?' he said.

'You mean . . . if we went home?' She held her breath.

'It wasn't just something you said in the meeting?'

'I meant it,' she said quickly. 'However I feel, he's missed you. He needs his father too.'

'But you won't let him live here.'

'Only if I can, too,' she said, hiding her frustration.

Duncan sighed, and dug a hand in his pocket. 'Here.'

He held out a small blue booklet.

'What's that?' Harry's voice made Mallory jump. She hadn't even heard him come back, too surprised by Duncan holding out Harry's passport.

'Take it,' he said, impatient.

Her fingers slipped over the cool textured cover, over the Australian coat of arms printed in silver.

'Can I see?' Harry asked.

Mallory handed it to him and he spun the pages, opening it out on the information panel with his photo. Harry then asked if he could show AJ, and Mallory watched him bolt away, brimming with life and unencumbered with doubts or responsibilities. She looked back at Duncan.

'I want him coming here regularly,' Duncan said. 'At least two trips a year. Maybe more.'

'As long as it doesn't disrupt his school, he can come as often as he wants. But I'll be coming with him. Or you can visit us.'

'I have a business to run,' he said, then, 'Yeah, okay. Maybe sometimes.'

Mallory scratched at her eyebrow. She had a sense that the whole chapter of her life with Duncan was writing its last page. She supposed this victory should be satisfying, in some way. But it wasn't. She felt like the host at the end of a big party: exhausted, and still with a hell of a mess to clean up.

'He's a good kid,' she said, looking over to where Harry was still proudly showing off the passport.

'Yeah, he is,' Duncan admitted.

Mallory snuck a glance at him, and caught that proud gleam of parental joy in his eyes. She bit her tongue to resist saying anything more, anything that sounded like reminiscing. They might say the same words they'd once said, but their love for Harry was independent of each other now. The realisation brought an immense sadness.

'Flights are more or less back to normal. Clearing a backlog, of course, but it's not crazy like it was,' Duncan said, then dropped his voice. 'I'll need your word that what you said the other night won't be repeated.'

'Not by me,' she said. 'I don't have any control over other people. That's out of my hands.'

He compressed his lips. 'Set up a time on Monday at the office. I'll muster the suits and we'll talk about how things go from here. If you do that, I'll give you the fare back home.'

'Just the fare?'

'We'll talk,' he said. 'Harry?'

Harry disconnected himself from AJ, who'd crouched to point out something in one of the glass cabinets.

'I've gotta go back to work, sport, but I'll see you tomorrow. I wanna hear about those pancakes, yeah?' Duncan straightened. 'You know, we could have worked this out, Mal. You didn't have to be so dramatic.'

Then, with a disapproving glance at AJ, he strode for the exit.

Mallory watched him go, her arm around Harry's small shoulders. Duncan's parting shot was so juvenile, she hardly had to absorb it. Still, she could never take him at his word again. Could only believe him when something actually happened. The only thing that convinced her he'd even been here was the passport now in her hand.

'So, he just gave it back?' AJ asked.

'Yeah. With a little persuading.'

'Huh. Man might learn a healthy respect for your persuading.'

Mallory called Livia with the news while they were waiting for the train back to New York.

'Quite the last grand gesture, coming down to DC. Must have wanted to make it all about him one more time. I've heard he's a poor delegator. Likes to be the one in the spotlight.'

'He always did like to do things himself,' Mallory said softly. 'He wants the credit, I suppose.'

'Still, his lawyer should have made it clear how the whole situation made him look. Plus, even if he hasn't been drawing much of a salary, he will sometime. That's a hefty child support debt that he's going to have to face eventually. He can only have wanted to go to court because he thought you'd give up. When he saw you weren't going away, maybe this seemed the best option.'

'Must be something like that,' Mallory said.

Livia paused. 'Do I want to know?'

'Probably not,' Mallory said. 'But I have the passport.'

'Yes, you do.'

Livia began talking about further steps, including contacting the Australian lawyer Mallory had spoken to before so that they could place Harry's passport on a watch list. As the conversation went on, gooseflesh crawled over Mallory's arms. What would have happened if she'd stayed in Brisbane, filed the paperwork and hoped? What if she was still stuck somewhere on the road? She saw all the myriad possibilities. And while those things hadn't happened, she could never quite return to the naïve, hope-for-the-best pond she had swum in before.

She watched Harry hauling AJ around the station to look at train paraphernalia. She needed to take him home, back to the cottage, and his school. She knew that he would be happy there, but he'd also had his whole world upended these past few weeks. Duncan had given him a different picture of his future, one that she would now have to deal with. And more than all that, Mallory would have to grapple with how she had changed too.

It would be a long journey home.

•

Mallory left calling Silky Oaks until after she'd organised all the return flights. She was glad to be going home, and yet she was uneasy, waking up at two in the morning for no discernible reason. She told herself it was simply the inertia of having been under stress for so long: her body hadn't yet realised it could relax a little. Or that the business of Ernie and Zadie nagged at her, like a loose thread her mind couldn't help picking at. Or that she was still sad about Jock.

She timed the call to Silky Oaks for the late afternoon in Australia, even though it meant staying up past midnight and making the call from the hallway so that she wouldn't disturb Harry.

'Hallelujah!' Bridget declared when Mallory said she was coming home.

'Flight's booked in a few days because of the backlog. I wanted to know if I can be on the roster for mid next week. I'm nearly through my pay.'

'We had a flu go through the staff last week, so the roster's been thin. Just to warn you, the board are still investigating how three people managed to leave without being noticed – and then for Jock to die! It's thrown everyone. They've told us not to talk about it, but of course everyone is, especially now the Flints are coming back.' She dropped her voice to a whisper. 'Can you tell me the whole story now?'

Mallory did.

'He was doing it because he wasn't a good husband?' Bridget asked. 'That's insightful for the old curmudgeon. And now they're swanning about in Nashville.'

'I don't know if it's swanning. Zadie isn't as well as Ernie. He was complaining about the cost of the health system here after the two visits on the road.'

Mallory then had to explain about Zadie's panic attack and the UTI. Halfway through, Bridget told her to wait, because she was going to the file room. After she came back, Mallory could hear Bridget flipping pages in the background.

'I have her file,' Bridget said. 'Yes, she's had two UTIs already this year.' A pause. 'Ernie's right – there are notes here suggesting a review for a move to a higher care wing, and his vigorous protests.'

Despite all that had passed between her and Ernie, Mallory felt a pang. 'She had some very good days on this trip, though. I can't imagine why she's never come to the kindergarten visit. You should have seen her at the rodeo with all the animals.'

'Uh-huh.'

Mallory went on, describing again the highlights of that day, and Zadie's face when she'd recognised Nashville. Bridget's 'uh-huhs' became increasingly distracted.

Mallory finally paused. 'And we saw a UFO in New Mexico,' she said.

'Uh-huh.'

'Bridge. *Bridge.*'

'Mmm? Sorry.'

'What are you reading?' Mallory asked.

'Notes from Zadie's admission. Says her husband asked for her not to be involved in any children's visits. Thought she'd find it upsetting.'

Mallory frowned. 'Why?'

'I'm looking. Oh, here. It says . . . oh.' A long pause. 'Psychologist's notes say that she had a stillborn daughter, and that her husband gave instructions that it wasn't to be discussed. The psych actually thought *he* might benefit from some counselling. Thought he was blaming himself. Why would he do that?'

Mallory closed her eyes and put a hand over her face. The hall seemed unusually quiet. 'He was an obstetrician,' she said faintly.

'I guess that'll do it,' Bridget said. 'The notes say Zadie was actually willing to talk about Mabel, even though it upset her . . .' Bridget flipped a page, 'but later, as the dementia developed, she seemed to forget about it. Isn't that awful? I don't know what's worse.'

Mallory couldn't make any response. Mabel. She'd thought Zadie was mishearing her name, or recalling a long-departed friend. Mallory had never imagined it was her daughter's name. And Ernie . . . God, all those things she'd said to him about not understanding because he didn't have any children. About being glad he didn't have any.

'Oh, no,' she whispered. No wonder Ernie had looked as though she'd shot him through the heart.

'Mallory?' Bridget asked, sounding worried. 'You still there?'

Mallory heaved a breath. 'Yeah.'

'I was saying, it doesn't make much sense. Zadie's long-term memory otherwise is good. It's the short-term stuff she has problems with. Why would she forget her daughter?'

'Maybe she wanted to forget,' Mallory said. But she didn't really know what Zadie thought, or remembered. She pressed her fingers into the tight feeling, right over her heart. She wanted to rush into the bedroom and put her hand on Harry's little chest, just to feel him breathing in his sleep.

After she ended the call, she lay down next to Harry and thought about Ernie's phone call, the plea to come to the wedding. She could choose to ignore his request. No one would blame her.

But she also wanted to believe that Harry lived in a world where he would find kindness and love among heartbreak. And if she believed that, then she knew what she had to do.

Chapter 24

NASHVILLE TURNED ON A SPRING DAY OF BLUE SKIES, perfect for a wedding. Sunshine bathed the Wightman Chapel's roof in gold, and dappled down through the trees nestled between each stone building. To Mallory, it was like an early summer day in Queensland, but inside the chapel, with its soaring gothic walls and windows, the air was cool and scented with lilies. Even so, it wasn't until the joyful organ music began the service that she was glad she had come.

She had managed to change their return flight to add a stop in Nashville before she and Harry travelled on to LA, and then home. Harry wasn't a problem; he had caught enthusiasm for travel like a disease, and relished the chance for another adventure. Belle bringing him a miniature tuxedo at Ernie's behest only cemented the deal.

Mallory herself had been cautious. Despite regret over what she'd said to Ernie, she couldn't help remembering his judgements of her. And when she saw the delight on Zadie's face at her reappearance, Mallory feared her leaving again might bring further upset. Mallory was also tired, right down to the marrow, exhausted from the travel and the worry. The only thing that could relieve that feeling now was seeing her little cottage again. At least she told herself that home would relieve it. Thoughts of AJ kept catching her at odd times.

He hadn't come with them. He'd left for Chicago to finish his trip. As Mallory had said goodbye to him, a pain had shot through her chest. He'd said that he hoped they would see each other again, but she didn't know how that would happen. She lived halfway around the world. He had things to do.

On the first notes of the organ, however, she couldn't help but be carried away with hope and compassion. Harry hung on to her hand as they slid into their seats. She was moved by the rows and rows of vacant pews. Some of the staff from the centre around the chapel had come down, but otherwise it was just Belle and them.

Zadie wore a simple dress of pale lavender, and someone had put flowers in her hair; Ernie appeared almost regal in a dark blue suit. Clearly, neither of them cared if no one else was here. Zadie gave Ernie a dazzling smile and a crinkle of her bright eyes, and tucked her arm in his.

Afterwards, Mallory and Belle stood to the side on the sun-dappled lawn watching while Harry stalked squirrels beneath a nearby tree and Ernie spoke with the pastor on the step of the chapel. Finally, he and Zadie came slowly across the lawn. Mallory had to admit that Ernie seemed to have lost ten years. His frown had smoothed, and his back was straighter, as if a great weight had lifted from his shoulders.

Zadie walked taller, too, casting glances at the stone walls of the campus buildings, as if remembering her time here so many years ago.

Ernie gave Mallory a curt nod. 'You look very nice,' he said.

'Really?' she said, surprised. She was wearing a red dress she'd seen in a New York vintage shop window, and suspected it was still showing the creases from being crushed in her bag.

'I appreciate you coming,' he said formally. 'Changing your plans like that.'

'Oh, I'm very good at changing plans, now,' she said.

He chuckled. 'I suppose you must be.'

All this time, Zadie had been watching Harry, whose shirt had come untucked as he crept up on a squirrel. 'He's a patient one,' she said, her voice slow but clear. Then Harry took a quick step and the squirrel bolted up a trunk. Zadie chuckled. 'Or maybe next time.'

Mallory beckoned Harry over and introduced him properly to Ernie and Zadie.

'Hello,' Harry said, twisting his toe in the grass, suddenly shy.

'What do you say?' Mallory prompted.

'Thank you for my tux, Dr Flint,' Harry dutifully recited.

'I made clothes for a squirrel once,' Zadie said, focused on Harry. 'Can you imagine how small they were?'

Harry's eyes lit. 'Was it a suit like this one?'

'A little pair of trousers, and a vest, too.'

'Was it for a pet squirrel?'

'He loves dressing up,' Mallory said to Ernie, as the squirrel clothes conversation continued, but she noticed the way all expression had left Ernie's face, the tightness of his lips. She spotted Belle coming back from the bathrooms.

'Ernie,' Mallory said, 'can I talk to you for a minute? In private.'

'I'd like to stay near Zadie today,' he said.

'We don't have to go far, just over by the wall. Harry and I are flying back to Australia tomorrow and I need to talk to you about Silky Oaks.'

Grudgingly, he allowed Belle to take Zadie's arm and came, and they stepped into the shadow of the chapel where the air was cool and earthy. Ernie rocked to a halt with his strong arm propped on his cane.

'Silky Oaks can't dictate terms to us,' he said. 'When we're ready to return, I'll call them.'

'That isn't why I wanted to talk to you.'

He raised his eyebrows.

She took a breath. 'I said some things, that morning in Memphis, that were hurtful. I was angry and upset but I shouldn't have said any of them. I wanted to say I was sorry.'

'Well, I—'

'Please, let me finish. You'll remember all those ideas I had for doing things differently at Silky Oaks that I talked about in the car. Mrs Crawley thought I was dreaming, but I thought I could see the complexity of all the residents. I prided myself on being able to work through any difficult situation, to be perceptive about what people needed.' She looked away, across the bright emerald lawn. 'But I never considered whether my ideas might actually distress someone. And then I said those things to you and made it all worse.'

Ernie's face sagged, as if it was a damp towel falling from its pegs. 'You read the file.'

'Parts of it.'

Ernie cleared his throat. 'I've been thinking about what I said since you left, too.'

'You have?'

A nod. 'This world's not the one I grew up in. Values I have aren't the done thing anymore. I should have minded my own business.'

'Okay.' It wasn't the sort of apology she would have liked, but she'd take what he offered.

'Ah,' Ernie said, raising a hand towards her face. 'See? I knew that wasn't the right thing to say.'

'It's fine.'

'You really shouldn't take up poker.'

Mallory smiled. 'That sounds like something Jock would have said.'

Ernie nodded. 'God rest him. He always did better at this than me.'

'At what?'

Ernie gestured around. 'The world, the changing. Feels like I'm living on a different planet, and I don't speak the language. While I was practising medicine, I had my work. I understood how to keep up with that. Now, I'm no longer relevant. I never had to think about, I don't know, children taking medication, or gays marrying. I don't even know what I think of those things, but they're obviously important issues now. I just can't keep up.'

Mallory thought a moment. 'Jock said you were sharp as a razor. I bet you could keep up if you wanted to.'

Ernie grunted, and asked her to tell him about the funeral. When she was finished, they stood with the warm breeze blowing over their skin.

'Do you think you'll come back to Silky Oaks soon?' she asked.

He blew out a long breath, then tipped his head towards another newly married couple having photos taken in the distance, big smiles, and their heads pressed together like a valentine heart.

'You see that?' he said, pointing his cane. 'One day, you're young and invincible, and the next thing you're old and regretful.' He shook his head, and looked across to where Zadie sat on a bench beneath a sprawling tree, her white hair twisted up behind her head, her dress flowing over the wooden seat, watching Harry race around on the grass.

'Happiest day of my life when she agreed to leave this place with me. She never let the disappointments be all there was. Even after . . . what happened. That's why she had many friends, and why I worked all the time and had none. She was the brave one. Always was.'

He closed his eyes. Mallory was aware he could have broken down in that moment, but when he opened his eyes again, they were dry. He had a steel in him, Ernie did. A man who'd held himself together when the world gave him every reason to shatter. He was an old rigid oak. Zadie must have been a willow, gracefully bending.

'And how do you feel, now that you've done what you wanted?' Mallory said. 'Makes quite a story. Everyone at Silky Oaks will be breaking out when they hear about it.'

Ernie gave a short laugh. 'Most out-of-character thing I've done in my life.'

'Better late than never.'

'You young people, you think that outlandish acts are what life is about. That's why you love Hollywood movies.'

Mallory laughed again, feeling the room he was allowing for her to jibe him. 'You were young once, I'm almost sure of it.'

Ernie chortled, then his expression turned serious. 'I looked up some of that research you mentioned in the car. About the different care models. Having pets, even children in the facility. Different terminology and ways of thinking. It wasn't all rubbish.'

'Really?'

He nodded. 'Well, Zadie appreciates you being here. When we come back to Australia, I hope you could take some time to visit her, even though I know we're not in your wing. Would mean a lot.'

Mallory leaned over, thinking to kiss his cheek, then patted his arm instead. The things they'd said to each other would always rub between them, like a grain of sand, but her life was ahead of her while his was behind him. She had compassion for that.

'Of course,' she said, watching Harry line up another squirrel, Zadie watching too. 'And you're wrong: sometimes, outlandish acts are just what's required.'

He gave her a long considering look, then one eyebrow rose in acknowledgement before he turned away down the church green. Mallory slid in to the bench seat beside Zadie, who was twisting one of the flowers from her hair in her fingers.

'That was a lovely wedding,' Mallory said. 'Belle did your hair very nicely. How does it feel to be home again?'

The flower stopped twisting. 'It looks much the same,' Zadie said, lifting her eyes to the chapel's stone walls. 'I always loved this place and I did want to be married here, once. But it hasn't been home for a long time.'

Mallory glanced across at Ernie, who was talking with one of the centre staff. 'I must have misunderstood.'

'Ernie wanted to come. He needed to. He feels better, now.'

Mallory looked at Zadie in surprise. She was so clear today.

'My grandmother was the one who brought me to this chapel first,' she said. 'She was a sweet woman, very bright, such a positive person. But before she died, everyone knew she was acting differently. I know that's happening to me too.' A small frown tugged between her brows. 'I'm not afraid of it. I saw my grandmother with it and she was lovely to the end. But Ernie's afraid.'

Mallory nodded. 'Yes, I think you're right.'

'I have blessings,' Zadie went on. 'I still have Ern after all these years. I could have lost him and been alone. And he organised all this, just for me.'

'He obviously loves you.'

'I did so enjoy the rodeo. I didn't think I'd see another one. I didn't think I'd see Nashville again, and this beautiful chapel. I miss my dogs. But I'd miss Ernie more, Mallory.'

Mallory hesitated. 'That's the first time you've called me Mallory. I, uh, didn't realise who Mabel was until a few days ago, when I spoke to Silky Oaks.'

'Ah.' Zadie looked down at her hands. 'Sometimes,' she said slowly, 'I liked to pretend that Mabel was still with us, what she'd be like. A positive person, I think. Dark brown hair, like mine used to be. If we went out, I'd look at all the girls and see if any of them were like I imagined her. Once at home, I saw this young woman with a group of children in the foyer. I thought, ah, there she is.'

Mallory swallowed. 'Do you remember meeting me in the airport in LA? In the bathrooms?'

Zadie frowned, and then slowly shook her head. 'I remember the rodeo. We sat in the stands, watching the barrel racers, and all those young brave people. Some days are like that. Some, I have no idea.'

Mallory smiled sadly. Zadie's heart was larger than anyone's she'd ever met, and on a good day she had insight and compassion and love, despite what life had dealt her. How hard must it be for her to know that her memories, everything that made her life, were slipping away? And for Ernie, having to watch? But Mallory also knew that memory could be as much emotion as it was facts. It was joy and grief, and anger and calm. Zadie could forget the facts, but maybe the love she and Ernie had forged so many years ago would endure.

So Mallory took Zadie's hand, and asked her about her dogs and horses, and all the things she'd done among these buildings as a girl. Zadie's smile spread as she spoke. She pointed towards the chapel, to this tree, and that nook. When Ernie came back, he listened for a while before Mallory rose. She left them there on the bench, Ernie's weak arm lifted across the back of Zadie's shoulders.

Harry rushed past, joined by a girl wearing a pink netting dress and a boy in a miniature suit jacket, both of them clearly poached from the other wedding party and drawn by the promise of squirrels. To a casual observer, Zadie and Ernie could have been grandparents. Mallory imagined the scene as a painting, an artist capturing the loyalty and love in Ernie's draped arm, the joy of the cavorting children, the way the sun made dabs of yellow on the leaves and bright spots on upturned faces. Harry vaulted off the boy's back and met the earth with a whoop, the three of them giggling and mucky – and, deep in her heart, Mallory thought about a gruff man in leather who rode a Rocket and suddenly knew she would see him again. For no other reason than that life was addictive in its promise of goodness and wonder, in its hope that even in the dark cracks of sorrow, something better could come again.

Epilogue

MALLORY AND HARRY ARRIVED HOME ON AN EARLY MAY
Friday just as the curling breeze off the sea was turning
frosty. The chooks heard the gate and came running. Mallory
counted and found all of them there. She'd have to buy
Bridget a box of Cadbury Roses to thank her for keeping
them in food and water.

Harry had been quiet on the journey from the airport,
morose after the realisation that his father's New York
promises weren't going to happen. Even when Mallory told
him that they would be visiting every year, maybe even twice
a year, this had failed to penetrate Harry's silence. But the
moment Harry saw his fluffy white bantam streaking behind
the larger chooks, he shed his sadness like a coat and scooped
her up, planting kisses on the soft feathers of her back.

Mallory relaxed. The cottage paint was peeling like
sunburn, the jasmine in desperate need of a prune, but she
threw open the doors and windows with fondness. Time to
let the stale air out. They were home.

The next Monday, Harry went off to his old school and came home talking about a field trip to the city museum, and what all his friends had been doing since he'd been away.

Mallory went back to work, despite jet lag that left her feeling like both her eyes were bruised. Silky Oaks was much the same, except the Easter decorations had been taken down, leaving faint Blu Tack blotches on the cream walls, which would be covered in a few months when Christmas activities rolled around.

Mallory expected a grilling over the events in the USA, but all that happened was Mrs Crawley asked her to write up any relevant medical notes. Mallory suspected Ernie must have really thrown his weight around to put out any fires. Her shifts ran as they always had, but even when the kindergarten children visited and brought the delight of spontaneity to the residents, she carried an ache in her chest, keener than what she'd felt when Duncan had walked out of their lives.

Something wasn't right.

She did her work – helped her residents to dress and eat, stripped beds and cleaned, and organised entertainments, and talked to them, and moved them between the lounge and their rooms, and outside for air and sunshine. She went home and collected Harry and made dinner, and the two of them would sit together, eating dessert and poring over books or making paper dinosaur models, or origami. Still, Mallory couldn't shake the sense that she was out of alignment, as if her internal compass had shifted course after the trip, and she was no longer travelling in the right direction.

One night, it was cold enough that Harry asked if they could light the fire. So the next day, they cleaned out the grate until their hands were black, and they laughed painting charcoal lines down their noses and cheeks. The fire warmed the house, and Harry went to bed with a smile rounding his cheeks into rosy apples.

And yet when Mallory slipped into the covers with a paperback mystery, she was restless. Duncan was sending a little maintenance money now, so finances weren't as stretched, and even though she still had to consider the formal legal process for a parenting order, it wasn't about money. Some of it was lingering stress from the trip, and grief over Jock, and thoughts about AJ, whom she hadn't heard from since they left.

But that wasn't everything.

She looked up into the Bayside night, shining with the full moon, and realised it was not the things she was dealing with. Like the space between the stars, something was missing.

•

Ernie and Zadie came back to Silky Oaks the following week, and the staff were in a flap with rumours of where they'd been.

'I heard Tasmania,' said one. 'Didn't he have family down there?'

'That was the other Ernie,' said someone else. 'I bet they've been on a cruise. Lucky buggers. Where's the third one, though?'

Mrs Crawley had clearly clamped down on the truth for there to be so much speculation.

Mallory said nothing. Eventually, everyone would have to know that Jock had died, and his room on the second floor would be assigned to someone else. She thought of Jock every time she passed the empty computer room, on her way up to visit Zadie. There, she would spend her breaks, and talk about what she and Harry were doing at the cottage: what mischief the chickens had been up to, how the roof had leaked in the last storm, and how Harry had made an impromptu mud slide in the wet grass and come in shivering but laughing.

Zadie smiled, but she didn't say much now – except that she would sing along to the sixties songs that Mallory put on the music player. Zadie had more problems with wandering, and being agitated at night. Medications were adjusted. Mallory would show her pictures that Ernie had taken of the road trip, trying to remember which songs had been playing in those places to best jog her memory. Once, Zadie stopped singing, right in the middle of 'King of the Road', and said, 'Turn it off, Mabel, dear. I'm done singing.'

That was the day Ernie stopped Mallory in the hallway and asked for a word. The next moment, Mallory found herself in his room, where stacks of fresh journal papers filled the desk.

'I want to get Zadie a dog,' he said. 'She's never got over losing Melville. What do you think?'

Mallory's instinctive surge of enthusiasm was tempered as she thought about it. 'I think it's the most fantastic idea. But you know the rules.' She shrugged, wondering what on earth she could do. 'I'm sorry, Ernie. If you want to smuggle one in I'll cover for you as long as I can, but eventually . . .'

She trailed off. Ernie had a glint in his eye she hadn't seen before.

'What are you up to?' she asked.

'I'm thinking about setting up a brand-new place, one that uses this, this—' he waved a hand at the stacks of paper '—"new model". Where Zadie can have a dog, and we can stay together. And make that possible for other people too.'

Mallory was so dumbfounded she couldn't speak for ten long seconds. A deep pang of jealousy flashed in her heart. 'I think it sounds like a marvellous idea. But how?'

'That's where you come in.'

'Me?'

'You were the one who found this idea. You're experienced in this industry.'

'But I don't know the first thing about setting up a new facility! There'd be buildings, and funding, and finances and – I don't even know what.'

Ernie was nodding. 'That's my area. I worked decades in the health system. I know about government departments, and who I can ask about funding. I've contacts at the university hospital – they might even be interested in a partnership. But my body can't do the physical work, and eventually it's going to need someone young at the helm, to keep it going. What do you say? I don't know if you've noticed, but we don't exactly have time to sit and think about it forever.'

'Are you making a joke, Ernie?'

His eyes crinkled. 'Oh, I would never do that.'

Mallory grinned. 'Are you really serious about this? Don't dangle the thing I've wanted to do and then take it away.'

'You see all this paper?' he said, lifting his weak hand again to the stacks of articles. 'I had to learn to use that damned computer to find them.'

Mallory laughed. 'Then you really must be serious!'

He shook his head, clearly uncomfortable with her delight, but she squeezed his arm anyway. He had tenacity. And he had love. She could admire that.

'I know why Zadie went with you all those years ago,' Mallory said. 'She wanted you above anything else. Who else would have loved her enough to make a daring breakout at your age?'

'Oh, at *my age*,' Ernie said, but his voice was thick with emotion. 'I don't want to lose her, Mallory.'

'I know.' Mallory paused. 'Bridget says that when people love each other like you do, their souls always remember each other.'

'Don't believe in souls,' Ernie said.

'Well, I do.'

'No evidence for it. It's just what people say to make themselves feel better.' But he said this uncertainly, as if he'd really like to believe it.

'Maybe there isn't evidence, not scientifically,' Mallory said. 'But I know there's some place in us that gives us strength when there's nothing else left. Call it whatever you like. I'm going to call it a soul.'

He made a sound in his throat that wasn't entirely dismissive. And while it was the last time that he openly showed how worried he was, he attacked the project of establishing a new facility with a ferocity Mallory thought a person half his age could not have matched.

•

After only a week, she handed in her notice to Silky Oaks. Ernie had started paying her a manager's salary, and wanted her out 'in the field', scouting for appropriate real estate, reporting back with photos, and checking his ideas about staff numbers and set-up times. Mallory leaped on faith. The whole thing could have fallen over tomorrow, but she knew an opportunity like this wouldn't come around again. The day Ernie secured his first private investment – through an old university colleague – Mallory took him and Zadie to collect a dog.

She was a little Maltese called Dixie with a fluffy white coat and happy, carefree face. At least, what Mallory interpreted as happy and carefree in a dog face. Within two minutes of meeting Zadie, she'd crawled up on her new owner's lap.

'I know she's not a greyhound,' Ernie told Zadie. Since learning of the prospect of a dog, Zadie had asked repeatedly for a rescue greyhound, like Melville. 'But we'll be able to keep her at Silky Oaks until our new home is ready.'

Zadie didn't show a single molecule of disappointment, petting and grooming Dixie until the dog was dozing with contentment. Mallory watched with equal parts satisfaction and apprehension. The idea of this dog had breathed such life back into Zadie, and Mallory was willing to bet other residents would be clamouring for pets too, probably led by Mr Burgundy's request for guinea pigs. Mrs Crawley might have a revolt on her hands, one that she could blame squarely on Mallory. Mallory tried to feel brave. She hoped not to need a reference from Mrs Crawley, and besides, maybe Silky Oaks would change after all.

After the bustle of her workday, where the new facility's agenda drove every decision and action, she arrived home on Friday night and had to stand in the doorway for ten minutes, just trying to think of what to do with the evening. The house was empty. Harry was on his first sleepover at a friend's house, so the cottage seemed dull and chilled. She paced around on the creaking floorboards, checked the windows were closed, put away the dishes in the strainer. She opened the fridge, surveyed the half-cabbage, leftover spaghetti bolognese, and a side of roast chicken of uncertain age, and closed it again. She wasn't hungry anyway. She'd go over the staff advertisement drafts and think about dinner later.

She set up her computer and rebuilt the fire, in a desultory mood. The night was going to be cold. She'd much rather have had Harry home so that they could toast marshmallows.

Because the truth was, even with her work and Harry, she was lonely. And when she felt it most keenly, she thought of Jock, and all the bitter and sweet moments of that trip across the States.

As she struck the match, her phone rang. Seeing a private number on the screen, Mallory answered, expecting it would be Ernie.

'Hello, is that Mallory?'

'Yes?' Mallory didn't recognise the woman's voice.

'Bridget gave me your number. I'm Caroline . . . I'm John Henderson's ex-wife—Jock, that is.' She sounded hesitant, as though this was a call she was unsure about making. 'I want to apologise for taking this long to call you.'

'Oh, that's okay,' Mallory said quickly. 'The news must have been a shock, and I understand you weren't in contact.'

There was a long pause. 'To be honest, I wasn't sure how to take it. We've only been in touch a few times in the past several years, and not at all in the decades before that. I don't know if you knew the circumstances.'

'He mentioned you'd split up when your children were very young.'

Caroline sighed. 'Jock had a lot of problems. I tried to understand, but those years were incredibly difficult. I couldn't take the disappearing for days, the mood swings, the disappointments. I was very glad when we split up. I don't know if I've ever recovered from it.'

'I think he knew that,' Mallory said slowly. 'He said he regretted what had happened.'

'I do have the sense he'd got some help in these past years,' Caroline said. 'I wish things had been different. I feel bad for saying this, but I didn't want to go to his funeral. Too many bad memories. But I did want to speak to you. I understand you were with him in the last few days.'

Mallory sank down on the couch, the silent air around the cottage burrowing into the lonely part of her heart that still missed Jock. 'Yes. He was heading back to his childhood home,' she began, and told Caroline about the journey, about everything that had happened. 'I think he knew that he might not make it all the way there,' Mallory finished. 'But he was trying to make amends. I think he'd want you to know that. And he was very kind to me.'

Caroline's voice was choked. 'I know. I do understand that. You see, we just found out today that he left the kids the house, the one he grew up in. It came with a note saying that he was sorry for all the things he couldn't be to us, but that he wanted the kids to have the house.'

'He did?' Mallory's eyes filled with tears.

'Yes. And well, the kids never did know him, but maybe now I can start to tell them.'

'I have all the letters he wrote his mother, and the ones she wrote him. Can I give them to you? Maybe that could help. Seems right you should have them.'

Just before it seemed the conversation should end, Caroline took a breath. 'Was it a good funeral?' she asked, a little tremulous. 'Was anyone there?'

'A whole posse,' Mallory said. 'A friend of mine knew a veterans' association, and they mustered their troops.'

'Good,' she said. 'It's awful what happened to him, please believe me that I know that. He always wanted to be with his brother. At least they'll always be together now.'

Mallory ended the call and sighed, taking a moment to let this news settle through her.

She couldn't help thinking of AJ. They had talked briefly about keeping in touch, but neither of them had yet followed through. Every time Mallory thought about sending him a message, it didn't seem enough. He had left an indelible impression on her heart, one that wasn't satisfied with pixels on a screen.

She picked up the matches and strode to the fireplace with purpose, trying to push all the intrusive wonderings about him back into the vault in her chest. As she struck the match, her phone pinged on the kitchen bench. She waited, holding the tiny flame up to the tinder, but something about that *ping* was making her heart thud, as if the universe had sent an answer to her thoughts. She left the fledgling fire licking over the logs and snatched up her phone.

The moment she saw the message, the thud became thunder.

AJ: *Hey.*

She couldn't help smiling stupidly. Her fingers trembled as she typed back. *Hey.*

AJ: *How's the weather down under?*

Mallory: *Cold. I just built the fire.* On impulse, she snapped a picture of the just-taking logs and sent it with the message.

AJ: *Cosy. Looks like a good spot for settling in.*

Haven't heard from you in ages, she typed back, trying not to imagine him sitting on her couch.

I know. Had things to sort out. Need to ask you something.

Mallory: *?*

AJ: *Can I see you tomorrow?*

Skype? she typed, amazed by how just the idea of seeing him on her computer screen lit her up like a bonfire.

Then, he typed: *No, not Skype.*

Mallory had to take two deep breaths, reading over the message before she wrote back, *AJ, where are you?*

Just landed in Brisbane. Figured I'd find a hotel. See if you were free tomorrow.

Mallory closed her eyes, little satellite fireworks going off in her head. Despite all the possibilities for disappointment, she typed back.

Come now.

A pause. *What about Harry?*

At a sleepover.

Send address, he typed. *Now, please.*

The hour it took the taxi from the airport was the longest of Mallory's life. She flew around the house, scooping up laundry that had missed the hamper, straightening cushions, wiping crumbs off benches, hanging on every noise from the road, boiling the kettle and finding a jug, and still the clock hands crept lazily around the numbers.

When the taxi finally bounced down the long uneven driveway, her whole body was trembling, and she couldn't drop the stupid grin off her face.

Then he was there, coming through the gate with nothing more than a black duffel thrown over his shoulder, tipping his head back to find the moon, which was pouring soft light down through the trees and over the cottage. He wore blue jeans and a grey t-shirt, his hair a little longer, but with his deadpan expression he still looked like a big man out to make trouble.

When he saw her waiting in the doorway, trouble dissolved into a broad smile. He didn't stop to say anything inane or awkward. He gathered her up in his arms and hugged her to him, and she pressed her cheek against his chest, and heard his heart racing, too.

'I missed you,' he said.

She pulled back and smiled into his face. 'So you just got on a plane?' she said, her voice all wobbly.

'Yeah. I heard there was this amazing fireworks night soon. Plus, I figured you might go for the grand gesture.'

'About time,' she whispered. 'You know how many nights I've had sweet tea waiting in the fridge since I came home?'

His eyebrows curved. 'Southern hospitality, a fire on a cold night, and a beautiful woman,' he said. 'Couldn't really ask for more.'

In that moment, Mallory saw the shape of a future before her, bright with possibilities. She had no idea what would come of any of it, but she knew to enjoy the good things when they walked through her door. So she led him inside to the waiting fire.

Author's notes

THE IDEAS MALLORY EXPRESSES ABOUT ELDER CARE ARE based on the work of Dr Bill Thomas and the Eden Alternative – you can read more at www.edenalt.org or listen to part of their story on the Reply All podcast episode #101, 'Minka'. The specific idea of intergenerational programs (like kindergartens visiting or being located in aged care facilities) was taken from examples like TIME at Tigger's Honeypot in NSW, Australia, and The Grace Living Center in Jenks, Oklahoma, USA. I'm fascinated by these ideas, and admire so much the innovators who are driven to improve the care of our elder citizens.

Some parts of this novel are set in real places or at real events (certain rodeos, for example) but dates of those events may be incorrect for story reasons. Funeral services at Arlington National Cemetery typically take much longer to organise than depicted in this novel. These and any other such alterations or errors that I have made with artistic licence are mine alone.

I want to extend grateful thanks to many, including the wonderful people I met on my research trip driving across the USA (proving you can make it from LA to Nashville in four days . . . it's just perhaps not advisable). Special mention to Lana Higgins and her colleagues, who brightened my day in Fort Smith, AS, and David Rosengarten, whom I met by chance in Katz's Deli in New York and who provided enthusiastic local knowledge, good conversation and wonderful places to eat. Many thanks also to Yasmin Dulley, whose help with Australian family law so informed the story.

Thanks always to Rebekah Turner for being such a pillar of help with the book and many other things, and to other friends and family who assisted when the going was very tough in 2017, including the lovely Christine Wells. Special thanks to my husband Kevin, my mother Isobella and stepdad Vic for your support. Finally to the publishing team at Hachette, who helped me reach the vision I had for the story, and who saw it out into the world. Thank you all.

Escape to the most fabulous city in the world
and fall in love with this heart-melting story
by bestselling author Charlotte Nash . . .

Available now from

piatkus

The Paris Wedding

Free trip to Paris: city of love, light, and clothes to die for ...

Ten years ago, Rachael gave up the love of her life. Now she's being offered an all-expenses-paid trip to Paris – the city she's always dreamed of living in – to watch to him marry someone else.

Paris has all kinds of surprises in store for Rachael, who's more used to countryside lanes than Coco Chanel, including a handsome photographer. But the sparkling city of love, hope and longing has a way of unlocking your heart's deepest secrets. And there's one question that just won't stop nagging at her – a question she'll have to find an answer to before her time in Paris is up.

One thing's for sure: it's going to be the trip of a lifetime.

Praise for Charlotte Nash

'I was enthralled ... Nash's skilled storytelling will keep
you turning pages until the very end'
Fleur MacDonald

'Nash's main characters are easy to love ... a thoroughly
enjoyable read that will make you laugh and cry'
The Daily Telegraph

'You will fall in love with this deliciously poignant story
about family and friends, and love lost and found'
Queensland Times

'Readers will be sure to laugh, reach for the tissue
box, grit their teeth in anger and fall in love with the
embracing character set of this unforgettable novel'
Mrs B's Book Reviews

'The most heartwarming road trip story
you ever did read'
Marie Claire

'As authentic as you will get, unflinching in its honesty, raw and beautiful. I just can't recommend this novel highly enough'
Theresa Smith Writes

'I enjoyed a previous book by this author but this new novel is on a whole other level ... I can't recommend this beautiful book more'
One Woman's Brief Book Reviews

'An uplifting drama leavened by gentle humour, blossoming friendships and a good, old-fashioned romance'
The Courier-Mail

'Fans of *The Unlikely Pilgrimage of Harold Fry* and *The Best Exotic Marigold Hotel* will enjoy this tale of friendship, family and the road'
The New Daily